The Circle Dance

Sarah Grazebrook

PIATKUS

Copyright © 1993 by Sarah Grazebrook

First published in Great Britain in 1993 by
Judy Piatkus (Publishers) Ltd of
5 Windmill Street, London W1

The moral right of the author has been asserted

*A catalogue record for this book is available
from the British Library*

ISBN 0-7499-0217-5

Typeset by Datix International Limited, Bungay, Suffolk
Set in 11/12 pt Times
Printed and bound in Great Britain
by Bookcraft (Bath) Ltd

Chapter One

Life did not begin at forty for Isobel Day. In fact it nearly ended.

Richard Day put down the phone. Irritation welled over him. She's done it on purpose, he thought. After all my efforts. This really is the last straw.

Over at the hospital Mr Jamieson was returning to his wife, who sat huddled on the end of a wooden bench. 'It's tea,' he informed her. 'Coffee's finished.'

Mrs Jamieson nodded. 'It's half-past three,' she said. 'Coffee would be finished by now.'

A nurse drifted by. 'Who are you for?' she queried, recalling that they had been there some while.

'We're witnesses,' Mr Jamieson explained. The nurse nodded indifferently and moved away.

'Well,' said Mrs Jamieson, and smiled at the ferocious-looking woman behind the tea urn stamped 'Friends of St Clare's'. She wondered what the enemies had been like.

Richard drove to the hospital. He had had to phone Jenny, telling her to put everything on hold. Jenny had been sympathetic and reasonable and had told him not to worry and that she would pick up the wine from the off-licence and pay for it with her Access card. She would then rush round to Diana's and help with the food, as arranged, because even if Isobel couldn't actually be present at her surprise fortieth birthday party, Jenny felt certain she would want it to go ahead anyway. She knew *she* would.

Richard knew with equal certainty that Isobel would not,

but felt unequal to the task of explaining this to Jenny who was a mere twenty-seven and had only been his mistress for six months. They were not yet on the 'honest opinion' footing which usually heralded the end of his affairs.

A fracture, they had said on the phone. That could mean anything. Images of a silent Isabel entombed in snowy plaster vied with the more likely vision of Isobel furiously nursing a bandaged ankle and cursing indiscriminately at the medical profession, the National Health Service and anyone unfortunate enough to pass within fifteen feet of her looking cheerful.

The truth was somewhat closer to his first imaginings than Richard had perhaps been prepared for.

Isobel was indeed silent as she lay beneath the coarse white linen in the recovery room. She was also deeply unconscious.

'But . . . don't you have to get my consent or something?' Richard floundered, unnerved by the smell of antiseptics and the rehearsed indifference of the staff. 'I am next-of-kin, you know.'

'Fortunately your wife was able to sign her own consent form before we operated,' the houseman told him. 'She was in a great deal of pain. We thought it best to go ahead.'

'Yes, but . . .' A sense of grievance was now setting in. 'I mean . . . someone might have said. All they told me was that it was a fracture. That's all they said on the phone.'

'We prefer not to go into too many details over the phone, Mr Day, as I'm sure you'll appreciate. It's really better if these things are discussed person to person. Ah, here's Mr Robertson now. I'm sure he'll be able to put you in the picture more fully.'

Richard followed the consultant into his cool grey office and allowed himself to be seated in the confection of steel rods which the new Trust Status at St Clare's had decreed suitably streamlined and cost-effective. Mr Robertson sat opposite in an old green armchair.

'Mr Day, I'm Hugh Robertson.' Richard nodded. 'This must have come as a bit of a shock to you.'

Richard shifted in his rods. 'Obviously, any sort of accident . . .' he began.

'Accident. Ah . . . yes.' Mr Robertson folded his hands as if in prayer and rested his forefinger on his chin, in accordance with soap opera technique.

'What's that supposed to mean?' demanded Richard.

Mr Robertson looked at him steadily. 'Your wife is an extremely lucky woman,' he said. Richard wondered fleetingly if the doctor was referring to him, but discounted the thought as premature. More silence ensued during which Richard clinked and the consultant creaked in their respective chairs.

Mr Robertson spoke again. 'Had there been any sign?'

'Sign of what?'

'That this might happen. Something like this.'

'Something like what? It may have slipped your memory but no one's yet found the energy to tell me exactly what did happen. Has she broken her ankle or what?'

'Yes, yes,' said Mr Robertson testily. 'A compound fracture of the fibula plus sundry contusions to the upper thigh and rib cage. That surely is not the point?'

Richard ran a hand over his brow. 'Perhaps you could tell me what the point is?' he asked quietly.

Mr Robertson, who had also done a mandatory human relations course, lowered his voice.

'The point is, why?' He leaned forward across the desk, seeking direct eye contact.

'How should I know why? Probably fell over the pavement, knowing Isobel. She never looks where she's going. Not that our pavements aren't a disgrace,' Richard added sharply, suspecting that the man would have contacts in the council.

'She was up on the cliffs,' persisted Mr Robertson. 'The stretch between St Margaret's and Kingsdown. Not many paving stones there.'

'Well, for heaven's sake it must have been a rabbit hole or something. What's so odd about that? Those cliff paths are in an appalling state,' Richard reiterated, sensing that the doctor was in some way seeking to apportion blame.

'Mr Day, we know what happened. Your wife fell over the cliff. Fortunately her fall was broken by a ledge some twelve feet below. Otherwise . . . Fortunately also, the incident was witnessed by a couple who were able to summon immediate help. What we don't know is why she did it. I had hoped you might have been able to shed more light, but obviously the problem lies deeper.' He sighed again. 'We shall just have to wait till Mrs Day feels able to tell us about it herself.'

Richard felt like the proverbial man who has been hit in the face by a wet fish. 'She fell *over*' he repeated like a zombie. '*Over* the cliff?' Mr Robertson's face exhibited the smallest gleam of triumph. 'Yes, indeed, Mr Day. She was seen to lunge forward and topple over the edge. As I said, had it not been for the outcrop which broke her fall . . . But we must put all that behind us now. The important thing is to find the root cause, and with your support that, I am sure, is what we shall be able to do.' Mr Robertson smiled his consultant's smile and rose, holding out a baby-pink hand. 'And now I expect you would like to see your wife?' He opened the door and shepherded Richard out to a hovering staff nurse who led him briskly back along the dark linoed corridor and into an airless ward full of women in quilted bedjackets, knitting and chomping biscuits with the gumless displeasure of the very old.

Isobel lay behind closed curtains at the far end. Richard padded self-consciously down the ward, aware of dry eyelids flicking noisily after him. A nurse went before him and, slipping through the curtains, motioned him to enter. Isobel gazed dreamily up at him.

'Er . . . Hullo, darling,' muttered Richard, painfully aware that he, too, was now in the realms of soap opera. The nurse disappeared. Isobel tried to say something but her mouth was too dry. Richard regarded her plaster critically. 'How long's all this going to take?'

Isobel shook her head. 'Don't know.'

'You would pick today of all days.' His wife acknowledged the awkwardness with her eyes.

'Some birthday.' Richard could feel the annoyance welling up again, now that he could see she wasn't badly hurt. Not all that badly, anyway. The way that fool doctor had been going on anyone would think . . . He said' – Richard could hardly keep the disbelief out of his voice. 'He said you fell over the cliff. Silly bastard! What's he on about? What were you doing up there anyway? I thought you said you were going to get your hair done. You haven't had it done, have you?' He peered disparagingly at Isobel's matted tresses. She smiled. Ever the economist, Richard. 'No,' she croaked. 'I changed my mind.'

'Just as well,' said Richard, 'bit of a waste.' He smiled sheepishly to show it wasn't the money he was thinking of. 'So, how do you feel?'

'Pretty awful.'

'Yes, well, you would. Foot hurt?'

'Ankle.'

'Yes. Hurts, does it?'

'Like hell.'

'Yes, well, it would.' Richard sat on the edge of the bed and wondered what to do. His mother would pick the children up and give them tea. That was a pre-arrangement anyway, to allow him to get on with the last-minute details and crises. No easy matter, a surprise party, particularly when most of the organisation is in the hands of your mistress and ex-mistress. Although Diana was quite a way back. There had been Yvette and Naomi in between. And Jenny was very capable in her slow methodical way, or if not capable, unquestionably willing.

Isobel tapped his arm. He looked up. She pointed to a water jug and passed a finger across her parched lips. Richard nodded vigorously and looked round for the nurse. She was down the ward wielding bedpans like a silver service waitress. He decided he could probably deal with this particular crisis on his own. Gingerly he dipped a paper hanky in the water and watched it dissolve into small blue flakes. He tried again with his own, and dabbed clumsily at his wife's lips, like a boxer testing an opponent's reflexes. Isobel sucked hungrily at the cloth, reminding him of what had first attracted him to her, namely her insatiable interest in sex. This had waned somewhat over the years, a fact which he put down to the ageing process, (Isobel's not his), rather than the fact that his repertoire had turned out to be rather more limited than he had given his wife to suppose.

'Better?' Isobel nodded.

'Richard . . .'

'Yes?' He glanced at her then looked away, aware that some sort of apology was in the offing. God, he thought, she *did* do it. She knows about Jenny! She's forty years old. Over the hill. She's going to tell me all about it.

He wondered briefly if it would be possible to ring Jenny first to tell her to put everyone back for half an hour, so that he at least would be there to greet the arriving guests, but he could hardly leap up and rush off just as his wife of seventeen years was about to tell him why she'd try to kill herself.

'There's something you ought to know . . .'

'Oh?'

He looks just like a frustrated schoolmaster, Isobel thought, noting the quizzically arched eyebrows and slight retraction of the nostrils. Still handsome, though. 'It's about today . . .'

Richard's feeble hope that she might be going to ask him to fetch the nurse evaporated. 'Go on.'

'I know.'

'Know what?' Goodbye Jenny.

'About the party.'

'The what?'

Isobel laughed, then winced. 'I'm sorry. I wasn't going to say, but . . . what with everything . . . I know about the surprise party. The off-licence rang to ask how many glasses you wanted. It wasn't their fault. They must have thought I was the maid or something . . . I'm glad you think it's so funny.' A little of the irascibility for which they were mutually renowned began to surface in Isobel's husky voice.

Richard, dizzy with relief, controlled himself and bent to kiss his wife.

'And you don't mind?'

'Why should I mind?'

'Well, you rather hate that sort of thing, don't you?'

'You know I do.'

'It was Jenny's idea. Jenny Holt from the Eastleigh Preservation Society. You remember her? I happened to mention to Jeremy after the meeting last month – that it was, you know, The Big One – and that I didn't know what to do for you, and she . . . well, she suggested a surprise party. I didn't think it would work at first, but she offered to organise the food and that – Diana's helping her.'

'Deeper and deeper in, thought Isobel, basking in the warmth of his invention. Richard rumbled on, feeding little details into his monologue, emboldened by her silence into explaining all the whispered phone calls and the sudden absences, till the nurse at last rescued him, or Isabel, depending on one's point of view, from further divulgences.

'What do you want me to do?' Richard took her bandaged hand and tried to look boyish. ' Shall I cancel? Of course I will. The wine's Sale or Return so that's not a problem. We'll be eating salmon pâté for a month. Pity the children don't like it. Still, not to worry. It's just so marvelous you're okay.'

'Of course you must have the party.'

'No. Wouldn't dream of it. There's no point without you.'

'I insist. What about the guests? It's a bit hard on them.'

'They'll understand.'

Isobel was getting tired of this pointless conversation. 'What about my presents? They'll take them all away again.' A look of pained indecision spread like honey across Richard's face. 'I hadn't thought of that.'

'Well, think of it now. I shall expect you to bring them next time you come.' She lay back and closed her eyes.

'I think she needs to rest,' murmured the young student nurse, who had never been left in charge of a suicide before, albeit a failed one.

'Yes, yes, of course. Goodbye, darling. I'll be in again tomorrow.'

'Give my love to the children.'

'Will do. Isobel?' She felt his breath hot on her ear.

'Mm?'

'It . . . This . . . it was an accident, wasn't it?'

'Of course it was.'

'I knew it would be. Goodbye, darling.' Richard strode triumphantly down the ward looking neither to right nor left. Dear Isobel. Poor Isobel. Still she would have hated the surprise party. He had known from the start it would be a disaster. Just an excuse to spend more time with Jenny, really. Lovely, solemn Jenny, who didn't know the meaning of sarcasm. And Jenny would be there tonight, standing timorously over her salmon pâté – apologising for its perfection – so humble, so sincere, so adoring. And Isobel would not. It had all worked out for the best, really.

Chapter Two

Richard drove first to his mother's where the children, forewarned by their grandmother that Mummy had 'hurt her foot', demanded immediately to be taken to the hospital to gaze upon their mother's wounds. Richard exerted what patience he could but finally snapped when eleven-year-old Patrick accused him of being a spoilsport and (under his breath) a nerd. This resulted in a clip round the ear for Patrick, a storm of abuse from his mother and loud and unwavering howls from both the children.

Richard apologised, gave Patrick a pound, Eleanour twenty p and his mother the half bottle of whisky he had bought to steady his nerves with before the party.

It was agreed that Patrick and Eleanour would stay the night with Grandma and that he would pick them up at lunchtime, the next day being Saturday, and take them to see Isobel and then to the swimming pool and McDonalds. This was generally agreed to be 'wicked', and he left the trio cheerfully watching a Tarzan film and eating popcorn out of plastic pudding bowl.

Isobel meanwhile slept the sleep of the heavily doped, drifting timelessly in and out of the events of her fortieth birthday, from Eleanour's thundering appearance at a quarter past six with a musical birthday card and a lavishly wrapped box of sherbet lemons, through Patrick's offering of a cup of tea and a pin cushion made from her own discarded shoulder pads, to Richard's beribboned presentation of a tie-dyed cotton nightdress and some rather ethnic ear-rings.

That a woman entering her forty-first year could reasonably be assumed to prefer silk to unshrunk purple cotton, Isobel let pass, but it was the sight of the earrings, long and strangely angled, that had sent her bolting to the cliffs with a half bottle of Moet et Chandon and the firm intention of spitting in Jenny Holt's eye at her surprise party that evening. The earrings were pierced. Isobel's ears were not.

There are doubtless tender tales of couples who have been married for fifty years and yet are still quite unable to remember each other's favourite colour or shoe size, but Isobel's ears had played a significant part in her relationship with Richard and it wounded her savagely that he should ever have entertained a vision of her with mutilated lobes. She was only too aware that one could feel a wind change in Siberia through the gap in Jenny's conches, backed up, no doubt, by the draught inside her head, but that Richard should have confused the two of them was something she could not forgive.

She did not dislike Jenny, any more than she had disliked Naomi or Yvette. Diana still annoyed her but that was because, having wearied of Richard, she had turned her attentions to Isobel, and when this had proved a dead end, had taken to keeping her up to date with her husband's various peccadillos in a manner both moralistic and sick-making.

Jenny, aside from her obvious predilection for other people's husbands and execrable taste in nightwear, had so far caused Isobel very little trouble. True, she had not yet learnt the art of lying convincingly or ringing off when Isobel chanced to pick up the phone, but on the whole she kept well in the background of the Days' domestic life and clearly made very small demands on Richard's libido, refining if not extending his sequential technique.

Isobel had more than once reflected that it would be perfectly possible to chart Richard's infidelities by the area of her own body to which he first addressed his attentions. This seemed to her slightly ungenerous, however, besides interfering with her own continuing pleasure. Anyway, she could always find out from Diana.

For herself, Isobel had remained remarkably faithful to Richard. Her only serious breach had been a rather dreary fling with her husband's ex-business partner, begun on a joint family holiday when the children were small and allowed to peter out naturally with the first frosts of autumn. She had also fallen prey to the charms of Lebanese drummer at one of the company's annual do's, but that had taken place strictly under the influence of too much champagne, and to that day Isobel was not entirely sure if she had actually committed the act or merely passed out with her skirt over her head.

Champagne had always been her downfall. Presumably because it was so infrequently available, particularly during the early years of their marriage. It was champagne that had rendered the drummer irresistible, champagne that had made her call Richard's father a fascist at Eleanour's christening, champagne (albeit a rather sickly Spanish version) that had set off the affair with Richard's partner, and now champagne that had landed her in hospital on her fortieth birthday.

A nurse came and looked at her.

'I'm forty,' Isobel told her, her lips cracking with the effort.

'Very naughty indeed,' the nurse agreed. She was opposed to mollycoddling the suicides. The beds were needed for genuine patients.

'Water.'

'You picked the wrong spot,' said the nurse, and hurried away to organise the drinks trolley.

Isobel tried to sit up but the effort was too great. She reached desperately for the plastic jug on her locker. Richard's paper hanky had now reduced to tiny strands of filament smearing the water like a sea mist. She tried to grasp the handle.

'Now look what you've done.' The pro-life nurse stood over the dripping Isobel, an expression not unworthy of Khomeini on her face. Just behind her hovered Isobel's neighbour who had ridden hotfoot on her zimmer to the galley in order to summon aid. Isobel, cold, throbbing and still parched, shivered miserably and thought about Richard, and Jenny, and the earrings.

*

Back at Shingle Cottage Richard wrestled angrily with the cork of a bottle. The house was full of women – Diana, ordering everyone about, two of Jenny's friends from the Green Party who seemed set on turning the sitting room into an arboretum, as they staggered back and forth with sawn-off barrels of foliage, and Jenny herself, demurely spreading pâté by the ice buckets. Staring bleakly into his favourite room Richard wondered if the plants were for people to hide behind, leaping out with cries of 'Surprise' and 'Happy Birthday' when Isobel walked in.

The fact that she would not now be walking in didn't seem to make the prospect any less likely.

'Richie . . .' Jenny's soft voice broke in. 'Richie . . . I was wondering if you could give me a hand with this banner? I want to drape it across the top of the mirror but Louise has got the stepladder to put the bay clusters in the cloakroom.'

Richard gulped the remains of his wine and followed Jenny reluctantly into the sitting room. She handed him a white plastic runner and a large lump of Blue Tac. 'We didn't want to use drawing pins,' she explained. 'They make little holes.'

Richard attached the banner as best he could, alarmed to see that it read 'Happy Fortieth, Izzy' in rainbow-coloured ink. That someone, even with so slight an acquaintance as Jenny had with Isobel, should ever have thought this appropriate, filled him with an encroaching sense of despair. He detected Diana's hand in all this. The message slumped to the ground. 'I say, Jenny, do you think we really need this? I mean if Isobel's not going to be here. And it does seem a bit heavy for this blue gungey stuff you've given me.'

'Oh, Richie, yes, we must.' Jenny's eyes pleaded beseechingly. 'Don't you see, otherwise it'll just be like *any* party.'

'I don't know about that,' muttered Richard, looking once more at the magic forest.

'Oh, please, Richie. I know it must seem silly to you, but,' the faintest flush of colour swept through Jenny's pastel cheeks, 'I want this to be Isobel's night.'

A small hiccup escaped from Richard as he contemplated the depth of his lover's stupidity. 'But, darling, poor Isobel isn't going to be here. I thought you realised that.'

Jenny smiled a silvery smile. 'I do, Flumpish, I do. But that doesn't mean we mustn't think about her, or remember her.' Her voice dropped away and Richard saw a minute tear forming in the corner of each eye. He shook his head. Anyone would think Isobel was dead. A tiny jab of doubt shot through his mind. 'All right, darling. Whatever you want. After all, you've worked so hard. It's your party.'

'And Isobel's,' came the reminder.

'And Isobel's.' Richard went to have a shower.

The Jamiesons went home on a bus. Having sat for nearly three hours in reception, they were finally interviewed by a young traffic cop who had called in for a cup of tea on his way back to the station. He was a little put out by the urgency with which the receptionist directed him towards the couple, but she, too, had a bus to catch and the sight of the pair of them crushed together in the deserted hallway was beginning to get on her nerves.

The young policeman's effort to transfer the case was abruptly halted by his reporting sergeant who bellowed: 'Get on with it, you berk!' down his radio when he called in for further instructions.

'What exactly happened?' asked the constable when he had noted their name and address.

'Well,' said Mr Jamieson.

'We were going for a bit of a blow,' said Mrs Jamieson, 'and as we came over the rise we saw her . . .'

'She was standing up,' interrupted her husband.

'More like reaching. Reaching forward. Her arms were out. Like a bird. And then she sort of . . . well, went over.'

'Over what?'

'Over. That was it. The cliff.'

'Over the cliff?'

Mr Jamieson nodded.

'And what happened then?'

'Well . . .'

'We went to see,' said Mrs Jamieson. 'We went as fast as we could.'

'We hurried.'

'And what did you see?'
'That was it. She was still there. It was a miracle.'
'A miracle.'
'The policeman shook his head. 'Are you saying you thought you saw the woman fall over the cliff, but when you got there she hadn't?'
'No.'
'What exactly are you saying?'
'She went over the cliff all right. No question of that.'
'There was a ledge. A little way down.'
'Quite a way.'
'Oh, it wasn't, George. Not if you consider . . .'
'No, not considering,' he agreed.
'And the woman was on the ledge?'
'Yes.'
'Was she conscious?'
'Yes. Oh, yes. She was shrieking.'
'I think she was scared,' Mrs Jamieson confided.
'And what did you do then?'
'We told her to hang on. We'd get help,' said Mr Jamieson.
'And did you?'
'Mr Jamieson drew himself up. 'We most certainly did.'
'How?'
'Well . . .'
'I stayed with her,' volunteered Mrs Jamieson, 'and George went back. There's a coastguard station just the other side of the rise. He went there and raised the alarm. They brought a helicopter.'
'A helicopter?' The constable looked impressed.
'Yes. They didn't need it, because she wasn't that far down. Two blokes went down with a stretcher and they put ropes round it and pulled her up. It was a miracle.'
'And did the woman say anything to you?'
Mrs Jamieson looked embarrassed. 'I think she was a bit hysterical,' she murmured.
'But did she say anything?'
'Well . . .'
'Go on, Dorothy. He's a policeman. He's used to all that sort of thing. Aren't you, lad?'

The policeman nodded.

Dorothy Jamieson stared fixedly at the buckles on her woven brogues. 'She said "Some bloody birthday", just as they were putting her in the ambulance. After that she closed her eyes. I think she was a bit ashamed. We sat at the back, near the door. She didn't say anything else, did she, George?'

'Not a word.'

The policeman closed his notebook. 'Thank you very much for your help.'

'Er, constable . . . ' George Jamieson stood up and took a tentative pace after him.

'Yes?'

'We were wondering how we're going to get home? We came in the ambulance, see.'

'Ah. I should have a word with the receptionist. Would you like me to speak to her for you?'

'That would be most kind.'

The constable crossed to where the receptionist was waiting, coat buttoned, for her replacement to take over. He exchanged several words with her and then came back. 'She says there's a bus station just across the road from here,' he told them. 'So you'll be all right. Thanks for your help.'

'Well!' said the Jamiesons in unison, and made their way out of the foyer.

Chapter Three

As Isobel dreamed and the Jamiesons ate pork pies and salad, Richard sang optimistically to a tape of *Rigoletto* and scrubbed away the tensions of the day. He shaved and splashed himself with Earth Body After Shave, which Isobel swore was a combination of sweat and pesticide. In actual fact he was not particularly fond of it himself, but it had been a present from Jenny, albeit under the guise of a free sample, along with Isobel's Pure Wind shampoo, which left nothing to the imagination.

He dressed carefully in amber silk shirt, as suggested by Jenny, and cream twill trousers. Opening the drawer to find a fresh pair of socks, he came across the flat black box containing his proper present for Isobel, an oyster silk teddy with matching camisole and French knickers. Richard sighed with the genuine depression of a man whom life is treating unfairly, then finished dressing and went in search of a drink.

While the unfairness of life to Richard Day may be open to question, its determination to screw him up was not. As he padded innocently through the trailing greenery which had spread faster than bindweed along the hall, his thoughts no deeper than whether to open another red or start on the champagne straight away, he was ill-prepared for what a passing moment of weakness in Jenny's arms had allowed him to set in motion. Later he would reflect that this was the day when his faith in women's transparency began to slip. The darkness of the kitchen surprised him, since it was south-facing and usually retained the last of the sun till quite late in the evening. Reaching for the light switch he leapt back in uncharacteristic revulsion as his fingers tangled with several pieces of warm hairy bone. Before he could recover from this there was a snapping of blinds and a burst of light as the room was instantly illuminated, not only by electricity but by the dismal sight of thirty-eight people dressed in varying shades of gold and orange.

'Surprise!' They stammered self-consciously, cheer-led by Diana and Jenny, themselves afire in scorched terracotta and saffron kaftans. 'Ha . . . appy Birthday . . .' Muttering and whispering ensued as couples turned to blame each other.

Richard stood for a moment, thinking what a mistake yellow was for most people, then roused himself and proffered his boyish grin. 'Crumbs,' he said. 'You got me that time.' There was laughter. He held up his hand. 'I'm sure you all know by now . . . Jenny will have told you, that all this is a bit, how shall I say, off kilter?' Uneasy laughter. 'Let me say first of all how truly grateful I am to you all. Firstly for showing up – or rather not – in view of the circumstances. Remind me never to leave a woman alone in my kitchen again . . .' Relieved laughter. 'Secondly for agreeing to take part in this circus. I know some of you might have preferred not to spend twenty minutes holed up in the freezer. All I can say is, imagine if Isobel *had* been here – you'd've been in there for months! We'd probably still have been eating some of you in February.' Delirious laughter.

'I'd just like to say I've been to see Isobel. She's fine, sends you all her love, and in case any of you are feeling a little bit . . . worried . . . about holding a party when the guest of honour's lying ten miles away in a hospital bed, she particularly asked me to tell you that she really wants everyone to have the time of their lives tonight. And that's from the horse's mouth. And she sends special thanks to Jenny and Diana for all the effort they've put into tonight's affair and she'd like us all to drink her health at midnight, and I think that's about it . . . Oh, yes. Jenny says if anyone needs a mini-cab she's been in contact with Crabbes and they're ready to send out the fleet tonight, so has everyone got a drink? Let the revels commence.'

There was a general cheer as limbs aching from the effort of keeping still, and jaws even more tortured by the same constraint fell into overtime.

'I can't see why in hell's name we had to spend all that time shoved together in the pitch dark if a) Isobel wasn't coming and b) she knew about it anyway,' complained a rather distant acquaintance who had been dragooned in to make up the numbers. Jenny had insisted that the party total forty, though this had been rather knocked on the head by Isobel's enforced absence. She had overcome this by placing one of the few comfortable chairs in the centre of the dining room and insisting that no one sit on it. She had mooted at one point how nice it would be if they could find a suitable photo of Isobel to lay across the seat, but even Diana had assumed a temporary deafness at this.

Richard roamed around accepting condolences on Isobel's behalf, staving off enquiries which bordered on the personal, and trying to work out how he had ever been so foolish as to let Jenny loose with his address book. Of all the names incorporated in the fat little tome, Jenny seemed to have garnered the least appropriate – how could she have possibly thought that twerp from the council would have been a friend? The only reason he was in the book was because Isobel had written several bordering-on-the-libellous letters to him about the abolition of the public lavatories in Swan Street. Why on earth should he have accepted? Revenge? Richard cast a scathing eye over the man's buttercup shirt. Presumably the woman dressed like a pumpkin with him was his wife. He began to wonder whose was the true revenge. Come to think of it, they all looked equally dreadful, except for Jenny who was younger than anyone present and looked positively Pre-Raphaelite with her cinnamon hair cascading artlessly over her narrow shoulders. He wanted to sweep her away and carry her upstairs to the bedroom. No, not the bedroom. That would be too insulting to Isobel. Besides he'd forgotten to put his socks in the laundry basket and even Earth Body could not have disguised the aroma of boiled Camembert erupting from those.

He contemplated the study, but a remembrance of Diana thumping 'Coats' on the door deterred him from that possibility. He'd just have to wait. The night was young. Anyway it would be stupid to disappear just as the champagne was beginning to flow. By the look of this bunch they'd have finished the lot and be on to the sparkling Saumur before he'd got his trousers down. He'd better have a word with Diana to hold some back for midnight.

'Richard . . . Darling, what a tragedy this is. A tragedy.' Richard gazed into the Aztec eyes beckoning to him from behind a plate of asparagus.

'Marjorie. How good of you to come. I know Isobel's been longing to . . .'

'Don't say a word. It's all forgotten and forgiven. Tell her, as soon as she's well, there'll be a part for her in our next production. Well, not our next – it's *Stepping Out* – but the one after that. Definitely the one after that.'

Richard nodded his gratitude, conscious that Isobel had walked out of the last Haywain Players' production after being asked to wash all the costumes and remove Eleanour from the workshop, where she had been happily painting the chairs black.

Mrs Carter was there from the school PTA without the husband who, rumour had it, had left her for a dinner lady from the neighbouring secondary. She was eating vol-au-vents as though going for some kind of record and pouring forth the less savoury details of her private life to a plump-looking woman whom Richard recognised from the Eastleigh Preservation bunch.

Where were all their real friends? Where were Mark and Alison, and Jeff and Sally, and Bob . . . Surely Bob should be here? He only lived next door. Yes, there he was talking to Diana with that back-against-the-wall courtesy that a formal upbringing and a terror of women had engendered in him. Richard went to the rescue. 'Thank God for a familiar face.' Bob's face brightened, or maybe it was the glow from his Mr Smiley sweatshirt. 'I say, Diana,' Richard turned to her, 'who are all these people? I would have thought you could've drummed up a few tried and trusted for Isobel's fortieth.' Diana shrugged huffily. 'Nothing to do with me, sweetheart. Jenny's the one with pocket book. Perhaps you should have colour-coded it for her. You know, red for rotters, blue for bores, black for poopers . . . oops, shouldn't have said that, should I? Isobel's favourite colour's black,' she explained to Bob, who already knew. 'I think Isobel looks very beautiful in black,' he replied with unfelt courage.

'Still,' said Diana, peeved, 'it's hardly what you want at a party, is it? Someone going round in black?'

'I think it would be blessed relief after this lot,' asserted Richard, wondering how he had ever fancied her. 'It's like driving into full beam on the motorway.'

'I think anyone who misses their own surprise party is a bit of a pooper anyway,' said Diana with an acid little smile to prove she was only joking.

'Diana,' said Richard irritably, 'she fell over a cliff. Twelve feet over a cliff. I think had she had the slightest conception of what you had in store for her, she'd've made bloody sure she went the whole way.'

There was a slight lull in conversation, but since practically no one there either knew or cared about Isobel, the party continued under its own freeloading momentum.

Bob led Richard away and produced a bottle of Scotch he had hidden in one of the mountainous plant pots. They retreated to the garden. Jenny continued to waft tantalisingly and ineffectively among the guests, stopping to exchange earnest syllables about the rainforest, most of which seemed to have been transported to Shingle Cottage, and to smile and dimple disarmingly when praised for her magnificent sorrel canapés and the delicacy of her All Fruit Punch.

'Isobel's well out of this,' said Richard, not for the first time, as he ferreted unsuccessfully for the whisky.

Bob watched him with kindly concern. 'It's not in that one,' he explained at last, when Richard's elbow had completely disappeared beneath the fresh organic soil. 'It's in the one by the door.'

'You might b. well have said,' said Richard without rancour.

Bob eased himself to his feet. 'I'll get it. I've got to have a pee anyway.'

'Why don't you go behind one of these? They're big enough.' Richard gestured to the giant fern which he had been so pointlessly uprooting.

Bob shook his head. 'Too much acid. Besides, suppose you get the wrong one again?' Richard acknowledged the sense of this and went in search of some more ice. A fluttering hand touched his arm.

'Richie . . . I've been looking for you everywhere. There's someone I want you to meet.' He looked round in surprise. He had rather forgotten about Jenny since his fourth glass of Scotch, but was pleased to find her so close to him. Benignly he reached for her buttock; swiftly she detached herself from him and slid away, trailing his fingers lightly in hers.

'Anita . . . Anita . . . Here's Richard. I've found him at last.'

Richard became aware of a vast gold expanse. Raising his eyes he looked up at a woman two inches his superior, wearing what appeared to be a metal breastplate and tin hat, reminiscent of the costumes in *Springtime for Hitler*. Closer inspection revealed that the breastplate was mostly composed of sequins, as was the hat, but the overall effect was anything but soothing to Richard's already tested nerves.

'Anita's the music,' said Jenny.

'Ah,' he said. 'The music, eh?'

Anita smiled and Richard half expected to see teeth like James Bond's Jaws sparkling from her mouth. They were the normal yellowing bent variety, however, and did not markedly detract from her face which was in itself strangely unappealing.

'I think, Richie, it might be best if we got everyone into the lounge, don't you think?'

'Erm, yes,' he said helpfully, wondering if it would be possible to seal the exits and pump carbon monoxide into the room at the same time.

'Can you say something, then?' persisted Jenny.

'What sort of thing?'

'An announcement. That there's going to be music. In the lounge.'

'Oh. Right.' Richard cleared his throat. 'If I could have everyone's attention for a moment. Jenny's asked me to say there's going to be some music – live, that is – in the sitting room. So if we could all make our way in there?'

He waved his glass of ice cubes enthusiastically in the general direction they were to go and Jenny, pressing his arm warmly in gratitude, flitted away, followed by the Amazon who could be seen to be producing various thin pieces of metal from the folds of her tunic.

Richard was about to return to the garden when the phone

rang. It was his mother to tell him Eleanour had lost a tooth, and how much did the tooth fairy usually leave her? Richard said he thought it was twenty p, and his mother ahaaed down the phone and said she hadn't believed it was really two pounds fifty, as sworn to her by Patrick.

'What is that ghastly noise, Richard,' she asked sharply as a thin piercing whine rent the air. 'Is this phone bugged?'

Richard debated whether to explain or merely deny all knowledge of the sound. His mother, however, had already solved the mystery to her satisfaction. 'I know exactly what it is,' she informed him. 'It's the noise they make when you get a dirty phone call. I read about it in the Yellow Pages. Has Isobel been getting dirty phone calls? No wonder she threw herself over a cliff.'

'She didn't throw herself over, Mother. She fell. As you very well know.'

'I don't know anything of the kind,' retorted his mother huffily. 'I think if I had to put up with that noise I might very well do the same thing.'

Richard contemplated securing a sixty-minute recording of Anita's music and presenting it to his mother at the earliest opportunity. He resisted the temptation, however, and reiterating the current rate for lost teeth, bade her a chilly goodnight.

It was getting late. Late enough for Richard to calculate that by the time he had removed his socks and aired the bedroom, turned off the central heating and issued these appalling people with their thimble of champagne, it would be near enough to midnight to drink Isobel's health, empty that disgusting sorrel stuff down the waste disposal and call an end to the frivolities. The public ones, that was. The best was yet to come. Jenny, twice in one day. Well, almost one day. The midnight bit was a technicality.

He still felt slightly guilty about sneaking off with his mistress when he should have been taking his wife out to lunch, but it had only been a half arrangement. 'If I can get away,' he'd said. And he had left her the Moet et Chandon in case things hadn't worked out. Of course if he had taken Isobel to lunch she would never have gone for her walk on the cliffs . . . but that was a ridiculous train of thought. No point in speculating on what might or might not have been. Sure fire recipe for disaster. The future. That was what counted. Never look back.

'Richie . . .' He started. 'Oh, sorry, darling. Did I wake you? You looked so sweet with your head on your hands like that. Just like a little boy in nursery school.'

Through the fog of alcohol and slumber Richard tried to perceive whether this could be turned to his advantage. He rather liked the idea of schoolmistress and pupil. Isobel was useless for set piece fantasies. She always giggled.

'It's nearly midnight.'

'Ah. Oh, yes.'

'I think we should get ready for the toast. Some people have got babysitters.'

'Really?' Richard was amazed to think that anyone in his house that evening was capable of procreating. He struggled to his feet. 'Better get the champagne.'

'Oh, it's all right. Diana's done all that. Everyone's just waiting for you.'

Richard grunted and, feeling rather as Neil Kinnock must have done at the 1992 election party, followed Jenny down the hall. He was annoyed to see that Diana had been unnecessarily generous with the champagne but, seeing the look of polite anguish on several of the faces, reflected that they had probably earned their drinks for sitting in silence through Anita's minstrelsy.

'Ladies and gentlemen, it's nearly the witching hour and time to drink the health, or perhaps I should say return to health, of our absent hostess.' Slight cheer. 'May I just say once more how grateful I am to you all for making what might have been a very lonely evening for me, such a joyful occasion. You all know and love Isobel and I'm sure I'm not making too great a case for it if I say her spirit has guided the festivities this evening.' Louder cheer. 'With or without her, the show has gone on. And now, do I hear the chimes of midnight?' Everyone craned obligingly. 'Not absolutely sure. But then, when have the clocks in Barnbridge ever been right?' Much laughter. Richard raised his glass. 'To Isobel. May this be the happiest fortieth birthday she'll ever have.'

*

Everyone drank.

'Fuck!'
  'Richie, darling, please don't swear.'
  'I'm sorry, darling, it's just one of these bloody twigs has gone right through my kidneys.'
  'Oh, darling, no. Are you hurt?'
  'I'll live.' He turned on his side, batting back the offending laurel as he sought to find a clear patch of carpet. He could understand Jenny's delicacy in not wanting to sleep in the bed he shared with his wife, particularly as he had not had time to remove the offending socks, but really he was getting a bit old to be flailing around on a living-room floor surrounded by rapidly dying hired plants. Jenny's suggestion that it would be romantic, 'like sleeping under the stars', together with his own memory of their earlier encounter al fresco, had led him to agree to the conditions, but whether it was an excess of wine, a dearth of desire or just plain old-fashioned weariness, he longed to be able to crawl, preferably alone, between the covers of his bed, and close his eyes on what would be forever for him Black Friday.

Miles away in her crisp white sheets, Isobel slept and dreamt she was a bird.

Chapter Four

'I don't like that.' Isobel, in considerable pain since the nurse in charge of the drugs trolley had been giving her a very wide berth all day, held up a picture of a man with one eye and a large red parrot coming out of his cranium.

'What shall I do with this, Mummy?' Eleanour, who was unwrapping Isobel's presents like a hyperactive piece worker, held up a mauve box containing two tablets of soap and a bath cube. 'Put it over there with the other bathroom stuff, darling.' Eleanour duly added it to the pile of talc, hand creams and embroidered guest towels rapidly mounting on the corner of her bed.

'I bet I know who this is from.' Patrick handed his mother a tall brown tube with a picture of a hedgehog on the side.

Isobel considered the card. ' "Love from Jenny." How sweet. What is it? An enema?'

Richard snorted with laughter. 'Here, let me see.'

'What's a nemena, Mummy?' asked Eleanour.

'It's what you have to make you poo, isn't it, Mum?'

'More or less. Who told you that?'

'Grandma. She said Grandpa had to have one once and he went all over the floor of the doctor's.'

'Did she really?' Isobel and Richard exchanged glances. They had more than once remarked on Renate Day's habit of giving explicit details of her late husband's descent into senility to the children.

'I don't want one of those for my birthday, please,' said Eleanour in a small voice.

'It's all right, darling. It's not what Mummy said. It's

cocoa butter. To help you go brown in the sunshine.' The thought of this did not greatly appeal to Eleanour either, and she turned her attention to the remaining presents, though with notably less enthusiasm than before.

A nurse came round with tea and two slices of bread and butter. Eleanour and Patrick ate the bread and Richard and Isobel sipped at alternate sides of the teacup.

'So the party was a success?'

'Roaring,' said Richard. His head was, anyway.

'Was I missed?'

'Of course you were. Everyone kept asking after you.'

'Liar.'

'To tell the truth, I'd never seen half of them before in my life. Why I let Diana talk me into it, I'll never know.'

'Diana?' Isobel looked genuinely surprised. 'I thought it was Jenny's idea?'

'Her idea, yes. But Diana did most of the organising. Well, she would, wouldn't she? Not that Jenny didn't work her socks off getting things ready.' Richard felt he had been a little disloyal, but he really was right off Jenny after that fiasco on the sitting-room floor.

'I suppose she acted as sort of liaison officer – between you and Diana?' Isobel lay back dreamily and contemplated her plaster cast. 'Otherwise you wouldn't have had to phone her so often.'

Richard laughed uneasily. 'One thing's for certain. Never again.'

Isobel looked at him. 'Was there much champagne left?' Richard took his cue to be indignant. 'Not as much as there should have been. Bloody Diana! Sorry, kinderlings. Dishing it out like there was no tomorrow. What are you laughing at?'

'Nothing,' said Isobel. 'Only there nearly wasn't.'

'How long's Mummy going to be in hospital?' asked Eleanour on the way out.

'I'm not sure. Why don't we ask one of the nurses? They're sure to know.'

Being Saturday they were mostly agency and knew nothing,

though their faces grew notably graver once they had established which patient Mrs Day was.

'Mr Robertson will be round on Monday,' said one. 'Perhaps you'd like to speak to him personally? I could make a note.'

'Yes, yes, you'd better do that,' sighed Richard. 'But surely you know how long patients usually stay in for a broken ankle?'

The nurse was non-committal. 'It depends on a lot of things, sir,' she said. 'How complex the fracture is, the patient's general state of health, circumstances at home – whether there's anyone to help her about.'

'I can sort all that out,' responded Richard brusquely. 'I can tell you something, she won't want to be stuck in here any longer than she can help. No offence, but hospitals are definitely not Isobel's sort of thing.'

The nurse lowered her eyes. 'No, sir,' she said. 'We can see that.'

The children spent an exhilarating weekend being alternately indulged and shouted at by Richard who, though deeply attached to them, was still suffering from the after effects of the party. Bob came round and took them both fishing on Sunday morning. Patrick caught a crab and found a dead herring, left over from one of the boats, which he gave to Eleanour who insisted on putting it in the frig 'to take and show Mummy'.

Richard's mother appeared with several tins and endeavoured to prepare a Sunday lunch with some frozen pork she had dug out of her freezer cabinet. The result was universally declared disgusting and Richard was obliged to make several toasted sandwiches before the four of them set off for the hospital, Eleanour proudly wielding her disintegrating herring, now wrapped in the sports pages of the *Independent on Sunday*.

Isobel was suitably effusive and Eleanour allowed her trophy to be taken away to be 'cooked' by the student nurse who had came hurrying over to see who had been sick.

Renate helped herself to the nicer pieces of soap and two

of the guest towels, meanwhile regaling Isobel with a story of someone in her late husband's ward who had developed gangrene after stepping off a moving bus and breaking three of their toes.

Patrick asked if his mother would be home in time to watch the Under Twelves football final the following Saturday and, having established that if not his grandma would definitely wash his strip for him, pronounced himself satisfied and turned his attention to bullying Richard for a video to watch that evening.

Eleanour, not entirely free of the odour of her herring, snuggled up to Isobel and told her that she was going to do a big picture for her to hang over her bed. Isobel professed herself delighted and Richard seized the opportunity to suggest that the sooner Eleanour got started, the sooner they could bring it in to Mummy.

'You're looking much better today,' Richard ventured, while his mother was shepherding the children back to the car.

Isobel inclined her head. 'So are you.'

Richard grinned sheepishly. 'I did rather overdo it. I was missing you.' Isobel smiled. 'Yes,' she said kindly. 'I expect that was it.'

Richard squeezed her hand. Isobel winced. 'God, I'm sorry, darling. Did that hurt? I thought it was your ankle.'

'Everything hurts. I can't wait to get out of this place.'

Richard cast a glance around. 'It is a bit stuffy, isn't it? Still, I'm seeing the doctor tomorrow, then we'll know what's happening.'

'How are you managing with Patrick and Elly?'

'Oh, fine. Mother's going to stay the night, and then once I've seen the quack we can decide whether we need to get someone in.'

'What sort of someone?'

'Well, you know – an au pair or whatever.'

'Over my dead body.'

'Yes, but be reasonable, darling. Even if they do let you out, you're not going to be all that mobile for a few weeks, are you?'

'That doesn't mean I want some eighteen-year-old nymphomaniac roaming round the house day and night.'

'Oh, come on, Izzy. They're not all like you were. More's the pity. Look at that girl the Phillips have got. She wouldn't disgrace a silent order.'
'That's even worse.'
'I can't see what the alternative would be.'
'Your mother. My mother. Anybody's mother.'
'Look, shall we talk about it in the morning? After all it's a bit academic at the moment, isn't it?'
'What time are you coming?'
'Early. About half-past nine. I don't want to miss that Robertson bloke.'
'Right then.' Isobel turned huffily on her side, the weight of her plaster dragging at her like an anchor. 'See you tomorrow.'
Richard bent and kissed her. 'Tomorrow,' he murmured.
'Richard . . .' Isobel's resonant voice followed him down the ward. 'Bring me some aspirin when you come, will you? They seem to have run out here.'
Richard swallowed and felt himself flushing. 'How many?' he mouthed.
'About two hundred,' Isobel bellowed defiantly. 'And a bottle of vodka.'
From all over the building nurses came racing.

'What do you mean, a psychiatrist?' Richard, normally admired for his sang-froid, was turning an unhealthy shade of pink. 'Since when did you need a shrink for a broken ankle? No wonder the NHS is bankrupt. I didn't have a shrink for my wisdom teeth. Why does she need one for her ankle? Bloody ridiculous. Never heard anything so daft in my life.'
Mr Robertson sat calmly in his green chair. Richard had long since vacated his. 'Mr Day, believe me, there is absolutely no stigma to be attached to seeing a psychiatrist these days. You may not believe these figures, but one in nine adults will suffer some form of mental illness in the course of their lifetime.'
'Yes, well, it looks like your turn's come round,' expostulated Richard, his head buzzing with the absurdity of the man's suggestion. 'I never heard anything so ridiculous.

What's he going to do? Teach her to walk on a broken bone? What is he, some form of faith healer? Pick up thy mattress and walk? I'll tell you something, the sooner my wife gets out of here the better, as far as I'm concerned. It's creepy, that's what it is. Have you seen *One Flew Over The Cuckoo's Nest*?'

Mr Robertson smiled to show he, too, had a sense of humour. 'Mr Day, if you'd just allow me to explain . . .'

'Oh, by all means explain. Right.' Richard sat sharply on his metal chair and fixed the consultant with the sort of stare that had caused many a team manager to wilt.

'As I say, your wife is under no obligation whatsoever to undergo any form of treatment to which she is averse.'

'Oh, marvellous. So she *does* have a say in all this?'

'But I have to point out to you the facts. Your wife, on her fortieth birthday, was seen – remember there were witnesses – to throw herself over a cliff some two hundred feet above sea level.'

'Yes, and look how far she got. Twelve feet! For God's sake, man, do you seriously think if she'd intended to kill herself she'd've picked the one spot in four hundred miles of coastline with a built-in safety net?'

'Exactly my point.'

'Eh?'

'Your wife not only made certain someone saw her go over the cliff, thus assuring rapid rescue, but she chose to jump from a spot from which she could be perfectly sure she would sustain no serious injury.'

'If you don't call a broken ankle serious . . .'

'Think, Mr Day. Think of what I'm saying to you.'

'What are you saying to me?'

'That it was a cry for help.'

'Of course it was a cry for help. Wouldn't you cry for help if you'd just fallen over a cliff?'

Mr Robertson sighed. 'Mr Day, you're not listening to me. Did you ever listen to your wife, I wonder? Is that why she was forced to make this dramatic gesture? To prove to you that she was still alive.'

'It seems an odd way of going about it. Killing herself,' said Richard stubbornly. He was beginning to feel the ground give way beneath him. The man was obviously mad. Barking up completely the wrong tree. Hadn't Isobel told him herself that it was an accident; that she had tripped, or slipped, or something? 'She told me herself,' he blurted out defiantly. 'She told me it was an accident. Good God, man, do you suppose that wasn't the first thing I asked her? And she said it was an accident. So where does that leave you?'

Mr Robertson sighed again. 'That's what she told us, too.'

'Hah!' Richard thumped the desk in triumph. 'So what's all this about?'

'It's about why your wife is afraid to admit what she did, even to herself, Mr Day. That's what it's about.'

Richard closed his eyes.

Chapter Five

Dorothy Jamieson shut the front door and carried her groceries through to the kitchen. George Jamieson was reading the paper. 'Need any help with that?'

'I can manage.'

'I'll put the kettle on.' He rose and filled the plastic jug kettle their daughter had given them for Christmas. Neither of them liked it. Little chunks of limescale were constantly floating to the top and speckling their drinks like dried milk. All very well it being economical. They'd preferred the old metal one. Their daughter had said it wasn't worth mending, but it was only the plug. Anyway, someone must have thought it was, because it had gone long before the dustmen came round.

'There were some people down the town.'

'No?'

'You know what I mean. Strange people. All in yellow. They were giving out leaflets.'

'Did you get one?'

'Somewhere.'

'Probably double-glazing. Or life insurance. Did they have a coloured umbrella?'

'Not that I remember. They might have done. I didn't see.'

'Probably life insurance then.' He made the coffee.

Richard sat on the end of the bed. 'All I'm saying, darling, is that it would do no harm to speak to the man. Who knows? He might be able to tell you about some grant your entitled to or something.'

'A free abseiling course, you mean? I absolutely categorically refuse to be interrogated by some jumped up pea-brained quack who's done a postal course in psychiatry and wants someone who can't run away to practise on. And if you ever so much as hint at any such thing ever again, I shall instigate divorce proceedings on the spot. In fact, I think I shall anyway. Oh, how could you do this to me, Richard? I always thought you cared about me, just a bit.'

Helpless sobs. Richard put an arm round Isobel's trembling shoulders. 'Now you're upset.' A nurse hovered. Richard swore savagely at her. Curtains were placed around the two of them.

'Wouldn't *you* be upset? I'm stuck here in this horrible boiling dump and I can't move and my ankle's killing me . . .'

'It's still hurting?'

'Well, no, it's not hurting exactly, but it's not very nice, is it, having a leg in plaster? It goes all the way up to my knee, you know. I shall end up with one leg thinner than the other. That's what happens. The woman in the next bed told me. She says they never recover properly because the other one's done all the work, so I shall have one leg like a Russian shotputter and another one like a matchstick.'

'A woman for all seasons.'

'It's nothing to joke about. Mind you, when I'm on the funny farm I don't suppose it'll matter all that much.'

'Isobel, for heaven's sake, no one's talking about you going anywhere. All they want is for you to have a chat to this bloke and tell him why you think you fell over the cliff. It's probably got more to do with the Highways and Footpaths Commission than sending you to Broadmoor.' Isobel sniffed. Richard handed her a wad of hankies. He bent low and whispered to her, 'The truth is they think it's my fault you had your accident. I didn't notice you enough or some such rot.'

'You'll notice me all right when I've got one fat leg and one thin one.'

'So I just think the best thing would be for you to play them along a bit – say we've had a heart-to-heart and I've seen the error of my ways etcetera, and that way you'll be out of here in no time. Otherwise . . .'

'Otherwise what?'

Richard shrugged irritably. 'Otherwise they're going to keep fussing away and you'll probably be in here a fortnight. And I'll have to get an au pair or something.'

Isobel's face darkened. 'Just this once. I'm only going to speak to him once. No more.'

'That's all I'm asking, darling. Just to get them off our backs.'

'What are you doing about the children?'

'They're fine. Mother's coming round to give them their tea, and they're going to Mark and Alison's tomorrow, and Jenny said she could pop round after work and cook me something so I don't starve while you're away.'

'I wouldn't count on it. Remember those nut cutlets she brought us?'

Richard grimaced. 'Yes, well, to be honest, I was thinking of suggesting an Indian takeaway – you know, as a sort of thank you for all she's done for us.'

Isobel reached for her hairbrush. 'What a good idea,' she nodded. 'I shall have to try and think of some way of thanking her myself.'

'Mrs Day?' A small thin man with metal-framed glasses stood at the foot of the bed. Isobel looked up from her crime novel. 'Yes?'

'I'm Dr Mahon. Simon Mahon. Just thought I'd pop down for a chat. Is this an awkward time?' Isobel closed her book but said nothing.

'May I?' Dr Mahon indicated a chair. Isobel nodded coldly. 'How's the ankle?'

'Broken.'

'So I gather. Nasty things, ankles. Broken ones, that is.' He smiled.

'Have you ever had one?'

Dr Mahon looked slightly uneasy. 'Not broken, exactly. I've had a couple of collar bones, though. Falling out of trees.'

Isobel smiled politely. 'And did they send a psychiatrist to interview you?'

'When?'

'When you fell out of the trees. I mean, it was obviously a suicide attempt, wasn't it? How many times did you fall out? Did you wait till one collar bone had healed up, or did you just turn round and go back up and keep leaping out till you'd broken the other one?'

Dr Mahon cleared his throat and wondered if he should call for curtains. 'I was only a child at the time,' he murmured cautiously. 'They were only childhood accidents.'

'And mine was a middle-aged accident. They do happen, you know. This ward is full of people who've had accidents. I don't see you talking to any of them.'

Dr Mahon smiled. 'Perhaps I should be. Very few things are as straightforward as they at first appear.'

'And very few things are as complicated as you would like to make them. Now, when am I getting out of here?'

'I'm afraid that's not my province. Mr Robertson will be able to tell you more about that.'

'Perhaps you could fetch him for me?'

A tiny flicker of irritation furrowed Dr Mahon's brow. 'I can certainly ask a nurse to pass your message on.'

'Please do.'

Dr Mahon rose. 'I expect you'd like to rest now. I've enjoyed our little chat.' Isobel eyed him disdainfully and reached for her book. Dr Mahon smiled ingenuously. 'I see you like crime novels.'

Isobel raised her eyes. 'Not particularly. The hospital library is very poorly stocked.'

The psychiatrist hurried away.

'Excuse me . . .' Isobel opened her eyes. A brawny man in jeans and a leather jacket was standing at the foot of the bed. He held a crash helmet under his arm. Isobel looked at him.

'I didn't mean to wake you up.'

'You didn't.'

'I'm looking for a Dr Mahon.'

'Why? Have you fallen off your motor bike?'

'Sorry?'

'Nothing. I don't know where he is. He was round here earlier. I should ask the nurse.'

'I did. She seemed to think you might know.'

'I know where I'd like him to be, but I don't think that would be much help.'

'He didn't say where he was off to, then? After you?'

Isobel sat up. 'What is this?'

'What's what?'

'How do you know he was talking to me? What are you? The follow-up?'

The man put up his hand in mock alarm. 'Hold off. I'm only looking for the guy. The nurse said she saw him talking to you and then he cleared off. She just thought you might know, that's all.'

Isobel scowled at him. 'Well, I don't.'

'Fair enough. Sorry I disturbed you.'

'You didn't.'

'Right then. Sorry I didn't disturb you.' With an unsuitably flippant wink he turned and strode away down the ward and out into the corridor where Isobel could just see him chatting easily to Pro-Life. What a nerve, she thought. They're all after me. She returned to her novel which was about a paranoid schoolmistress who thought the devil was trying to steal her mind.

'And so you're coming home on Thursday.' Richard sat cheerfully on the end of the bed. As far as he knew Isobel had spoken to the shrink who, he assumed, was completely satisfied with the outcome, and since her x-rays proved that the bone was knitting satisfactorily, Mr Robertson had expressed his willingness for her to be discharged as soon as possible. The children were sorted, he could still have his dinner with Jenny, and he had arranged – or rather, Marjorie Bennett had – for a part-time cleaning lady to take care of the more cumbersome domestic details until Isobel was able to get about on her own. With this in view a physiotherapist had appeared briefly just before tea and measured Isobel for crutches. Her first lesson was set for the following morning.

Isobel, too, felt decidedly more cheerful at this news, especially as she had been promised a proper wash by the little student nurse, who was fast becoming quite proprietorial as she found that her charge showed none of the tendencies to slash her wrists with the cutlery that she had been told to watch out for.

'How's my picture coming along? Has Elly started it yet?' Richard grinned. 'Oh, certainly. She's doing it at school. She's says Mrs Butt thinks it's very good. It may go in The Gallery.'

Isobel smiled. 'I'm glad all this has served some purpose. Tell her to remember what I said about falling over.' Isobel had often made a point of the fact that all the local warning symbols seemed to have been designed by someone with mirror vision. People fell up stairs, tripped backwards and slid with their noses two or three inches above the ground. Of particular irritation to her was the sign for crumbling cliffs, which involved a Tin-Tin lookalike apparently in the process of going into orbit, surrounded by a small cluster of rocks tumbling resolutely back into the cliff face.

Richard stretched. 'It'll be good to have you home. I hate hospitals.'

'So do I.'

'Do you think you'll be able to manage on those crutch things?'

'Of course I will. Why shouldn't I?'

'Only asking. What shall we have for dinner on Thursday night? Something special.'

'You choose. I can't think that far ahead. Nothing with pureed swede.'

'Mr Day . . .' the staff nurse clopped across to him. 'Could you just pop into sister's office on the way out, please? One or two details . . .'

She trotted away. 'It'll be about physio, I expect,' yawned Richard. 'God, it's hot in here. Do you mind if I clear off? There's a film I want to watch at nine o'clock.'

Isobel shuffled her pillows. 'No, you go. I've got this book. I'm quite enjoying it. Hugs and squeezes to the children. Tell them to get Grandma to buy a big cake for Thursday. Whatever you do, don't let her make one,' she added hastily.

Richard smiled. 'Message received. I'll give her the money, then there'll be no excuse.'

'Mr Day . . .'

Richard had forgotten all about the staff nurse's request as he walked back into the relative cool of the corridor. 'Oh, yes. Sorry. Miles away.' He went into the little office. The sister was tidying papers into a filing cabinet.

'Mr Day. Thank you. Do sit down. I won't keep you a minute. It's about Mrs Day.'

Richard smiled. 'I imagined it would be.'

The sister looked at him gravely.

'Yes. . . . Mr Day, you know she spoke to Dr Simon Mahon, our resident psychiatrist today?'

'I gathered she had.'

'Did she say anything to you about the interview?'

'Not as such. I gather she wasn't frightfully impressed with him.'

The sister smiled apologetically. 'I'm afraid it's a bit more than that. Your wife exhibited signs of positive animosity towards Dr Mahon. So much so that he felt it best to leave the matter in abeyance for the time being.'

'Wise man. There's no talking to Isobel when she's in a mood.'

'And does she often have these "moods", Mr Day?'

Richard sensed trouble. 'What precisely are you getting at, Sister?'

'I'm not getting at anything, Mr Day. Mr Robertson just asked me to mention that, although he is perfectly satisfied with your wife's physical progress following the accident, he is a little anxious about her mental state. Dr Mahon fears she may be undergoing some sort of breakdown – minor at present but possibly opening up avenues for a more serious collapse if not monitored carefully at this stage. What he proposes is that your wife should continue to attend at St Clare's for group therapy. He runs a voluntary Depression Session on Tuesday afternoons between two and four, and he thinks it would be an excellent idea if you could persuade your wife to take part.'

Richard stared at her coldly. 'You mean people actually volunteer to come along and be depressed for two hours every Tuesday afternoon? Can't they do that in the waiting room? There's usually time.'

The sister stiffened a little. She was very proud of how St Clare's waiting time had improved since Trust Status.

'I think you know what I mean, Mr Day. As I say, it's a group session and there's absolutely no compulsion to attend. Patients are able to talk about any problems they may have, freely and in a sympathetic atmosphere – something they may not always find at home,' she added sharply.

Richard stood up. 'Well, if it's that good perhaps you should talk to her about it yourself,' he said brusquely. 'Now, if you'll excuse me, I have to go home and beat the children.'

Isobel, watching as Richard stalked out of the sister's office and away down the corridor, wondered what had passed between them. The sister did not immediately appear, and when she did, looked as inscrutable as ever. She cast a quick glance in Isobel's direction, shook her head almost imperceptibly, and made her way quickly down the corridor in the direction of the main hall.

Chapter Six

Isobel liked her crutches. They were not as unwieldy as she had feared, and once the physiotherapist had accepted that she was never going to negotiate the stairs in any other position but on her bottom, they made good progress. So much so that after lunch Isobel decided the thing she needed most was a walk in the fresh air.

It took her longer than she had anticipated to get down to the ground floor without the verbal encouragement of the physio, and by the time she got there she was feeling decidedly jaded, but a cold blast of air reminded her that freedom was within her grasp, so gingerly she hopped her way past the trolleys and x-ray machines lining the corridors until she found herself by a fire exit opening on to a small dark quadrangle of grass and wooden seats. Stealthily she eased her way through the rubber-lined door, shivering as the cool spring breeze swept through her dressing-gown. She hobbled over the uneven ground to the nearest seat and slumped triumphantly on to it. All around the quiet buzz of hospital life – the clang of pans from the kitchens, someone whistling, a woman's laugh ending in a spasm of coughing, the hum of the generator – encircled her. She leant back and closed her eyes. Somewhere high above a bird sang. Isobel, who knew nothing about birds and cared less, thought how lucky it was to be free and able to fly away from this ghastly prison where she was trapped by a leg iron of plaster.

A strange moaning sound broke the air from one of the ground-floor rooms. Gradually it increased. Isobel listened anxiously. It came from the direction of the boiler room. She only hoped there wasn't going to be an explosion. Awkwardly she levered herself up, fighting down a growing sense of panic. Trust her to pick the day the hospital blew up to be sitting ten yards from the blast. Not that the noise was exactly mechanical in nature, in fact it had a distinctly human aura to it, but it was certainly odd and Isobel felt sure she would feel happier away from it.

It was as she was squeezing her way back through the recalcitrant rubber doors that the sister spotted her. For a moment she stood poised in profile outside the x-ray department from which she had come, staring at Isobel like Gary Cooper in the shoot-out of '*High Noon*'. Isobel was equally transfixed, and hesitated to lift her crutch for fear of being beaten to the draw.

'Mrs Day. Isn't anyone with you? Oh, poor you. Well done.' The sister padded steadily towards her, murmuring encouragement like someone attempting to capture a wild horse. 'But this is excellent. All down the stairs as well? Not such a good idea to cut across the quad, though. I'm afraid we'll have to go the long way round. Never mind. Not far now.'

She herded Isobel gently but firmly along the corridor and back past the main stairway to the passage marked PSY and PATH. The thrumming sound was increasing again. It certainly wasn't motorised, Isobel conceded. More like a swarm of angry bees.

'What is that sound?' she asked as they approached.

The sister gave a deprecating laugh. 'Oh, that's just everyone relaxing. They start every session with a few exercises. It's class-led. Obviously you'll be a bit restricted to begin with . . . but the voice patterns are very soothing, so I'm told.'

A sense of horrible foreboding gripped Isobel as the sister's hand reached for the round black knob of a door marked PSY 1.

'Look . . .' she began. The sister smiled and placed a reassuring hand on her arm.

'Don't worry about a thing,' she murmured soothingly. 'They're a very friendly bunch.'

*

If the members of Dr Simon Mahon's Depression Session group were indeed friendly, they were making an excellent job of disguising the fact, as they lay in screwed-up wodges on the scrubbed wooden boards of the therapy unit. They had ceased buzzing and were now grunting noisily in short compressed snorts, at the same time slapping the floor with varying degrees of brutality. Isobel forgot for a moment that she was on crutches and swayed perilously in an instinctive desire to get away. The sister caught her expertly and smilingly placed a finger to her lips, at the same time contriving to look at her watch.

The snorting seemed to be dying a natural death as the participants gradually uncurled and lay flat on their backs, panting rhythmically like a congress of Heavy Breathers. Eventually even this petered out and the room became silent, bar the occasional rumble of a still depressed stomach. Isobel raised her eyes from the occupants of the floor and saw for the first time Dr Mahon, knotted into a corner of the room, every muscle of his body reflecting the tension from which he sought to free his disciples. Furtively he rubbed his temples and shook out his hands with wild flexing movements. Isobel noticed that everyone had their eyes shut. Just as well, she thought.

Gradually the group righted itself.

'Thank you, Meg,' purred their mentor, 'for a very . . . telling relaxation.'

A pale freckled woman of about forty-five, wearing a brilliant turquoise track suit, smiled nervously and dipped her eyes to the floor. People were beginning to get up, stretching and shaking their limbs in a way similar to Dr Mahon's, or someone with St Vitus' dance, depending on your point of view. Curious glances were aimed at Isobel, standing apart in her cream dressing-gown and matching nightdress, a snowy plaster protruding from one side and a panda slipper from the other.

The sister stepped forward. 'Dr Mahon, Mrs Day has very bravely come all the way down on her own to find you. I'll leave her with you, shall I? I'll send a junior down for her at four o'clock.'

With that she disappeared back along the echoing corridors into the labyrinth that was St Clare's. Isobel thought for a moment of following her, but the prospect of a three-point turn on crutches was more than she felt able to undertake on her first day out.

'Mrs Day . . .' Dr Mahon, all smiles, came sidling over. 'Come and sit down. Can you manage?' Isobel thumped self-consciously across the floor, feeling more and more the inadequacy of her nightwear. Installed in a chair she had a chance to survey her fellow depressives. They certainly looked the part, by and large; the only person who seemed out of place was a stocky woman with untidy grey hair and amused intelligent eyes who sat leaning against the wall, a jacket rolled up to cushion her back.

'Shall we introduce ourselves?' suggested Dr Mahon. There was a clearing of throats and a general shifting of position. Isobel wondered why they were all sitting on the floor when there were chairs ranged all around the room. They were none of them particularly young, although the woman with the mane of hennaed crimson hair was probably only in her thirties. Isobel smiled involuntarily at the thought that the thirties sounded young.

'This is Leonie.' Dr Mahon gestured to the woman, who tossed her head balefully, reminding Isobel of a horse that has lost its rider. 'And next to her is Hilary.' Hilary was a man. He, too, had a good head of hair – silvery and brushed back from his temples, revealing a high forehead and aquiline features. His eyes, pale and disinterested, swept over Isobel registering no reaction. She stared back, equally unmoved. 'Meg . . .' The woman in the track suit lifted her eyes briefly, essayed a smile then sank back into mortified contemplation of her feet. 'Maureen.' The grey-haired woman nodded cheerfully at Isobel and lifted her hand in salutation. Isobel returned her smile, amused to see the woman's eyes roll fleetingly towards the ceiling.

Dr Mahon turned to his final protégé. 'And this is Ken.' Ken jerked his head so violently that Isobel was uncertain whether the gesture was a greeting or the beginning of a fit. She smiled again and waited for the next stage in the proceedings, badly hoping that it might be tea. This was plainly too much to ask and, after Dr Mahon had revealed her own name to the assembly, various items of news and information were imparted, including the dubious revelation that Ivan, 'from the September group', had yet again felt able to discharge himself from the Reach Beyond Clinic in Berkhamstead, and that the orderly in question had been persuaded not to press charges. There was a rumble of satisfaction at this outcome and from Leonie a full-throated cry of, 'Thank God.'

Discussion then turned to any problems that had come up during the week. Ken said he had had a panic attack while waiting to change his library book and this was gone into at some length, with Leonie suggesting they should all hold wrists and hum for a while. Dr Mahon explained for Isobel's benefit that this would allow them to find each other's pressure points and release the build-up through their oesophagi. It seemed rather a long way round the problem to Isobel, who thought it would be much easier to stick with the same library book till the attack had passed, but she could see that the idea appealed to several of the members, and was only grateful that she was too far away for any of them to reach her wrists.

Dr Mahon said they would come back to that as time was pressing, and meanwhile advised Ken to breathe deeply on his own count. This proved extremely distracting, as Ken seemed quite incapable of counting at all as far as Isobel could see, going rapidly from three to one and back to six while punching himself in the abdomen and sucking in air like a drowning man.

Maureen shook her head and smiled benignly when asked if she had anything to bring up, but Meg was plainly in some difficulty, sighing and half beginning sentences till Leonie, who clearly saw herself as some kind of Distress Sixer, told her to stop hogging the limelight. This so horrified Meg that she retreated to the end of the room, weeping pitifully. Dr Mahon immediately instigated 'group comfort', which involved the entire ensemble descending on the unhappy woman and endeavouring to hug her to death. Isobel watched fascinated from her chair as Meg was variously pummelled and crunched between her colleagues, reflecting that the exercise looked about as comforting as the culmination of *Lord of the Flies*.

Dr Mahon terminated the exercise while she was still breathing, and Meg confessed herself to be feeling 'much better'. Isobel concluded that, under the circumstances, she had probably made the right decision, and they now moved on to Leonie who, apparently, was still suffering from a recurring nightmare wherein she was gang-raped by a legion of Roman soldiers and forced to run naked through a marble palace, being pelted with peeled grapes and ambrosia.

Isobel privately considered that this was the kind of nightmare most women would give their eye teeth for, and was more than a little suspicious since Leonie seemed unable to give Maureen a precise description of what ambrosia looked like when so questioned.

There was general agreement that Leonie's dreams were very vivid – and long, thought Isobel, if she can get through a whole legion. She wondered if Leonie took sleeping pills. It might be worth asking the night sister for a couple that night. Nothing venture, nothing gain.

Hilary said he was fucked if he was going to tell a group of twats like them what his fucking problems were. They were too fucking screwed up to fucking well sort themselves out, let alone him.

With this he clambered to his feet and strode across the room, slamming the door as he went. There was a short silence, then Dr Mahon smiled and said he was happy to say he really felt Hilary was coming out of himself at last. And Leonie asked if he was still writing his poems. Dr Mahon said as far as he knew, yes, but it was always difficult to tell with Hilary. Maureen said mildly that she wondered if writing was the ideal career for the man, since his vocabulary was rather more limited than her neighbour's three-year-old grandson's, but this observation was greeted with scant enthusiasm.

Far away a church clock chimed four. 'There is just one thing . . .' Dr Mahon's hands soared prophet-like to gain their attention. 'There is something I want to tell you. It's a great pity Hilary had to leave. This would have been of particular interest to him, I suspect. Never mind. I shall get in touch with him during the week to gauge his reactions. I have had a proposition put to me.' He paused dramatically.

Isobel stifled an urge to say she wasn't at all surprised. The others sat motionless, watching him. 'I have been approached ... approached, only, may I say ... by the producer of a television company ... independent, may I add ... with a view to making a "fly on the wall" documentary on my methods and treatments.' An excited rustle ran through the group. 'So far my discussions have only been preliminary, but the plan is, should you be willing, for the crew to film a few of our sessions – quite naturally – they promise we will be entirely unaware of their presence, to be shown nationwide at some later date.'

Leonie held up her hand. Dr Mahon continued, 'Now I don't have to tell you how much this would mean for me personally – a chance to present my methods to a wider audience, perhaps to encourage funding. Above all, to encourage a growth of my practices in similar clinics throughout the United Kingdom, and, dare I say it, the world? But, and it's a very big but, what really matters in all this is not me. Not me, but you. You, who have trusted me and placed your lives, albeit for a little time, in my hands. And it is of you I think when I consider this proposition. Not of publicity, not of recognition for myself – in fact that is one aspect which fills me with a slight sense of dread –'

Very slight, thought Isobel. What a creep.

'But think of the benefit it will bring to you. The confidence, the sense of self-worth it will encourage, and most of all the knowledge that, by sharing your suffering with those unfortunate millions who know nothing of my therapy, you will become a partner in your own healing process.' He bowed his head. 'Think about it. We will talk about it again next week when the director will be here to answer any problems you may be experiencing with the concept. Yes, Meg?'

'What if ... what if ...?'

'Yes?'

'What if ... we don't really want to take part?' Her voice had faded to nothing. Dr Mahon smiled sweetly.

'Naturally, Meg, there is absolutely no compulsion for anyone to take part in this unique opportunity unless they wish to. Heaven forbid.'

Meg looked vastly relieved.

'I must add, however, that there is a minimum requirement for the number of participants to make the series viable over the period of time involved. And should anyone feel that he or she is unable to avail themselves of this wonderful offer, I should naturally have to replace them from my very considerable waiting list.'

Meg's mouth worked in several directions at once. 'And ... would that person be able to rejoin the group once filming had finished?'

Dr Mahon looked like a man torn. 'I think it would be only fair,' he said slowly, 'for the person who had turned down the opportunity to return to the end of the waiting-list. Don't you?'

Meg sank into her track suit.

There was a sharp tap on the door which opened almost immediately to reveal an agency nurse, sent to retrieve Isobel.

'How'd you like it?' she asked in a strong Australian accent as Isobel thumped up the stairs on her bottom.

'Not a lot,' said Isobel.

'Bloody nutter, if you ask me,' said the nurse cheerfully. They achieved the ward without further conversation.

Chapter Seven

Jenny sat by her pile of envelopes. It was a pity that Diana hadn't been able to help her after all. Especially when she'd seemed so enthusiastic at the party the other night. It wasn't even as though Jenny had suggested it to her. She'd just happened to mention that she had two hundred envelopes to address and mail for the Eastleigh Preservation Society and Diana had practically fallen over herself in her desire to assist. Still, Diana was a very busy woman. Jenny, though busy, was nothing like so busy as Diana. She just wished she hadn't turned down that offer from Marjorie Bennett quite so firmly. Diana had made her do it, saying the woman was a menace and she would rather be hanged, burned or drowned than spend an evening in the same room with her. Presumably that excluded the party, since she was the one who had insisted Jenny ring her in a council meeting to invite her. Oh, well.

These recycled envelopes seemed to be everso slightly smaller than the regular brown they used to get from the wholesalers. She only hoped the mailshot pointing out the horrors of a new supermarket only three-quarters of a mile from an ancient monument would not be irreparably damaged by the extra fold she had been forced to introduce.

Jenny sighed and went to pour herself some herbal spring water. Opening the frig, she caught sight of the freshly ground nuts she was going to use for the walnut roast she was making for hers and Richard's dinner tomorrow night. Darling Richard. How magnificently he was coping under the strain of it all. How many men could have gone ahead the way he had with a surprise fortieth birthday party for a wife who had fallen over a cliff at lunchtime on the very day it was planned for? He had such . . .guts. Other people in her position would have said 'balls', she knew, but that was the marvelous thing about Richard – you'd never describe him in those sort of terms. He was a man of iron, of principle – a modern day hero. He just was. Of course, not everyone would agree that a married man with two children should be involved with another woman, but with Richard it was different. He was above all that. There had never been any question that he would forsake his family ties. He knew where his duty lay. Theirs was far more of a platonic love affair, with bodily communication. She was his muse, his Psyche, his bondwoman.

Isobel was his bondwoman too, but not in the same way. With Jenny his spirit, the very soul of the man, could fly free. With Isobel he was trapped. He was the hunter not the poet. The provider not the salvation. What a shame it was they couldn't both be with him, sharing the caring, the nurturing. Jenny would have loved to have borne him a child. Isobel could have helped with the delivery; the two of them together, sisters serving their lord.

Jenny hoped to be reincarnated in fifteenth-century Spain. Failing that, in a Mormon community. She had once gone out with a Mormon and been very tempted by the prospect of sharing a home with three sister-wives. Unfortunately things had not worked out quite as planned, owing to her lover's tendency to perspire rather more than the national average, which seemed to have affected his ability to attract the requisite number of helpmeets. Moreover, once his four-month ministry was over he had had to return to Salt Lake City whence he came and, despite fervent promises to the contrary, Jenny had heard no more from him and had been forced to transfer her affections to a rather dogmatic father of three who worked in the office next to hers, in the Town Planners' Department. That was before she had met Richard. Richard who one day had appeared like a sun god, standing storming in the corridor outside Parks and Planning as she tiptoed past to fetch a coffee. He'd hardly noticed her. Why should he? It was only when, stepping back to emphasise a point in his row with the Clerk of Works, he had pinned her against the wall, covering her with scalding coffee and ruining her paisley smock, he had acknowledged her existence. How dexterously he had spun to her rescue, dabbing tenderly at her tingling breasts and stomach. The coffee hadn't really burnt her, the smock was far too voluminous for that, but she was definitely shocked by the incident, and his gallant suggestion that they adjourn immediately for a light lunch had completely won her over.

Jenny sighed, pondering the inevitability of Fate. They had been destined to meet, of that she had no doubt. It was just unfortunate that destiny had not seen fit to spill the coffee some seventeen years earlier, thus avoiding the presence of Isobel in the equation. That Jenny herself would have been only ten, and thus not so irresistible to a man of twenty-eight as is a woman of twenty-seven to a man of forty-five, played little part in her fantasy. Besides, in a way it was better having Isobel around. At least she knew what she was up against. Not that Jenny saw it in those terms, but at the back of her mind there occasionally lurked the suspicion that she had not been Richard's only transgression in the years of his marriage. It wasn't anything he said exactly; more what other people said, particularly Diana who, brilliant and exciting though she was, could occasionally be a little indelicate in her remarks.

No, there was nothing wrong with Isobel. Jenny liked her; admired her; looked up to her, even. There was something so strong and independent about Isobel. She never seemed to defer to Richard before making up her mind. In fact sometimes it seemed as though she wasn't even listening to a word he said. Jenny supposed that was part of the semaphore by which long-married couples communicated. They didn't have to sit attentively trying to scratch some meaning from each other's garbled predictions; they just knew.

Jenny longed to be on that sort of footing with Richard. Of course six months was nothing compared with seventeen years, but she was beginning to sense a sort of oneness between them. For instance, she had known instinctively that Richard would want to make love to her on the floor of the living room the other night; entwined together amongst the verdant luxuriance, they had become as plants, burgeoning sinuously in the fruit of their passion. How wonderful it would have been if she could have become pregnant. Sadly, Richard was rather a stickler for safe sex. He had hinted once that he had been the victim of some form of unpleasantness down below and that this had made him doubly fastidious in the matter. It was a bit of a pity this wholly commendable solicitude did not extend to his feet, which seemed to be occasionally forgotten in his pursuit of bodily hygiene. She wondered how Isobel put up with it night after night. Perhaps she was used to it. Perhaps after seventeen years she didn't even notice. Jenny ruefully acknowledged it would probably take her at least fifteen to reach that happy plateau.

But then, Isobel was a much harder woman than Jenny. Not hard in the nasty way, although it was difficult to see how else to describe it – tough, a little insensitive. Very insensitive, if you thought about her walking out on the Haywain Players. Selfish, even. She certainly didn't seem to put Richard's welfare above her own. Sometimes he'd get home from a long day in meetings and things and Isobel wouldn't even have begun to get the supper. It wasn't as though she worked. She only had the children and the house to look after. Richard had often had to rush away from their snatched moments together because he had to get to the cleaners before it shut. Admittedly the cleaners was only half a mile from Richard's office, and a ten-mile round trip from Barnbridge, but it was Isobel's job to see to all that sort of thing. Jenny was as liberated as the next woman, but if Isobel hated housework as much as Richard said she did, perhaps she should have thought twice about getting married.

Well, she'd be all right now because Richard was getting someone in to do the cleaning till her ankle was healed. Knowing Isobel she'd probably make friends with the woman and then insist she couldn't do without her, even after her foot was mended. In fact it wouldn't surprise Jenny to hear she'd broken her ankle on purpose just to get out of clearing up after her party. No, that was hardly fair. Isobel had known nothing about the party. She was being irrational. It just did seem that some people had all the luck.

With this philosophical conclusion Jenny set aside her envelopes and went to soak the lentils for tomorrow night's roast.

Richard could tell from the carefully foil-covered loaf tin that meat was not on the menu. 'Here, let me help you.' He took Jenny's bags and peered despondently amongst the protruding greenery. Not a chop in sight. She'd bought another of those dreadful loaves full of bits again, too. They got stuck in his teeth. He'd spent half their last evening trying to dislodge them out without looking like Dracula on speed.

'I got one of those loaves you like,' smiled Jenny as she followed him in.

Patrick was in the kitchen spooning jam on to slabs of smouldering toast for himself and Eleanour. 'Hullo, Patrick, Eleanour. I've come to cook supper for Daddy while Mummy's in hospital. Are you going to have some too?'

'What is it?' asked Patrick warily.

'It's a walnut roast, with black bean salad and braised celery.'

'No, thank you,' said Patrick formally. 'We had it for lunch today at school.'

'Fibber,' squeaked Eleanour indignantly. 'It was mince and mashed potato.'

'No, it wasn't.' Patrick threw her a life-threatening glare. 'You have packed lunch. You don't know.'

Richard intercepted. 'I think perhaps it's a little sophisticated for these two. I'll open a tin of spaghetti for them and they can get an early night.'

Groans greeted this suggestion till Richard declared unceremoniously that it was that or the walnut roast, whereupon the protests subsided to muttering, and Richard was able to dismiss them to the television room while Jenny got on with her preparations and he opened a bottle of wine.

'I think it's wonderful the way you manage the children,' said Jenny, cheerfully pounding some yellow seeds into a paste.

'Oh, they're no trouble. Jolly nice kids.'

'Yes, of course they are. Marvelous. Well, they would be, wouldn't they?'

'Why?'

'They're yours.'

Richard smiled disarmingly and handed her a glass of wine. Sensibly he avoided adding, 'And Isobel's'.

'I expect you're longing to have her home?' Jenny, snuggled against Richard's feet.

'Who?' Richard dragged his attention back from Friday's meeting with the auditors which somehow the consumption of large lumps of pulverised walnut had brought painfully into focus.

Jenny struggled to free her hair, which Richard was knotting rather fiercely round his finger. 'Isobel, goosey. She's coming home tomorrow, in case you'd forgotten.'

'Oh.' Richard stifled a burp. 'Yes. No.'

' "No" you hadn't forgotten, or "no" you're not longing to see her?'

'Well, of course I hadn't forgotten, sweetness. But that's tomorrow. And tonight's tonight.'

Try as he might, Richard could not avoid adopting Jenny's AA Milne approach to love-making when in her company. Personally he preferred something more earthy. There was only room in his loins for so much foreplay. All this pussyfooting around with 'flumpish' and 'diddums', or whatever it was Jenny liked him to call her, was beginning to have a deleterious effect on their relationship.

He still yearned for her waif-like innocence, the yielding quality with which she submitted to his desires. It was just that too much time spent in conversation with her tended to blight his lust, throwing a pall of technicality over his endeavours – not helped by the leaden clumps of steamed soya regularly weighting down his vital organs.

'Isobel was telling me,' he said impassively, 'that the shrink at the hospital is going to star in a television series. One of those "fly-on-the-wall" jobs.'

'Goodness.'

'Yes. Apparently a whole television crew moves in and just films all the headcases while they're waffling on about their problems and such. Can't see how it can possibly do any good telling five million people you want to sleep with your mother.'

'Do they want to sleep with their mothers, the people at the hospital?' gurgled Jenny in some horror.

Richard sighed. 'Of course they do. All men want to sleep with their mothers. That's why they hate their fathers. Didn't you know that?'

'No.' Jenny felt slightly sick.

'Elementary psychology. Freud.'

'Oh, Freud,' said Jenny, much relieved. 'I thought you meant for real.'

They retired to the study. The children had long since gone to bed, having fended off Jenny's offer to read them a bedtime story. Patrick, at eleven, scorned all such things and Eleanour, though only six, was much of the same opinion preferring to lie under the bedclothes with a forbidden Kit Kat and a tape of The Addams Family.

They made love on the sofabed, Jenny murmuring about little piglets and Pooh Bears and Richard trying to work out what he would do with Isobel's plastered leg while performing a similar function with her. Later Jenny drove home, her heart thumping with bittersweet happiness. How magnificent her strong grizzly bear had been. She was just the softest pinkest kitten in his paws. How lonely she would be, now that the She Bear was coming home to claim him.

She swerved to avoid a jay picking desultorily at a crisp packet in the centre of the road. She must be sensible. She must not let Isobel's accident upset her. It was just that Richard was such a tender-hearted man; he'd be bound to feel he must spend more time at home, at least until Isobel was able to fend for herself. On the other hand, Isobel was very independent. She'd probably be up and about in no time. She certainly wasn't the sort to cling unnecessarily. Neither, of course, was Jenny. Richard would never put up with that kind of woman. He needed strong, free spirits around him. Emancipated creatures.

Feeling strong, free and emancipated, Jenny parked her

car, removed the pile of ironing Richard had given her to see to, and went inside to phone her mother who liked her to call her every evening.

Chapter Eight

Isobel's homecoming was every bit as chaotic as Richard had anticipated. He had taken the afternoon off to pick her up from the hospital, only to find they had lost her notes and that Mr Robertson had been called away to an emergency ...ochtomy of some kind, and would not be round before half-past three.

He phoned his mother to pick the children up, and was informed that she had been unable to get into town, owing to the non-appearance of the gas man, but had made a very nice cake from a packet she had found at the back of her larder, requiring only an egg and four tablespoons of hot water. Richard debated asking her to be sure and return the five pound note he had given her, but decided it was a lost cause.

He found Isobel dressed and sitting crossly on the end of her bed while a black male nurse endeavoured to take her blood pressure. Richard could see from the end of the ward that this was rocketing by the second. His wife had never been a patient woman, and hanging around for an absentee consultant was not at all her kind of thing.

The notes were found at last and various pills and unctions loaded into Isobel's bag. Mr Robertson had still not materialised and Isobel was all for leaving without seeing him. The sister threatened to give her an appointment for the following morning if she didn't wait, so Isobel sat on, fuming, while Richard went in search of tea – no longer available from the trolley, since Isobel had been crossed off their list.

When he returned Mr Robertson, struggling for serenity

but obviously very annoyed, was explaining to his wife the necessity of check-ups and physiotherapy. Isobel, who held the man largely responsible for her entanglement with the Depressives, had fixed him with an obdurate stare, concealing none of her contempt, and was refusing to answer any of his questions.

Mr Robertson turned as Richard approached, plainly hoping for a little cooperation and expecting none. 'Mr Day, I was just asking your wife if she will require to be fetched by ambulance for her physiotherapy treatment? I've arranged for her to come in on Tuesdays at eleven. The session lasts an hour. If she liked she could get some lunch and then go on to Dr Mahon's group in the afternoon.'

Richard gave the consultant a peculiar look. 'Does that appeal to you, darling? An hour waggling your foot in the morning, then two hours brain-washing in the afternoon?'

'Put like that, how can I resist?'

'Mr Day, I really must protest. You are obviously entitled to your own opinions on medical ethos, as practised at St Clare's. As a Trust hospital we naturally welcome constructive comment of any kind, but I cannot stand idly by and listen to you abuse a highly professional member of the staff. Dr Mahon's qualifications are second to none, I can assure you. Your wife is very fortunate to have been offered a place in his therapy sessions. Particularly at this present time.'

'You mean she didn't have to fall over the cliff first?'

Mr Robertson snorted in disgust and turned back to Isobel. 'You have your appointment card, Mrs Day. I shall look forward to seeing you in Out Patients next Tuesday.' He swung on his heel and strode purposefully out of the ward.

'That was well worth waiting for,' said Isobel loudly, as preceded by Richard she thumped cheerfully out of the ward to freedom.

'And my picture is up in the gallery. When are you coming to see it? Mrs Butt says it's very interesting.' Eleanour, crumbling pieces of her grandmother's equally interesting cake down the front of Isobel's tee-shirt, sat clamped to her mother, regaling her with all the news of which six days' enforced seclusion had deprived her. 'Patrick got sent in for calling the dinner lady a nerd.'

'Oh, Patrick, you didn't?'

'Well, she is.'

'That isn't the point. You must show respect for your elders. It's not very nice to go round calling people names. How would you like it?'

'She said you were crazy.'

'What?'

'She said, "Just because your mother's lost her mind, there's no need for you to do the same", when I forgot which side of the playground we were meant to be in.'

'You're joking!'

'I'm not. That's what she said. So I called her a nerd.'

'Quite right. Which one is it? I shall call her a nerd myself next time I see her.'

Richard handed her a cup of tea. 'Don't you think that will tend to exacerbate things? I should forget all about it. And Patrick, I don't want to hear you've been calling anyone names again. Do you hear me?'

Patrick bit huffily into his cake, which shattered in a fine explosion of crumbs all over the carpet.

'This is very nice, though I say it myself,' said Renate Day happily. They all agreed.

'I can't understand how she would even know I'd had an accident,' mused Isobel, skilfully deflecting the offer of a second slice.

'Oh, that's peasy,' chirped Eleanour knowledgeably. 'I told Mrs Butt all about it, and she must have told Mrs Pashman.'

Isobel made a note of the name. She didn't really believe Mrs Butt, who was the soul of discretion, would have said anything to anyone, but there were twenty-nine children in Eleanour's class, and six year olds were not renowned for their circumspection.

'What exactly did you say, darling?'

'Everything, mostly. How you went for a walk and got sad so you jumped off the cliff.'

Isobel stared at her. 'Who told you that?'

'Grandma. She said she didn't blame you at all, and if she was married to Daddy she'd jump off a cliff too. Didn't you, Grandma?'

Renate Day smiled benignly at her offspring. 'Something like that, I expect. Now, who's going to have the last piece of cake? It's only a little one.'

'Are you all right?' Richard turned to Isobel who was wriggling uncomfortably about in the bed, her leg propped up on several pillows, the duvet flung back to accommodate them.

'No, of course I'm not all right.'
'Do you want a pill or anything?'
'Have you got cyanide?'
'Isobel, I wish you wouldn't keep making these macabre jokes all the time. It's no wonder these stories are flying around.'
'What stories?'
'These stories. Like the dinner lady.'
'That's your mother's fault.'
'Yes, I know, but there's no need to keep feeding her ammunition. You didn't have to say I'd tried to have you committed.'
'You did, as good as. You were the one who said I ought to see that madman. Now look what's happened. They want me to star in the floor show. Who knows, I might be the next Cilla Black if I play my cards right.'
'Yes, well, ask them to get you a booking in Australia, will you? Honestly, Isobel, I know you've had a bad time and all that, but really I sometimes wonder if you *do* need a psychiatrist. You're getting paranoid. I mean, whoever believes a word my mother says?'
'Eleanour, plainly. And half the staff at Hopefield Primary.'
'Do you care? About the staff, I mean?'
Isobel sighed. 'Not really. I just feel so . . .put upon. Everyone seems to be telling me what to do. Worse than that, they're telling me what I have done. When none of them were there. Only that little old couple who came and rescued me. They never said I'd tried to kill myself. And they saw me jump.'

Richard sat bolt upright. 'What do you mean "jump"?'

Isobel shrugged. 'Fall. Whatever. I can't even remember myself what happened. One minute I was there, on top of the cliff, and the next I was there, not on top of the cliff. Will that do? God, my foot aches. Five more weeks of this thing. I shall go mad.'

She lay back and closed her eyes. Richard listened to the rhythmic sigh of her breath as she slept. Late into the night he stared up at the white glow of the alabaster moon. Shall go. Go. Has gone, he thought.

Chapter Nine

'Mummy...' Eleanour's delighted face came rushing towards Isobel as she stood, propped up on her crutches, at the school gate. Her mother's temporary indisposition did not prevent Eleanour hanging coat, lunchbox and copy of prayer for assembly over Isobel's already occupied arms. So laden, she was then presented anew to Eleanour's classmates, most of whom knew her, as 'My Mummy, who's broken her ankle.' Isobel could see from the confusion in the diminutive faces that several of Eleanour's acquaintance were trying to decide whether 'Mummy with a broken ankle' was different from 'Mummy', and if so, in what way?

Patrick ambled up and added his satchel and a pair of worn-out trainers to the cache, so that Isobel was left standing like the winner of the Crackerjack Cabbage Game, while Eleanour dashed off in search of Mrs Butt to see if she could open up the school hall again to show Isobel the famous painting.

Mrs Butt duly appeared, looking anxious and motherly, and hurried over to Isobel, remonstrating with the children as she came for burdening their mother thus.

'How are you, Mrs Day? You poor thing. Patrick, how could you ask your mother to carry your bag like that? You should know better. And you, Eleanour. You're meant to be looking after Mummy.'

Eleanour beamed, and Patrick took back his bag but not his trainers as Mrs Butt led the way to The Gallery.

'Are you all right, Mrs Day? I never know how anyone manages to cope with those crutch things. I must say you're doing awfully well. Have you had them before?'

'No, no I haven't. I expect it's just that I'm getting used to them. It's not too bad once you've got the knack. These are good.'

They were inside the school now, walking down the gloomy corridor between the two rows of paintings, starting with the fourth-form children of Patrick's age and working down to the four-year-old Reception pupils. About two-thirds of the way along the passage they stopped. The wall was divided by the door of the school kitchen and there, in full view of the dinner ladies and anyone else who cared to see, was Eleanour's picture. Isobel took a breath. Mrs Butt watched her with sympathetic concern.

'She's managed to convey an excellent sense of movement, don't you think?'

Isobel nodded. 'Oh, yes.' She turned to the excited Eleanour. 'It's beautiful, darling. You are clever. And you've remembered what I told you about not falling backwards. Has Daddy seen it yet?'

Eleanour shook her head. 'I can bring it home next Friday, can't I, Mrs Butt?'

Mrs Butt nodded. 'If you really want to, I think we could let you take it home now, Eleanour.'

Eleanour's face clouded with indecision for a moment, then cleared as she shyly shook her head. 'No, thank you, Mrs Butt. I like having it in The Gallery.'

The two women exchanged glances.

'Right you are, Eleanour. You take it home next Friday. Daddy can see it then.'

'It wasn't all that good,' grumbled Patrick ungenerously. He was now carrying his own and Eleanour's bags, plus the shoes.

'I think it was absolutely lovely,' panted Isobel, who was not as used to the crutches as she had thought.

'Will Daddy like it, too?' asked Eleanour, aware that her parents' tastes did not always coincide.

'Sure to, darling. It's excellent.'

'Which bit did you like best?'

Isobel considered. Difficult to decide from the florid face of the woman toppling headlong downwards to a waiting crocodile, the streaming witchlike hair, and the oversized goldfish swimming incuriously in the azure depths below. Had her daughter asked which bit had affected her most, Isobel would have had no problem replying. It was without doubt the title – a huge banner of black and red lettering splayed across the sky like a streamer from a bi-plane: MY MUMMY KILLING HERSEL BY ELEANOUR DAY.

'I liked it all,' said Isobel. 'What shall we have for tea?'

Richard was late home. There had been some kind of rally or demonstration in the town centre and this had led to abnormal congestion on the back road he used. He arrived hot and cross.

Isobel dispatched Eleanour to run him a bath. She was not in a particularly good mood either. Marjorie Bennett's cleaning woman had not arrived and when she had phoned, she had been palmed off with some excuse about a sickly aunt in Rye.

Isobel, not one of those who swear by the integrity of domestic helps, had been brusque with the husband, thereby ensuring weeks of undusted mantelpieces and resentful sniffing for herself, plus a half promise that Mrs Beasley would be with her on Monday, 'unless there's a relapse.'

Isobel half hoped there would be, since she had no wish to have a stranger prodding around in her home, and even less one sponsored by Marjorie Bennett.

The more she thought about it, the more likely it seemed that Mrs Bennett had installed the woman specifically to spy on her and report back on any furniture which might do for future Haywain Players' productions. Still housework was ghastly at the best of times, and there was no way she was going to triumph over adversity by learning to hoover on one leg. She gave Patrick a glass of wine to take up to his father and set about defrosting the lasagne she had found in the freezer. She supposed she would have to do some shopping at some point. Perhaps she could get a minicab and ask the man to wait while she hobbled round the supermarket. The thought did not greatly appeal. Perhaps someone would do it for her if she made a list. Not Jenny. It was bad enough to have survived six days of hospital gudge, without commissioning someone to recreate the menus in one's own home.

Richard came down much refreshed. Isobel wished she could have had a bath. Stand-up washes were not at all the same, particularly when faced with the recurrent danger of toppling sideways in mid-splash.

She thudded into the sitting room and sat down. Richard looked up from a file he was reading. 'How's your day been? Did you manage all right?'

'Not too bad. Everything takes so much longer to do. It's a bit exhausting.'

Richard nodded solicitously. 'It's bound to be to start with. Did that woman turn up? Mrs Thing?'

Isobel shook her head. 'She's got a sick aunt in Rye – according to her husband.'

'How sick?'

'How should I know?'

Richard shrugged. 'I just thought you might have asked. After all, if she's going to be nipping off to Rye all the time...'

'I don't suppose she is, unless the aunt's very sick or very rich.'

'Or both.'

'Exactly. Anyway, I've been thinking, I'm not at all sure I want one.'

'One what?'

'A cleaner. She's bound to say we've got all the wrong stuff and she can't use an upright hoover and she doesn't do windows and her last lady paid for a taxi both ways. You know what they're like.'

'Sounds suspiciously like my carrier service. Well, there's no point in worrying about it now. See if she turns up on Monday and we'll take it from there. What are we having for supper?'

'Lasagne.'

'Not those frozen ones?'

'Why? What's wrong with them?'

'Don't you remember? Mother got them from that friend of hers whose husband was fired from the Italian restaurant.'

'Oh, God. Yes, I forgot. Well, there's nothing in the frig. At least there is. There's a sort of grey thing with bits of yellow. I think it may be Patrick's fishing bait. I do wish he wouldn't put it in there.'

'Actually it's a bit of walnut roast. Jenny – you know, Jenny Holt – came round last night and cooked it for us. I think I mentioned she'd said she might?'

'Yes, you did. Was it nice?'

'Not terribly. I'm a meat man, as you well know.'

'Still, it was nice of her to offer.'

'Yes. Everyone's been very kind. Picking up the children and so forth.'

'So it was the least you could do.'

'What?'

'Have her. Round.'

Richard studied his accounts sheet. 'Yes,' he mumbled. 'How about a takeaway?'

Mrs Beasley arrived at a quarter to ten on Monday morning.

Isobel had just settled to her library book when there was a series of rings on the front door bell. Awkwardly she lowered her leg from the arm of the settee where it was resting and groped for her crutches. By the time she got to the door the chimes were assuming peal proportions, determining her to replace them with a knocker at the earliest opportunity.

A plump grizzled woman wrapped in a quilted jacket and carrying a large plastic shopping bag stood in the porch. 'I was beginning to wonder whether you was in,' she accused, and without preamble marched past Isobel and deposited her bag on the hall table. Isobel closed the door. 'Mrs Beasley?' she enquired pleasantly.

'That's right. You'll be Mrs Day.'

'Yes. How's your aunt? Your husband said . . .'

Vera Beasley fixed Isobel with a critical eye. 'As well as can be expected, thank you. I don't know if Mrs Bennett told you, I can only do Thursdays along with the Monday. I can't do three days.'

Isobel said that would be perfectly satisfactory. There really wasn't all that much to do. Mrs Beasley's lips twisted upwards in an expression of unmitigated contempt as her eyes flicked along the bookshelves lining the hall recess.

'Houses with books are always the worst,' she said unequivocally and gave Isobel her quilted jacket to dispose of.

Isobel showed her the kitchen and the utility room and offered to make her a cup of tea. Mrs Beasley said she thought she knew how to make a cup of tea, thank you, and she would need to leave early to catch her bus. Isobel contemplated asking her whether her bus always ran at a different time on Mondays and if so, whether she wouldn't prefer to change her day or consider catching a later one, but the prospect of less Mrs Beasley was infinitely more attractive than more, so she left her to it and returned to her book.

It was some time before Mrs Beasley emerged from the kitchen and this was to tell her that none of the Days' household cleansing agents were in any way adequate to the task before her and that, with Mrs Day's permission, she would purchase a fresh set and bill her accordingly. Isobel agreed to this with the stipulation that they should all be ecologically friendly, which brought a return of the twisted lips and a sound not unlike water being poured on hot fat. Mrs Beasley then went upstairs where the distant and infrequent moan of the hoover could be heard for a while, followed by the reappearance of the lady saying she didn't change sheets on account of her back.

Isobel was within two strokes of saying did she think she herself should apply for the job, since it was obviously best suited to people with ongoing infirmities, but refrained on the grounds that she did not want to prolong their conversation.

Mrs Beasley left at ten to twelve saying she would try to come early on Thursday and she liked to be paid weekly in advance. This was too much for Isobel who bestowed on her an angelic smile and said, 'Wouldn't everyone? However in the real world . . .'

Mrs Beasley sniffed with genuine flair, and said she was only doing it to oblige Mrs Bennett and Barnbridge wasn't on her usual route. Isobel replied that she would be certain to inform Mrs Bennett of her kindness and closed the door rather firmly in her face. She clattered slowly into the kitchen in search of sustenance. Mrs Beasley had managed in the course of her labours to rearrange the dried goods tins so that the cornflour now stood where the coffee had been and the rice where the biscuits belonged. Further inspection revealed that she had emptied the dishwasher and hung the tea towels on the radiator. She might or might not have swept the floor.

Isobel opened a tin of soup and made some toast. She had forgotten to ask Marjorie Bennett how much the treasure charged. Bound to be in double figures, she reflected. Upstairs there was some evidence that Mrs Beasley had cleaned the bath but none for the basin. The little of jar of bath pearls that Eleanour had bought her for a coming home present seemed rather depleted, but that could easily have been one of the children. Tired by the effort of hauling herself up the stairs, and more so from the effort of being polite to Mrs Beasley, Isobel slumped on to the bed, heaving her plaster cast after her, and lay like a log, staring at the ceiling. What a mess! To think she'd been so anxious to get home. To escape from the prison of her hospital bed. She was more in prison here than there. At least there'd been people there. Here she was in isolation, apart from the dreaded Mrs B.

She reminded Isobel of Mrs Danvers – not physically, any more than she herself could be compared with *Rebecca*'s mouselike heroine, but the relationship was startlingly similar. The sinister chatelaine, the incarcerated madwoman, the reckless unfaithful lord of the manor, returning by night to wreak his wicked will upon his crippled prisoner.

An involuntary sigh escaped her as she realised how she would welcome just such an intrusion at that very moment. It was ages since she and Richard had made love. At least ten days. While her ankle had been hurting she hadn't given it a lot of thought, but it was all right now, apart from being set in concrete. She wondered how they would manage. Whether Richard would even fancy her embedded in plaster. Still, he liked a set piece. Perhaps she should cut up one of the old pillowcases and make a nun's head-dress for herself? He'd certainly like that. Also it would give her something to do till it was time to fetch the children. She thought about it then discarded the idea. She hated sewing and anyway she'd be bound to giggle, and that always annoyed Richard.

Instead she set about rigging up a permanent rest for her ankle. The pillows were all right on a temporary basis, but they tended to sag in the night so that her legs were practically parallel by morning, making her ache from foot to thigh.

That done she turned her attention once more to the immediate problem of her future. What was she going to do all day? She couldn't drive, she couldn't cycle, she couldn't play tennis. She couldn't even walk very far. Perhaps she should try and get a part-time job. They'd be bound to look on her more favourably with her wounded leg. Besides, weren't employers meant to accept a certain percentage of disabled workers nowadays? What would happen, though, when her ankle healed? Would she be out on her ear? Did she care anyway?

Weren't people who'd had a close brush with death meant to see life so much more clearly? Surely things should be falling miraculously into perspective? She oughtn't to be lying here worrying about how to do the shopping and whether Jenny and Richard had screwed in her bed while she was away. She should be studying the petals of wayside primroses, and basking in the smell of new mown grass and the song of birds in the telegraph wires. You couldn't send telegraphs anymore. Only silly messages over the phone, that arrived on Patience Strong notepaper, long after you could have rung the person in question and said all you had to say for half the price. What did she have to say anyway? Quite a lot really. Not everyone knew what it was like to plunge over a cliff half full of champagne on their fortieth birthday. Perhaps she should write a book, dealing with her experiences. What had led her to this watershed? Whither now? She knew from the television chat shows people wrote and sold books about much less. Only the other week there had been that horrid old goat from Dorking who had been given twenty minutes prime time to plug the story of his mother's affair with a Ghurka in the nineteen thirties. If he could, why shouldn't she? Her story had far more contemporary pulling power than yet another 'Home, home on the Raj' saga. Of course, the mother had been the daughter of some top knob over there, but the son, who was he? An ex-geography master from Dorking.

He must have known someone to get all that publicity.

That was the problem. Exposure. Isobel didn't really know anyone in publishing, if you discounted that creepy friend of Jenny Holt's who ran a loss-making rag for green poets – as if there could possibly be any other kind. Richard knew a couple of blokes at the BBC but they were in current affairs. Did her accident count as a current affair? Possibly not, and definitely not by the time she'd written it up. What she needed was an immediate contact who could plant her firmly in the public consciousness. Now. Some hope.

But hope is not lightly erased from the human heart and, as Isobel rolled on to her side, prior to working her way downstairs for a cup of tea, her appointment card for St Clare's fell out of her pocket. 'Eleven o'clock. Mr Robertson', she read and in brackets underneath 'Two – Four. Dr Mahon'.

Chapter Ten

The minicab taking Isobel to St Clare's had to make a detour round the town, since there was a 'happening', as the driver described it, in the market square. Isobel, intrigued that anything, even a fruit stall, should happen in this, the quietest town on the Kent coast, accepted the news philosophically.

They were late at the hospital but so, too, was Mr Robertson whose Daimler had also been caught up in the closure of the main street. True to medical tradition the receptionist had booked four other people for eleven o'clock, so Isobel was sent to x-ray and then back to the waiting room where she squeezed herself into a seat in the corner and thought about titles for her autobiography.

'Mrs Day. . .' Isobel turned. 'Mr Robertson is ready for you now.'

Isobel hauled herself up and followed the nurse across the corridor to the consulting room.

'Good morning, Mrs Day. How are you feeling today?'

'All right,' said Isobel. Then, remembering her purpose, 'Much better, in fact.'

Mr Robertson smiled. 'Your x-rays are looking very promising. I must say, for someone of your age . . .' He hesitated. 'That is, in their forties . . .'

'I've only been in them ten days.'

'Quite. Well, yes, exactly. The bone is knitting very well. Remarkably. Not that forty is any age at all these days. Goodness, women older than you are having babies. Every day.'

'I don't think that would suit me,' said Isobel mildly. 'Not every day, anyway.'

Mr Robertson harrumphed. 'Everything all right at home?' he asked offhandedly.

Isobel was silent for a moment. 'Yes.' She stared at her hands.

Mr Robertson frowned. 'I don't suppose you've thought any more about attending Dr Mahon's therapy sessions?'

Isobel let her eyes slide quickly to his face then down again. She sighed.

'Mrs Day, is there anything you want to talk to me about? Please feel perfectly free. I can assure you anything you say will be treated in the utmost confidence.'

Isobel took a breath. 'It's just . . .' She sighed again and shook her head.

'What?'

'Just . . . I'd like to join Dr Mahon's group, but I don't think he'd want me. Not after what I said.'

A delighted smile lit the consultant's face. 'Mrs Day, of course he would. Dr Mahon is not a man to hold grievances. Goodness, he hears a lot worse than anything *you* could throw at him in the course of his work, I can assure you. This is excellent news. Will you be able to stay today?'

Isobel demurred. 'I don't know. Perhaps I'd better discuss it with my husband?'

Mr Robertson's face became grave. He put both hands on the desk and leaned towards her. 'Mrs Day, I think that would be a mistake. You have made this decision – may I say, a very wise one – on your own. I think you should stick to it. The longer you delay, the less inclined you will feel to follow it through. Believe me, I am a doctor, I have seen this happen time and again. With very serious consequences.'

Isobel's eyes rose to meet Mr Robertson's. She wondered if she should tremble a little, but decided it might be dangerous on crutches. Slowly she rose. 'Thank you, Dr Robertson,' she murmured. 'Thank you for everything.'

Mr Robertson also rose. 'Thank *you*, Mrs Day. And I shall see you in a fortnight's time, if you'd like to make an appointment at reception.'

Isobel limped into the corridor. The sun was shining on the polished lino. She felt irresistibly cheerful.

Mr Robertson put a call through to Simon Mahon's office. 'Just to say, the Day woman's agreed to put in an appearance this afternoon.' Dr Mahon haaed enigmatically. Mr Robertson rang off. That philistine Mahon got on his wick. Still, at least it looked as though he'd be bringing some money into the hospital with this television lark. Thank God he'd got him a suicide to mess around with. Not bad-looking either, for forty. They'd never have bought it with that bunch of failed alkies and fruit cakes. A self-denying suicide, now that was something for Mahon to get his teeth into. If he couldn't get them in the Jictar Ratings with that ... There was a tap at the door as a nurse appeared to ask if she could bring in the next patient.

Isobel ate her sandwiches in the little grass quad she had discovered the week before. There was no one else out there and a bird came and hopped around a few yards from her feet. Just as Isobel was deciding she quite liked birds after all, it flew away, disturbed by the swish of the doors behind her. She looked round. It was the man with the crash helmet, without it this time, but still in the same faded jeans and leather jacket. What a poseur, she thought.

'Mind if I join you? It's so hot in there.' Isobel made no attempt to shift her crutches. The man moved them out of the way and sat down. He fished a can of beer from his jacket pocket it and opened it. 'Want some?'

'No, thank you.'

'D'you work here?'

Isobel stared at him disbelievingly. 'Well, yes, of course I do. It's local policy to employ people with broken ankles to run the hospitals round here.'

The man glanced down at the plastercast protruding beneath her skirt. He laughed. 'Sorry. Didn't see it. Just had the feeling I'd seen you here before.'

'You have. I was in bed last week. You were looking for Dr Mahon.'

Realisation dawned. 'I remember. Sorry, I didn't recognise you.' He hesitated.

'Go on. Say it.'

'Say what?'
'I look different with my clothes on.'
'Not really.'
'Thank you very much.'
The man swigged his beer. 'It's a pity,' he said at last.
'What is?'
'That you don't work here.'
'I don't think so. I hate hospitals.'
'Me too.'
'Why are you here then? You don't look all that ill.'
The man turned to her solemnly. 'I have six weeks to live.'
Isobel's mouth fell open. 'I'm so sorry. I had no idea. Oh, how awful. Really?'
The man laughed. 'No, not really. At least, not as far as I know. Had you going, though, didn't I?'
'I think that's a horrid thing to do,' said Isobel, furious in her relief.
The man nodded. 'You're right. Sorry. Bad taste. Failing of mine. No, I'm on the crew for this documentary. Cameraman. Harry Peters.' He held out his hand. Isobel took it cautiously.
'You mean the one about the therapy session, the depressives . . .'
Harry nodded. 'That's the one, God help us.' He got up. 'Pity it's not about broken ankles. I might have enjoyed that.' He winked at her and made his way back indoors.
Isobel watched him wandering cheerfully round the corridor till he came to PSY 1 and disappeared through the door of it. This is not going according to plan, she thought.

Harry Peters aside, the crew from Arachne Productions came painfully close to Isobel's expectations. It was a small unit comprising the director, his PA, one sound and one cameraman, and a general dogsbody, Luce, who seemed to fulfil all those functions normally the lot of twenty-seven union stalwarts. There was also an invisible power known as the producer, who had neither name nor sex as far as Isobel could determine, but existed on some sort of higher plane, like the god of the Ancient Hebrews.
At five to two, having spent a difficult half hour trying to

find a ground floor Ladies and then to manoeuvre herself in and out of it without falling over, Isobel made her way round to Dr Mahon's therapy room. She had butterflies in her stomach, but also a sense of delicious anticipation.

The rest of the group were there already, apart from Leonie, along with the strangers, at least two of whom looked like prime candidates for ECT. One, a gaunt creature with spiky blonde hair and a small but drooping bosom, was talking earnestly to Harry Peters as he fiddled with a handheld camera. The other, a reed-like man with a greying pony tail and sallow complexion, was sitting cross-legged in front of Simon Mahon, nodding with the intensity of a brand new spring as the doctor expounded the details of his treatment programme to him.

A jolly-looking man with a purple nose was tinkering with his sound equipment while a pale pretty girl of about twenty handed round polystyrene cups of coffee.

The participants themselves seemed to have been relegated to the position of onlookers for the time being as they sat warily round the wall, occasionally murmuring to each other but in the main just watching. Only Maureen Hart seemed unaffected by the excitement of it all as she sat placidly completing her crossword.

Isobel nodded to the others and thumped her way across to her. Maureen looked up and smiled as she lowered herself beside her. 'Hullo. Didn't expect to see you here.'

Isobel felt herself blushing. 'I was curious. I doubt if I'll stay. It's not really my sort of thing.'

'Mine neither.'

'Why do you come? Oh, I'm sorry. I didn't mean to be nosy.'

Maureen laughed. 'You may well ask. Badgered into it by my GP. He didn't know what to do with me. Didn't want to keep giving me pills. I got a bit down after my husband died. I said I'd give it a go, just to get him off my back, really. Then I found out it's handy for the big Tesco's. They do special offers on Tuesday, you know. So I pop in after the session and get a lift home in the ambulance. Couldn't be better.'

Isobel smiled. 'But how do you put up with all the moaning and groaning?'

The older woman shrugged. 'It doesn't bother me. Keeps them happy. I get my shopping. Nothing's for nothing, is it?'

Isobel had to agree, but she couldn't help feeling the price of a television launch for her autobiography might have been placed a little high as Dr Mahon rose portentously and raised his hands for silence. The feeble rustle of Meg's voice died away and all was quiet, bar the cheerful humming from the sound engineer as he juggled his various gauges indiscriminately under the psychiatrist's chin. 'Just going for a level,' he explained.

'Good afternoon, everyone. Welcome. Now, as I believe I mentioned to you last week, we have with us this afternoon a television crew.'

Whatever happened to 'just a preliminary'? Isobel wondered.

'Now,' a soothing smile, 'I don't want any of you to panic. The word is they're not going to film anything this week. That is, not for public consumption.' Sighs of relief. 'What the director – I suppose this would be the appropriate time for me to introduce him to you – Mr Julian Joffe. I expect some of you will be familiar with his work? "The Panels of Southern Ecuador" comes immediately to mind.'

'Is that a soap opera?' whispered Maureen. Isobel spluttered with laughter and was rewarded with a forgiving look from their mentor. 'And many other documentaries. He is very highly thought of in his profession and we are doubly lucky that he has chosen our little group at St Clare's for his thrilling new series. "Mind: The Steps".' He paused. Isobel noted how the doctor's previously indeterminate lilt was rapidly becoming a full-blown Irish brogue as the sound man waved his meters. Was this intentional, she wondered, or a nervous reaction?

'The plan for this afternoon is that we all get to know each other. That way, when filming starts for real – hopefully next week – we shall be able to carry on quite naturally with our classes without anyone feeling under pressure or nervous. All perfectly natural reactions, I can assure you. Even I feel nervous sometimes.' Who would have guessed? thought Isobel, watching him thread and rethread his fingers.

'So, what I suggest is . . .' What Dr Mahon suggested was

never to be made clear, for at this moment the door flung open and there stood Leonie, like Vivien Leigh at the burning of Atlanta. Her hair if anything a deeper shade than the week before, her earrings twice as long. Silently she stood, one hand resting expressively on the doorhandle, her eyes both proud and submissive as she gazed upon the assembled group. 'I'm late.' The dark melancholy of her statement fell upon the abyss and was allowed to hang there. 'God, the bloody traffic. Where shall I sit?' Isobel saw her taking in the new faces, her grey eyes lingering for a moment on Harry Peters. She saw too that he was watching her with some interest and felt an inexplicable twinge of resentment.

Dr Mahon stepped forward. 'Over here, Leonie. Come and sit by Meg. I'd like you to breathe for a moment. Nothing to worry about. We've only just begun. I was just explaining what's going to happen.'

Leonie trailed her purple skirt across the floor and sank into a chair beside Meg, who immediately began to rustle at her, reminding Isobel of a gnat.

'I've talked to Julian about this – Julian is our director, Leonie.' She inclined her head. Julian returned a tight-lipped smile. 'What we'd like to do is start with an informal session – a little breathing – nothing too exhaustive, then introductions. No one need be nervous. Remember we're all on your side here. Support, that's the name of the game.' Isobel noted that Meg had gone very pale. 'What we've decided – no panic, now – just to get us used to the cameras, is that each of us will talk a little bit about ourselves. Why we're here, what we hope to achieve from the sessions etcetera, and Harry here will film it.' Gasps. Leonie closed her eyes. 'Now no one is to worry. I shall be here to help you if any of you need it. Remember, none of this will be used in the final product. You have my word for that. There is absolutely nothing to worry about.'

The pale girl reappeared with more coffee. Seeing the look on Ken's and Meg's faces, Isobel fervently hoped it contained some form of sedative.

Simon Mahon must also have detected a potential problem with the imminent suicide of two of his clients for he instigated a quick panting session followed by some heavy breathing which seemed to produce the required anodyne, albeit temporarily.

Mingling was encouraged while they drank their coffee. This meant that Harry and the sound man, who was called Jock, went into deep discussion at the end of which Luce, the dogsbody, was dispatched to place bets over the phone. Julian Joffe, whom it appeared could only be addressed through a third person, in this case the spiky PA, Fran, was led round the room like a sacrificial goat and introduced to his cast. He said very little, but pressed a long clammy hand against those offered before returning to Dr Mahon and engaging once more in earnest conversation.

Leonie and Hilary were on their feet, talking in loud theatrical voices about the appallingness of life in general and the traffic round the ring road in particular.

Isobel wondered if Leonie worked, and if so, as what. She had the air of a third-rate actress which, if true, might account for her availability in the middle of the day. Hilary was probably rich, she decided. His designer dinge was too carefully arranged to be the genuine product of indifference or poverty. Meg – it was impossible to say. A part-time secretary? How would she ever answer the phone? Maureen, she imagined, was retired. Poor Ken looked too fidgety to hold down a job. He was probably the only person there in genuine need of help. It would be interesting to see how media exposure would affect him. Not that she would be around to see it. One look at Julian Joffe had convinced her that he was not the man to launch her earth-shattering revelations. Still, it had been worth a try. And she might go to Tesco's on the way home. Maureen would help her, she felt sure of that.

'Didn't expect to see you here.' She looked up. Harry was grinning down at her.

'No.'

'Seems a queer way to mend a broken ankle.'

'What?'

'Rolling round on the floor and reading poems and that.'
'I see you've done your homework.'
'I always do my homework. Tell me why you're here.'
'I want to be the next Gloria Hunniford.'

Harry glanced around the room. 'You've got some competition.' Isobel laughed. He crouched down and began to peel her skirt slowly up her leg. She slapped him hard on the shoulder. 'What the hell do you think you're doing?'

Harry retreated. 'Just wanted to see if it was a real plaster. I mean, if you had a thing about pretending you'd broken your ankle, you'd be well advised to contact a shrink, wouldn't you?'

There was a slight hush as Julian glared at Harry. He put his hand to his mouth. 'Sorry, guv. Forgot. Not meant to call them "shrinks",' he said in a stage whisper. Maureen chuckled into her crossword.

'Harry, if you're about ready?' said Julian. His voice was high and slightly petulant. It accorded very well with Isobel's image of an arty director.

Harry rose and went back to his camera. Dr Mahon had 'volunteered' to go first, much to everyone's relief. He introduced himself, reeling off a long stream of qualifications, none of which anyone had heard of, and a number of doctorates and degrees from remote and American-sounding universities, which bore the same distinction. He then went on to express his purpose in undertaking this 'unique experiment'. This quite interested Isobel, since to her certain knowledge programmes of this nature had been going on at regular intervals since the late-sixties, but she was curious to know what he expected to get out of it, apart from his own column in *Woman's Own* and intermittent invitations from Breakfast TV.

None of this was forthcoming, however, and the monologue was eventually brought to a close by Jock raising his hand to say he was running out of tape.

There now followed the dreadful quandary of who should go next. Dr Mahon wanted it to be Meg, on the reasonable grounds that she would probably die of fright if she had to wait much longer. Meg, however, was quite unable to see it in this light, and had to be escorted to the lavatory by Luce. Discussion then ensued between Hilary and Leonie, each seeking to persuade the other, and modestly decrying the suitability of their own personalities to such intimate perusal. While this was going on, Maureen quietly folded her newspaper, wandered over to where Harry was standing staring into space, spoke to him briefly, and sat down in the chair vacated by Simon Mahon.

The camera rolled as Maureen explained that her name was Maureen Hart, that she was fifty-nine, had been a widow for eight months, had no children and had joined the group in the hope of readjusting to life as a single person after all her years as a married woman. This seemed perfectly reasonable to the class, though perhaps not worthy of the riotous applause triggered by Dr Mahon and avidly continued by Julian Joffe and Fran.

The time for modesty was clearly past as Leonie, without so much as a sideways glance, swept into Maureen's seat and with a toss of her crimson mane, flung her leg provocatively across her knee, revealing a surprisingly long slit in her floor-length skirt, as she beamed upon Julian and then gave Harry her most seductive smile.

She explained that she was Leonie Carter, a poetess by trade (Maureen and Isobel exchanged glances), and that she had enrolled for therapy to find herself. Isobel considered that it would be very difficult to lose her in those ear-rings, but decided to keep the observation to herself. Hilary was plainly sulking and said he'd be fucking well damned if he was going to talk to a fucking camera and a fucking tape recorder. Harry shrugged and said it was fucking well all right by him, so Hilary was relegated to behind Ken and Meg, who had come tiptoeing back from the Ladies with an anxious-looking Luce holding her elbow.

Ken stammered so badly that it was hard to get hold of his name, let alone his problem, but it was finally established that he was called Graves, and that he was forty-seven and had recently been made redundant from his job. He was divorced and also childless which began to make Isobel feel like a freak of nature, till Meg was eased into the chair and confessed to having both a husband and a son of nineteen, and also her husband's mother living in her house.

It was at this point that Dr Mahon's manner changed. 'Tell us about your relationship with your mother-in-law, Meg,' he commanded softly. Isobel saw her baulk. This was obviously no part of Luce's agenda for enticing her out of a locked lavatory.

'I . . .' she began, her eyes fluttering desperately round the silent faces.

'Come along, Meg. Remember what we've said. You must learn to face up to problems if you want to solve them. Tell us about your husband's mother. Do you like her?'

'I . . . Nn . . . Nnn . . .'

She's going to be sick, thought Isobel. What a bastard.

'We didn't come here to talk about mothers-in-law.'

There was a stunned silence. Everyone looked at Maureen. Her face remained implacable but Isobel caught the tiny glint of steel in her calm brown eyes. Simon Mahon caught it too, for he smiled at her genially.

'Perhaps you're right, Maureen. After all, tempus fugit. Thank you, Meg. Let's hope you manage to get the hang of it next week.' He held out an arm. 'Mrs Day. Your turn, I think.'

'No, thanks,' said Isobel.

'Yes, please.' He gave a little laugh to demonstrate his use of wit. Isobel remained where she was.

'We're waiting.'

Isobel smiled. Hilary intervened. 'Oh, for fuck's sake, why don't I go next? Save all this effing hanging about.' Dr Mahon waved his hand imperiously. 'I've asked Isobel to go next.'

Hilary turned to her. 'Go on. Get it over with.'

'Yes, go on,' intercepted Leonie. 'We want to move on.'

Meg leant forward. 'It's not too bad really,' she whispered encouragingly. Ken croaked something.

Dr Mahon turned to Maureen. 'What do you think, Maureen? Do you think Isobel should let herself down like this?'

Maureen was silent for a moment. 'I don't think she is letting herself down,' she said finally. 'I think she's one of the few people here who is in control of her own feelings.'

'You are a group.' Mahon thumped the table to emphasise his point. 'You must act collectively – together. That is the point of the therapy.'

'Trained in China, did you, guv?' asked Harry, adjusting his lens and swinging it round threateningly towards the doctor's hairline. Mahon was at once alarmed and infuriated. His glance fled to the director who was watching the entire encounter with a rapt expression on his naturally gloomy face.

Harry swung the camera back. 'Either she does or she doesn't. It's all the same to me.'

'It's got nothing to do with you,' squeaked Mahon, then pulled himself together. 'If Isobel would rather sit this one out, that's perfectly acceptable to me. It's just the group I'm thinking of.'

'That'll be a first,' muttered Maureen under her breath. Isobel watched as Hilary edged himself towards the chair. Slowly she hauled herself up. 'All right,' she said politely. 'I don't mind.' A look of sly triumph spread across Mahon's face. He smiled but said nothing as she took her place. Hilary once more subsided, burping loudly as he disappeared behind the pages of a *Morning Star*.

Harry leaned forward. 'The camera's pointing at the floor,' he murmured, 'so you can say what you like.' Isobel sat down. Dr Mahon was on his feet. 'If I could just stop you for one minute...' He turned to Joffe. 'Could you ask... Fred, is it? ... to focus the camera on Mrs Day's face. Not the hem of her skirt.'

Harry emerged from behind the apparatus. 'Look, guv, would you like to take over this thing and I'll do what you're doing, which is getting up everyone's nostrils? I *am* pointing it at her face. It's called a Number Three, okay? Not every mugshot starts with the wart on your nose. Did you know that?'

Harry had moved several paces forward as he spoke, with Mahon retreating accordingly. It was Jock who calmed the atmosphere by demanding in a thick highland accent whether anyone was wearing handcuffs because he was getting a clink on his boom. Harry returned to his position and Isobel adjusted her skirt, just in case he was working some sort of periscope system.

'My name is Isobel Day. I am married with two children: Patrick who is eleven, and Eleanour who is six. My husband is a marketing manager. His name is Richard.'

'How old are you, Isobel?' came the wily Irish voice.

'I'm forty.'

'And why have you agreed to take part in this experiment?'

Isobel looked straight into the lens of the camera. 'I've got the hots for Harry,' she said.

They went again, Harry having apologised for dropping the light meter on Jock's spare tapes.

This time Isobel said that she felt she had a lot to learn from her fellow volunteers, and that she hoped Dr Mahon's therapy would enable her to become a more fulfilled and caring person.

Julian led the applause for this. He had been seriously alarmed by the flippancy of her previous reply, and though he had been warned to expect the unexpected, had laid no plans for the onslaught of humour in his series. This was something that had to be nipped in the bud. Mind you, he could always edit the dratted woman out if she was going to behave like a comedienne. But even that would present problems because she was the promised suicide attempt. True there was another, but that was only pills, not a full-blown leap over the cliff like the Day woman.

Trouble was she looked so well-adjusted, apart from her ankle. Of course, that was possibly the exciting part – the fact that she looked normal. Very Hitchcockian. He was looking forward to the bit when Simon Mahon forced her to confess what she had done in front of the whole group. That should be some show.

Isobel relinquished her seat to Hilary, who said he really didn't give a toss whether they filmed him or not, whereupon Harry said 'fine', and put the cover on his camera. Hilary looked distinctly shocked by this, and said he didn't mind if they really insisted, so Harry took the cover back off and Hilary let fly with a stream of invective about his several sodding wives and his bleep bleep father.

Isobel reflected that it was something of a gift to be able to express one's frustrations in terms of 'bleep bleep', particularly if appearing on television. This fueled her suspicion that Hilary was not without media connections of some kind, but she was more concerned with asking Maureen if she could accompany her to Tesco's than pondering the finer points of Hilary Bell's background.

Dr Mahon rounded off the session by saying they had all done very well and could Meg stay behind for a minute? He then suggested that they breathe through one nostril to a count of ten before dismissing them and turning his attention to Julian who was hovering over him with a line of creases in his forehead that would not have disgraced a professional pleater.

Maureen professed herself delighted to escort Isobel round the supermarket. 'We can share a trolley,' she said. 'I don't want much. We might even get a boy to push it for us.'

'Push what?' asked Harry who had packed up his gear and was holding the door open for them.

'Our trolley,' said Maureen. 'We're going to Tesco's.'

'I'll push it for you. I need some beer.'

'Cheerio.' Isobel waved to Maureen who was going back to Reception to wait for her ambulance. She gazed at the trolley, piled high with provisions to keep Jenny Holt at bay. This was a mistake.

'Where now?' asked Harry, unfastening a beer from his six pack and opening it with his teeth.

'I'll have to phone for a minicab. There are some phones over by the kiosk.'

'Where do you live?'

'Barnbridge.'

'Far?'

'Too far to walk.'

'The curb's too far with this lot.'

'It's about eight miles.'

'I'll take you.'

'No. Thank you. I couldn't possibly. I mean, you must have to get back to London. You'll hit the traffic as it is.'

'Birmingham.'

'Birmingham?'

'Going to see my daughter.'

'Oh, well . . . all the more reason to get going.'

'Eight miles isn't going to make any difference.'

'It'll be sixteen by the time you've gone both ways.'

'You don't want me to?'

'I didn't say that. I just don't want to be a nuisance. This blasted ankle. I know now how invalids feel. Always depending on other people.'

Harry took a swig of his beer. 'Invalids love it. It's handicapped people can't stand it.'

He drove fast along the winding lanes.

'How did you get involved in all this?' asked Isobel. 'Turn left at the next signpost.'

'Needed the work. There've been a lot of cutbacks.'

'Did you know the director before?'

Harry shook his head. 'Jock got me on it. There's not much doing these days.'

'Won't you go mad?'

'Will it show?'

Isobel laughed. 'I hate that man, Mahon.'

'Is that why you're there?'

'It wasn't. I think now maybe it is. I was going to write a book. I thought I might make some useful contacts.'

'What sort of book?'

Isobel hesitated. 'Fiction.'

Harry nodded. 'Not much call for that when you've got that bunch for real. There's two wouldbe suicides amongst that lot. Did you know that?'

Isobel looked at him. 'Do you know who they are? Turn right here.'

Harry swung round the corner. 'Nope. But I bet I soon will.'

'How much do you bet?' asked Isobel. 'This is where I live.'

Harry slid to a halt. 'How much is it worth?'

'Nothing,' said Isobel.

Richard opened the door to them.

Chapter Eleven

Harry and Richard unloaded the shopping. 'Thanks,' said Richard. 'How much do I owe you?'
'That's all right,' said Harry. Richard stared at him oddly. 'What do you mean?'
'You don't owe me anything.'
'Are you from the hospital?'
'You could say that.'
Isobel returned from greeting the children. 'Richard, this is Harry. He's the cameraman on Dr Mahon's series.'
A look of deep suspicion furrowed Richard's brow. 'What's that got to do with you?'
'I'm in it.'
'You're what? Isobel, I hope this is a joke.'
Isobel grinned at Harry. 'I wouldn't call it that exactly. Aren't you going to offer Harry a beer or something? He's gone right out of his way to bring me home.'
Harry shook his head. 'No, thanks. I'd better get going. Well,' he held out his hand, 'nice to meet you.' He turned to Isobel. 'See you next week?'
'I don't know. I'm going to think about it.'
He turned to Richard. 'Try and persuade her, will you? That plaster's got a lot of potential.'
Richard nodded curtly.
Isobel watched Harry drive away. 'It was nice of him to bring me home.'
'Anyone would have done the same.'
'They didn't though, did they?'
'What's all this about you being in that maniac's series?

You swore blind you were having nothing to do with it.'

'I'm allowed to change my mind, aren't I?'

'Not about things like that. Have you any idea the harm you could do yourself, appearing in a television programme with a load of nutcases?'

'They're not nutcases. Not all of them anyway. If you ask me Dr Mahon's the one who needs to be locked up. The man's a bastard.'

'There you are then. Let's hear no more about it. Jenny thought it was an appalling idea when I told her. And you know how liberal she is.'

'What the hell's it got to do with her? I'll thank you not to discuss my personal affairs with every Tom, Dick and Harry that sticks a nut cutlet under your nose.'

'That's not fair. Jenny's a friend. She's only got your best interest at heart.'

Isobel turned on him. Richard did not like the look in her eyes. 'Anyway,' he waffled, 'perhaps you're right. I shouldn't have mentioned it. I'm sorry. It's just she was there and it sort of came out. I'm sorry. I'll be more careful in future.'

Isobel continued to stare at him. 'Good,' she said at last, and left the room.

True to her word, Vera Beasley arrived three or four minutes early on Thursday morning. Richard had not long left for work since he had a meeting to attend and hadn't thought it worth going into the office first. Thus he had been able to help Isobel sort out some tasks to keep herself occupied with during her enforced incarceration in the sitting room which they had agreed would best serve as a retreat from Mrs Beasley. Isobel was seated by the window with her foot on the pouffe when the woman arrived. She was trying to work out which of the bills should be paid first, and which would have to wait till the end of the month. It was all very boring. She sustained herself with the thought that when she had done this she could start on her book.

She had decided to press ahead with it, despite her misgivings about its projected launch. After all, quality would out. The only thing that stopped her discounting the Mahon circus altogether was the knowledge that Jenny Holt thought it a bad idea. That alone would be sufficient reason to persist through hell and high water – a fairly apposite metaphor – plus the possibility of revenging herself on that charlatan, Simon Mahon. She wasn't sure how, but felt it within her grasp. And that creepy consultant who had got her into all this in the first place. Yes, it was too soon to give up yet.

'I've brought you one of these.' Mrs Beasley thrust a sheet of pale yellow paper into Isobel's hand. 'I thought it might help.' She received it gratefully, hoping it might contain the names of several alternative cleaning ladies. It was, however, merely a list of forthcoming rallies for a group called Apocalypse 2000, citing various ecological disasters in the offing, the majority of which seemed destined for the east coast of Kent if its message was to be believed.

'This house will be under water in twenty years' time,' Mrs Beasley continued with stoic satisfaction. 'There are too many wicked thoughts floating around. The sea is angry.'

It seemed a little hard to Isobel that the sea should have singled out her particular house as a recipient for its venom, especially when her own was so amply justified. 'Ah, well, I expect the damp course guarantee will cover it.'

'See what I mean?' Mrs Beasley rebuked her. 'Man shall not live by bread alone.'

'Indeed not,' Isobel agreed, edging her way back towards the sitting room.'

'People don't realise.'

Isobel smiled, hoping to convey both realisation and the lack of it. 'I'd like you to concentrate on Patrick's room this morning, please. Don't worry about the rest. I'm getting the hang of the hoover now.'

'S'more than I ever will,' muttered Mrs Beasley darkly. 'I was in bed all evening with my back after I got home Monday.'

'I'll leave you to it then, shall I?' said Isobel brightly and made a positive bid for sanctuary.

'I was going to do your frig for you,' came a doleful rejoinder.

'No need,' countered Isobel through the door. She sat for

some moments, anticipating a rearguard action, but when none was forthcoming, returned to her paperwork.

Bills completed, she wrote a couple of thank you letters to friends who had sent flowers, poured herself some coffee from the flask she had persuaded Richard to prepare for her, and opened the pristine reporter's notebook. 'My Life', she wrote neatly at the top of the page and underlined it twice. 'By Isobel Day'. There was something about this that reminded her of Eleanour's painting, but she let that pass. It might even be a good idea to use her daughter's picture for the cover. It was certainly very eye-catching.

'Notes', she wrote, and underlined it once. 'Unfaithful husband. Vegetarian mistress. Middle-age. Madness. Suicide.' She looked at what she had done. It was pleasingly concise. She wondered if she should try to write some character sketches, but there didn't seem much point since she knew the people involved and would merely have to transcribe them to paper as the time arose.

She poured herself some more coffee, rearranged the flowers in the vase on her desk, and re-read a letter from an uncle dated 1985 which had fallen out of one of Richard's A – Zs.

The door opened to reveal Mrs Beasley holding the bottom half of Patrick's pyjamas and asking what Isobel wanted her to do with them. 'Are they dirty?'

'They're not clean.'

'Well, no, they wouldn't be clean. Do you happen to know where the top half is?'

'Under his pillow.'

'Is that clean?'

'It's about the same.'

A sense of being in a Pinter play invaded Isobel. ' I should just put the trousers under the pillow too then, Mrs Beasley. Was there anything else?'

'I wondered if you'd decided?'

'Decided what?'

'Whether to go to the meeting. The one in Barnbridge. It's tomorrow evening. Only I need to let them know.'

'Let who know? I'm sorry, I've no idea what you're talking about. Which meeting is this?' Marjorie Bennett must have given the woman a message for her and she'd forgotten all about it.

Mrs Beasley lifted a vase on the piano and began to polish underneath it. 'The Appoclix 2000,' she said in an offhand way. Isobel gawped. 'You mean that leaflet you gave me when you came in?'

'That'd be it.'

Isobel didn't know whether to laugh or cry. 'Actually, no, Mrs Beasley. It isn't something I think I'd be interested in. Whatsoever.'

Mrs Beasley raised her eyebrows and replaced her duster in her apron pocket. 'We're none of us beyond help,' she said reprovingly.

I wouldn't count on it, thought Isobel. She smiled politely. 'I'm sure we're not. Is Patrick's room finished now? You might like to just do the bathrooms.' Mrs Beasley seemed about to reply but changed her mind and plodded laboriously out of the room.

To think I've voted Labour all my life, Isobel chided herself. But how else was she to get rid of the woman? She hadn't wanted her in the first place. She certainly didn't want her now. It was all Marjorie Bennett's fault. How she loathed that woman. When her foot was better she was going to sneak Eleanour and all the Rainbow Brownies into the Haywain Players' workshop and let them loose with cans of spray paint. That would teach her to be helpful.

She turned to her notes. She seemed to have got the nub of it there. Neatly she added 'End of World' and 'Sinister Charwoman'. She felt quite exhausted. To think people said writing was easy. Never again would she sneer at The South Bank Show. She looked at her watch. Half-past eleven. Mrs Beasley would be wanting to be paid. Idiot that she was, she'd forgotten to get in touch with Marjorie Bennett about the woman's wages. She fished in her bag. She had a ten pound note. Surely the creature wouldn't want more than that for waving Patrick's pyjamas in her face? Isobel doubted she'd done much more all morning. Perhaps she should have let her clean the frig after all. Jenny's walnut roast was still in there, festering gently. Neither of them could bring themselves to throw it out; Richard out of peak and Isobel out of a long-held ambition to discover a cure for Aids.

She sighed, put her notebook in her bag and went in search of Mrs Beasley. She found her, not as suggested, in the bathroom, but outside delving feverishly amongst the pile of charcoal, tongs and accoutrements Isobel had exhumed from the garden shed with a view to barbecuing on the first warm evening.

'Are you looking for anything, Mrs Beasley?'

She raised herself slowly. 'No,' she said, and put her hands in her apron pockets.

Isobel smiled curiously. 'I forgot to ask how much you charge,' she said.

'She charges nine pounds a morning. I had to give her a cheque. She was most put out. I think she thought I'd have a biscuit tin full of used fivers stashed away somewhere. She certainly gave Elly's elephant a good look.'

'Nine pounds isn't all that much nowadays,' said Richard impartially. 'Not for a full morning's work.'

'No, not for a full morning's work, I agree. Unfortunately I don't think Mrs Beasley works to the same time system as most people. Her morning starts at twenty to ten and ends at a quarter to twelve.'

'Well – if she gets it done.'

Isobel gave up. 'I don't like her coming. She interferes with my work.'

Richard raised his eyes from his newspaper. 'What work?'

Isobel hesitated. 'It's just something I'm doing. And I don't like being constantly disturbed.'

Richard sighed. 'Just tell her then. Honestly, Isobel, I don't know what's come over you. You never used to be so feeble.'

'Oh, thank you. Well, thank goodness you're still a knight in shining armour.' Isobel made a creditable attempt to flounce from the room, somewhat impeded by her crutches.

Richard closed his eyes and laid his head on the back of the chair. God, this was worse than he had imagined. How long would her foot be in plaster? The quack had muttered something about five weeks. He didn't think he could stand another four. What was he supposed to do? He'd got her a home help, albeit not a very efficient one, from the sound of it. He'd arranged for the butcher to deliver. Patrick was bringing Elly home from school on the days his mother couldn't manage it. She had the phone, she had books. What was the matter with her? She'd never been this bloody useless before.

A ghastly thought struck him. Suppose it was her age? Suppose it was true, all the things they said about women reaching forty? Jenny had shown him a book about it. She seemed to think it was perfectly normal. Well, she would with thirteen years in hand. If that were the case the broken ankle would merely be incidental. Five weeks! He gave an involuntary laugh. Fifty years, more like. He was a doomed man. Isobel would become progressively more fractious, more demanding, more accident-prone. Images of his wife bouncing off bridges, flyovers and highrise flats flashed before him. She would lose all interest in sex, be covered in facial hair, take up peculiar causes . . .

Isobel reappeared in the doorway. 'I'm making a risotto,' she informed him defiantly.

Richard opened his eyes. 'Lovely,' he said politely. 'Do you want any help?'

Isobel gave him a long cool look. 'No, thank you,' she said. 'I'm enjoying the challenge. Oh, by the way, Mrs Beasley left this. I don't know if it's of any interest to you?' She flicked a piece of yellow paper at him.

Richard read it. 'Why on earth should it be? Load of cranks.'

Isobel smiled serenely. 'It's always good to keep an open mind, isn't it?'

Chapter Twelve

'What's the matter, Flumpish?' Jenny lay across Richard's body, tickling his nose with a paintbrush of hair.
'Nothing. Why should there be?'
'I don't know. You just seem a bit . . . far away.'
Some hope, thought Richard, struggling to stretch his left leg which was buzzing with pins and needles. It was not that Jenny's room was small; in fact it was the largest of the three in the house which she shared with divorced music teacher and a rather glamorous travel agent, who always seemed to be away. It was just so unbearably cluttered. Richard liked straight lines, open spaces, tall rectangular windows which could be flung open and breathed through.
One of the things that had first attracted him to Jenny, as opposed to the travel agent whom he had met very early on in the courtship, was the size and scope of her french windows. But Jenny, ever true to the rainforest, had covered the wretched things with some kind of climbing shrub, practically obscuring the light and making it quite impossible to open them.
Richard sighed. Jenny tickled harder. Richard sneezed. 'Oh, darling, now you've caught a cold. I knew we shouldn't have opened the bathroom window. I could see you were in a draught.'
How erotic can you get? mused Richard. 'Good God, is that the time? I'd better be off. We promised the children a barbecue. I don't want Isobel messing with it. She'll end up like Joan of Arc.'
'Dear Richie. You're so thoughtful. What are you going to cook?'

'Steak,' said Richard with relish, and in a moment of inspiration, 'Isobel wanted to invite you, but you don't like that sort of thing much, do you?'

Jenny smiled sadly. 'How sweet of her, but you're quite right. And I don't think you should be eating so much meat. It's not good for you. It makes you all grumpy. I can always tell when you've had meat for lunch. You didn't know that, did you?'

'No,' said Richard, thinking he was a lot grumpier when he hadn't had meat.

'Anyway I'm going out tonight.'

'Oh?'

'Yes. It's a meeting by the pier. Apocalypse 2000. I don't know much about it. Anita asked me to go with her. You remember Anita, don't you?'

'Very well.'

'She is nice, isn't she? She's very interested in all that sort of thing – the spirit of the earth and that. She knows quite a lot about it. She once went out with a Natural Law Candidate.'

Richard got dressed, thinking how lucky he was to have married a cynic. Perhaps Isobel was not falling to pieces quite so much as he'd imagined. After all, having a leg in plaster was not the easiest thing, especially with two children to look after. Sympathetic though they undoubtedly were to Isobel's plight, Patrick and Eleanour just couldn't be expected to appreciate the limitations it placed on her. It had been quite unreasonable of Eleanour to throw a tantrum when her mother refused to take them to the White Knuckle Theme Park the other day, and Patrick's habit of turning on the bath then going to watch television was unnerving at the best of times, let alone when it took you ten minutes to get up the stairs. No, perhaps he had spoken out of turn when he'd called her feeble. She was probably just tired. And this Beasley woman did sound rather a pain, and there was certainly no evidence that she ever cleaned anything.

'How is Isobel?' Jenny's lavender eyes gazed anxiously up at Richard as he sought to extricate himself from her embrace.

'She's fine. Considering everything, she's doing very well.

It's a bit of a strain, of course. She gets tired, but you would, wouldn't you?'

Jenny pattered over to her stencilled dressing table. 'I've got something for her. I'm sure it will help.' Strands of green string were placed in Richard's hand.

'What's this?'

'It's seaweed. Tell her to put a teaspoonful in a cup and just add boiling water. She'll notice the difference.'

'To the cup or to her?'

'To her, silly. It's a pick-me-up. Anita swears by it.'

'Well, it's obviously done wonders for her.'

'There you are then. Kiss.' She stood on tiptoes. Richard kissed her. He still felt a stab of lust at the softness of her mouth. How wonderful it would have been if she'd been foreign. Not a word need they have exchanged. Better still dumb. His mind dallied with oriental slave girls. Not tongueless, of course. He was brought up sharply by this ghastly extension to his fantasy.

'Bye bye, my love. Must be off. Have a nice meeting. Regards to Alice.'

'Anita. My love to Isobel and the children.' She watched him canter down the stairs and heard the front door slam. She really didn't feel much like going to a meeting with Anita. Richard was so wonderful but he did rather exhaust her sometimes. He was so ferocious. Of course it was extremely exciting at the time but afterwards she often found she tended to feel a little drained. She rose and put the kettle on. A cup of seaweed infusion would revive her, but she really must see what she could do about getting Richard to eat less meat.

Isobel had started the barbecue when Richard got home. Billows of yellowy smoke were belching over the top of the house as he drove up the drive. He parked the car and tore along the side path to the back expecting to see, if not the charred corpse of his wife, at least the desecration of his lawn. Neither was visible, however, and he found Isobel and the children cheerfully laying out sausages and hamburgers beneath a fine cloud of ash which hovered over the patio like a presage of storms to come.

'I told you not to start till I got here,' he spluttered. 'What have you put on that? It's blazing like a funeral pyre.'

'Paraffin,' said Isobel blandly. 'I couldn't get it to go with those firelighters. I think they must be damp.'

Richard fussed around the fire, opening vents and making useless and dangerous thrusts with the poker, till the flames died down of their own accord and the coals at last began to glow grey and then white.

'Will it be long, Mum? I'm starving,' called Patrick, starting on his third packet of crisps.

'Not long now. Stop eating all those crisps and go and fetch the salad. It's on the top shelf in the frig. And bring me that bottle of wine that's in there too, will you, please?'

Patrick departed and Richard went to change his clothes. He did wish Isobel wouldn't try and do everything just because he was a few minutes late getting home. She really shouldn't be lighting barbecues with a leg in plaster. Suppose a spark had fallen on it? Did plaster burn? He suspected it would. Very likely combust, in fact. The thought of Isobel helplessly trapped while her leg was roasted before her sent him leaping back down the stairs, arriving in the garden even hotter than when he went in.

Isobel was sitting with her leg, as yet uncooked, propped on a tool box, a large glass of wine in her hands. She looked at him curiously as he stood panting by the wizened wisteria, victim of her perennial indifference to all things growing. 'Do you want some of this?' She gestured to the bottle.

Richard nodded. He was feeling a little unsettled by the sudden violence of his imagination. Perhaps Jenny was right. Perhaps he should eat less meat. His gaze fell upon the slabs of porterhouse Isobel had had the sense to cover with cellophane. The juices of his mouth gushed unabated round his tongue. Tomorrow, he thought, I will have fish for lunch.

The barbecue was successful. The children wandered around dropping food indiscriminately on themselves and the ground, much as they did indoors but with less nuisance value. Isobel and Richard drank too much and devoured their steaks like cannibals, snorting with laughter over

Isobel's account of Mrs Beasley's attempt to make her raid the children's piggy banks, rather than submit her to the ordeal of cashing a cheque.

'She really is a bit odd,' Isobel gurgled, pouring the dregs of another bottle into her glass. 'She came stalking in and thrust that thing about the sea having terminal PMT under my nose before she'd even taken her coat off. Not that it's worth her taking her coat off because she's not in the house long enough.' They both cackled helplessly at this. 'Apparently she's been to one of their meetings, you see, and now she's touting for converts. It must be on a commission basis.'

'I wonder if it's the same lot that's causing all the traffic jams.'

'Probably.'

'The sooner they're swallowed up the better. It was mayhem by the roundabout. Odd-looking bunch. All in yellow. Reminded me of . . .' Richard stopped.

'What?'

He'd been going to say 'your fortieth birthday party', but decided against it. 'Oh, I don't know . . . runny butter.'

Isobel smiled. 'It's hard to imagine Mrs B doing that sort of thing.' She paused. 'Actually, it's quite hard to imagine her doing anything.'

'I must meet this Mrs Beasley.'

'I wish you would.'

'Why?'

'Well, for one thing you wouldn't keep telling me I'm exaggerating . . .'

'For another . . .?'

'It would stop you fantasising about Attila the Hun.'

The distant wail of sirens caught their attention. For a few moments they listened as the sound got nearer and more frantic, then reached its peak and subsided with a few rogue shrills into silence. 'I was beginning to think they were for us,' said Richard.

Isobel looked at her watch. 'An hour and a half. That would be about right,' she said.

'Something must have gone up. There was definitely more than one.'

'Probably the warehouse again. It burns down every other month now.'

Richard began to pile the plates. 'Come on, you two. Come and give me a hand to clear up.'

'Can't we go and watch the fire engines?' asked Eleanour, picking up one crisp packet and handing it to Isobel.

'They've gone now. Anyway, it's time you were in the bath. Patrick, come and take some of these dishes in.'

Patrick let go of the washing line along which he had been attempting to swing and rolled across the grass commando-style, firing indiscriminately at his family with a broken piece of fencing. 'Can we just have a quick look?' he asked, taking two plates off the pile and starting towards the house.

'Very quick,' said Isobel. 'I expect they've gone by now.'

The children disappeared, leaving the two adults to clear away the rest.

'Mark and Alison's children always clear up after meals,' grumbled Richard, who hated housework of any kind.

'They're older.'

'They did it even when they were younger.'

'They also do their music practice and visit two old ladies on a regular basis.'

'Little prigs.'

'Take your choice.'

'Yes, but our two could do a bit more. Especially now you've got your leg.'

'My leg's fine. I hardly notice it now. At least I wouldn't if people didn't keep going on about it.'

'Last time I offer you sympathy.'

'Good.'

'I have to tell you, Isobel, you've been extremely bad-tempered since your accident.'

'And before?'

'You were extremely bad-tempered.'

'Well, at least I can't have banged my head. Where have those children got to?'

'I'd better go and grab them or they'll be messing around out there half the night.'

Richard was saved the necessity by the return of Patrick and Eleanour with the rather dull news that the fire engines had now gone and nobody seemed to be dead.

'Elly. Bath,' said Richard.

'One man had his hair all burned off though, didn't he, Patrick?' submitted Eleanour, as if this might advance her case for staying up.

'We don't know that,' countered Patrick with the irritating disloyalty siblings often display in times of crisis.

'Well, he hadn't got any, anyway,' persisted Eleanour sulkily. 'It looked all burned off.'

'How do you know what burned off hair looks like?' demanded Patrick.

His sister stuck to her guns. 'I just do. It was all brown underneath and he only had his nightie on so he must have been.'

Isobel, who had long since lost track of the argument, shooed them inside and hobbled off to make some coffee which she felt both she and Richard would need if they were ever to get the children to bed.

'I'm not sure about this,' muttered Richard after he had banged his knee for the third time.

'I thought you liked pain,' said Isobel accusingly. She resented his criticising the inverted sock drawer covered in a towel she had erected with such care and deliberation.

'There's pain and pain,' sighed Richard. 'There's a difference between being smacked on your bare bum and having your cartilages displaced by a block of wood.'

'You must explain it to me some time,' retorted Isobel peevishly.

'Oh, come on, darling. Don't go all huffy on me. It's just . . . What was wrong with the pillows?'

'They went all soggy in the night.'

'Them and me both,' said Richard, now thoroughly off his stride. Isobel began to giggle.

'That's right. Laugh at me.'

'I am.'

'You know what you are, Isobel? You're a ball breaker. You're enough to render a man permanently impotent. Do you know that?'

'I do now you've told me,' said Isobel with a touch of asperity. 'What a pity I didn't know six years ago.' Richard groaned and buried his head in the pillow. 'That was six years ago. I thought we'd agreed it was in the past.'

'It is,' said Isobel, staring at the ceiling. Richard forked himself up on to his elbows and gazed down at her. 'I do love you, Isobel. You do know that, don't you?'

Isobel rolled on her side and put one arm round his neck. Richard, ever grateful for his steak, felt the juices returning.

'And you love me, so that's all that matters.' He eased himself on top of her. 'Isn't it?'

Later, lying beside the sleeping Richard, Isobel continued to stare at the ceiling. Yes, she thought – if it's true.

Chapter Thirteen

The phone rang on Monday morning while Isobel was getting dressed. Richard was in the bathroom and so it was answered by Eleanour who came galloping up the stairs to report that Mrs Beesknees would not be coming that day because she'd been shaken.

The prospect of anyone having the courage or indeed the strength to shake Mrs Beesknees, as she was ever after to be called, was more than Isobel could absorb at that time of the morning but she was immediately filled with an immense sense of freedom. A reprieve. She would not waste it. As soon as was reasonable she would phone Marjorie Bennett – in the council offices if necessary – and tell her to inform her protégée that her services were no longer required at Shingle Cottage. She knew she should do it herself but her strength was not yet up to it. Whether it ever would be was not something to concern herself with at that particular moment.

'You look cheerful,' remarked Richard as he drank his coffee. He, too, was feeling rather good. He reckoned he'd finally got the sock drawer sorted. By coming in at an angle, a bit like a Harrier landing, he had experienced the double satisfaction of avoiding damage to his kneecap and at the same time rubbing up against Isobel's plaster, which was cold and smooth and accorded very well with his long-held ambition to rape his wife on a tombstone.

The sun shone. The children set off for school, also happy because it was crisp day, and Isobel made herself fresh coffee and carried it, without spilling, from the worktop to the kitchen table.

The phone rang.

'Isobel?'

'Yes?'

'It's Marjorie. Marjorie Bennett. I'm at the office. Had to come in early.

Hope I haven't got you out of bed or anything.'

It irritated Isobel that Marjorie always assumed no one else had anything to do but her. She smothered an urge to say she had been making love to the postman and offered a simple negative.

'Good. Bad news, I'm afraid. I've just had Jenny on the phone. Jenny Holt – you know?'

'I know,' said Isobel wearily.

'Well, apparently she was at some meeting on Friday. One of those weirdo things she's always getting involved in. Druids or some such. She went with that peculiar woman who played on those awful tin whistles at your party . . . Oh, I forgot . . . you weren't there, were you? Oh, well, never mind, you probably won't know the one I mean. Friend of Diana's, I wouldn't be surprised. Lovely party, by the way.

'Anyway, things apparently got a bit out of hand on Friday. Lots of chanting and all that. Billy Graham sort of stuff. And the gist of it is – according to Jenny, but she was in such a dither I couldn't understand half of what she said – that these people, for reasons best known to themselves, started some sort of fire on the beach and it got out of control and set fire to the pier fencing. Anyway they had to call the fire brigade, or someone did. and that was that.'

She paused for breath. I'm glad I'm not paying for this call, thought Isobel, then remembered that she was probably was since it was council offices.

'But . . .' Marjorie's timing owed much to her years with the Haywain Players '. . . one of the people there was taken "a bit quar", as they say, so Jenny and her friend went to help – took her back to Jenny's for a cup of tea – and it turns out it was none other than Vera Beasley. What she was doing there I'll never know. The woman's obviously completely off her rocker, but then we all knew that, didn't we?'

'I didn't,' said Isobel with some feeling.

'Oh, didn't I tell you? Probably forgot. Still she's an excellent cleaner I've been told.'

'Not by me,' said Isobel. 'In fact I was planning to ring you about her myself this morning.'

There was a slight pause. 'Has something gone missing?'

'Only bath bubbles so far. That's not the point. It's very kind of you, Marjorie, and I know you mean well, but I never wanted a home help – I'm quite capable of surviving in my own squalour for a week or two and so is my family. I've had a phone call from Mrs Beasley already this morning to say she won't be coming in – presumably in connection with this meeting you're talking about – and I want you to get in touch with her and tell her her services are no longer required. I'm very sorry if she needs the work, but really I cannot cope with having her in the house.'

There was a silence.

'Well, if that's how you feel . . .'

'That is how I feel. And by the way, how did Jenny know this Vera Beasley was meant to be coming here?'

'She didn't at first. That was what I wanted to warn you about. Apparently the woman was still rather agitated by the time they got her home. She kept insisting she'd had some sort of mission. A "purging", I think Jenny said it was called. Well, you know how worked up people can get at these things. You've only to see Geoffrey after a one day match at Lords to see how it can happen. But the gist of it was that she seemed to think you were in some way responsible for the fire or something. Don't ask me how. But Jenny wanted me to let you know, just in case.'

'Why didn't she ring me herself?'

'How should I know? I expect she was trying to save money. It was an internal call, you see. She's only on the fourth floor. Speaking of which, I must go.'

'And you will tell Vera Beasley I don't want her to come any more, won't you?'

'Well, if you really want me to. Though if you say she hasn't taken anything . . .'

'I don't want her to come.'

'Very well then, Isobel. But I don't know if I'll be able to find you anyone else at this short notice.'

'I don't want anyone else.'

'You must have someone.'

'I must not, Marjorie. And if you send anyone else I shall personally set fire to them on the doorstep. Do you understand?'

Marjorie's voice went quiet. 'I understand, Isobel.'

Isobel replaced the receiver.

In her office in County Building Marjorie Bennett turned to the chief architect who had been waiting to speak to her for ten minutes. She shrugged deprecatingly. 'One does one's best.' Reaching for her personal notebook she began to dial Diana.

Isobel passed a pleasant day. She spent twenty minutes on her book, ten on the title which she decided should be either *A Brush With The Angels* or *Watch Out Below*, eventually opting to leave it as *My Life* for the time being, with the others in brackets to show she was undecided. She then moved on to rough plot details which included a section on Mrs Beasley entitled 'Hellfire Corner' and some lines on Jenny and Diana whom she had rechristened the Twat Pack.

The familiar writer's block set in at this point and, taking her library book and what remained of the Sunday papers, she thudded out into the garden and spent the rest of the morning in a deck chair.

The phone rang several times but she didn't attempt to answer it, secure in the knowledge that she had forgotten to turn the Answerphone on so would not have to deal with them later.

After lunch she ironed a shirt to prove to Richard that she did not need another home help, and then fell asleep listening to the radio, to be awakened by the return of Patrick and Eleanour bearing identical letters from the school on the subject of forthcoming parents' evenings.

Richard came home early. He had not been able to face calling in on Jenny on the way, having received a frantic call from her at the office to the effect that she was seriously afraid she had spilled the beans about their affair to Marjorie Bennett *of all people*. When Richard had asked her why she had felt the need to talk to Marjorie Bennett at all, let alone confide in her the innermost secrets of her heart, Jenny had come very close to tears and explained, between hiccups, that she had had to phone her because she couldn't possibly have rung Isobel and she hadn't known what else to do, what with Isobel being all alone in the house, and if anything had happened to her she, Jenny, would have killed herself.

Richard had managed to calm her down sufficiently to ascertain that 'anything' referred mainly to the arrival of Mrs Beasley on their doorstep, and since he knew from Eleanour that the woman had no intention of putting in an appearance that day, his immediate fears were somewhat relieved. He therefore concentrated on getting Jenny to reveal exactly what she had said to Mrs Bennett, which seemed to involve a great deal of talk about brushfires and not much else. Nowhere could he detect anything that might be construed as an intimate confession, and saying as much, he managed little by little to calm her down. Jenny finally rang off amid fresh assertions that if anything had happened to Isobel she would do away with herself and if anything came between her and Richard she would simply die. There didn't seem a lot Richard could offer, faced with two such complementary alternatives, so he suggested she treat herself to a bun at coffee break and promised to call round at the house at the very first opportunity.

Replacing the phone he wondered what the switchboard would have made of that. This business of dying seemed to figure very large in women's imaginations. First Isobel, although that of course was an accident – anyone who knew Isobel would know that – and now Jenny. Maybe it was him? Maybe his was the kind of personality that attracted suicidal females? Was this a good thing or a bad? It was certainly very wearing, of that he had no doubt. Faced with such profundities Richard rang up his squash partner and arranged for a game in the lunch hour, then feeling decidedly more postive, he returned to his accounts.

*

The evening passed quietly. They watched a programme about schizophrenics which reminded Isobel of her conversation with Marjorie Bennett and the apparent State of Grace in which Mrs Beasley now found herself. Richard didn't mention Jenny's call to him, but listened sympathetically to his wife's insistence that no more domestics be allowed to cross their threshold. 'I expect you're right. It was worth a try. I just don't want you overdoing things – putting your recovery back or whatever.'

'I never overdo things. It's not my style.'

'Yes, well, all right. Why don't you pop up and see Mother tomorrow? She could give you lunch.'

'No thanks.'

'You could probably survive a cup of coffee or something. I don't want you getting trapped in the house. You could take a cab. Don't let Mother drive you whatever you do.'

'You're very solicitous all of a sudden. I'm perfectly capable of occupying myself, if that's what you're worried about.'

'Yes, but you're alone all day in the house. It can't be much fun. Why don't you ring Alison and see if she'll take you over to Russell Gardens or something? It's nice there at this time of year.'

Isobel contemplated Richard suspiciously. 'What am I supposed to do in Russell Gardens? Feed the ducks? Dribble? Stop treating me as though I was on the verge of senility. If I want to go out, I shall go out. If I want to lock myself in the bike shed and sniff glue, I shall do that. I am a free agent. I haven't just got rid of the Venerable Beasley to have you take over as chief minder.'

Irritation swept over Richard. 'I tell you what you are, Isobel, you're a bloody nuisance! I've got the doctor breathing down one ear telling me I drove you over the cliff by not noticing you.'

Isobel burst out laughing. 'Did he tell you that? Mahon?'

'Not him. The other chap. With the carnation.'

'Robertson.'

'And now you screaming at me because I'm noticing you too much.'

'I'm not screaming. I may feel like it sometimes, but I don't do it.'

'Perhaps you should.'

'Perhaps I should.'

'So, what are you going to do tomorrow?'

'I haven't made up my mind. I shall see what tomorrow brings.'

Richard put his arms round her waist and hauled her along the couch towards him. Slowly he put his tongue in her ear. 'How about seeing what tonight brings?'

He carried her up the stairs, no mean feat on the winding period staircase, and laid her delicately on the bed. Then he undressed her and, placing her leg strategically on the landing stage, removed his own clothes.

'I can see,' said Isobel, pulling the duvet over her and shivering slightly, 'that this sock drawer is going to become an essential part of your equipment.'

'Would you care to rephrase that?' murmured Richard sleepily. 'You make me sound like a travelling salesman.'

Isobel watched him for a moment then leant over and kissed his forehead lightly. 'Good night,' she said.

Chapter Fourteen

Isobel had resolved she would not return to the hospital for Simon Mahon's therapy session. Much as she disliked the man, stitching him up did not seem sufficient reason to get involved in something which could only, as Richard had said, do her harm.

She spent the morning sorting out the washing, making endless slow and ineffectual trips between the machine and the garden, small bags of wet clothes dripping from either crutch and slapping uncomfortably against her as she wobbled over the uneven ground.

She dropped a whole load of socks into a flower bed and cursed with frustration as she manoeuvred to pick them up. Inside the phone was ringing. By the time she got back it had stopped. She rinsed the socks and started out again. Again the phone rang. Isobel made no attempt to turn back.

She abandoned the laundry after the sock episode and concentrated on lowering the hems on Eleanour's school dresses which had shot up remarkably since the previous summer, reminding her of the child's plaintive cry that her shoes were squeezing as she set off for school that morning. Patrick needed new swimming trunks, too, and he'd ripped a hole in his jumper. Isobel was hopeless at darning. Children were an expense, she decided. The sooner she got her autobiography on the bestsellers shelves the better. She went and found it, added two sentences about the cost of living, juxtaposed rather neatly with the cost of dying, added Naomi and Yvette's names to the Twat Pack and hunted around for another biro as hers appeared to be running out.

There was a ring at the door. Isobel froze. Surely not? For some reason she felt convinced that Mrs Beasley had returned to haunt her, or worse still, clean her house. Feverishly she rammed her book back into the drawer and closed it. Another ring. Stealthily she ducked below the window and eased herself down on to the rug, lying flat out, her hands covering her head, eyes tight shut. The bell chimed angrily. Footsteps along the side path. They stopped. Isobel waited for what seemed an eternity then very cautiously opened her eyes and looked up. A piercing scream escaped her. There, nose pressed against the pane, her face hideously distorted by the glass, stood Diana Greenslade, peering down at her in mute alarm.

That's all I need, cursed Isobel, rolling awkwardly on her side as she groped for a crutch to lever herself up. With as much composure as she could muster she staggered round to the front door and let Diana in.

'Christ, Isobel, I thought you were dead.'

What's new? reflected Isobel. 'It's a relaxation exercise. Very good for the stomach muscles. They gave it to me at the hospital. I have to do it every day.'

Diana eyed her disbelievingly. 'Anyway, I've had old Marje on the phone, bleating away. What's this about the char coming looking for you with an axe? I tell you, I thought maybe she'd got here already when I saw you lying on the floor like that. Are you sure that's good for the stomach muscles? I'd've thought it was more for the lumbar region.'

Isobel shrugged. 'I expect you're right. You know more about these things than I do.'

Diana flexed her well-honed body and led the way into the kitchen. 'Anyway, I've come to sort you out. Can't stay long. Took an early lunch. Where's your pressure cooker? I'm going to run you up a casserole. Just stick it in the ov for half an hour when Richard gets home. You'll have to make do with fruit and cheese for afters. Haven't got time to do a pud. Christ, Isobel, what do you do with these saucepans? The handle's spinning round in my hand.'

'It's a bit loose,' Isobel explained.

'I can see that. Don't tell me you haven't got a pressure cooker?'

Diana was ferreting in the frig. She hauled out the butcher's carrier bag and began to root through it.

'I haven't actually.'

'Oh, Izzy, Izzy, Izzy . . .' Diana took Isobel's face in her strong hands and shook it reprovingly from side to side. Isobel retreated. 'It's all right. I'm not making a pass.' She selected the blade steak. 'Now, what are we going to cook this in?'

'Honestly, Diana, there's no need for you to do all this. I'm perfectly capable of cooking. I'm perfectly capable of doing everything except running long distance and playing football.'

Diana turned on her a knowing look. 'Of course you are, lovey. We all know that. But let's face it, you've had a bit of a crack, and this is the time for all of us mates to rally round a bit. That's all.' Her rosy face grew serious. 'We're not trying to undermine you, Isobel. You mustn't think that. It's because we care about you we're doing it. And Richard. We care about him, too.'

'I don't think that's ever been in doubt,' said Isobel a trifle sharply.

Diana plunged into the vegetable rack and occupied herself with chopping onions at speed. This made them both cry and caused a temporary lull in the conversation.

'What you need is a food processor,' observed Diana as she thrust the remaining carrots into a pot with the meat. 'Of course they're a bit of a price.'

Isobel conceded inwardly it would be worth any price to be spared these endless invasions of her privacy. There was another ring at the bell. Isobel groaned.

'You go,' ordered Diana, sweeping feverishly round her feet. 'I'll just have a quick whip round with the hoover and then I must be off. I could call in again tomorrow after work. Are you all right for necessities? I can always do a quick shop before I come.'

'I'm fine, thanks.' Isobel groped her way through the chairs Diana was piling up in the doorway. She could see a tall shadow through the frosted glass panels of the front door. It certainly didn't look like Vera Beasley's silhouette, she noted with some relief.

The relief turned rapidly to dismay as she opened the door. 'Oh, no. What do you want?'

'Is that any way to talk to your chauffeur after I've come all this way?'

Isobel gazed at Harry's grinning face. 'But what have you come for? I'm not going to Dr Mahon's classes any more. I've decided. I told you I might not. You should've rung before you came all the way out here.'

'I did. You didn't answer.'

'Oh, was that you? I was down the garden.'

'Anyway I didn't think you'd want to go. That's why I came.'

'That makes absolutely no sense at all.'

'Yes, it does. I've brought a blanket and some chloroform.'

'I should keep it for yourself if this week's anything like last.'

Harry laughed. 'What about your shopping? They've got cutprice chickens at Tescos this week.'

'Who are you?' Diana, sleeves rolled stylishly to just below her elbows, stood behind Isobel gazing with unashamed relish at Harry's solid frame.

'I'm Lady Isobel's lover,' said Harry, returning her gaze. It was the first time Isobel had ever seen Diana lost for words. The reprieve was short-lived. 'Oh, how marvelous,' she chortled. 'Wait till I tell Richard.'

'He knows,' said Harry. 'It was pistols at dawn.'

'Goodness me, an early riser, too,' said Diana with revolting coyness.

Isobel turned to Diana. 'I thought you had to get back to work?'

'Yes, I do. Well, I suppose I'd better love you and leave you both. Don't forget, Izzy my pet, anything you want me to pick up, just give me a bell. And you,' Diana turned her most vampish smile on Harry, 'can give me a bell anyway. Iz will give you the number, won't you, love?' She squeezed past them both and was soon to be seen hurtling away in her brand new company car.

Harry leaned on the doorpost. 'So – you don't want a lift.'

'No thanks. Look, I'm sorry you came all this way for nothing.'

He shrugged. 'Worth a try. I don't suppose you fancy

lunch? I could do with some cheerful company before the ordeal.'

'I'm not that cheerful,' warned Isobel, then shook her head. 'Look, I'm sorry. It wouldn't work.'

Harry looked at her curiously. 'What wouldn't?'

Isobel felt embarrassed. 'Anything. Having lunch. Besides, there's nowhere round here, and if we go into Eastleigh that means I can't get back.'

'I'll bring you back.'

'You can't. You've got to be at the hospital by two. It's all too complicated.'

'Rubbish. What else are you going to do? Stomp round the house like Long John Silver all afternoon? Suppose Boadicea comes back? She'll have you pegged out on the line by the time the kids come home. I tell you something, you're a sitting duck in this house. I bet everyone in your phone book's going to have a go at doing you a bit of good. Shopping, cleaning, picking up the kids – all so's they can have a poke round the inside of your house, and the inside of your head, I wouldn't be surprised. At least with old Mahon you've got the choice of what you tell him.'

'I'm not so sure about that.'

'Not some of them, I grant you. But you have. You should use it. Show the others they don't have to let that Irish berk duff them up like that. You and the old girl, you could do that. Play him at his own game. Strike a blow for the nutcases.'

Isobel laughed. 'You have a telling way with words.'

Harry grinned. 'You know what I mean.'

Isobel sighed. 'It's not that easy. He's trained. He knows how to catch people out, and once it's been filmed he's not going to let it go.'

Harry's face became serious for a minute. 'You're right,' he said softly, 'but you see, I've got the film. And things can go wrong with film.'

Isobel fetched her coat.

'I don't know if I should have anything to drink if I really am going to this afternoon's session.' They were seated in the garden of The Collier's Arms, a lively pub not far from the main centre of Eastleigh.

'One won't hurt. What do you drink?'

'Wine, please, white.' Harry got her a glass and a beer for himself. They ordered shepherd's pie and sat basking in the late spring sunshine while they waited. 'You don't have to go,' said Harry at last.

'After being practically kidnapped? Anyway it'll annoy Richard.'

'Do you want to annoy him?'

'Not so much him as . . .' Isobel stopped herself. She'd been about to say 'his girlfriend' '. . there are other people too, who said I shouldn't do it. I just get so sick of people trying to decide things for me. God, I'm forty years old. If I can't decide now, when will I be able to?'

Their food arrived and they ate in silence for a while. Isobel watched Harry. He was older than she'd thought at first. Late thirties, she surmised, maybe even forty. 'Can I ask you something?' she said when they had finished.

'You can ask.'

'Did you really ring this morning?'

Harry's face broke into a grin. 'No. Did you think I had?'

'Not really. So why did you come all that way?'

'I fancy you.'

Isobel shook her head. 'That's not a proper reason.'

'Since when?'

'You know what I mean. You're the kind of man, I'd guess, who fancies anything in skirts. You can't spend your whole life scooting round the country after them.'

Harry laughed. 'That's all you know. But you're right. I did have an ulterior motive, as they say.'

'Are you going to tell me what it is?'

Harry considered. 'Not yet. If I'm right I'll tell you.'

'And if you're wrong?'

Harry was silent for a moment. 'I hope I am,' he said.

Chapter Fifteen

Tension hung in the air of PSY 1 as Harry and Isobel entered. It was only ten to two but already the group was assembled, even Leonie, who had plaited coloured beads into her hair, the kohl around her eyes creating a passable likeness to an Egyptian princess.

Large bottles of mineral water had replaced the coffee on Luce's tray, but she was making no attempt to offer it round, and no one seemed particularly interested in helping themselves.

Fran was making frantic telephone calls, arm crooked dramatically over her head as she sought to make her point to whomever was on the other end. There was a great deal of 'I know, love, but . . .' and 'of course I see your point'ing, making it perfectly clear to the casual observer that she was getting absolutely nowhere. Calls finished, she slid off the desk and hunted feverishly in her bag for cigarettes. Isobel saw Simon Mahon lean towards her. With a look of total despair, she replaced the cigarettes and went to bully Luce, who was helping Jock sort his equipment.

Harry was now talking to Julian Joffe. Isobel saw him frown. She wished she had asked him about their director during lunch, but the subject of the crew itself had been rather overshadowed by talk of Dr Mahon and his acolytes.

Harry was of the opinion that Leonie was oversexed; that Hilary Bell was a fart of the first order; that Meg was in for a thoroughly bad time; and that Ken would probably be the only one to derive any benefit from the enterprise.

'What about Maureen?' Isobel had asked. Harry shook his head. 'She's got me foxed. I can't think what she's doing there.'

'She told me she did it to please her GP. And for the shopping, of course.'

Harry shrugged. 'I don't know,' he said.

'And why am I there?'

'That's easy.'

'Oh?'

'You're there because I forced you at knifepoint.'

'Oh, yes,' said Isobel. 'I forgot.'

'Are we all here?' Dr Mahon had adopted his Moses-with-the-Tablets pose. Fran counted them hoarsely under her breath. Dr Mahon rubbed his hands together. 'Right now, everyone. Today is, as they say, The Day. Now I want you to remember everything I've said to you. One: we are all on the same side. This is not in any way a competitive exercise. It is a session, the same as any other session. The only difference being that Julian and his crew will be recording us. But that need make no difference – in fact I will go further – I will say it *must* make no difference to anything. I want you to forget they are here. It won't be easy at first, I realise that, but I think as the afternoon goes on you will begin to feel more at ease and then, hopefully, we shall be able to start to get some real value out of the experience. Now are there any questions before we start?'

Hilary raised a hand. Isobel noticed for the first time how beautifully his nails were manicured.

'Yes, Hilary?'

'I would just like to establish a few fucking guide lines before we begin.'

'Yes?'

'For a start, what is our position vis-à-vis editorial control?'

A look of surprised concern came across Mahon's face. 'In what way, Hilary?'

'In the usual bloody way, for fuck's sake. Do we or do we not have a right to give the yea or bloody nay to what goes into the final cut?'

'Well, I . . .' Mahon flashed a savage look at Julian who rose creakily from his cross-legged position on the floor.

'Got you.' Joffe nodded vigorously. 'Good point. Naturally there would be no question of our including anything that might cause real distress or, dare I say it, offence to the viewing public. After all,' a strange hissing noise came down Julian's nose, Isobel watched in alarm, before realising it was an attempt to laugh, 'we don't want Mary Whitehouse on our tails.' His face returned to its natural melancholy. 'Does that answer your question?'

'No, it fucking doesn't,' said Hilary. For once Isobel thought he had expressed himself quite well.

Leonie was up, waving her arm like a reed in the wind, the soft jangle of her bracelets enhancing the impression.

'I think what Hilary's trying to say is how much say do *we*, the humble guinea pigs, have in the final version? Is that right, Hilary?'

'I think I made that perfectly clear,' snapped Hilary. 'Either they understand the Queen's bloody English or they don't.'

Leonie raised her eyes to heaven and gave a small deprecating smile, mostly directed at Harry, whose face betrayed not the slightest reaction as he returned her gaze.

'Ah.' They were reminded that the director had not yet furnished them with a satisfactory answer, nor did it seem likely that he would. Simon Mahon stepped in again to say that he felt sure, just as they entrusted him with their hopes and fears, so they would be happy to trust so distinguished a director with the ability to reproduce only that which was valid and worthwhile from the therapy sessions. He then led them rapidly on to breathing exercises which Harry filmed from start to finish, without anyone being remotely aware of it.

Isobel, who had been highly suspicious of the much-vaunted 'fly-on-the-wall' technique began to see that it was possible to function without an anguished consciousness of the camera, given the will to do so, which some of the group had and some of them most definitely did not. She herself was excluded from the rolling and grunting on account of her ankle, so had plenty of time to observe the others in this so-called relaxation period.

Meg and Ken were rigid with tension. Leonie flung herself around like a panther on heat, moaning and gasping. A thin film of sweat was forming on Jock's brow as he recorded this. Hilary lay very still and took deep rhythmic breaths, forefingers pressed against his temples, occasionally making little circling movements round his eyes. He looked supremely smug. Maureen, Isobel suspected, had gone to sleep, so peaceful she looked curled in her corner. Dr Mahon tiptoed amongst them, occasionally lifting elbows and letting them drop. 'Foetal,' he murmured to Isobel as he came past, pointing to Maureen. 'She is waiting for the rebirth. The others are not yet ready.' Isobel looked at him but said nothing.

Gradually the group revived. Leonie stretched like a cat and made a great show of rearranging her skirt which had mysteriously risen way above her thighs. Jock was drinking a cup of the mineral water. Fran sat beside him, glaring at the back of Leonie's head.

When everyone was sitting up Dr Mahon again asked them each in turn if they had anything they wanted to bring up. Isobel avoided Harry's eye. Ken, surprisingly, for he rarely completed a sentence, had a poem that he wanted to read. As it turned out it was not so very surprising since the poem was quite without verbs and not dissimilar from much of his prose. It seemed to Isobel to concern the contents of a dustbin, 'broken', 'fetid' and 'rancid' featuring a lot. They clapped encouragingly when he had done, Maureen particularly because 'rancid' fitted one of the crossword clues she had not yet managed to get.

'And this is your own work, Ken?' asked Mahon gently. Ken affirmed that it was. 'Ah.' He turned to the others. 'And what do we learn from this – outpouring of thought? What does it teach us about Ken?'

There was a silence. Slowly Meg's hand trembled into the air. 'Yes, Meg?'

'He's depressed.'

Ken nodded emphatically.

Mahon smiled at Meg with the kindness people reserve for deaf mutes. 'Yes, Meg, but we knew that before. What fresh things does it tell us about him?' Meg subsided into her chair, fierce pink patches appearing on her freckled cheeks.

'He feels trapped,' asserted Leonie, with some justification.
'And crushed,' added Hilary.
'Broken by life's experiences,' Leonie was away, 'trampled on, kicked about . . . gutted.'
'Fucking gutted,' chorused Hilary.
The two of them smiled at each other triumphantly.
'Yes, yes.' Mahon was on his feet. 'At last we begin to sense how Ken is feeling. We begin to sympathise, to empathise – to *feel* with him and *for* him. Now at last he knows he's not alone.' Isobel saw Harry swing the camera towards Ken. I bet he wishes he was, she thought.

It was now Maureen's go. She said she was afraid she was going to be very boring and say that she had nothing to put before the group again. Simon Mahon pressed as best he could, asking if she was still taking sleeping pills, and having received a negative, if her seeming indifference to the 'slings and arrows of outrageous fortune' was not, in fact, a coverup for more deeply rooted pressures which, if allowed to fester, would in time curdle and rise to the surface like a boiling volcano?

Isobel watched to see if Maureen, as a crossword addict, would be able to tolerate this pot-pourri of metaphors, but she merely smiled as at a child's enquiry and answered 'If you say so.' The psychiatrist passed on.

Hilary managed to displace Leonie for once, by informing them all in a resounding voice that he 'couldn't see his way out of this one'. Everyone waited politely to see if there was more to come or if Hilary's statement had been finite. For the first time Isobel became aware of the steady whirr of the camera, then realised that Harry was crouching beside her. 'Couldn't organise a piss-up in a brewery, let alone the rest,' he muttered before moving on to get a better view.

'What appears to be the problem, Hilary?' purred Dr Mahon at last. 'Do you feel able to tell us about it?' Just try and stop him, thought Isobel, and shifted her good leg which was getting stiff. Hilary sighed. Isobel saw Jock stifling a yawn. Luce was writing feverishly in a notebook. Fran looked as though she would kill for a cigarette. Julian Joffe was folded like a Jack-in-the-box, waiting for someone to release the lid.

Maureen nudged Isobel. 'The Thinker,' she nodded in Hilary's direction. It was true. Hilary had perfectly recreated the heroic pose, his blue-silver hair swept back to reveal the noble profile as he sought for an answer to his suffering.

'More like "The Wanker",' whispered Isobel. The two of them began to shake with laughter. Gradually the others became aware of the disturbance and watched them in awe as they coughed unconvincingly into their handkerchieves.

Harry filmed them remorselessly, occasionally panning round to the astounded faces of the rest, before returning to Maureen and Isobel who were now hiccoughing with the abandon of the condemned.

Hilary gazed at them with ill-concealed loathing until finally they regained control. 'I'm so sorry,' whinnied Maureen. 'I don't seem to be able to stop.' This set Isobel off again.

'Perhaps the ladies would like a glass of water?' suggested Mahon, plainly preferring the idea of cyanide. Luce rushed to provide some. Isobel asked if a window could be opened and Luce rushed away to find a window-pole. Gradually calm was restored but Hilary had clearly lost all interest in being helped, and had vacated the chair in favour of the furthest corner of the room where he sat knees akimbo, ostentatiously sipping from a hip flask and glaring unseeing at a pornographic paperback.

Meg was once more ordered into the hot seat and, rather than offend the doctor further, complied, albeit with a look of such despair that even Leonie managed a small smile of encouragement.

Mahon began quite gently, asking how her week had been, if there had been any particular problems at home she would like to talk about. Meg, who had obviously psyched herself up to some extent, said yes, her mother-in-law had been very awkward about her cooking.

'Go on.'

Meg hesitated, reaching for words which would render her mother-in-law rather than herself the villain of the piece. 'Well . . . On Wednesday I made a steak pie – Neil's very fond of it. .'

'And who is Neil?'

Meg looked genuinely surprised. 'He's my son,' she said.

'Go on.'

'And my husband likes it, too. My husband's name is Michael,' she added helpfully.

'What has that to do with a steak pie?' asked Dr Mahon, still very kindly.

'I . . . Nothing.'

'Go on.'

Meg began to fumble with a handkerchief. Julian tapped Harry on the arm and indicated that he should focus on this.

'Erm . . . she, my mother-in-law, just sort of picked at it, and when Michael, that's my . . . er . . . asked her if there was anything wrong, she said it was full of gristle and she couldn't digest it.'

'How old is your mother-in-law?'

'She's seventy-nine.'

'Do you think it was altogether fair to feed an old lady of seventy-nine gristle?'

Meg spluttered at the injustice. 'It wasn't gristle. It was pie steak. It was very tender.'

'But she couldn't eat it?'

'She said she couldn't.'

'And then?'

'The next day it was the same. It was fish and she pretended she had a bone stuck in her throat and choked and choked.'

'Pretended? Is it not a very common thing for elderly people to choke on fish bones? Their eyes, remember, are not what they once were.'

'There weren't any bones,' whimpered Meg as though pleading for her life.

'It was Birds Eye. The steaks. They don't have any bones.'

'Go on.'

'And then it was the same all week. Something wrong every meal time. It got to the point where Michael said he was going to do the cooking himself if I couldn't get anything right.'

Dr Mahon nodded sagely. 'And Neil. How did he feel about all this?'

Meg shook her head helplessly. 'He ate out after the fish. He didn't come in for meals after that.'

There was silence for a moment. Dr Mahon sighed, his

fingers forking into each other, chin resting lightly on top of them. 'Do you wear turquoise a lot, Meg?' he asked suddenly.

Meg baulked. 'I . . . you . . . not very . . . for here.' Her voice trailed away.

Mahon smiled round at the rest of the group. 'Did anyone understand that? I'm sure I didn't.' No one spoke. 'I ask Meg a simple question, requiring only a "yes" or "no", and what do I get? A burbled string of monosyllables. How can I help you, Meg, if you can't even give me a straight answer? Now, I'm going to ask you again, and this time', his voice became low and coaxing, 'I want you to tell me the truth. Do you wear a lot of turquoise?'

Meg sat for a moment, her breathing was sharp and noisy. Slowly she got control of it. 'I wear turquoise when I come here,' she said painstakingly, 'because you told me to wear bright colours. You said it might help my depression.'

'Because I told you to.' Dr Mahon beamed as though he had just heard the best joke ever. 'So you do everything I tell you, is that it? If I told you to walk in front of a bus, you'd do it, would you? If I told you to put your head in a lion's mouth, you'd do it?'

'I should think it would be preferable to this.' Maureen's clear voice cut through Mahon's probing. His eyes flicked furiously over to her. 'If I could have silence when I'm working with a patient. It is very destructive to destroy the concentration process.'

Maureen met his gaze with calm contempt. 'I think what you're doing is very destructive.'

'I know what I'm doing, believe me.'

'I do believe you. And I think it's wrong.'

'What's it got to do with you?' The doctor's voice had risen to an unseemly pitch. He recovered himself. 'Maureen, I understand your alarm, but you must trust me. I am a doctor. This is part of my therapy. It is what makes it different from other forms of psychoanalysis. You'll see, by allowing Meg to talk through her anxieties I shall be able to begin the process of regeneration. But I can't do that if I'm not allowed to complete the treatment.'

He smiled affably. Maureen sat back. Mahon returned to

Meg. 'I think's that's enough for now, Meg. Can't have you hogging all the limelight, can we? Leonie, I think it would be nice to hear from you now.'

Meg slid out of the chair and scurried to a seat by the wall. Isobel could see that she was shaking. 'And Meg,' the steel frames glinted after her, 'no more turquoise, eh? It doesn't actually suit you very well.'

Leonie, too, had written a poem for the occasion. It was certainly more lyrical than Ken's but didn't manage to convey much more. At least not to Isobel. Death figured very largely, as did sex, the two inextricably entwined in a series of rather graphic images which had Jock salivating. She saw Harry's eyebrows rise slightly once or twice and noticed that the camera was dipping more and more frequently to the point where Leonie's sarong parted company with her legs.

Dr Mahon asked if the poem was a direct outcome of any of Leonie's nightmares. She agreed that it was, but with becoming reticence explained that words would never capture the violence, the sheer brutality of her dreams. There was a rustle of expectancy from all three males in the crew at this, but Dr Mahon passed on to her use of flowers as analogies for the invasion of her body, and since these mostly centred on bees and pollen which they had all heard a million times before, interest waned. Leonie was finally prised out of the chair when Harry had to change his reel. Hilary thought he might be ready to talk about his problem again, but was given short shrift from Dr Mahon who said he had an important announcement to make. The group waited attentively. Dr Mahon glanced across at Julian Joffe who nodded imperceptibly and reclasped his hands over his knees.

'There's been a slight change of plan.' He paused, obviously expecting some sort of reaction, but since no one had the faintest idea what his plan was in the first place they remained stoically silent.

'Julian has asked me whether, in view of the short time available to him – five weeks is no time, no time at all in terms of therapy, as I'm sure we all appreciate – whether it might not be possible to so shape the sessions that some positive conclusion might be reached? Merely in terms of viewer comprehension, you understand. No one pretends that a cure to all our problems can be found by magic to coincide with the length of the series.'

But we'll have a damn good try, Isobel reflected.

'I have naturally given the matter my deepest thought, and I have to confess at one point it seemed to me that the only option might be to cancel the whole thing ... But after consultation with my colleagues at the hospital I have been persuaded that would not be the answer – in fact it might even be designated "the easy way out". And that is not our way. Is it?'

From the look on most of the faces, including the crew, it appeared that that would decidedly be the preferred exit, but the question was plainly rhetorical as Mahon continued, 'And so I have decided that, while continuing to follow our own paths, we shall mould our therapy to a recognisable form of consummation, and to this end I have enlisted the help of a very dear friend and colleague who will be with us next week.'

'And what precisely is this fucking consummation?' growled Hilary, who was still peeved at being denied his spot.

'Ah. I think this will appeal to you, Hilary, particularly. It is, in fact, a circle dance.'

There was a stunned silence.

'What's that?' whispered Isobel to Maureen.

Maureen shrugged. 'No idea. Probably ring-a-ring-a-roses. You won't be very good at that, will you?'

'I'll be all right at the falling down,' said Isobel. They began to giggle again.

Dr Mahon shot them a very sharp look. Meg was watching them in terror. 'Can anyone tell me what I mean by that?' he asked like a school inspector.

No one could. Dr Mahon smiled. 'It is a form of dance developed in the East originally, mainly performed by women, but by no means exclusively so.' He smiled comfortingly at Ken and Hilary, who belched. 'It was used to soothe the pains of labour and childbirth and from that was gradually incorporated into the way of life, as a means of expressing a need for peace and rhythm within. A sort of coming together of the body and the spirit – a unifying.'

Leonie recrossed her legs. 'And you say you have engaged someone to come and instruct us in this thing?'

Dr Mahon shook his head as though a wasp had landed on it. 'No, no, no, – nothing so formal. No, an old old friend of mine from my days at St Caspin's – she specialises in music and drama therapy – has promised to come over and explain the basics to us. We shall take it from there. There's nothing whatever to worry about. As I say, apparently anyone can master the technique – with the possible exception of Isobel who will be a little constrained till her plaster comes off. How long does it have to go, Isobel?'

'Months,' said Isobel.

Dr Mahon gave a tinny little laugh and looked at his watch. 'I see we're nearly out of time. I'd like to finish with a little oral expansion.'

Jock's eyes lit up. It was not as exciting as he had hoped, however, and after ten minutes of Leonie and Hilary whooping and humming, with a very low tremor from Ken and Meg and nothing at all from Maureen and Isobel, he pulled the plugs on his recording machines and began packing away his gear. Julian saw this and opened and shut his mouth several times, but without an interpreter, Fran having disappeared to smoke a cigarette in the lavatories, he was forced to let the matter go.

'Are you going shopping?' Isobel asked Maureen as they escaped.

Maureen shook her head. 'I'm all right this week,' she said. She seemed a little subdued. 'What about you? Can you manage on your own?'

'I don't really need anything either. I bought enough for the eighth army last week. I didn't think I'd be coming again.'

'Why did you change your mind?'

'I didn't really. Harry came and kidnapped me, and since I was in the middle of being done good to, it seemed like the best way out.'

Maureen smiled.

'Do you fancy a cup of tea while you're waiting for the ambulance?' suggested Isobel.

Maureen considered for a moment. 'If you don't mind, I don't think I will. I've got a couple of letters I need to write.' She patted her bag as if to prove her integrity.

'Oh, right,' said Isobel, feeling slightly disappointed. She would have liked to talk to Maureen without the rest of the group around. There was something about her that was interesting; Isobel wasn't sure what. It was as though they had known each other for a long time and didn't have to conform to the niceties of normal social intercourse. A sort of shorthand, but why that should be, she couldn't imagine.

She turned back towards Reception. Maureen was making for the little quad, a small rather weary figure all of a sudden. In the main hall Isobel approached the phones. They were all in use. She saw Harry talking to Leonie who was flinging arms and hair all over the place. If he's not careful she'll catch him one with her beads, Isobel thought spitefully. He's certainly not wasting much time. Then she thought how petty that was. Just because he was talking to her. But she knew already that Leonie and Harry could have only one topic in common.

She ordered a cab before Harry could offer her a lift as she knew he would, since he had brought her and could hardly avoid it. He accepted her refusal without dismay. 'I'll pick you up next week, shall I? Ballet shoes and all.'

'There's no need. I may not come.'

Harry frowned. 'You said that last week.'

'Yes. I meant it.'

'Right. About twelve suit you? We could try that Italian place we drove past.'

'Harry, I'm serious. This whole thing is getting out of hand.'

'Give it one more week. For my sake.'

'For your sake! You'll survive well enough without me.'

'You're my muse. My hand goes all wobbly when you're not there.'

'Yes, well, there's obviously plenty of work for wobbly cameramen or you wouldn't have got this far.'

'I'm a man of ambition. I want to shoot an unwobbly film.'

'Oh, shut up, Harry,' said Isobel, laughing.

'Cab for Mrs Day.' A weaselly-looking youth in a cut-away tee shirt and sawn-off jeans stood by the receptionist jangling his keys.

'There's my cab.'

'Sure you don't want a lift?' asked Harry, casting a wry look at her driver.

'Sure.'

'See you next week then.'

'Well . . .'

'I'll be on the bike.'

Chapter Sixteen

'Oh, Richie, *thank* you, darling, for coming. You can't imagine how awful it's been, just sitting here, worrying and worrying all the time.'

'I thought that sort of thing was meant to stop you worrying,' said Richard with asperity as Jenny unthreaded her limbs from a matsyasana fish position and rose to greet her transient lover. 'Yes, it does. But I'm not doing it properly because I can't empty my mind.' Richard said nothing.

'How is Isobel? Is she all right? Did Marjorie let on about . . . about what I said to her? Oh, I wish I'd never rung her. Whatever possessed me to be so stupid?'

Richard hoped this too was a rhetorical question. 'Isobel's fine. I don't know what all the fuss was about. Actually I'd say you'd done her a bit of a favour.'

'Me? How?'

'You see, she was going to ring Marjorie Bennett anyway to tell her she didn't want the Beasley woman to come any more, so you saved her the trouble. It all worked out very well in the end.'

'Really, Richie? Or are you just saying that to make me feel better?'

'Darling, of course I'm not. Come here and let me give you a cuddle.'

Jenny flew to him. 'I've got the most marvellous news.' Richard stiffened. Maybe he watched too many mini-series, but in his experience that remark always prefaced an announcement of pregnancy.

'You remember Anita?'

Richard relaxed. 'No.'

'Oh, Richie, of course you do. She's the one who played that marvelous flute solo at the party.'

'Oh, yes. The one with the tin whistles.'

'That's what's so clever. She does it all on those. She can play Elgar's Cello Concerto.'

'I'm impressed.'

'Anyway, that's not the news. She rang me at work this afternoon, and the most marvelous thing. She's going to be in a television series.'

'As what?' asked Richard, genuinely mystified.

'As a sort of adviser.'

'You mean like "Masterclass"?' Richard's mind hovered on Elgar and the tin whistle.

'No, no. Well, yes, not exactly,' quivered Jenny. 'She's been asked to advise on a documentary series in a hospital.'

'What on earth for? Is she qualified?'

'Not in a hospital way, but she does music therapy. She's trained for that.'

'What's that?'

'It's when people are distressed and you go and do sort of music with them and things and it helps them. She's awfully good at it.'

'Obviously.' Richard had noticed most of the hired plants had been dead when the van arrived to collect them. He'd assumed it had had something to do with the heating. 'I still don't see the connection between hospital documentaries and music therapy, though. I mean, I don't remember music in "Your Life in Their Hands" or that thing about having babies underwater.'

'It's a specialist group. Under a psychiatrist. Apparently there's a film crew making a documentary about people who've had nervous breakdowns or are very depressed – some of them have even tried to kill themselves, the doctor told Anita, and anyway, they were at college together, and he's asked her to come and work alongside him, doing music and dance.' She paused expectantly. Richard struggled to banish the image of televised group suicides as Anita passed amongst them playing her Pied Piper whistles. 'That's excellent,' he managed. 'She must be very pleased.'

'Oh, she is. We all are. It's her big break. She's going to compose some new pieces' specially for the show.'

'That's marvellous, darling . . .'

'And the best bit of all is, she says – she can't promise, mind– but she thinks it might just be possible for me to go along and watch. Not be in the film or anything. I couldn't bear that. But just to observe. It would be so useful for me . . . Richie are you all right? Are you too hot? I could open the window if you don't mind holding the azaleas . . .'

What am I worrying about? Richard thought as he hurtled down the back lanes terrifying the jays from their perennial stalking grounds in the centre of the road. Isobel had packed it in. And in any case the odds of Jenny being allowed to watch the filming were fairly remote, and even if she were, she wouldn't actually get to talk to anyone. Would she? And even if she did there was no chance of their saying anything to connect Isobel with them, and even if they did, there was no reason to suppose they would let on why she was there. Not that she was there because of that. But they thought she was, or they wouldn't have wanted her there in the first place.

A rabbit ran across the road. Richard swerved instinctively and caught his wing mirror on an overhanging branch. It rattled ominously. He swore and changed down. The slowing of the car soothed his fevered brain. This was ridiculous. He was the one who needed therapy. What the hell did it matter if Jenny did find out why Isobel had been seconded into the group? Who was she going to tell? Only him. And he knew. And what did it matter if she did find out why, since it wasn't true anyway?

Thus encouraged he changed back up to fifth and roared through the village and back again, since he'd forgotten to pick up the children from his mother's where they regularly went for tea after school on Tuesdays.

'Sorry we're late. I was a bit slow getting to Mother's. Traffic, you know. And then there was a queue at the fish shop.'

One of the best parts of these weekly trips to their grandmother's for Patrick and Eleanour was the subsequent visit to the fish and chip shop. Much as they adored their grandmother, which they unquestionably did, she frequently forgot to buy anything for them to eat, and they had long since come to accept that 'tea at Grandma's' meant television, Cluedo, chewing gum, Morning Coffee biscuits, and a fish supper in the back of the car. Sometimes Richard got some for himself and Isobel as well and then they all ate together round the kitchen table, wine, vinegar and ketchup plonked unceremoniously amongst the paper wrappings.

Tonight, however, Richard did not feel like fish and chips. He felt like steak. He needed steak.

Part of the reason for his anti-social zoom through the countryside was that Jenny's news had had a strictly unbargained-for effect on his libido, and it was only through the most ardent concentration that he had been able to pick up where he had left off before the bombshell. This would not do. He had had gammon and pineapple for lunch. Not one of his favourite meats. Clearly this was to blame for tonight's little fiasco, but he would have to be careful with his diet in future. He had noticed with some delight that Isobel's flagging sexual interest had been much revived since her accident. Maybe it was the degree of ingenuity required to effect a result that had lent spice to their endeavours. Whatever it was, it was certainly worth hanging on to and he couldn't afford to let a pitiable lack of Vitamin C or whatever steak had in it interfere with things.

'How was your day?' he asked. 'Did you phone Alison?'

'No, I didn't have time.'

Richard glanced at her to see if she was being sarcastic, but Isobel looked perfectly equable, if a little tired. 'So what did you do? Did you go anywhere? I was thinking we might have supper out, if Bob'll babysit for us? We could go to The Collier's Arms or something. We haven't been there for a long time. That's if you haven't started cooking.'

'That would be nice. Not The Collier's Arms, though. It gets so crowded.'

'Not on a Tuesday.'

'Still.'

'Truth is, I rather fancy a steak. That's the only place you can get a decent one round here without paying the earth.'

'All right, then. I don't mind.'

'Unless you'd rather go somewhere else.'

'No.'

'Good. I'll go and see if Bob's in.' Richard went next door and returned ten minutes later with the news that Bob would be perfectly happy to babysit and would come round about half-past seven.

Isobel went upstairs to have a wash. She'd got quite good at it now, having rigged up a sort of pen for herself with the wooden towel rail and the laundry basket. She found if she leant right forward into the shower stream the water ran down her left leg while leaving her plaster dry, thus creating the illusion of a proper soaking and she could shampoo her hair at the same time.

It would be nice to go out to supper, albeit she would have preferred somewhere different. Still she didn't have to have shepherd's pie again. And it wasn't as though there were any harm in her having had lunch with Harry. There was nothing secret about it. She just hadn't got round to telling Richard yet. She would in a minute.

'So what have you been doing with yourself all day?' asked Richard as they settled into a corner table.

'Actually it's been quite hectic. Diana came round.'

'What did she want?'

Isobel's hand went to her mouth. 'Oh, my god, I knew I'd forgotten something. She made us a casserole. We were meant to have it for supper.'

'Is it still in the oven? I could ring Bob.'

'It didn't get as far as the oven. You know what she's like—always doing a dozen things at once.'

'How long did she stay?'

'Too long. She said it was her lunch hour. Anyway . . .' Isobel did a violent double take as Harry Peters appeared at the foot of a stairway leading from the pub accommodation. He saw her and raised his eyebrows in surprise, before making his way through to the lounge bar. Richard followed her gaze.

'Isn't that that bloke who brought you home from the hospital last week?'
'Yes.'
'I thought you said he came from Birmingham.'
'I didn't say he came from Birmingham. I said he was going to Birmingham.'
'Not much sense of direction, obviously. Mind you, it's Tuesday today. He's probably back down again.'
'Yes. Richard . . .'
'Mmm?'
'I went to the hospital today.'
'I thought your appointment was next week.'
'It is. I went to the therapy thing.'
'You what?' Any fear of anaemia was immediately negated by the rush of blood to Richard's face. 'What the . . .'
'There's no need to throw a fit.'
'But you said . . . You swore . . .'
'I know. I had no intention of going, honestly. But then Diana turned up and started driving me mad.'
'You can say that again.'
'If you're going to be unpleasant, I'm not going to tell you about it.'
'Well, honestly, Isobel.'
'And then, while she was hoovering, Harry turned up.'
'Who? You mean him? That bloke over there? I'll break his bloody neck.'
'Oh, for heaven's sake, Richard. Stop being so ridiculous. He came to see if I needed a lift. He didn't know I'd decided not to go, did he?'
Richard shifted crossly in his chair. 'What's it got to do with him, anyway? If you wanted to go, surely you could have got there under your own steam?'
Isobel stifled her irritation. 'Yes, of course. I was thinking of cycling in.'
'You know what I mean. You could have ordered a cab. I could have taken you, come to that. I don't suppose you thought of ringing me?'
'No,' said Isobel with perfect veracity. 'You're usually busy in the lunch hour, aren't you?'
Richard prickled with guilt. 'What's that supposed to

mean?' Isobel looked at him coolly. 'What would you like it to mean, Richard?'

Richard shuffled round in search of an imaginary wine waiter. 'How did you get home? I suppose he drove you back as well?'

'No, as a matter of fact. I got a cab.'

'How much did that cost?'

'Rather less than your steak.'

'I just don't understand why you agreed to go in the first place.'

'Because I was bored, Richard. Do you understand the meaning of the word? I was bored with bloody Diana, and the house and the garden and my ankle . . .'

'And me as well, I daresay. Go on, say it.' With the perverseness of the guilty, Richard thundered into the attack. 'The next thing you'll be saying is he took you to lunch first.'

'He did.'

'He what?'

'Did. Yes. Take me to lunch.'

Richard sat back as though he'd just scored the winning penalty.

'Marvellous. I leave my wife alone in the house for a few hours, and what happens? Some bloody brummy comes and whips her away to a five star restaurant, loosens her up with alcohol, no doubt, and then sticks her in a room full of lunatics and films what goes on.'

Isobel began to laugh. 'Very *Marat Sade*. I wish it had been half so exciting.'

Richard's sense of threat began to evaporate. 'Well, what did you do then?'

'We came here. I had shepherd's pie and a glass of wine and Harry had . . . he had shepherd's pie as well, I think, and a half of beer, then we had coffee and I ate Harry's mint imperial because he doesn't like them.'

Richard poured more wine. 'I suppose the afternoon was a disaster? The filming and that.'

'You could say that.'

'I hope you've made it quite clear you're not going to go any more? And you don't want any more lifts?'

'My very words.'

Richard squeezed her hand. 'I'm sorry. Perhaps I did over-react a little. It's just I worry about you. Particularly now you're stuck in the house. I mean, you used to be so active, always off somewhere playing tennis or swimming or whatever.'

'Yes, well, I'm not Douglas Bader, Richard. The sun may yet rise on my tennis racquet. It's only three more weeks till this plaster comes off and then I'll be as good as new.'

Richard smiled winsomely. 'You will keep it, won't you?'

'What?'

'Your plaster. After they take it off. It's just I've rather got to like it . . . you know . . .' Isobel gazed at him in amusement. 'Richard, you are positively perverted.'

Richard beamed. 'I know. But you will ask to keep it?'

Isobel grinned. 'Actually I've got a feeling they break them to get them off. Take a hammer to it or something.'

'Who told you that?'

'Diana, I think.'

'Diana takes a hammer to everything,' said Richard with some feeling. 'I must have a pee. Tell them to bring me some extra chips if the food comes while I'm gone, will you?' He wandered off and Isobel reflected on the strangeness of coincidence. Why was Harry still here? Perhaps she should go and have a quick word with him, point out how annoyed Richard had been and how impossible it would be for her to continue with the therapy. She had just about made up her mind to do that when Richard returned. 'I had a quick word with your mate.'

'Oh, no. What did you say?'

Richard laughed. 'It's all right. I didn't throw down the gauntlet. I just thanked him for picking you up today, and said you'd definitely decided to give it a miss from now on.'

Isobel felt a stab of annoyance. 'Why did you do that?'

'Because you have.'

'No, I haven't. You have. I do wish people would stop trying to make up my mind for me. What little officially remains of it.'

'Oh, don't start, Izzy. You're hungry, that's what the problem is. You're always like this when you're hungry. I am, too. Where's this bloody food? Shall I order some more wine? By the way, I said we'd join them for a drink after we'd eaten. Show there's no hard feelings. Was that a good idea?'

Isobel stared at him. 'They?'

'Yes, he's got a woman with him. I think he said you knew her. She's from the filming thing too. Must say she doesn't look as cracked as I'd've imagined. Oh, here's the food.' The waitress set it down. Richard smiled at her beguilingly, 'I say, I don't suppose I could be a perfect rotter and ask for some extra chips, could I?'

Isobel was not much enamoured of the prospect of drinks with Harry and Leonie. She knew for a fact that Richard's suggestion would have depended entirely on the physical appeal of Harry's companion, and also that Leonie had the kind of daffy sensuality that characterised so many of his girlfriends past and present. Would that be such a bad thing? Surely no one could be more trying than Jenny? Leonie could. Of that she had small doubt. Still, it would be rather a laugh if Richard, who had argued so vehemently against her continuing the group sessions, were suddenly in the position of begging her to keep them up.

'Do you want coffee now, or shall we get some before we go?'

'Before we go, I think, please.'

'Right. They're in the lounge bar. We don't have to stay long.' Richard paid the bill and helped Isobel to her feet. The landlord gave her a strange look as she hobbled across the restaurant. He was used to seeing women with different men and men with different women, but to have one in each bar seemed a little modern for his liking.

Harry rose as they entered and fetched a couple of chairs from a neighbouring table. 'Hullo again,' he said cheerfully. 'What would you like?'

'I'll get these,' said Richard. 'I owe you one, and what would your friend like?' He leaned forward attentively. 'I'm sorry, I don't know your name. I'm Richard, by the way.'

The woman in the corner pulled her chair aside to make room for Isobel. 'Maureen,' she said. 'Maureen Hart.'

Chapter Seventeen

It took some time for Isobel to get over the surprise of seeing Maureen there. Richard and Harry sized each other up and fell to discussing the cricket scores, Harley Davidsons, and the merits and demerits of travelling north on the A1.

Maureen spoke very little but sipped her whisky placidly while the two men parried road junctions, her brown eyes twinkling with silent amusement.

'Is this your local?' asked Isobel. Maureen shook her head.

'No, Harry brought me up here. The ambulance was delayed so he said he'd take me home, and we had a cup of tea, then he suggested we have supper together. This seemed like a good place since he needed to book a room anyway.'

Out of the corner of her eye Isobel could see her husband working his way round to something. Harry rose to get more drinks as he turned to Maureen. 'I gather you're a friend of Isobel's from this . . . filming thing?'

Maureen caught Isobel's eye. 'Yes,' she said pleasantly.

Richard tried again. 'Do you . . . that is . . . are you . . . Have you been going to this doctor bloke's classes for very long?'

Maureen shook her head. 'About two months. I don't know. Is that long?'

'But what do you actually get out of it? I mean, according to a friend of mine it's mainly for people who . . . that is . . .'

'Yes?' asked Maureen with perfect directness. Richard looked flustered.

'She . . . they . . . didn't seem to know a great deal about it, but a friend of hers – theirs, apparently, – has been asked to help out with some sort of music. Would you know anything about that?'

'I think Dr Mahon mentioned something about a circle dance. It's to please the director. You'd be better off asking Harry.'

'Asking me what?' Harry set down the tray of drinks.

'About the circle dance,' said Isobel. 'You know, Mahon was rabbiting on about there needing to be a conclusion to the series. By the time he's finished it'll look more like *Under The Greenwood Tree* than a fly-on-the-wall doc about depressives.'

'Wasn't Thomas Hardy a depressive?' said Harry.

'How are you going to dance with your leg in plaster?' demanded Richard.

'They've erected a kind of pulley,' said Isobel. 'I hop round on my left leg, and this thing trundles round beside me holding my other leg up.'

Richard's face registered utter horror followed by slight irritation. 'Very funny. I only asked. It seems a perfectly logical question to me. I daresay after two weeks in that nut's clutches logic's a bit out of the window for you.' He turned to Harry. 'What do you make of all this?'

'It's a job.'

'Do a lot of this kind of thing, do you?'

'What kind of thing?'

'This ... filming people ... not actors, I mean. Real people?'

Harry considered. 'About half and half.'

Richard drained his glass. 'Well, Isobel's out of it now, if you're going to be dancing around all over the place. Can't say I'm sorry.'

'You very rarely do,' said Isobel, resentful of being spoken for in her presence.

'What I can't understand,' Richard focused his attention on Maureen again, 'is why a perfectly intelligent woman such as yourself would get mixed up in this kind of thing.'

Maureen smiled. 'They're very persuasive at the hospital,' she said. 'I think you'd agree your wife is hardly a likely candidate, but she's there. Perhaps it's got something to do with keeping an open mind.'

Richard acknowledged the truth of this. 'It's not that I'm against it, you understand. I'm sure it can be very helpful for some people, but for God's sake . . . Isobel . . . I mean, she only broke her ankle – not that that's not a rotten thing, before you have a go at me – but anyone would think she'd done it on purpose the way they go on.'

'I suppose there's more than one way of looking at most things,' said Maureen mildly. She turned to Harry. 'I'm afraid I shall have to be getting back, if you don't mind. I can always get a cab if you'd rather not turn out again.'

Harry shook his head vigorously. 'Nonsense, my love. It's no problem at all. It's been great of you to come.'

'Maureen says you're staying here.' said Isobel.

'Yes, that berk, Joffe, landed it on me this afternoon. We've got to do some exteriors tomorrow morning. Think he's afraid he'll end up with too many of Ken's poems if we don't have a bit of grass to pad it out with.'

The two women laughed. 'Mind you,' said Isobel, 'it could be worse. We haven't been subjected to any of Hilary's yet.'

'Nor will be if I get my way,' muttered Harry. 'Jock owes me a favour, I think I'll get him to blank out all the tapes every time the nerd opens his mouth.'

'Which nerd are you talking about now?' asked Richard ingenuously. 'Are there a lot of them?'

Isobel burst out laughing. 'Above the statistical norm, I'd say. Look, Richard, I've had a thought. Why don't we take Maureen home? It's only down the road to Eastley, and it'll save Harry having to get his car out specially.'

'No need for that,' protested Harry.

'Yes, honestly. It's the least we can do after you picking me up and everything. Isn't it, Richard?'

Richard voiced no objection, thinking that it would be just as well to clear any obligations.

'Well, if you're sure? Only it's in the opposite direction.'

'Not much,' said Isobel. 'Not as far as we were for you.'

'Yes, but you've got your leg,' put in Maureen. 'You don't want to be jolting around down there. It's pretty bumpy along Clitheroe Gardens.'

Richard raised his hand. 'I have it. I shall take Maureen home. Isobel can stay here and I'll pick her up on the way back. It's only five minutes each way. It'll take her that long to get to the door, won't it, my sweet?'

'Probably. Unless Harry carries me.' Richard shot her a look.

Harry grinned. 'In that case it'd take fifteen.'

When they had gone Isobel glanced at Harry. He seemed far away, staring dreamily into the last of his beer. He stirred himself. 'Sorry, miles away. Do you want another drink?'

'No thanks.'

'Coffee?'

'Coffee would be nice.'

Harry got up and went over to the bar.

'She says she'll bring it over. Do you come here often?'

Isobel laughed.

'What's so funny?'

'I was thinking you must be older than I thought.'

'Why?'

'Don't you know?'

'No.'

Isobel sighed. 'That means you're younger than I thought.'

'I'm thirty-eight. Does it matter?'

'No. All I meant was there's a line in *Look Back In Anger* – the John Osborne play – it was quite well-known at the time. He says: "Do you come here often?" And then she says—no, it's not her, it's the other one – the friend says . . .'

'What does the friend say?'

Isobel hesitated. 'Oh, something or other . . . I forget.'

' "Only in the mating season",' said Harry.

The waitress arrived with the coffee.

Harry poured two cups. 'You still haven't answered the question.'

'What? Oh . . . no, we don't. Not really. I didn't want to come tonight, only Richard fancied a steak and it's really quite reasonable. I certainly didn't expect to see you here. Or Maureen. Do you make a habit of picking up depressed women and luring them to pubs for meals?'

'Yes,' said Harry. 'They're not so choosy as cheerful ones.'

'I think Leonie might be. I bet she's a vegetarian.'

'She's a cannibal,' said Harry. For a moment their eyes met.
'You should know,' said Isobel, trying not to sound piqued. 'What about Meg? How are you going to lure her up here?'

Harry smiled ruefully. 'I think a packet of crisps would probably catch Meg. Poor cow. I can just imagine her old man. And the son.'

'And the mother-in-law,' added Isobel.

They fell silent, pondering the awfulness of Meg's domestic situation. The landlord called 'time'. The girl behind the bar looked over to them and shook her head.

'It doesn't matter for you, love. You're a resident.'

'Let's hope she is, too,' murmured Harry, staring openly at the girl's cleavage. Isobel glared into her coffee.

'Does it annoy you?'

'What?'

'Me talking like that?'

'Why should it? In my experience it's usually the sign of a very small dick.' Harry burst out laughing. 'How deep is your experience?'

'Deep enough.'

'Pity. Speaking of which, shouldn't your husband be back to claim you by now?' Isobel looked at her watch. It was a quarter to eleven. 'I expect he stopped for petrol,' she said.

'Are you going to come next Tuesday?'

'I doubt it. I've got an appointment with that Robertson chap in the morning so I shall have to go in, but I don't think I'll stay. I thought it might have been useful to start with, but I can see it's not going to be, especially if they all start morris dancing or whatever.'

'I can pick you up for the morning bloke.'

'There's no need. Actually, I'd rather you didn't, if you don't mind.'

'Why not?'

'Because it makes for difficulties.'

'I don't see why it should.'

'No, nor do I. But it does. Even this evening I got into some ridiculous sort of situation with Richard, with me wondering if I should pretend I didn't know you and I hadn't been to the session and you hadn't given me a lift, and it was all so unnecessary. I don't want to be put in that situation any more, that's all. I've got enough problems without adding to them.'

'But you hadn't done anything wrong, had you?'

'No, of course not. But I felt as though I had, don't you see?'

Harry sat back. 'So I won't see you any more after tonight?'

Isobel looked up, surprised. 'Well . . . no, I suppose not. If you put it like that. Does it matter? I mean I'm sure Dr Mahon will find a suitable replacement, if that's what you're worrying about. He could probably arrange for her to have a false plaster on her ankle if you think it would help, cinematically speaking.' She waited for him to laugh, but he didn't.

A thundering on the locked pub door announced the return of Richard. Harry stood up and handed her crutches. His hand touched hers as she slipped her fingers into the straps.

'Sorry I was so long,' called Richard who had left the car engine running.

'Maureen insisted on making me some coffee. Daresay she thought I needed it.'

'She thought right,' Isobel called back. She half turned to Harry. 'Well, thank you for everything – the lifts and lunch and everything.'

'Give me your number,' said Harry almost angrily.

Isobel hesitated. 'I really don't think . . .'

'Give me it.' She did.

'That Maureen's a nice woman,' said Richard as they drove home.

'Talks a lot of sense. We had quite a chat on the way back. She likes you. Says you shouldn't be wasting your time on therapy. Says she'll miss you, mind. She was on the point of chucking it in when you turned up. Says it would be nice if you and she could stick around long enough to wreck that quack's chances. Apparently he's got shares in the TV company. Stands to make a fortune if it gets networked.'

Isobel closed her eyes. 'But you wouldn't want me to, would you?'

Richard thought. There was still the awful danger that Jenny would turn up at the hospital and see Isobel, and even if she didn't, she seemed very thick with this Alice bod who played the tin whistles. On the other hand, the prospect of Isobel's being thoroughly occupied each Tuesday afternoon for the next month laid out endless possibilities for a more leisurely approach to his philandering. Not that he saw it as such, just a masculine urge which needed satisfying, same as any other. Jenny was on flexi-time, so she could work late on the other days and take Tuesday afternoons off. Also, if she was with him, she couldn't possibly be spying on Isobel and the nutcases. And Maureen Hart seemed a thoroughly responsible sort of person. No harm would come to Isobel while she was with her.

'Richard, you don't want me to go, do you?'

Richard reached across and took his wife's hand. He was surprised to find that it was trembling a little but assumed that she was tired.

'It's up to you, darling,' he said amiably. 'But I don't see that it would do any harm.'

Richard, bolstered by his porterhouse, was amazed and delighted at the energy and passion of his wife that night. As he sank back exhausted, having considerately readjusted Isobel's footrest to her liking, he reflected that perhaps he should take her out more often, and that definitely he should eat steak more often, and that if he were to be required to perform twice a day on a regular basis, he should perhaps try to come to some budgetary arrangement with the butcher.

Isobel, burning with guilt, lay beside her husband, unable to cast out the image of Harry which had fired her lovemaking. She felt ill with contempt for herself. Why had she given him the phone number? She could so easily have walked away from him. He knew where she lived. He knew her name. If he had wanted it that badly he could have found it out for himself. But she had given it to him, and in doing that she had crossed the line between the possible and the inevitable.

Useless to tell herself it was not too late; that she had done nothing wrong; that tomorrow or whenever he rang, if he rang, she could say it was all a mistake, that she had had too much to drink, that she did not want to meet him again, in her home, at the hospital, anywhere. Even if she never saw him again she had given in to him. She had admitted that she was his for the asking, something which had never happened before. Not with Richard's partner, or the Lebanese drummer, or the six or seven undergraduates on whom she had progressively foisted her virginity. Not with Richard, even. But with Harry, bloody Harry, who probably got as much pleasure from chatting up a folding chair as a woman. It was perfectly clear that he did it from habit. He had no tastes or preferences, he just adjusted the controls to meet the particular situation. Look at today. He had called for her, ogled Diana, sweet-talked that drip, Leonie – even wormed his way into Maureen's for a cup of tea, and who knew what else, except that Maureen was too sensible to be taken in by that phoney charm – and then made a pass at the barmaid, right in front of her, Isobel, and finally, when all else had failed, been reduced to fumbling her crutches and demanding her phone number with menaces.

With these frenzied and not entirely accurate reflections Isobel fell into a troubled sleep.

Meanwhile, in the kitchen of her terraced house in Clitheroe Gardens, Vera Beasley cut the buttons off Richard's amber silk shirt and moved them nearer to the edge. She was pleased with her new kettle, less so with the tea she had removed from Jenny Holt's kitchen dresser. Wondering whether the sea would reach as far as Clitheroe Gardens, she drained her cup and went to bed.

Chapter Eighteen

Harry didn't ring. Isobel spent a wretched morning, first avoiding the phone, then hovering over it like a distraught vulture. When it finally did ring she stood paralysed, unable to pick it up. She realised she should have put the answerphone on, then she could have listened to what he had to say without committing herself further. But she hadn't. On the sixth ring she snatched it up and babbled their number, including the code, in an attempt to sound detached and calm. It was the butcher to say his van was having trouble and he wouldn't be round till the afternoon. Was that all right? Isobel said it was with such relief in her voice that the butcher wondered privately if last week's order had been up to scratch.

She thought about attacking her autobiography, but phrases such as 'faithless woman' and 'harpy' began floating through her head with such persistency that she put it aside and concentrated instead on tidying the desk drawer, which was full of bent paperclips and brown envelopes with things like 'bank' and 'Dijon mustard' written on them. It was while engaged in this that there was a tap on the window. Isobel's immediate fear was of a return visit from Diana. Images of the casserole still uncooked on the stove flashed across her mind, then fled as she looked up and saw Harry's tanned face peering down at her. He had his crash helmet with him, just as on the first day she had seen him. She wondered that she hadn't heard the noise of his motorbike, then realised she had and had dismissed it as next-door's lawnmower.

A horrible sense of chlaustrophobia gripped her as she sat looking at him. She felt hot and trapped and guilt-stricken all over again. This was ridiculous. She would get rid of him, then the thing would be done. Sorted. Harry pointed to the front door. Slowly she reached for her crutches and hobbled round to open it.

Having done so she positioned herself firmly in the doorway, making no attempt to invite him in. Harry watched her for a moment, then reached inside his jacket and produced a leaflet. 'I'm sure, like most of us, madam, you are very worried about the siege of Babylon,' he said.

'What?'

'I thought as much.' Placing his foot deliberately in the door, he flapped the leaflet under Isobel's nose. Instinctively she backed away. Harry stepped rapidly into the hall and closed the door.

'What is this?' asked Isobel crossly, her nervousness evaporating.

'Dunno. Some woman dressed as a pomegranate gave it to me when we were filming in the square this morning. Thought you might be interested.'

Isobel considered the pamphlet. 'It doesn't say anything about the siege of Babylon here.'

Harry glanced at it. 'No, well it wouldn't. There's not a lot to say. What is it? Jehovah's witnesses?'

Isobel shook her head. 'No, it's those Apocalypse 2000 people. They're holding some kind of gathering in the area. Mrs Beasley was very thick with them. Tried to get me to go to one of the meetings.'

'Did you?'

'No, of course I didn't.'

'No "of course" about it. You're a very suggestible woman.'

'No, I'm not.'

'Are you sure?'

'Yes.'

'Damn.'

Isobel laughed. 'Don't start. You do know that was all a mistake last night, don't you?'

'What?'

'You know. Me giving you the phone number and that. I mean, not that there's anything wrong with you having our phone number. You're welcome to give us a ring or call in any time you're in the area. You know that. But, you know – the way I did it was a bit . . . I just didn't want you to think . . . What I'm saying is . . .'

'I know what you're saying, Isobel. Think no more about it.' With these sage and adult words Harry took hold of her and kissed her long and passionately, Isobel clinging for dear life to him as her crutches crashed to the floor beside her.

'You shouldn't have done that,' she accused him unsteadily when he finally released her tongue.

'Me? What about you? I've never been hung on to so hard. You're insatiable.'

'I'm not at all,' said Isobel defensively, 'my crutches fell down. I couldn't let go.'

'A feeble excuse. Tell you what, we'll try it again and this time don't hold on.'

'No . . . Oh . . .' The crutches really had very little to do with it.

'Do you always make love in the hall?' asked Harry after a while. He was getting past the point of wanting to stand up. Isobel was shocked by the realisation of what she was doing. What on earth had gone wrong? She was meant to be getting rid of him, not leaning against a wall with her clothes half off like some fifth form scrubber behind the bike shed.

'I . . . this . . .' She made an ineffectual attempt to retrieve her blouse.

'Wait there.' Harry moved swiftly to the sitting room and, sweeping the curtains together, littered the floor with cushions from the armchairs and couch. Returning he lifted Isobel up and deposited her in the middle of them. 'Harry, we can't. Please. It's the middle of the day. Suppose someone comes.'

'Someone is coming,' said Harry, a touch unromantically. 'How do you undo this?' He fiddled impatiently with her skirt.

'It's elastic. It just pulls on and off.'

Harry wrenched it off and gazed in unconcealed lust at her injured leg. 'That's gorgeous,' he murmured, running his fingers voluptuously up and down the smooth white surface.

'Sorry about the other one,' said Isobel, wondering what it was about plaster of Paris that was proving such a turn on for the men in her life. Perhaps she should have gone the whole hog and jumped off a bridge over a motorway. Her body might never have seemed more beautiful. It made sense of necrophilia. Harry, however, had got over his initial interest and had turned his attention to the more receptive parts of her anatomy.

He was an amazing lover, much gentler and more intuitive than Isobel had imagined, the outward bullishness of his manner completely lost in the sensitivity of his touch. Isobel closed her eyes and sank away into her fantasies. She would have stayed there for ever.

'I have to go.'

Isobel reached up to him. 'Not yet, surely? What time is it?'

Harry glanced at his watch. 'Ten to three. We've got another couple of shots to get in. I said I'd be back by four.'

Isobel sat up. 'You didn't tell them you were coming here?'

Harry laughed. 'Didn't I say? They're all out there waiting. I said I'd only be five minutes.'

They got dressed. Isobel remembered she had had no lunch but she wasn't hungry. She supposed she should offer Harry some kind of refreshment. He had certainly earned it, but somehow it seemed a bit trite. 'More tea, Vicar?' she said.

Harry laughed. 'I'd better be off.' He put the room to rights, Isobel instructing him on what belonged where. 'Don't draw the curtains,' she said. 'Just in case anyone's outside. I'll say I've been lying down with a migraine.'

'I've been called some things,' said Harry. 'Never a migraine, before.'

'How long are you staying down?' asked Isobel as he picked up his jacket. She hoped she sounded casual.

'Just tonight. I'm going to see my daughter tomorrow. She's got her exams coming up. I like to be around.'

'How old is your daughter?' asked Isobel, realising she knew nothing about him.

'Seventeen.' Isobel nodded and stared at her fingernails.

Harry put a hand on her shoulder. 'Divorced,' he said and, kissing her lightly on the cheek, opened the door and was gone.

Richard was pleased to find Isobel still in a good mood when he got in. If anything, she was even more affectionate than the night before. He inspected the butcher's offerings which she was unpacking on the kitchen table, and decided there was quite enough there to keep him in training. The children had been making shortbread and, having eaten a fair bit of it on the way from the oven to the tin, didn't want much supper. This was a good thing because it meant they would probably have beans on toast in front of the television, allowing him and Isobel to have a more leisurely dinner à deux when the two of them had gone to bed.

Looking at Isobel as she hopped around the kitchen, (she had long since dispatched with crutches for short journeys), he was amazed that he had never really appreciated how good-looking she was. Her hair shone in the evening sun and her skin sort of radiated health and happiness. He was a lucky man. Of course, she was pretty lucky too. It wasn't just coincidence that they had a decent life style with two smashing children. He'd worked hard to put them where they were, and Isobel had worked hard with the children, making sure they had reasonable manners and weren't spoilt – not very, anyway. He still couldn't get over the price of Patrick's mountain bike. Yes, altogether they were very lucky to have what they had, the house, the children, and each other. How many couples in their forties, for they were both in their forties now, he thought with burgundian relish, were still happy in each other's company, enjoyed such a thriving sex life, – loved each other, in fact?

He supposed they loved each other. It was hard to tell after seventeen years. Not like being in love. He could hardly remember what that felt like. He had certainly been in love with Isobel once, and several other women before that – none since that he could remember, because it was all such a rush once you were married, especially happily married. No time for the delicious subtleties of courtship and seduction, just a few drinks in a hotel bar or, in Jenny's case, vegetarian moussaka and a bottle of Retsina in the lunch hour. He would have liked to be in love. Perhaps he would fall in love with Isobel again. She certainly seemed like a different woman these days – since her birthday, in fact. Perhaps there was something to be said for a woman in her forties, after all. They had more confidence, more grace, even with a leg in plaster, more style. Yes, he would give some thought to this. Maybe it was time to ease himself away from Jenny a little and spend more time at home. Jenny would understand. She was more worried about his domestic set-up than he was. Or Isobel for that matter. Which reminded him, he must ring Jenny and fix up about next Tuesday afternoon. After all, it was only for three weeks, and there was no point in wasting a god-given opportunity. Besides it would give him more time to prepare her for a possible break.

'Would you like a drink, darling?' he asked solicitously. 'Do you want me to give you a hand with the supper? I could scrape us up a bolognese if you're tired.'

Isobel turned on him a ravishing smile of perfect wifely contentment. 'I'm not tired,' she said. 'Not at all tired.'

Richard smiled back.

Chapter Nineteen

For Isobel being in love was perhaps not such a novel experience as it might have been for Richard. She had often, during the course of their marriage, allowed herself the luxury of imagining life in the arms of another man. That she had not pursued these fantasies, even where it was patently a possibility, whilst Richard had barged happily from one affair to another, with none of the moral justification which liking and not lust might have lent to his escapades, was presumably a reflection either on their characters or their sex. Impossible to tell.

Nonetheless, the effect on Isobel, as a woman of forty, mature and sexually experienced, might reasonably have been expected to be a little more muted than that on a girl of sixteen. This was not the case, however.

She woke each morning that week to a feeling of inexpressible excitement and nervousness. She ate less, laughed more, played sixties tapes to herself all day in the house, forgot to put the oven on, the washing in, the shopping away. She denied the children nothing, ate slice after slice of Renate's jam sponge, and listened to Jenny expounding the value of zinc in an ageing woman's diet for twenty minutes, when she called round with a fresh supply of seaweed for Isobel's infusions.

With Richard she was a temptress, a nymph, a whore. Whatever could be essayed with a broken ankle and two children in the house was done. Richard's head spun with delight and confusion. How could he have neglected this creature for so long? He began to think that he would renege on his arrangement with Jenny for Tuesday and spend the afternoon instead in the bosom of his wife. Jenny, however, had looked so crestfallen at the first hint that he might not be able to get away, that he had relented, especially when she had meekly pointed out that she had had to take the time as part of the Queen's Birthday Holiday, and would have to start at eight each morning for the rest of the week.

By Saturday Isobel's euphoria was turning to restlessness. Harry had neither phoned nor written. Not that she had anticipated the latter, but she had expected a call. His daughter was doing exams, he had said, and he had had to get all the way to Birmingham to be with her. Maybe they weren't on the phone. Did he actually live in Birmingham? She had got the impression not. Why? He was divorced. But Birmingham was a very big place. Big enough to have call boxes, she thought with sudden fury. Why hadn't he given her his number? Because he didn't want her to ring. Perhaps he wasn't divorced after all. But why say so, if it wasn't true? Idiot! Men always said that, because women felt guilty if they thought they were harming someone's family. How could he do what he was doing if he was still married, though? He wasn't an unkind man. He was gentle and funny and strong ... Isobel felt her insides beginning to tremble again. No, Harry would never hurt anyone like that. He was too intelligent. But look at Richard. He was intelligent, too, and kind and funny and all the rest, and yet he regularly deceived her – or thought he did. And yet it didn't seem to hurt. Perhaps because she always knew. Ever since that woman at the conference in Bath, just after Eleanour had been born, the one who had rung him at home and hung up when Isobel, baby clamped to her like a plug, had struggled across the room to hear the dull click of the receiver being replaced, and Richard had come hurrying down the stairs with an enamel brooch he had spent a fortune on in an antique shop and forgotten to give her till that moment.

She had never seen the woman. Margaret. A nice sensible name. Something of a high flyer, according to Richard. He seemed to think that superiority on the work front would in some way endear her to Isobel, suffering the throes of postnatal depression – justify his choice. Whatever it was, it had set a barrier between them which the intervening years had smoothed but not erased. Whether Margaret had been the first, Isobel did not know. She only knew she had come at a time when she herself had needed Richard, perhaps for the first time in her life, and that he had not been there, and because of that things could never be the same again. It was not necessarily a bad thing. It had taught her not to rely on anyone, to judge them as mortals not as friends, and with her sights so substantially lowered she had been able to enjoy a certain sense of contentment. It also helped her now, for with the actual act of adultery had flown all her misgivings and self-doubts. It had been absolutely meant to be. Nothing could have been righter or more perfect. Thinking of this Isobel's fears disappeared again and a new burst of delirium sent her hopping round the garden, picking everything that would yield to her lopsided snatches.

'Where's Mummy?' Richard had been attaching new windscreen wipers to the car and was mysteriously covered in oil.

'In the garden.' Patrick was watching her dispassionately through the kitchen window, a long trail of chewing gum dangling from his mouth.

'And get rid of that disgusting stuff before Mummy sees you. You know she'll go mad.'

'She's down the bottom,' responded Patrick. 'I've got ages yet.'

Richard sighed and tried ineffectually to remove the oil with washing up liquid. 'I thought we might go down to The Meadows in Eastley. There's a cricket match this afternoon. Would you like that? We could take a picnic.'

'Can I take my bike?'

'Hardly, to a cricket match. You could take your bat, though, and I could bowl to you for a bit.'

'What about Elly?'

'Elly'll be all right. She can take something to play with. I'll go and see what Mummy thinks.'

Isobel was greatly in favour. She liked cricket. Or rather, she liked what went with it on a sunny afternoon – wine, food, a decent thriller, along with Richard's commentaries which were spiteful and funny.

When they were first married, before Patrick was born,

they used to sneak off somewhere and make love in the bushes, shaking with laughter at the encroaching cries of 'Howzat!' which became something of a byword with them for a while. Isobel suspected it was on one of these occasions that Patrick had been conceived though when she had told Richard, he had looked a little nonplussed that so portentous an event should have come about so haphazardly.

They set off shortly before one, Elly with a friend and her roller boots, Patrick also with a friend and the sponge tennis. They had offered to take Richard's mother, but she had declined on the grounds that she was planning to restock her fish pond that afternoon and, rather more ominously, that she had some cooking to do.

The afternoon passed peacefully, with the children off in the thicket playing murder and Richard and Isobel reclining luxuriantly on the grass, she reading, he murmuring capriciously at the umpire's every ruling. After a while it became too hot for Isobel's liking. The plaster cast, though impervious to temperature, weighed her down. She hunted round for her crutches and hauled herself to her feet. Richard looked up. 'All right, darling?'

'Yes, I was getting pins and needles. I think I'll go for a hobble. It's a bit shadier round the other side.'

'Do you want me to come with you?' asked Richard solicitously, sound in the knowledge that his offer would be rejected.

'No. Keep an eye on the children, though, will you? I don't want Elly and Clare going out of sight.' Richard agreed to do this, though both of them knew he couldn't tell one small girl from another at that distance.

It was round the other side that Isobel came across Maureen, sitting in one of the deck-chairs laid out by the groundsmen for these occasions. She was wearing sunglasses and Isobel almost passed her by, but Maureen, for obvious reasons, had less trouble recognising Isobel and called out, indicating the vacant chair beside her. Isobel was not at all sure that she would ever be able to get out of a deck-chair, once in, but there were plenty of burly men available, their being only a stone's throw from the pavilion, and if the worst came to the worst she could always send a runner to fetch Richard.

'I didn't know you liked cricket,' said Isobel, thinking what an absurd remark that was, since she didn't know anything else about Maureen either.

'I used to come with Jim – my husband,' Maureen replied. 'We used to bring a picnic and make a day of it if the weather was nice.' Isobel saw the sad remains of sandwiches for one lying on top of Maureen's newspaper, opened as always at the crossword. 'We came all last summer,' Maureen continued. 'They played right up to September.'

Isobel involuntarily calculated that Jim must have died very shortly after that, since Maureen had mentioned eight months at the hospital and it was now the beginning of June.

Maureen reached for a flask. 'I have to say, it's not quite the same without him. Would you like some of this tea? It's not long made. I don't really like tea from thermoses, but this seems to be okay.' Isobel accepted gratefully.

A cry went up from the wicket keeper and after some deliberation a sandy-haired man was given out, much to the annoyance of the crowd round the pavilion, which roared its disapproval in a manner more reminiscent of a cup tie final than the sedate setting of a village green.

'Is Harry picking you up on Tuesday?' asked Maureen after a while.

Isobel almost jumped at the mention of his name. 'I don't know,' she stammered. 'We hadn't really arranged anything. He just sort of turned up last time. I . . . don't know what his plans are really.' She glanced quickly at Maureen to see if this feeble effort had passed muster, but she was gazing benignly at the cricket and showed no hint of suspicion.

'I like Harry,' Maureen continued. 'He talks a lot of sense.' Isobel recalled that that was exactly what Richard had said about her. She wondered if it was going to come full circle, with Harry avowing her own rationality and her swearing by Richard's. It didn't seem likely.

'I don't know much about him,' was all she could manage. Maureen sipped her tea.

'No, nor do I. He's travelled a lot, because of his job. Jim and I used to do quite a bit of globetrotting when we were younger.'

'What did your husband do?' asked Isobel.

'He was a chemist,' said Maureen. 'I met him when I was

teaching, just after the war. Those days we used to hitchhike everywhere. We had no money. It was a lot safer then, obviously. We went to Greece, and all round Italy and Spain. Turkey, one year, I remember. That was interesting. Then Africa. I'd come into a bit of money when my father died and we blew it all on the air fares. Air Ethiopia. It went everywhere. We certainly got our money's worth. It took us a day and a half to get there. That was before the days of inflight videos and duty free. When we got out I could hardly move I was so stiff. I was the same shape as the seat. Jim laughed so much I thought he was going to burst.' She smiled at the memory. 'Of course we neither of us knew . . .'

'Knew what?' asked Isobel. Maureen shook her head. Behind the sunglasses Isobel could see the brown eyes staring miserably ahead. 'That that's how he would end up.'

Isobel sat in silence.

'Multiple Sclerosis,' said Maureen after a moment. 'It took a long time. To start with you could hardly notice it. In fact we began to think they'd made a wrong diagnosis, but then it started to get a hold. Some days he could hardly lift a cup to his mouth, others he was fine. I used to push him up here to watch the cricket, and apart from the wheelchair you wouldn't have known there was anything wrong. After all, you sit down to watch cricket, don't you? I used to love those days. Then last October – the ninth, it was – he had a heart attack. They kept him on life support for a couple of days, but once we knew he wasn't going to get better, I told them to take him off it. We'd discussed it before. It's what he wanted. It's what I'd want. No point in hanging on if you've nothing to live for. And he hadn't. He was going to be on tubes and drips forever more. It wasn't the life for him. He wanted to be up, swinging from the chandeliers, swimming naked in the sea like we used to – the sea, not the chandeliers.' She laughed. 'I'm sorry to go on like this. I'm sure it's the last thing you wanted at a cricket match.'

'Don't be sorry. I'm glad you told me. I only wish there was something I could say that might be of any use to you.'

Maureen hunted for her cardigan. The sun had gone behind a cloud and the air was suddenly chilly. 'I'm glad I've told you,' she said. 'You and Harry. I shan't tell anyone else.' A pixieish grin lit her face for a second. 'I certainly shan't tell Dr Mahon.'

Isobel rubbed the goose pimples on her arms. 'I'm surprised anyone ever tells him anything,' she said.

Maureen nodded. 'I'm not sure that they do.'

'What? Not even Leonie and Hilary?'

Maureen smiled. 'What do you think?' she said.

The cricketers were leaving the pitch. Someone had apparently won. Across the grass Isobel could see Richard gazing vaguely around. The children were nowhere to be seen. He spotted Isobel's waving crutch and came loping across the field to join them. 'Hullo again,' he said to Maureen. 'I don't know where the children have gone. One minute they were there . . .'

'They're over by the swings,' said Isobel who could see the top of Eleanour's head protruding from the sandpit. 'You'd better go and round them up. It's nearly six o'clock. They must be starving.'

Richard did as he was bade. Isobel made several fruitless attempts to lever herself out of the deck-chair, then sank back exhausted. Maureen offered her arm, but Isobel shook her head. 'I'm too heavy, especially with this ball and chain. Wait till Richard comes back. He's used to it.'

'So am I,' said Maureen, but she made no further attempt to assist. Richard returned and duly extracted Isobel from her chair, the children offering advice and criticism till he swore at them, causing much giggling, and a look of prudish amazement from Clare who went to Sunday School.

'Nice woman, that Maureen,' said Richard again in the car going home. Isobel nodded. 'I daresay she gets a bit lonely on her own,' Richard continued. 'Why don't you ask her over for a meal sometime? I could pick her up if transport's a problem.'

'Yes,' said Isobel. 'I might.' But for reasons she couldn't explain, she didn't really want to bring Maureen into their circle of shared acquaintances. She wanted to keep her separate; a part of a different world, the world of Harry, and the group, and people who tried to kill themselves.

Chapter Twenty

Harry rang on Sunday evening. Patrick answered the phone, calling nonchalantly to his mother that there was a man who wanted to speak to her. Richard was in the garden, asleep under the Sunday newspapers, after a hefty Sunday lunch and too much red wine.

Isobel took the phone quite innocently. She knew he wouldn't ring at the weekend. 'Hullo?'

'It's Harry.'

'What? Why are you ringing now? What's happened?'

There was a pause. 'Nothing's happened. I just wanted to talk to you. Is it a bad time?'

'Well, of course it is. It's Sunday.' Isobel realised her voice had taken on the note of a conspirator. Rather like Richard's when he'd been planning her abortive party.

'I didn't know you were religious.'

'I'm not.' Isobel concentrated on sounding casual although Patrick had gone upstairs and Eleanour was out to tea. 'It's just it's the weekend. Richard's in the garden.'

'Give him my best.'

'He's asleep,' said Isobel testily.

'Well, what's the problem then?'

'It's just it makes me feel nervous you ringing when everyone's here.'

'Shall I ring off?'

'No. I'm sorry. I wasn't expecting it to be you. That's all. Where are you? Birmingham?'

'Shepherd's Bush.'

'What are you doing there? Have you broken down?'

She could hear Harry laughing the other end. 'I live here.'

'In Shepherd's Bush?'

'There's no need to sound so disapproving. I'm not the only one.'

'I wasn't. It's just . . . I didn't really know where you lived. I hadn't thought of Shepherd's Bush.' For an illicit phone call between lovers this lacked a certain fervour.

'How was your weekend?' she asked, hoping to up the pace a little.

'All right. I'm coming down tomorrow.'

'Tomorrow?'

'Tomorrow. Old Horse Hair wants a shot of the sun setting over the hospital, would you believe? This thing's going to look like *Lawrence of Arabia* by the time he's finished.'

'The musical,' added Isobel.

'What I wanted to know is are you around in the day at all?'

'Yes,' Isobel paused. 'Well, I could be. I'm meant to be helping my mother-in-law choose curtains, but I could put her off.'

'No, don't do that. It was just on the offchance.'

'It's only in the morning,' said Isobel quickly, cursing herself for her eagerness. 'I'll be back by twelve.'

'I'll see you then, then,' said Harry. 'Bye, Isobel.'

'Bye.'

'Who was that?' Richard stretching and yawning came staggering in from the garden.

'Your mother,' said Isobel before she could stop herself. 'About the curtains. We're going round to L. and G.'s in the morning.'

Richard nodded, then frowned curiously. 'She really is going round the bend,' he said. 'I could have sworn she asked me to tell you she'd found something in the market and not to bother, when I rang her about the picnic yesterday.'

Isobel's face burned furiously as she tidied the hall table. 'Oh, well, she's probably decided they won't do after all,' she burbled desperately.

Richard shrugged. 'I expect so,' he said. 'I'm just going to put the garden chairs away.'

Isobel watched him walking down the path. He was tall and suntanned and handsome and unfaithful. And she was small and pale and injured and unfaithful. But the real difference was that his feet were planted firmly on the ground, and she was walking a tightrope over a chasm. And if she slipped this time she didn't think she'd get a second chance.

Harry arrived about a quarter past twelve on his motor bike. It occurred to Isobel if this were to be a regular event it could only be a matter of time before the neighbours began to notice.

Bob was out all day so that wasn't a problem, but the woman three doors away was in. Not that it mattered because they didn't really know her apart from saying good morning, but it was such a small village. A man on a motor bike arriving at noon and leaving at three was bound to cause some sort of flutter before long. That's if he continued to call. Isobel's heart jerked at the possibility of anything else. Oh well, one day at a time. She let him in.

'I've bought us a picnic,' said Harry before she could speak. 'There's some nice woods you come through on the way here. I thought we could go there.'

Isobel stared at him. 'But you're on your bike.'

'Yes?'

'How am I supposed to get there. Walk?'

'You can come on the bike too.'

'Harry, I've got a broken ankle in case you hadn't noticed.'

'I'm not asking you to drive it, am I? There's masses of room. You just stick your leg out at the side.'

'Oh, yes? What happens when we turn the corner? I'll end up wrapped round a lamp-post.'

'Nonsense. Trust me. Have you got a bottle opener? I've bought you some wine.'

'I'd better drink it now if I'm going to die,' said Isobel lugubriously.

'Anyway, look, I've been thinking . . . It looks . . . well . . . a bit bad . . . You sort of turning up and not going away . . . if you know what I mean. On a motor bike.'

'I am going away on a motor bike. You're coming with me.'

'Harry, I can't. Think about it. Apart from the fact that I shall be dead before we get to the roundabout, what's it going to look like? You turning up and me going off with you? Someone's bound to see. It'll get back to Richard, I know it will.'

Harry considered. 'It's not like this in Shepherd's Bush,' he said. 'No one gives a toss what you get up to.'

'This isn't Shepherd's Bush.'

'I can see that. There are similarities though. Tell you what, we'll disguise you.'

'What as? A bollard?'

'You're very kinky, Isobel. Do you know that? I'm going to have to screw you before I take another step.'

'No ... Oh, Harry, you mustn't ... Not standing up ... I don't like it standing up. ... Oh!'

They compromised on the departure. Harry left five minutes before Isobel, and with all the sangfroid of someone embarking bareheaded on a desert crossing, Isobel locked up the house and clumped casually along the seafront in the opposite direction, two large and conspicuous brown envelopes poking from the bag slung round her neck. 'Just going to the post,' she rehearsed under her breath, 'just going to the post.' She met no one they knew, which was just as well, because in her haste she had forgotten to address the envelopes.

They met at the turn off for Eastley. Harry was already waiting, having done as silent a circuit of the village as he could manage on a 1000 cc motor bike. Isobel was exhausted, both with the walk and the strain of looking casual.

Had she thought about it, it would have been abundantly clear that the last thing anyone with their right leg in plaster on a hot summer day should look is casual. That's if they don't want to attract attention. However she had failed so abysmally in this respect that those who had seen her felt merely pity or surprise, and very little of that.

'What time do you call this?' demanded Harry, glaring at his watch. 'I thought you'd stood me up.'

Isobel scowled at him. 'I'd like to stand you against a wall and shoot you. What a stupid idea. I'm exhausted.'

Harry got off the bike. 'Poor girl. You do look a bit hot. Never mind. You don't have to walk any more. Here.' He reached into the box at the back and pulled out a spare crash helmet.

'Oh, god, have I got to wear one of those?'

'It's the law.' He lowered it carefully on to Isobel's head, adjusted the straps and stood back to consider her. 'You look like Madonna.'

'I feel like King Kong.'

'A bit like him, too,' Harry agreed. 'Now, give us your leg.'

'Which one?'

'The bad one, goon head.'

'If you're going to call me names I'm going home.'

'I'm sorry. I thought it was obvious, that's all.'

'Nothing's obvious about these things to me.'

'No, all right. Give me your leg. It's all right, I won't drop you.'

Isobel gingerly heaved her leg off the ground. Harry grabbed it and proceeded to lever it upwards towards the saddle. Isobel shrieked and grabbed hold of him. 'I'm falling. Oh, Harry, catch me. QUICK.'

Harry caught hold of her. 'Don't panic. I think it would be better if I lifted you on. Ready?'

'Ready.'

Harry picked her up bodily and swung her on to the postilion seat. Isobel swayed dangerously, her right leg straight out in front of her. 'What do I do now?'

'Stay there. For god's sake don't move. I'm coming round the other side.' Gradually, his hand pressed firmly into the small of her back, Harry edged himself round to the nearside curb. Carefully he lowered Isobel's right leg on to the pedal. 'How does that feel?'

Isobel wriggled cautiously. 'All right, I think. What do I hold on to?'

'There's a bar at the back.' Harry took her hands and attached them to the rod. 'But I'm leaning backwards.'

'That's all right.'

'It isn't all right. I'm frightened. I'm going to fall off. If I fall off when we're going along you won't even notice.' Harry sighed and shook his head. 'Do you want this Wall of Death job, or don't you? Hold on to me then. Put your hands round my waist.' He swung his leg over the saddle and settled himself easily in front of her. 'Go on. Put your arms round my waist.'

'I can't. I can't let go of this bar now. I've frozen,' she added, hoping that this piece of technical jargon would convince him of her seriousness.

Harry took his hands off the controls and reached round behind her. Gently her prised her fingers off the back rod and clamped them round his waist. 'Okay?'

Isobel pressed her head as close as she could to Harry's back. The smell of the leather was intoxicating.

Harry pulled on his gloves. 'Ready?'

'Do you mind if I don't come with you, Harry?' pleaded a small voice behind.

'Just trust me, Isobel. Would I let anything happen to you?'

'You might.'

'Well, I won't.'

Isobel began to mention ways in which she thought Harry might inadvertently maim her for life, but her words were drowned in the roar of the engine as he turned up the throttle and slid gently away from the pavement.

'Help,' screamed Isobel, clinging to Harry with all her strength. 'I'm falling off. Don't go fast. My leg's stuck. I don't feel very well.'

By the time they had cleared the last outlying house of the village Isobel was beginning to enjoy herself. She found that she had not yet fallen off, lost her leg, or been struck in three different places by passing traffic. She certainly liked the feel of Harry's solid back against her nose. Harry, sensing the vice-like grip begin to slacken, smiled to himself and made a private resolution. If this were to become a habit, he would buy Isobel a smaller, lighter helmet, since the pressure of her present one on his spine was becoming quite painful.

They had their picnic in a shaded woodland glade with the last of the bluebells scattered obligingly round.

Isobel had got cold on the bike and now sat shrouded in

Harry's voluminous jacket while he wrestled with the twisted corkscrew she had grabbed from the kitchen drawer. He seemed to have bought up most of the village shop. Memories of Ratty's picnic from *Wind in the Willows* came to mind as she watched him spread out the chicken, ham, salami, bread, tomatoes and macaroons. These struck her as an odd choice till she saw the way he got through them.

When they had eaten Harry lay with his head in her lap, and Isobel turned her thoughts to Hamlet and Ophelia, reflecting how difficult it was to be original.

'This is nice,' said Harry. He was squinting up at the sun filtering through the trees.

'Better than Shepherd's Bush?'

Harry turned his attention to her. 'What have you got against Shepherd's Bush?'

'Nothing. Well, I've hardly ever been there. I don't like London at all really.'

'Don't knock it till you've tried it.'

'I have tried it. I worked there for eight years when I left university.'

'Working's not living.'

'No.'

Harry rolled over on to his front and buried his face in her crotch. Isobel gasped with pleasure and anticipation as he slowly lifted her skirt and slid his tongue between her legs. I'm going to die, she thought, as he pulled her down to meet him. I can't keep this up. I shall have a heart attack. I shall go into spasm inside my plaster and hit my ankle and break it again.

'What are you thinking about?' Harry was drinking a beer, his jeans on the ground beside him. Isobel was lying with her hands behind her head thinking she didn't care if she broke every bone in her body if Harry was what she got for it.

'Nothing much.'

'You don't want to tell me.'

Isobel closed her eyes and smiled. 'Rude thoughts,' she said.

Harry laughed. 'To think I thought Leonie was the raver.'

Isobel tossed her head. 'She just talks about it.'

'You reckon?'

'Yes. If she was doing it, she wouldn't be there in the first place.' She sat up on her elbow. 'She's a classic case of frustrated spinsterhood.' Harry smiled and sat back against the tree, his eyes half-closed.

'Are you staying at The Collier's Arms again?'

Harry hesitated. 'I'm staying at Maureen's.'

'Maureen's?'

'That's right. She's got a three-bedroomed house. I'm going to pay her.'

'Maureen's?'

'Do you mind?'

'No. Goodness, why should I? I'm just surprised, that's all.'

Harry was chewing a twig. 'Well, it was her or Leonie's.' Isobel shot him a look then lay back again. 'No, that's nice,' she confirmed. 'I saw Maureen at the cricket match on Saturday. She was telling me about her husband. That's very sad.'

'Yes,' said Harry. 'How much did she tell you?'

'About him having Multiple Sclerosis. And dying of a heart attack. It was only last October. She's very well adapted, isn't she? Considering.'

Harry said nothing as he threw the twig into the ragged patch of bluebells. He got up. 'Come on. Time we got back. I can drop you by the greengrocer's. It's not so far to walk.'

Chapter Twenty-one

Harry and Isobel had agreed that she should go by cab to the hospital the following morning. It would create something of a hiatus in Out Patients if she turned up on a motor bike and, besides, Harry had agreed to give Maureen a lift. Isobel had experienced a pang of anxiety at the prospect of Maureen being asked to ride pillion, but Harry said she had been most emphatic in her desire to try it, and if he could transport a lunatic with a wooden leg without harm, he had no fears for Maureen's safety. Isobel accepted this in the spirit in which it was intended and said she hoped he landed up in a ditch.

Harry was to stay down the following night, Maureen having decreed that she would cook dinner for him in repayment for their outing the week before. It would therefore be possible for Harry to call in on Isobel on Wednesday morning before going back to London. Things were going well, Isobel decided as she hopped through the entrance to Reception at ten to eleven that Tuesday.

Things were also going well for Richard. He had managed to confirm a new contract with the council and under the guise of hastening the details to them, had managed to extract Jenny half an hour early from her corner of Health and Housing.

He had decided to take her to a decent restaurant for lunch. Poor Jenny. She existed on sandwiches and herb pâté. It wasn't her fault her culinary tastes were so excruciating. She had never been exposed to decent food. Part of Richard's plan for this swansong month of their affair was to introduce Jenny to a better style of life, so that when they parted, as he had decided they should, she would be the equipped to find herself a decent substitute, and to keep him. What finer token could a lover offer a departing mistress than the opportunity to hook another like himself?

With these lofty thoughts Richard waited in the car park for Jenny to join him.

'Richard...' A large woman in petrol blue was tramping purposefully towards him.

'Marjorie... How are you?'

'I'm fine, Richard. Rushed off my feet, as always, but that's not what I wanted to see you about.'

'You wanted to see me?' Sick thoughts of black chairs and unsewn codpieces flashed across his brain.

'How is poor Isobel? I sent Diana round. Did that help?'

'Yes. Oh, yes. She was a great help. Lovely pie...' Richard floundered, trying to see what was coming next. Marjorie Bennett did not function on past references.

'I've been meaning to get round to you myself. I haven't had a moment, what with the whitelining fiasco and this damn Council Tax hooha. I'm so sorry about the Vera Beasley business, by the way. You are absolutely sure nothing was missing?'

'No, no, I'm sure there was nothing like that. They just didn't see eye to eye, that's all. It was very kind of you to try and fix it, but really Isobel's managing perfectly fine on her own. She's not nearly as immobile as we thought she'd be at first. Positively scooting round on those crutches.' Out of the corner of his eye Richard saw Jenny come out of the building then scurry back again as she spotted Marjorie. 'Look, I really must be going, Marjorie. Very busy with this new contract. Thanks again. We must have a drink together some time. Perhaps when Isobel's better?' He fumbled for his keys.

'Yes, yes. Good idea. But the thing I wanted to talk to you about, Richard, is Isobel's mind. How is that?'

Richard regarded her with some irritation. 'Much the same as ever, Marjorie, thank you. She's stark staring mad. Now you really must excuse me.' He went round to the driver's seat and got into the car. Jenny was performing a sort of solo square dance in the foyer as panic that she would be left behind vied with a proper desire to avoid all contact with Marjorie Bennett.

'Diana says she'll try and make it at the weekend,' called the redoubtable councillor as he reversed savagely and swung the car away towards the exit. Back in the foyer Jenny wrestled with tears of frustration as she pondered the choice of ordering a taxi or returning to her office and pleading to have her Queen's Birthday Holiday rescinded. How she wished she had not offered to lend Anita her car for the day.

Marjorie Bennett, stalking energetically back into the building, saw Jenny skulking by the rubber plant. 'Hullo, Jenny,' she bellowed cheerfully. 'Richard's just getting some petrol. Why don't you cut across by the Goods Entrance, save him coming back for you?'

Isobel's visit to Mr Robertson was a complete waste of time, at least from her point of view. The x-rays continued to 'look promising' and since she could offer him neither gangrene nor thrombosis Mr Robertson turned his attention to her general health, asking if she was suffering from abnormal tiredness or having trouble keeping food down. To both enquiries Isobel gave a clipped negative, and silence then ensued while Mr Robertson smiled at her solicitously and Isobel glared back.

Eventually, realising that his patient had no intention of pouring out her heart to him, and also bearing in mind that he had fourteen other patients to see before lunch, Mr Robertson leant forward and asked, sotto voce, if she felt her sessions with Dr Mahon were helping at all.

'Helping what?' asked Isobel.

Mr Robertson sat back. 'Do you feel you are beginning to open up at all? To come to terms with what has happened, Mrs Day?'

Isobel thought. If she said no, he would only start lecturing her again, but if she said yes, god only knew what track he might go off on.

'It's difficult,' she began.

'It's always difficult, Mrs Day. These things are always difficult.'

Especially when you won't let me finish, thought Isobel. 'But ... I don't know ... Perhaps a bit more time?' An idea struck her. 'I'm thinking..'

'Yes?'

She raised her head. 'I'm thinking of trying to put my thoughts down on paper.'

'An excellent idea. A sort of diary, you mean?'

'More like a book.'

'A book. Oh, excellent. Excellent. Does Dr Mahon know about this?'

'Not yet.'

'Oh, I think you must tell him. This is a grand step forward.' He gave a sniffy guffaw. 'A step forward in every sense of the word. Well, two weeks' time, Mrs Day. And next time we shall be dispensing with this nasty old plaster cast. I expect you're looking forward to that?'

Isobel smiled agreeably. 'Just a bit,' she said.

'Isobel . . .' She looked up from her seat in the quadrangle to see Maureen approaching.

'Am I disturbing you?'

'No, of course not. Come and sit down. Have you had lunch? Have some of these rolls. I've brought far too many, but my stomach keeps rumbling during the quiet bits. I bet Jock's picking it up. It must sound as though there's an earthquake on the way.'

Maureen laughed. 'I can't think of anything more suitable.'

'Did you come on the motor bike?' Isobel stopped, realising she was not supposed to know, but Maureen evinced no surprise. 'Yes, it was marvellous. Harry is wicked. He goes far too fast.'

Isobel tried to sound disinterested. 'Where is Harry? Is he here?'

'He had to go and sort out his stuff. He was going to buy us some beer and bring it out here, he said. We had lunch on the way at that pub by the quay, but the beer wasn't very nice, so he's gone to get some more.' Isobel nodded. She felt uneasy talking about Harry as though he were just anyone, especially to Maureen. This was because she sensed with an almost telepathic certainty that Maureen knew what was going on. Whether or not Harry had confided in her, she couldn't tell, but that this conversation smacked of a charade, she was absolutely certain.

'The circle dancing should be interesting,' remarked Maureen after a while.

'Oh, god,' groaned Isobel. 'I'd forgotten about that. Imagine a female version of Mahon. It's too horrible to contemplate.'

'Well, perhaps she'll be a bit more pliable.'

'If she is he'll make mincemeat of her as well.'

Maureen reached in her bag for a handkerchief. 'Not much of a choice, is it? A bully or a jelly.'

'Still, if it takes the pressure off Meg for a bit. I'm beginning to feel quite protective of her.'

'Me, too. Mind you, I half wonder if it's what she wants. She feels guilty about hating her mother-in-law, and this is a kind of penance.'

Isobel bit into a roll. 'I think you've been coming here too long.'

A shadow crossed Maureen's face but it was gone as quickly as it had come. 'Not much longer,' she said cheerfully. 'Here's Harry.'

He hasn't told her, thought Isobel, half relieved, half disappointed, as Harry nodded to her and slumped down on the grass opposite. He handed Maureen a can of lager, apologising for the lack of a glass. She took it gratefully and swigged without embarrassment. Harry offered Isobel one, which she accepted, despite not liking it much, and the three of them drank in silence till a shrill and ghastly piping roused them from their private reveries.

'What the fuck's that?' asked Harry.

'It's coming from over Mahon's way,' said Maureen. 'You don't think . . .'

The three of them gazed at each other in mute horror. 'Here,' said Harry, 'have another beer. You're going to need it.'

The effect of two lagers on Isobel was insufficient to blot out the sense of acute dismay with which she saw two o'clock approach. Maureen and Harry were discussing cricket tours and hotels in Bulgaria, both of which seemed close to their hearts. She felt almost like an interloper sitting there beside them. At a quarter to she hauled herself up. 'I'm just going to the loo,' she murmured. 'I can't take Dr Mahon on a full bladder.'

There was a queue in the Ladies and when Isobel finally got round to PSY 1 the huffing and puffing was in full progress, but for one rather obvious addition. The breathing was accompanied by a thin reed-like trill produced by an inordinately tall woman on a battered-looking recorder. Isobel immediately recognised it as a variation of the sound they had heard in the garden.

She propped herself in the corner, surveying the unlikely scene. She wondered what it must look like through Harry's lens. Perhaps he would let her have a look sometime. Perhaps it was better not to know.

Dr Mahon's colleague drew her attention first. Besides being tall, she was shaped like a shoe box, completely angled at the shoulders, hips and feet. Her haircut was also cubist in conception, reminding Isobel of a Prussian soldier's helmet, lacking only the silver spike on top. She was dressed entirely in black, clearly to Leonie's annoyance, who had also opted for mourning that week, although hers was of a more flowing nature than the tight serge costume encasing the newcomer.

From the expression on the woman's face Isobel assumed she was experiencing equal, if not superior, pain to that her notes were inflicting on those present.

The exercise finished. Dr Mahon waved Isobel to a seat and began his customary homily. He made no mention of the woman at all at first, then introduced her almost as an afterthought. She was Anita Craven and she would be 'doing her thing' after coffee. For a ghastly moment Isobel thought she too would be treating them to her innermost sufferings, but since these had been so eloquently expressed in her music, she entertained the hope that not too much else need be revealed. She felt a flicker of pity for the poor woman who had plainly expected a little more build-up and now sat folded like a garden chair, her giant knees perfectly parallel to her chin.

Harry, having taken some footage of the woman, now sat

abstractedly in a corner, much to Simon Mahon's annoyance, who obviously assumed his every utterance should be recorded for posterity. He could hardly break off in mid-platitude, however, so was forced to content himself with directing fiercesome glances at Harry which, had he anticipated them, he would undoubtably have filmed with relish.

Confession time brought forth a second instalment of Ken's poem, detailing such activities as 'jerk', 'jump', and 'toss'. Isobel began to fear he had taken a leaf out of Leonie's book, albeit on a more intimate scale, but it appeared these verbs related to the state of Ken's stomach, shortly before his latest panic attack, which had taken place at a bus stop just past Sainsbury's in the high street.

Leonie followed on with some more of her own saga which was fast assuming the proportions of the *Iliad*, with most of the costumes in tow. Maureen, either as a result of too much lager or infinite boredom, had fallen fast asleep, and Dr Mahon decreed that she should be left so, since it was 'part of the healing process'. Isobel had a sneaking suspicion that it had nothing at all to do with healing, and a great deal to do with keeping her quiet. Hilary grabbed the chair next with the purposefulness of a large man in the search of a luggage trolley at Heathrow.

He seemed to have forgotten about 'not seeing his way round this one', and launched instead into a stream of profanities from which the words 'father', 'mother' and 'soddingwife' could occasionally be extricated.

Dr Mahon asked for suggestions. Leonie, characteristically, went for the hug, Ken stuttered his way towards 'getting in touch with himself', which was the last thing Hilary needed telling, and Meg, surprisingly more relaxed in a beige jersey and pale blue skirt, thought a sympathetic ear might be all that was required. Isobel saw Mahon's eyebrows soar sarcastically at this, but for the time being at least, he let it pass. 'And what does Isobel think?' he asked affably, jerking his finger towards her for Harry to turn the camera.

'Nothing really. A thesaurus might help,' said Isobel dutifully. There was silence while Isobel's intransigence was taken account of. This might have continued for some time but for a sudden screeching blast from Anita in the corner. Everyone turned to her, Simon Mahon' eyes, the size of pins, being the most terrifying. To Isobel's eternal joy, the woman stared right back with total equanimity. 'So sorry, Si,' she growled. 'Just cleaning my reeds. It's meant to be inaudible to human beings.'

Isobel was surprised that Mahon made no move to get Meg into the confessional. She too seemed a little bemused that no summons was forthcoming, but was clearly not going to volunteer. He asked Isobel if she had anything she wanted to say. Isobel accordingly asked if it would not be possible for someone to bring an electric kettle so that they could make their own coffee, since the stuff from the tea bar was undrinkable. Dr Mahon said this was a significant step forward and ordered a round of applause, nodding emphatically at Julian Joffe the meanwhile.

The director, who looked rather older than at their first meeting, cracked his knuckle joints in a slightly tormented way and whispered something to Fran, whose wild eyes rolled like gobstoppers as she dispatched Luce on yet another errand.

While this was going on Hilary and Leonie had embarked on a heated discussion, more accurately a squabble, about the pros and cons of anal intercourse. Hilary, surprisingly, being less in favour than Leonie, who maintained all contact was positive, however painful, while Hilary, with more sense than usual, said she didn't effing know what she was talking about and if she'd ever been to Charterhouse she might take a different point of view. Leonie pouted ferociously, having realised the attention was on them, and said her girls' grammar had had the highest academic achievement level in the Home Counties. Hilary immediately suggested that she ask Edward II how academic a red hot poker up his bum had felt, and Leonie countered that he might just as well ask a fish how it liked having a hook in its mouth. Hilary said he'd probably get more sense out of it than he would from Leonie, who retorted it was a pity his only example had been dead for six hundred years. Hilary said that shouldn't bother Leonie, whom everyone knew was a witch, whereupon Luce came bursting in with something under a cloth. This she presented to Simon Mahon with the fervour of a knight revealing the Holy Grail.

It turned out to be an electric kettle of indeterminate age which was duly passed to Isobel 'to see what she would make of it'. Isobel, assisted by Meg, made of it two pints of boiling water, Luce having omitted to commandeer any coffee, sugar or milk on her raid of the student nurses' staff room. She was once more dispatched and returned with the requisite extras some five minutes later, her pale face redder than usual, having been subjected to some decidedly graphic suggestions from a couple of the porters who had shared the lift with her.

After coffee Anita Craven, who had spent the break fitting lengths of pipe together like an apprentice plumber, and sipping bleakly at her cup of hot water, rose and crossed to where Dr Mahon was in yet another discussion with his director.

Isobel noted that, despite the amount of time the two spent, eyebrows interlocking, in passionate discussion of the next vital step, nothing ever seemed to emerge from it. Each week had followed precisely the same pattern, with precisely the same result. Zilch. She wondered how the public would react to a month of mooing and thumping on prime time television. Very Peter Brook. No doubt the critics would rave and the viewers would switch to 'L. A. Law', much as they did with Peter Brook.

She wondered if she would watch the programme when it came out. So far a transmission date had not been mentioned. Presumably it depended on the outcome. It was unlikely that any company would want to buy a series like this on spec. She imagined the selling spiel – 'makes *Marat Sade* look like a tea party. Come with us on a nightmare journey into the depths of a mind torn apart by madness. Explore with us the dark dark corners . . .'

'If we're all quite ready . . .?' Isobel was dragged from her new career as horror film blurb writer to see Anita towering over Simon Mahon who, even with his hands outstretched, barely reached to her earlobes. 'Anita is going to give us a little explanation of the purpose behind the circle dance, its function in society, and its use in modern day therapy. Anita.'

He stepped aside and sank cross-legged beside Julian on the floor. The rest of the group joined him, apart from

Maureen who showed every sign of falling asleep again, and Isobel who could not have crossed her legs if she'd wanted to, and most certainly didn't.

Harry was rigging a tripod for his camera. He obviously realised that without standing on a chair there was no way he would be able to include Anita's head in the filming. Though this would doubtless add a certain surreal dimension to the enterprise, it was apparently not what the director had in mind. In a whispered conversation Harry had made clear that Joffe could either have her head or her feet, or her head as far as her eyebrows and her ankles or, by reducing the focus to long distance, all of her, but only as a Liliputian. Joffe had opted for the first, preferring to go for the head while she spoke and the feet when she danced, pulling back to the whole as necessity dictated.

Anita stepped forward, immediately displacing all the technicians' plans, and began to explain her purpose. The circle dance, as previously mooted, took its origins from the Middle East and was used as a form of soothing pain both physical and mental, and creating inner harmony in the participants, while the continuity and contact of the movements assisted in the destruction of alienation trauma and the restitution of harmonising inner rhythms. There was a pause before Anita lowered her voice still further and suggested that in future the coffee break be replaced by herbal tea, which she herself would be only too happy to prepare. This was generally assented to, though Fran could be heard whispering loudly about 'budget considerations' to no one in particular.

Now came the point they had all been waiting for. Anita would demonstrate the dance in all its beauteous simplicity. In order to do this she had pre-recorded some of her own music to accompany herself. Jock accordingly started the tape, which Isobel recognised as the sound they had heard in the quadrangle. It was difficult to see how such close exposure to the birth of a banshee could induce inner harmonies in any but the totally deaf, but Anita looked serenely peaceful as she placed first one foot then another in front of each other, swaying her scalene hips, eyes closed, head slightly tilted, first one way then the other as the group looked on entranced, waiting for her to bump into the tripod.

Harry would not allow this to happen, however – whether from professionalism, or a genuine desire not to see her wreck his camera. He whipped it off the stand, folding the tripod away and followed her movements manually till the music ran out just as Anita rounded the corner by the tape deck for the third time.

She opened her eyes, the dreamlike smile evaporating, and cast them around her audience. 'You see. It's easy. Now I'd like us all to try.'

There was a pause, then a scraping of chairs as Meg, Leonie, Hilary, Ken and Maureen struggled to their feet. Anita spaced them out, fingertips on shoulders, looking more like a sergeant major than a choreographer. Her eye fell on Isobel. She turned to Mahon. 'What about this lady?'

Mahon shrugged. 'Isobel's a little indisposed. She has a leg in plaster.'

Anita turned to her. 'That doesn't matter,' she said emphatically. 'We shall be going very slowly at first. I'm sure you'll find it beneficial.'

'I'm sure I would too,' responded Isobel, 'but I'm not so sure that the others would.'

Anita's eyes positively sparkled at the challenge. 'You mustn't worry about them,' she decreed. 'This is for *you*. The inner self, remember. Your inner self isn't in plaster. Set it free.' There was a loud snort from Leonie, who already felt that space was at a premium if her garments were to flow to full effect, and a belch from Hilary, who had not yet come to terms with the idea of herbal tea.

'Come next to me, Isobel,' said Meg, her round face aglow with excitement. 'Come between Ken and me.'

Simon Mahon raised his hand. 'If I might step in for a moment ... While not wishing to interfere in any way with this little exercise, I feel I should point out that Isobel, though doubtless wishing to free her inner self as much as anyone, will only impede the progress of the others. Perhaps it might be better if the release of Isobel's inner thoughts were left to me as the ... shall we say ... instigator of this project?'

Anita opened her mouth to protest but was quelled by such a look of venom from her colleague that she closed it again and stood in silent wrath while circle reclosed.

Isobel hauled herself to her feet. 'Actually,' she said, 'I would like to have a try. That's if no one in the group objects?' She smiled demurely around.

'But you won't be able to keep up,' protested Leonie. 'You'll hold us all back.'

'Leonie,' broke in Maureen with a kindly smile, 'we're a support group, remember. We try to help each other.'

'Yes,' whispered Meg, hardly daring to lift her eyes.

'I know that,' snapped Leonie, 'I'm only thinking of Isobel. She'll feel awful if she cocks the whole thing up, won't she? I know I would.'

Once more Dr Mahon stepped in. 'Leonie has a point,' he insisted. 'We have to think of the effect on Isobel's wellbeing if she senses she is harming the group as a whole. What do you think, Ken?'

Ken hugged himself painfully and stuttered something about 'deciding for herself.'

Hilary said he didn't care what anyone did so long as they fucking well got on with it. So Isobel, with the sole intention of frustrating Simon Mahon, laid aside her crutches and, assisted by Jock and Luce, was winched into position between Ken and Meg, who flashed her a smile of such undisguised admiration that Isobel felt a sharp twinge of guilt. This was rapidly dispelled by one glance at Leonie, who was glowering at her with equally undisguised loathing.

Anita, blooming like a desert flower at this unexpected victory, implanted herself between Maureen and Hilary and marked out the basic steps on the floor for them. These consisted of a variation of barn dance dosey-doeing, with a soupçon of Zorba The Greek. The tape was rewound and rehearsal commenced.

As she had suspected, Isobel was almost incapable of moving. Though her left leg served her perfectly well, her right one remained static so that her efforts to dance resembled nothing so much as a small dog attached to a lamppost. Somewhere behind her she could hear Harry and Jock trumpeting into their handkerchieves.

In keeping with a lamp-post, Isobel's handicap had a far more detrimental effect on those who crashed into it, than on the obstacle itself. It presented no problems to Ken on her right, who only seemed capable of going one way and that, fortunately, away from her. It was very hard on poor Meg, however, who, overcome with solicitude and panic, endeavoured to skirt round Isobel everytime she failed to move, thus bringing complaints from Leonie that her arm was being pulled from its socket. Throughout this Anita, eyes once more closed, swayed and plodded to the shriek of her music, oblivious to the encroaching mayhem in the room, which was beginning evermore to resemble a casualty station for the dispossessed.

'That was very good,' she murmured when the tape had finished. 'Excellent for a first try. What did you think, Si?' Without giving him the chance to answer, she swung back to her pupils. 'We'll try it again, now that you've got the movements, and this time I want you to concentrate on your innermost thoughts and problems. Then I want you to try and let them drift away with the music till all you can feel is the rhythm of your own body in time with the beat. Close your eyes, everyone. I'm going to accompany you myself this time. If someone could just pass me my ocarina ...' Julian Joffe glared at Luce who hunted feverishly amongst Anita's bags for anything that might answer to this name. Eventually she admitted defeat, having come up with a can of Orangina, which was Fran's, and two bottles of lethal-looking homeopathic remedies.

The ocarina turned out to be a small terracotta instrument capable, along with most of Anita's equipment, of producing truly horrible sounds, which Anita duly proceeded to do.

The 'eyes closed' business was clearly a mistake, since Leonie took it as carte blanche to externalise one of her more space-invading nightmares, and managed to sock Julian Joffe comprehensively on the jaw. This led to a temporary adjournment while Luce rushed frantically in search of cold water and tissues – a rare commodity in a hospital – and the others, lost in their private worlds, sank down on their haunches forgetting about Isobel who keeled over at a Pisaesque angle before Fran noticed her and came tearing to her rescue with a window pole.

Once Julian had been attended to it was decided that the group had possibly done enough for one day and they were consigned to the chairs round the wall while Anita 'played them down', as the jargon appeared to have it. This consisted of two or three pieces of varying tunelessness during which they were instructed to think of warm sun and softly waving corn. Isobel immediately added herself and Harry, thrashing naked, to the tableau, thus depriving the exercise of its relaxation value.

Leonie had turned from a supporter of the dance to a violent antagonist in the space of one badly bruised elbow. 'I can't see the point of any of this,' she grumbled, casting unsisterly glares at Anita's back as she worked to dismantle her pipes. 'It certainly hasn't relieved any of my stress factors. I mean how long are you supposed to do it for? Till you drop? How does it end? There's no pattern to it. It's not a proper dance at all.'

Anita, who had finished packing her equipment, turned to Leonie with a genuinely forgiving smile. 'Oh, yes it is. It's just that you haven't quite got the hang of it yet. Don't worry. It'll come. The others had it very well. I expect it's to do with being a bit top-heavy. But you mustn't let it bother you. We can't all be graceful.' She gave a deprecating little laugh to show that she too had her weaknesses. This was too much for Leonie.

'Actually,' she intoned, 'I was nearly asked to audition for the Royal Ballet School. The fact that I plumped for academia doesn't mean I don't understand the form. There *is* no visible form to this circle thing whatsoever. How do you know when it's finished?'

'More to the point, how does the audience know?' put in Hilary with a bellow of laughter at this shaft of wit.

Anita reached deep into her pocket and pulled out enough keys to run the Bastille with. 'It's quite simple,' she told them mildly. 'It finishes when you get back to the beginning.'

Chapter Twenty-two

'What did you think of that?' asked Maureen, dipping a biscuit into her tea. Isobel followed suit. She was waiting for her cab, Maureen for Harry.

'It gets dafter and dafter. If I hang around here much longer I shall end up in the madhouse.' She hesitated. 'The awful thing is it no longer seems so crazy. I'm getting used to them all. That must be the beginning of the end.'

Maureen smiled. 'like the dance,' she said.

Harry joined them just as the weaselly youth arrived for Isobel. 'I'll walk out with you,' he said. The two of them set off slowly across Reception in pursuit of the boy who had disappeared without a backward glance. 'I'll come about ten in the morning,' Harry said. 'Can't stay long. I've got to go to . . .'

'Birmingham,' Isobel finished.

Harry shrugged. 'It's a difficult age, seventeen.'

'Wish I could remember,' said Isobel. She felt suddenly deflated, playing tenth fiddle to Harry's daughter, the motor bike, Julian Joffe, Shepherd's Bush. Even Maureen had him to herself for dinner, while she must go back to Richard and the remains of the cold lamb. So she was a bit surprised when Harry suddenly steered her into the dank cold recess by the hospital bins and kissed her with a desperation not previously detectable in his manner.

'I've been wanting you all day,' he muttered, ferreting inside her blouse.

Isobel struggled. 'For god's sake, Harry. What are you doing? The man's waiting for me in the cab. We can't. Stop it.' This time Harry did, though his expression was anything but acquiescent as he let go of her.

'Oh my god.' Isobel pointed a wavering finger. Harry followed her gaze.

'What?'

'That car. Next to the taxi. It's Jenny's.'

'Jenny who's?'

'Jenny Holt's. Richard's . . . Oh, nothing. Supposing Richard's . . . No, he wouldn't . . . Oh, god, what a mess. Do you suppose she saw? She's sitting in there.' The little red Fiat made retching sounds and bumped away towards the coast road. 'What do you suppose she was doing here?' Isobel agonised.

'How should I know? I don't even know who she is? I don't see what all the fuss is about?'

'Ooh . . .' Isobel was frantic with agitation. 'I knew this would happen. She must have been watching. Oh, what am I going to do?'

'Calm down for a start. She's gone now, whoever she is. Anyone would think it was your mother.'

'My mother wouldn't have mattered,' moaned Isobel.

'Well, there's not much we can do about it now.' Harry opened the door of the cab for her. 'I'll see you in the morning. We can talk about it then.'

'Oh, Harry, I don't know. Look, give me Maureen's number in case it's not all right.'

'It will be all right.'

'It might not be. Please. Please give it to me.'

Harry shrugged and scribbled a number on the back of a cleaning ticket. 'Do you want me to ring you?'

'No, don't do that, whatever you do. Promise me you won't ring.'

Harry regarded Isobel curiously. 'What's the matter with you, girl? I've never seen you in such a state. Who was that woman?'

Isobel shook her head. 'I'm sorry. I'm tired. I'm so sick of all this cloak and dagger business. I'll tell you tomorrow. I've just got this feeling . . .'

'What?'

Isobel hesitated. 'Oh, nothing. We'll talk about it tomorrow.'

Harry watched her. 'Whatever you say.'

The youth removed his headphones, slung his paper nonchalantly into the passenger seat and, turning the ignition, zipped away through the car park. Isobel leant back and closed her eyes. What was there to talk about? People with a future talked. What future did she and Harry have? No future, no past. Only a pretty rocky present. And that for not much longer. In a fortnight's time she would lose her plaster. Back to normal, albeit with one stalk and one tree trunk. In three weeks' time they would record the last programme, and Harry would zoom away to Birmingham or Shepherd's Bush or Bulgaria. What did it matter? She wouldn't be going with him. And he wouldn't be coming back. She assumed he wouldn't. But why was she so certain? Why did she know with such surety that something awful was going to happen?

Richard welcomed Isobel with open arms. He, too, had had a trying afternoon. Jenny had revealed an unsuspected propensity to sulk. He realised that this had a lot to do with being stranded in the council car park for three-quarters of an hour (Marjorie Bennett had been quite wrong about the petrol; Richard had merely done a circuit of the building, thus missing Jenny at every turning till an accidental encounter by the Bottle Bank), but for her to have refused any wine at lunch and stuck out rigidly for a tuna salad when he had taken her to the best carvery for miles, smacked to him of pettiness. This had in turn caused him to drink too much, adding terror to Jenny's querulousness as the car shot along the back lanes to the Days' house. There she had sipped cold water and sniffed in a distinctly unerotic fashion till Richard had made a formal apology for his behaviour and she had allowed herself to be led to the spare room. Even this had been without its usual satisfaction, since Jenny had decided she was suffering from PMT, and issued brave little moans at precisely the wrong moments, leading Richard to suspect that it was perhaps after all possible for a woman to fake an orgasm occasionally.

He had had to drive her home as she had lent her car to

someone, and had encountered the glamorous courier on the doorstep, just back from Cyprus, as she informed them, dark hair sleek against her olive skin, scarlet shift clinging to her warm body like a vest.

He drove home fantasising about Jenny's flat mate and wondering if it would be possible to come to some sort of arrangement with the two of them, especially as things were definitely cooling off between himself and Jenny, and besides, Andrea (the courier) was away most of the time so there would be no need for Jenny to lose out. Andrea looked as though she could eat a fillet of beef to herself.

The phone was ringing as he opened the front door. It was Jenny to say she had been a meanie beanie and she love love love love loved him. And could he ever forgive her, adding that she was telephoning him in the hall with absolutely no clothes on, having rushed out of the shower because she couldn't bear not to tell him how sorry she was? Richard forgave her, mainly on the grounds that it was easier than not to, and also that the image of Jenny naked in the hall made it quite impossible for him to finish the affair just yet.

He picked up the children and listened with glazed eyes while his mother explained the precise cause of her quarrel with window cleaner and led him from room to room to examine the damage to the paintwork.

Since it was on the inside Richard suspected it was probably the work of his own children rather than some hapless cowboy, but knowing his mother would never countenance a word against either of them, he contented himself with nodding and left secure in the knowledge that if his accountant could get away with half what his mother did, he would die a rich man.

The sight of Isobel, albeit a touch dishevelled, gladdened his heart. He poured her a drink. 'How was the filming?'

Isobel grimaced. 'The filming is supposed to be incidental. You make me feel as though I'm in a soap opera.'

'Sorry. How was the session?'

'Just like being in a soap opera.'

Richard laughed. 'You ought to be in one. You'd be good. You've got the right sort of face.'

'And the right sort of life style.'

Richard laughed again but a little uneasily. 'What did the doc say about your ankle? The real one, I mean.'

'Seems to think it's okay. I have to see him in two weeks and then they'll take the plaster off.'

'Did you ask him about . . . You know . . . keeping it?'

Isobel shook her head. 'It didn't seem the moment. Tell you what, you come with me next time, and you speak to him about it. You can say I want to keep it as a dreadful warning or something. How about that?'

Richard looked dubious. 'I don't think he likes me very much. It might sound better coming from you.'

Isobel held her glass out for more wine. 'Well, don't count on it. I shall play it by ear.'

Richard touched her ear.

'I love your ears.'

'You used to.'

'I still do.'

'You just can't remember what they look like.'

'It wasn't the look I was thinking of. It was the taste.' He bent down and put his tongue gently under Isobel's lobe. She shuddered with delight and spilt half her wine.

'Now look what you've made me do.'

'You'll have to take that off.'

'Richard, hang on. Where are the children?'

'Watching television. They won't budge.'

'Yes, but . . .'

Images of Jenny naked by the phone and Andrea, sweating in her scarlet suit, combined with the scent and taste of Isobel, swirled through Richard's thoughts as he peeled away her wine-soaked blouse. Not a complete waste of an afternoon, he reflected.

'Your blouse was on the wrong buttons. Did you know that?' he told her cheerfully as he tossed her a clean tee-shirt.

Isobel blushed. 'Was it? How stupid. I bet that's the only bit of me there'll be in the whole series. The Woman Who Couldn't Button Her Blouse, I'll be on the credits.'

'Better that than your real name. God, Isobel, they don't use real names, do they?'

Isobel considered. 'I've no idea. No one's really discussed it. I suppose they must use Simon Mahon's. I mean the whole farce is an ego trip for him, isn't it? I can't see much point in them calling him "Dr X". I don't know. I'll ask Harry.'

'Why would he know?' Richard's voice hardened slightly. Isobel caught the change.

'Or Jock. I couldn't ask any of the others. They're all mad, too. Except for poor little Luce, and she'll probably be dead from exhaustion long before we finish.'

Richard pulled his shoes on. 'What are the other people in the group like, apart from Maureen?'

'Mixed. There's a man with a stutter called Ken, a very shy woman called Meg that Mahon's always picking on. I must say she seemed a bit more cheerful this week. Perhaps because she's got rid of that ghastly turquoise tracksuit. A poser called Hilary. I think he's probably queer but doesn't want to admit to it. Maureen. And Leonie.'

'Who's Leonie?'

'A nymphomaniac poetess.'

'Sounds promising.'

'You haven't heard the poetry.'

'How do you know she's a nymphomaniac?'

'Harry said.'

'Harry seems to know a lot. Has he tried her out?'

'No, of course not. That is . . . how would I know? It's nothing to do with me, is it, what he gets up to?'

'I suppose not.'

'Richard . . .'

'Mmm?'

'Is there anything wrong with Jenny?'

'What?' Richard's eyes opened wide with alarm. 'Jenny who?'

'Jenny Holt.'

'Jenny Holt? What sort of thing? Is she ill?'

'I don't know. I thought you might.'

'Me? Why should I know? I hardly know the girl.'

'I know. But you do go up to the council offices quite a bit. I just thought you might have heard something. I'm surprised Diana didn't say anything the other day. She's pretty thick with her.'

'I don't understand. What do you thinks the matter with her? She looked all right to me . . . the last time I saw her.'

'When was that?'

'I'm not sure. Not all that long ago.'

'Not today anyway?'

'Good god, Isobel. Why should I have seen her today?'

'Because you were up at the Planning Department this morning. It's just . . . it's probably nothing – a coincidence.'

'What?' Richard was prickling all over. Why did she have to find out now, just when he was on the point of breaking off the affair? Why couldn't she have waited another couple of weeks when he could have denied it utterly, or passed it off as a brief flirtation?

'I saw Jenny's car in the hospital car park this afternoon, when I was getting into my cab. She couldn't have had an accident, could she, or she wouldn't have driven herself? Perhaps she was just visiting someone in one of the wards.'

Richard felt a supreme sense of relief. 'No, it's not that. She lent it to someone for the afternoon. That's why . . .' He stopped.

'Yes?'

'I met Marjorie Bennett up there this morning. She told me. Said Jenny had lent it to someone or something. I wasn't really concentrating, to tell the truth. By the way, she's threatening to come round some time. She's very worried about your mind.'

'Who isn't? Honestly, Richard, I begin to wonder if it is my mind at all, the number of people who want a slice of it. Marjorie Bennett, Mahon, Robertson, Vera Beasley, I wouldn't be surprised – mind you, she could do with a bit extra – Diana, she'll be back, I bet you.'

'This weekend,' broke in Richard.

'That settles it. I'm going away.'

'Perhaps we should just board up all the windows and write "Unclean" across the front door.'

'In the dust,' said Isobel.

'Truth is truth.'

Isobel sighed. 'And, of course, there's Jenny.'

Richard sat up again. 'What about her?'

'Oh, she's very worried about me. She plies me with potions.

Didn't you see that bag of green string she sent me? I'm meant to drink that. It looks like a Do-It-Yourself Tonsilectomy kit.'

Richard laughed and put his arm round Isobel's shoulders. 'She is a bit earnest. She means well.'

Isobel snuggled up to him. 'Does she?'

Richard looked at his wife's enquiring face and kissed her softly on the mouth. 'We all mean well,' he said. 'We all want you to be happy.'

Chapter Twenty-three

The urgency having gone out of the situation, Isobel did not phone Harry the next day. It all seemed rather ridiculous with hindsight. Even if Jenny Holt had been driving her car, or had seen the two of them together, what could she have made of it? Besides, it was hardly in her interest to tell Richard his wife was having an affair, unless she thought it would bind him more tightly to her, and anyone who knew anything about Richard would realise immediately that that would be the very last effect it would have. Richard philandered because he disliked the idea of being trapped in a monogamous relationship, rather than from any passion he felt for the women with whom he conducted these liaisons. He loved Isobel. The prospect of her behaving in a similar fashion was not one he had ever countenanced. He knew, or rather suspected, that there had been one or two falls from grace, but he accepted these as mere lapses, undertaken more in the spirit of revenge than desire. He knew her too well. He was her man, just as she was his woman. They both understood that.

Harry looked tired. Observing him Isobel was struck by how attractive the thin lines round his eyes were. How unfair that hers were not. Or perhaps they were. Unlikely.

'How was your evening?' she asked brightly, hoping, despite her fondness for Maureen, that he had been unable to eat for thinking of her.

'Interesting,' said Harry.

'Oh?'

'There was a flood.'
'At Maureen's?'
'No. Old bird next door went out and left the bath running or something. Anyway there was water pouring down the stairs by the time she came back. Bubbles, too. Must have looked like a Guiness factory. Apparently her old man was watching the telly and never heard a thing. First we knew about it was when she came haring into the back garden screaming about a tidal wave and the end of the world.'
'In Clitheroe Gardens? It's two miles from the coast.'
'Maureen says she's always at it.'
'Being flooded?'
'Not just that – some disaster or other. She keeps getting involved in causes and things. One time they had to get the vicar to come and exorcise a ghost.'
'You're joking. What happened?'
Harry shrugged. 'He sealed all the windows and then everyone in the street had to kneel on the pavement with garlic round their necks till the tormented soul came shooting up the chimney.'
'What happened then?'
'They fried it in batter and had it for tea.'
Isobel thumped him. 'Poor Maureen. It can't be very restful having neighbours like that.'
'No. She says the worst of it is the houses are in such poor condition, some of them, that there's no way of knowing whether yours'll be the next, and they've had the services out so often to number forty-four, she doubts whether they'd take much notice of a genuine emergency.'
'Perhaps she should move.'
'My guess is she'd like to. Move right away from the area. Few too many memories, if you ask me. Anyway, what with one thing and another, by the time we'd eaten and put the world to rights it must have been four o'clock when I got to bed. I feel like death warmed up.'
'You look like it,' said Isobel kindly.
'Would I say that to you?'
'I think so.'
'You're probably right. Now, tell me, what was all that about last night?'

Isobel hesitated. 'Oh, that. It was all a mistake, thank god. Not that it would really have mattered all that much. But it just seemed as though it would at the time, if you see what I mean.'

'So what was it?'

They were sitting in the dining room, the windows facing on to the garden out of sight of curious eyes. Harry had his legs stretched out in front of him. Isobel sat opposite, her own interlocking with his. He held out his arms.

'Come and sit on my knee.' She swung herself across. 'Now, tell me all about it.'

Isobel sighed. 'Richard's got a mistress.' She paused, but Harry said nothing so she continued. 'That was her car in the car park yesterday. I assumed it was her driving it and was worried that she might have seen us together, you know...'

'Snogging by the dustbins?'

'If you have to put it like that.'

'It's what it was.'

'Yes, well, all right. Anyway that's it. But it turns out she'd lent the car to someone else, so I needn't have worried.'

Harry was silent for a moment. 'Doesn't it bother you, Richard having a bit on the side?'

'Not really. He's always doing it. He thinks I don't know.'

Harry shook his head in disbelief. 'He must be fucking mad.'

Isobel looked at him. 'Oh, well, it's all right that way, if you see what I mean. I mean, we don't not... well...'

'You're still screwing him?'

'Well, yes.'

'Even since...'

Isobel sensed she was being disapproved of. 'I can't not, can I? I mean that would make him suspicious.'

'Do you enjoy it?'

'Oh, god, Harry. How do I know? Yes, probably. It's not the same. It could never be the same as with you.'

'No?'

'No, of course not. Why are you being like this? You've been married. Don't you know the way things are? You have to go on as normal, whatever happens. That's what marriage is.'

Harry stared out of the window. He looked genuinely upset. 'I got divorced,' he said.

'Do you want me to get divorced? Is that what you're saying?'

Harry shook his head. 'I'm sorry. It's your life. You do what's right for you. It's got f all to do with me anyway.'

'Yes, it has.' Isobel could feel tears beginning to come. Her throat ached with holding them back. 'I love you. I know I'm not meant to, but I do.'

She felt Harry's body stiffen. 'How can you love me? You don't know me?'

Isobel thought about it. 'You can't love someone you do know,' she said slowly. 'That much I've learnt.'

Harry shook his head. 'You're crazy, Isobel. Do you know that?'

'I'd be crazy if I didn't, the way people are queueing up to tell me.'

'Crazy and sexy and horny. Do they tell you that?'

Isobel tried to smile.

'Not all of them.'

'Well, you are. And I'm glad I met you. Does that help?'

Isobel wiped away the truant tears. 'Not a lot.'

'I didn't think it would. Come on, Mrs Day. I haven't got long. Where shall we go?' Isobel said the spare room would be best. Harry carried her up there.

'What's this?' He handed her a bright blue bead which had rolled out from under the pillows. Isobel looked at it. 'It's a bead, isn't it? I don't know how it got there. Eleanour or one of her friends, I suppose.'

'I thought it might be the Kentish form of contraception. The ancient Egyptians used to do that, you know. Beads or stones.'

Isobel shuddered. 'What a lot you do know.'

'I did a doc about the pyramids once. You pick up a lot in my job.'

'I've no doubt,' said Isobel, thinking of Leonie's beaded hair.

When Harry had gone Isobel cursed herself for telling him

she loved him. She knew it had upset him, more than the business about sleeping with Richard, and that had been bad enough. It was always a mistake to tell people what you were thinking, she knew that of old. With her confession she had handed over the reins to him. They were no longer equal in this affair. Oh what the hell! They never had been. She'd got this far in spite of the odds. She was one of life's survivors, albeit not in perfect shape. Time would tell.

With this philosophic persuasion she bumped downstairs and thudded out into the garden where she lay face down on the lawn and cried for a quarter of an hour.

It was here Diana found her as, at Jenny's behest, she made a flying visit with a large bunch of feverfew. 'Good god, Izzy, do you spend all your time flat on your face? Or is it only when I call round?'

'A bit of both,' snuffled Isobel, dragging herself up and wiping her nose on a leaf. 'Hayfever,' she added in explanation of her red-rimmed eyes.

'Can't see breathing in grass is going to help. Is it a saturation cure?'

'Something like that,' agreed Isobel. 'This is very kind of you, Diana. What is it? Spinach?'

'Feverfew. Jenny asked me to drop it in. There's something wrong with her car.'

'What do you do with it?'

Diana shrugged. 'God knows. Try soup. Oh no, you haven't got a pressure cooker, have you? Mornay sauce. Never fails. I must go.' She strode off down the path then returned. 'By the way, I haven't heard from that stud of yours yet. You haven't got his number by any chance, have you? I might give him a ring.'

'No,' said Isobel, more shocked than annoyed. 'He's not a stud, he's a cameraman.' Diana really was incorrigible, and yet she got away with it. Perhaps that was the way to be. After all she was very successful. She wondered what Harry would do if Diana did ring him up. Maybe she should give her the number just to see. But would she ever know? Not from Harry, presumably. Diana would never be able to keep quiet about it. No, she couldn't bear it. If Diana were that interested let her find out for herself.

She went inside. There was a message on the answerphone. It was from Harry, obviously in a call box, saying he'd forgotten to tell her he'd be staying down till Thursday next week because Julian Joffe wanted him around for the editing. His voice sounded gruff and matter-of-fact, as so many people's do on answering machines. Still she wondered that he'd taken the risk. Richard could easily have played it back. Perhaps that was what he had wanted. Then everything would have come to an end. Either that or she would have been forced to choose between them.

She shivered and erased the tape, checking twice to make sure it was clear. Then she rang her mother-in-law and arranged to meet her for lunch at the local pub. She needed a dose of domesticity. They could talk about the size of Patrick's trainers and whether Eleanour was old enough to take proper care of a hamster. In the event they discussed the plight of the Kurds and the corruptibility of the police, but Isobel returned home much refreshed, determined to put Harry entirely out of her thoughts, at least until bedtime.

Harry rang on Friday morning, plainly hungover. He muttered something about Monday, but it sounded so vague that Isobel put the receiver down no wiser. Either he was coming at lunchtime, or ringing, or not ringing. She would just have to wait and see. She thought about ringing back, then realised she still hadn't got his home number. Poor Diana. She certainly hadn't meant to tell her the truth. Mind you, Diana had probably got it by now. That would be the supreme irony. She considered ringing Diana and asking her if she'd had any luck, but even as a confirmed cynic, this seemed a little over the top. Instead she went upstairs and began a concerted effort to tidy the bedroom. It was all very well getting rid of Vera Beasley, but her own contempt for the domestic was getting a little out of control. She started with the chest of drawers, plunging her arm the length of her stock of tights to see which ones were laddered. Most of them appeared to be. She had kept them to wear under trousers in the cold weather but that could no longer be justified in the middle of June, as it would be when she was finally rid of the plaster.

She wondered what her leg would look like. Probably white and flaky and covered with hair. How revolting. She must remember to take a razor the day they took it off. It was a good thing they didn't make body searches of patients entering the hospital. That would be all Robertson and Mahon required: the mad woman from Barnbridge with a deadly weapon in her bag. Serve them right if she used it on them. A little shiver of delight ran through her at the prospect. She shook herself. Had she always been this bloodthirsty? Probably.

She moved on to Richard's cupboard. In the third drawer down she found a flat black box, fastened with a slim satin bow. She opened it. Inside lay an exquisite set of oyster silk lingerie. She fingered it delicately. A teddy – she loved those – a camisole top and French knickers. The bastard! She snapped the box shut. So that was the kind of stuff he bought for Jenny Holt. And what had he got for her? On her *fortieth* birthday? The most significant date in a woman's calendar. A tie-dyed pillowcase with armholes. Right.

She hopped furiously across the room to the bathroom, seized the nail scissors and returned. Opening the box she took out the teddy and, cutting it neatly into ribbons, replaced it. She did the same to the camisole and knickers, fitting the lid neatly over the whole and returning it to its exact place in the drawer, hidden under a sweatshirt which Richard never wore.

She felt liberated, justified, for everything she had done and would do. Richard had gone too far this time. Richard was out as far as she was concerned. With a flash of brilliance she remembered the ear-rings. She fetched them and dropped them amongst the confusion of torn silk and lace. Now thoroughly inspired she hurtled down the stairs on her bottom and hopped into the kitchen. Jenny's bunch of feverfew was languishing in the vegetable rack. Savagely she grabbed a handful and made her way back up to the bedroom. Panting, she removed the lid once more and crushed the herb into the box. This done she went and had a shower. Then, purged of the evidence, she once more descended the stairs, ready to greet the world in her role as wife and mother.

*

Richard noticed that Isobel was a little remote at first that evening, but she soon softened up when he told her about the hilarious episode when the auditors had got trapped in the lift for half an hour. The weekend passed peacefully enough. Diana, as promised, appeared briefly on Saturday afternoon on her way to a golf match. She asked how the feverfew had gone down as Jenny had something of a plague of it, and was anxious to find as many outlets as possible.

Isobel had replied that that was all too apparent and for a moment Diana had been silenced, before beginning anew on the subject of them all writing the council about a proposal to build a lavatory opposite the village war memorial.

Isobel had subsequently boiled up the feverfew and served it with chops and fried onions. The discovery that it tasted almost entirely of toothpaste was in no way displeasing to her. It was worth it to see Richard's face. When he had returned from the herbaceous border where most of the herb was now deposited he had remarked, somewhat pale-faced, that Jenny had rung him at the office to see if she could pop over on Sunday afternoon for a cup of tea if they weren't doing anything special.

'Why didn't she ring me?' asked Isobel pleasantly. 'Surely it would have been simpler?'

'She's got this thing about not disturbing you. I know it's daft.'

'It is a bit,' Isobel agreed. 'Seeing as I spend most of my time praying to be disturbed.'

Richard looked chastened. 'Not much longer now. It's only just over a week. I tell you what, let's go out to dinner the night it comes off. A real dinner. Not just the local pub. We could go to Fletchers. Would you like that?'

Isobel smiled. 'We couldn't possibly afford Fletchers. You know that.'

'Yes we could. Why not? It's a special occasion. Besides it'll make up for your birthday. Missing the party. A belated celebration, that's what it'll be.'

Isobel looked at his eager face. 'All right,' she said. 'A belated celebration.'

Richard beamed. 'Oh, there was just one thing Jenny said ... if it was all right for her to come over?'

'Of course it is. What's that?'

'Apparently she's having a bit of trouble with her car. You know I said she'd lent it to a friend? Well, it seems the stupid woman overloaded it or something. Anyway there's a problem with the clutch. She wondered if I could nip over there and pick her up – have a look at it at the same time. I said I didn't mind, provided you hadn't got anything planned for us. I know it's a bit of an imposition at the weekend, but she has done quite a few things for us one way and another. . .'

'Isobel snapped the wire down on a crumbling piece of cheddar. 'She has indeed,' she said.

Chapter Twenty-four

'You're sure she doesn't mind?' Jenny, statutory oily rag twisting in her hands, hovered over Richard as he fiddled with the engine of her car. 'No, of course not. When did you last have these plugs done?'
'I'm not sure.'
'They're in an appalling state. Give me that cloth a sec.' Jenny handed it to him. 'Bugger.'
'Oh, darling, have you hurt yourself? Let me look.'
Richard peered accusingly at his torn thumb. 'Bloody gaskets,' he muttered, before retreating once more under the bonnet.

'That should do it.' Some forty minutes and two cups of cooling lemon tea untouched on the path beside him, Richard slammed down the bonnet.'Try that.' Jenny padded meekly across the gravel and got into the car. 'Shall I start it?' Richard closed his eyes for a moment. 'Yes. Start it. That was the idea.' Jenny turned the ignition and revved the engine furiously. For a moment it caught, then spluttered and died away. 'Shall I try again?'
'Yes. Try again.'
Ten minutes of choking grunts and spasmodic rattles later Richard ordered Jenny out of the car. She slid out, silky hair damp with perspiration, eyes dark with mortification. 'I'm so sorry, Richie,' she murmured, standing by the Fiat like the mother of a juvenile mugger. 'It's never done this before.'
'I'm buggered if I know what it is.'

There was a loud harumph from the other side of the hedge where the ex-colonel and his wife were trying to read the Sunday papers.

'I think you're going to have to get a garage to it. How will you get to work tomorrow?'

'Bus,' said Jenny with such poignancy that Richard almost relented and offered to drive her himself. He caught himself just in time, however. If he really intended to pack this affair in he must stop behaving like a built-in handyman. Jenny must learn to stand on her own two feet.

'Come on. Let's go and see what Isobel and the kids are up to.'

'Do you still want me to come?' Jenny's wide blue eyes gazed humbly up at him. Richard softened. 'Of course I do. So does Isobel. So do the children. They're looking forward to it.'

Jenny sighed. 'They're so lovely,' she said yearningly. ' I wish I had children.'

Richard cleared his throat. 'I expect you will one day,' he said, immediately regretting it. 'What I mean is, you're still very young. Plenty of time yet.'

'I'm twenty-seven. I'm an elderly primipara. At least I would be if I had a child.'

'Who told you that?'

'Diana. She said anyone over twenty-three was an elderly primipara. She's going to have a baby next year.'

'Diana? Pregnant? Who's the poor sod?'

'Richie, don't be so mean. Actually, there isn't one yet. But she's looking around now. She's going to choose a man and then have a baby by him. She isn't going to live with him or anything.' Again the wide eyes focused longingly on Richard. He looked away quickly.

'But that's ridiculous. Typical bloody Diana. Trust her to think she can just pick and choose. How's she going to decide? Stick her hand down every bloke's trousers till she finds the right-sized cock?'

'Richard, that's horrible. I don't want to speak to you if you're going to talk that way. Diana's not like that a bit. You know she isn't.'

'Isn't she just?' responded Richard with some relish.

'No. She's kind and brave – yes, brave to do a thing like that. I only wish I had the courage.'

'I'm bloody glad you haven't.'

'What's that supposed to mean?'

Richard could see his chances of a quick screw receding. He put his hands on Jenny's shoulders. 'I've got nothing against Diana,' he said soberly. 'She's a very nice woman, in her way. Let's just say she's not my type. Whereas . . .' His eyes gazed eloquently at Jenny's dimpled face. 'Shall we just go inside and cool down for a few moments? Would that be a good idea?'

'I don't know . . .'

'I need to wash my hands. I'm all hot and oily.'

Jenny hesitated. 'Yes, all right. Not for long, though. Isobel will wonder what's happened to us.'

'Isobel's all right. She's got a book. She always reads on a Sunday afternoon.'

Isobel was weeding a small patch of flower bed at the end of the garden. She hauled herself up as Richard's car drove in and came to meet them. The children had made a camp of the deck-chairs with an old tarpaulin and were fighting raucously inside it.

'No luck?'

Jenny shook her head remorsefully. 'I feel terrible. Poor Richard spent *hours* trying to fix it but it just kept making this awful noise and wouldn't start. Would it, Richard?' She looked for corroboration to her accomplice. Not for the first time Richard wished she would learn not to over-act. Too much time spent near Marjorie Bennett, he supposed.

'Needs a garage,' he said briefly. 'Any chance of a cup of tea? I'm parched.'

'I'll go and put the kettle on,' said Isobel with breezy charm. 'What about you, Jenny? Can you drink teabag tea, or would you like something else?'

'Oh, anything,' Jenny avowed. 'I don't take milk, though. Would you like me to come and help? Richard, you shouldn't expect Isobel to be waiting on you. She's the invalid, remember.'

'Do her good,' said Richard. 'Don't want a vegetable on my hands, do I?' Isobel looked at him over Jenny's head.

'Richard, how can you talk like that?' She turned to

Isobel. 'I'm sure he doesn't mean it. He's just hot and bothered because of my naughty car. I feel so guilty, messing up your Sunday afternoon.'

'You haven't messed it up. I've had a lovely time. Very peaceful.' A piercing scream from the camp, followed by Eleanour's emergence in tears, seemed set to give the lie to this, but a plaster and a piece of cake wrought their usual panacea, and the afternoon settled back into its sleepy rut.

Jenny insisted on carrying the tray, which was far too heavy for her and intended for Richard. They sat outside and ate bought walnut and coffee sponge, which Jenny pronounced 'scrumptious', and the children decried as 'yukky'. Discussion was made of Marjorie Bennett's forthcoming production about a group of women learning to tap dance. Jenny was of the opinion that ambition had at last got the better of her, since there had been four resignations – two from the cast and two from backstage. 'Diana's in it,' she added tentatively, fearful that Richard would mention their earlier conversation. He said nothing, however, but merely reached for another slice of cake. 'I think she'll be awfully good,' added Jenny, gaining in confidence as Richard took a large bite. 'She plays the teacher. She has to teach all the others the routines, so she has to know them.'

'I shouldn't think Diana's short on routines,' said Isobel pleasantly. Richard choked very slightly on his cake.

'When will your plaster come off, Isobel?' asked Jenny, thinking a change of topic might be advisable.

'A week on Tuesday if all goes well.'

'What does that mean?'

'Nothing really. I suppose they have to x-ray my ankle before they take it off to make sure it's mended all right, but they seem to think it's okay so far.'

'I bet you're dying to be back to normal.'

Isobel smiled.

Harry was in a sparkling mood when he called for her on Monday morning. The weather was still fine and he had brought another picnic. 'I've had an idea,' he said after a pleasingly effusive greeting. 'I think you're right.'

'What about?' asked Isobel, unused to such acclamation.

'Not walking. You don't want to walk all that way to the edge of the village. It's much too hot. You get a cab up to The Ploughman. I'll meet you there and we can go on on the bike. Yes?'

'No,' said Isobel.

'Why not?'

'Because it doesn't matter.'

'What doesn't?' Harry looked confused.

'Whether anyone sees us. I don't care if Richard finds out anymore.'

Harry laughed cautiously. 'Oh, come on, Isobel. You know you do really. Anyway, my way will work. You won't have to walk at all, if that's what's worrying you.'

'It isn't. Watch my lips, Harry. I don't care. Right? And you needn't look so frightened. I haven't decided to set up home with you in Shepherd's Bush, so that's you off the hook.'

Harry stood back. He looked unhappy. 'What's all this about, Isobel?'

'Nothing. Shall we go? Or would you rather not be seen with me?'

'It's not me I'm thinking about.'

'Yes, well, don't think about me either. Then we'll both be happy.'

Harry shrugged. 'Whatever you say.' He picked up his helmet and went to fetch hers.

'I think I shall get a motor bike.' Isobel was lying on her back. Harry had remembered to bring a rug this week and the sun flashing intermittently across its red-gold pattern gave it an exotic air which suited well with Isobel's newfound feeling of independence. 'Then I shall just take off and go round the world.'

'What about the children?'

'They can come too. I'll get a sidecar. Somewhere hot. No more grey. I hate grey.' She sat up on her elbow. 'Do you know, the White Cliffs of Dover are grey. People come all this way just to look at them, sing songs about them, romanticise over them. And they're grey. It's all a con.' She lay back. 'Everything's a con.'

Harry lay down on his stomach beside her. 'You're very cynical this morning. Has something happened?' Isobel turned her eyes towards him for a moment then looked away. She took a breath. 'It wasn't true, what I said last week. About loving you. It was a mistake.'

Harry was silent. Isobel felt him watching her. At last he turned over on his back and lay staring up at the trees. 'Right,' he said. 'I didn't think it was.'

Isobel felt she should say something. 'Is it true you're staying till Thursday?'

'Looks like it.'

'With Maureen?'

'That's the arrangement.'

'Will you be very busy?'

'Probably.'

'So shall we be able to meet?'

'Do you want to?'

Isobel stared at him aghast. 'Don't you?'

Harry looked at her. 'Yes,' he said casually, as though she were offering him a cup of tea. 'I don't mind.'

This was too much for Isobel. 'Oh for Christ's sake, Harry, what was I supposed to say? I don't know what you want from me. Whatever I do is wrong.'

Harry sat up. 'I just wish you'd tell the fucking truth for once. Like you used to do. That's what I admired about you. You told the truth. Now what do I get? "I love you. I don't love you". I don't give a fuck whether you love me or not. I'm just sick of all this pussyfooting around. I thought we understood each other. I thought for once in my life, I'd come across a woman I fancied, I could actually talk to, laugh with. Now all of a sudden I get all this. One minute you're coming on strong, the next you're sounding like the Speaking Clock. You just tell me what you want and I'll try to provide it, right. Jesus, I'll be gone in a fortnight. Isn't that soon enough for you? And don't cry. I hate women who cry.'

'All women cry,' whimpered Isobel between sobs. Harry reached in the picnic basket and pulled out a paper bag. He upended the tomatoes from it.

'Blow your nose. Let's have some lunch. I suppose you're going to tell me you're not hungry now.'

Isobel blew her nose. 'I am hungry.'

'Good. Well, at least you're not a total failure.'

Isobel smiled weakly. 'That's the nicest thing you've ever said.'

Harry looked at her reprovingly. 'It's better than you deserve. You want to live for the day, Isobel. You can't hope for more. Maureen knows that.

She's got her head screwed on. More than I can say for you.'

Isobel put down her piece of chicken and slowly rolled her skirt up round her waist. 'I'm not Maureen,' she said.

'It's better in the open air,' Isobel opined, as she sat half-naked trying to peel an orange.

'What is?'

'Everything. Making love, eating, drinking. Living.'

Harry leant over and licked the dribbling orange juice from her breast.

'What about dying?' he asked.

Isobel looked at him as he smiled up at her. 'I wouldn't know about that,' she said.

When Isobel phoned for a cab the next day to take her to the hospital she was informed that no one was available. By 'no one' she took the girl to mean neither the weasel nor the owner, since they seemed to comprise the entire workforce of the village fleet.

'Oh dear,' she said plaintively. 'Only I have to go to the hospital.'

'Hang on,' said the girl solicitously. 'I'll see what I can do.' There was the customary buzz in the background overlaid with twang of the local radio before the girl returned. 'One of my drivers has got a hospital drop at one-thirty. He's going to see if the client would object to you sharing the cab. What time was you meant to be there?'

'Two o'clock,' said Isobel, 'but one-thirty would be fine.'

'Give us your number. I'll come back to you.'

Isobel did and was rung some ten minutes later to be told that the client had agreed and that the cab would call for her at one o'clock. Isobel thanked her and went to get ready.

As she had suspected it was the weasel who screeched to a halt outside at ten past one and proceeded to honk infuriatingly till she appeared. What she had not suspected was that the other passenger would be Anita Craven, complete with armoury of instruments, which seemed if possible to take up more room than her.

Anita, recognising her, was immediately suffused with enthusiasm and apologies as she fought a courageous duel with a long tin tube wedged diagonally across the back seat. 'It's my shawm,' she explained. Isobel, mishearing, thought she had said 'It's my turn' and, alarmed that it might be her turn next, opted to go in the front, despite the difficulty of finding enough room for her rigid leg amongst the pile of junk on the floor.

'I really must get a car,' Anita's contralto voice boomed from the back. 'It's hopeless trying to get around with my equipment.' Isobel agreed, thinking a removal van might better serve her needs. 'It's very very exciting, don't you think?'

'What?' asked Isobel.

'The project. The whole brilliant idea. I'm so glad Si called me in. It's such a privilege, you know, to be connected with a scheme like this. I think you're all doing marvelously well,' she added, 'especially you. I mean it takes a lot of guts to stand up and dance like that, when you can't even walk.' Isobel noted the faintest flicker of curiosity on the weasel's face before his customary torpor displaced it.

'Can I ask you something?' asked Anita.

'Of course.'

'Which bit did you like best?'

Isobel, who had been reliving her picnic with Harry in somewhat vivid detail, was momentarily fazed by this query. 'Umm?'

'Of the music. It's just I have to go up to Ashford with Julian tomorrow to do some post-synching, and I just wondered if you had any preference between the adagio and the glissando?'

'The glissando was very nice,' said Isobel, wondering what the hell it was.

'You prefer the glissando?' A note of disappointment entered Anita's voice.

'The other one was interesting, too.'

'Interesting. Yes, I thought that. Mind you, it was more or less a continuo. I don't know if I could recreate it to order.'

'Ah,' said Isobel. 'That's a shame.'

'I've got most of it,' said Anita, her enthusiasm mounting once more. 'If that's the one you'd go for.'

'I couldn't possibly take the responsibility,' pleaded Isobel. 'Why don't you ask Julian what he thinks?'

'Oh, yes, I shall of course. I just wanted to get a sniff of how everyone felt before we got to the actual taping bit, if you see what I mean.'

'Yes, of course,' said Isobel, grateful for the first time to see the hospital gates looming.

Chapter Twenty-five

Isobel had no desire to arrive early for the session, so she refused Anita's anxious offer of 'a chance to run through the movements' and went off in search of coffee.

Reception was extremely full that afternoon and she had to wait some time to get served. It was while she was standing there that she saw Leonie swanning across the hall towards her. She looked more than usually pleased with herself in her vermilion harem pants and matching smock.

'Isobel,' she whooped.'Quick, quick. Disaster. Julian has to go to Africa.'

'Now?' asked Isobel, slurping her coffee in surprise.

'Not now. But soon, very soon. It's complete and utter chaos. Leave your coffee. You're needed.' Isobel left her coffee, more because it was disgusting than because Leonie so ordered. 'Is that as fast as you can go?' exhorted Leonie, hustling her round the corner.

Along the corridors came the fretful howl of Anita tuning up. Several of the ordinary patients exchanged frightened glances, the staff merely smiling with grim resignation as they went about their duties.

'Ah, Isobel . . .' Dr Mahon came scampering across the room to greet her. 'We were wondering what had happened to you.'

'Really?'

'Yes. Anita said you came with her, so naturally . . .'

Isobel nodded and sat down.

'There's been a change of plan.' Mahon turned to the others as he spoke. 'Ladies and gentlemen, I've been talking to our director – unfortunately he can't be with us till later on. Some external filming. But he has decided – we, I should say – that things must be speeded up a bit. Now this doesn't mean that I intend to vary your therapy in any way, so there's absolutely nothing to concern yourselves about. All that will happen is that certain of our discussions will be, as it were, compressed a little.' He paused.

'What the fuck's that supposed to mean?' asked Hilary suspiciously.

Dr Mahon sighed. 'It means basically that Julian will require a little more pace than we had at first considered desirable. He may also, occasionally, want to retake certain of the shots – purely from a technical point of view, you understand. There's no question of anyone being obliged to put on some kind of performance for the camera. I'm sure you all appreciate that. Anyway I thought I'd have a quick word with you while the crew are absent, just so that you could prepare yourselves internally. After all,' he smirked conspiratorially, 'we do want to show ourselves to best advantage, don't we?'

Isobel wondered what possible viewpoint could present Mahon as anything but a jumped-up quack. 'Fly-on-the-wall' was looking more and more like 'sponsored swim in the soup bowl' with every passing moment. Mahon took them rapidly through their breathing exercises then suggested Anita spend a few minutes rehearsing the circle dance as he himself had some urgent business to attend to.

This was the first time Isobel had seen him leave the group during a session and she was curious to see if they would immediately break into spiteful gossip behind his back. He had them too well trained, it seemed, for no one said anything, although Hilary did produce his pornographic novel with which he seemed to be making alarmingly slow progress, and steadfastly ignored Anita's plea that everyone should 'take their places and space out'.

Isobel noted that Leonie looked pretty spaced-out already. She certainly had a faraway look in her eyes as she swayed sensuously to the impossible dirge of Anita's pipes.

Meg had obviously been practising, and entered quite joyfully into the spirit of things. Perhaps it does work, Isobel mused in some surprise, seeing the almost peaceful expression on her normally tense face. Ken, too, seemed soothed by the movements, albeit he was still stuck in the one-way system. A general understanding appeared to have been reached, whereby no one moved very much at all, thus imposing a voluntary damage limitation clause on the participants.

Maureen as always gave herself up to events. She danced, neither well nor badly, her attention all for Leonie's flailing arms and sharp-edged bangles.

Isobel merely stood and wiggled her hips, which she liked doing anyway, eyes closed, thoughts in the long grass with Harry. She wondered where Julian had carted them off to this time. There couldn't be much of Eastley he hadn't filmed by now. Perhaps he was making a travel documentary at the same time. She pondered what the Tourist Board would make of the town being touted as a haven for suicidal drop-outs.

The music ended. Anita pronounced them all much improved. 'I think,' she added tentatively, 'it might be an idea for you to take the beat from Meg. You don't have to open your eyes very much. Just sort of glance at her from time to time. It might make all the difference.' It certainly did for Meg who glowed a becoming pink and promised to do her best. She reminded Isobel of a Brownie being enrolled.

The sound of voices outside heralded the return of Simon Mahon and the film crew. Anita asked if they would like to do it again, but nervousness took over and the group disintegrated, except for Leonie who continued to oscillate with erotic abandon as the newcomers crept stealthily round her, Jock apologising profusely as he was accidentally buffeted in the rear.

Isobel glanced at Harry whose air of studied indifference she now knew signified annoyance.

Leonie had re-opened her eyes and was making great play of being frightfully embarrassed.

'Right, everyone.' Dr Mahon's hands were up. 'We have a small crisis.'

Everyone stared at him, less from any great interest in his crisis, than for the fact that he had changed colour. Not from white to puce, as had happened once or twice, but from fawn to mocha. 'What on earth's he done to his face?' whispered Maureen behind cupped hands.

Isobel shook her head. 'You don't suppose he's been for radiation, do you?'

'Microwave, more like,' said Maureen. Isobel began to giggle. Maureen stared fiercely out of the window.

'The problem is,' continued their mentor, blissfully unaware of the alarm he was inspiring, 'that we shall have to go straight into indepth discussion. You needn't worry. The camera will be on myself throughout this part of the programme. You will be merely extraneous voices. Then, after the break, we shall invert the process, but more of that anon. We'll start with Leonie, shall we? No, not that chair, Leonie. I shall be sitting there. Where do you want Leonie, Julian, or doesn't it matter?'

It did matter. Julian wanted Leonie just behind Harry so that Mahon's eyeline would give the impression of a face to face encounter, which it was in all but the presence of thirteen stone of cameraman between them. This seemed to unnerve neither of the protagonists, however, since Mahon had no intention of wasting his meaningful glances on a patient, and Leonie was plainly more interested in Harry's buttocks, from which her gaze scarcely faltered throughout the interview.

Jock shot forward and, with much fumbling, implanted a pin mike just inside the bosom of Leonie's smock. No such apparatus appeared necessary for Dr Mahon.

Isobel watched with mounting irritation as the psychiatrist probed, nodded and sighed, while Leonie dramatised, exaggerated and inched her body ever closer to Harry's thighs in her desire to be 'totally honest and straight' about her problems.

Not a possessive woman by nature, Isobel became transfixed by whether or not Harry was wriggling his bottom on purpose, or whether he felt genuinely crowded by the two thespians emoting either side of his private parts.

'And how do you feel in your relationships with men now, Leonie?' asked Mahon, after she had rehearsed her usual catalogue of being lashed to a tree and soaked in honey which the marauders then licked from her in batches of three till she was wet all over and shivering. Isobel shivered too, and wondered if it was permissible to take notes. She didn't dare catch Harry's eye.

There was a pause. Leonie sighed pitifully. 'I feel so vulnerable,' she confessed with the helplessness of she-tiger. 'I feel . . . that they want to do things to me that are wrong . . . sinful . . . basic.' Her head drooped.

'Is it all men you fear these things from? Or just certain of them?' coaxed Dr Mahon, gazing supportively into the lens of the camera.

'Nearly all,' admitted Leonie. 'Sometimes I meet a man and I think, 'Yes, – with you I could be safe. You would protect and care for me.' But . . . I know I must never tell him.'

'Why not?'

'Because if I do, he, too will become like a brute and seek to hurt me.'

'Why are you so sure of that?'

'I'm not . . . I . . . Oh, how I long to be free of all this.'

You and a dozen others, thought Isobel, looking pointedly at her watch.

'And how can you free yourself, Leonie?'

'I don't know.'

'You do know. You have it within yourself to free yourself. All it needs is a little courage. What must you do?'

Leonie's head was now so low that Isobel half expected it to appear through Harry's legs. She whispered something which even the pin mike was at a loss to record.

'Louder, Leonie. Louder.'

'Tell him.' The hoarse croak of a woman whose entrails have just been drawn.

Mahon nodded sagaciously. 'Tell the man. The very next time you feel like this about a man, tell him. He's human too. Men are not beasts, you know. They are warm, caring, loving creatures like some women. Can you understand that?'

'I think so.'

'Have you met anyone lately who made you feel like that?'

'Well . . .'

'You have, haven't you?'

'Yes.'

'And are you going to speak to him? Tell him how you feel?'

'Oh, Dr Mahon, I can't. Suppose he turns on me? Treats me like a slave? Forces me to do things against my will?'

'That is a risk you will have to take if you are ever to be free. Remember, you have the support of the group behind you, whatever happens. They will help to sustain you through this crisis. Is he here now?'

Leonie was silent.

'He is, isn't he?'

A small nod.

'Speak to him now, Leonie. We are all here. We will all support you.'

'It's Harry.'

That's twenty per cent of your support out of the window, vowed Isobel, you hard-nosed slut.

The fact that Harry continued to film with total insouciance was less of a surprise to the group than Simon Mahon's own reaction. Beneath his Californian tan, which they now perceived to be moist with perspiration, the psychiatrist was plainly experiencing some annoyance. Huffily he rummaged in his pocket for a handkerchief and pressed it against his temples then, with all the warmth of the Spanish Inquisitor, demanded of Leonie whether she did not think she was getting a little old for such juvenile fantasies. Leonie did not reply to this but rose and, folding her hands demurely in front of her, returned to her seat without a backwards glance. Hilary was looking at her very curiously, Isobel noted. The others seemed decently embarrassed and studied their hands with intensity, which was just as well or they might have noticed that Dr Mahon had two white patches either side of his forehead.

'Meg.'

She started as from the judicial black cap. 'Me, Dr Mahon?'

'Yes.'

'I'm not sure . . .'

'That is why we are here, Meg. To help you gain assurance.' Mahon rose and gestured to his chair.

'Hang on.' Harry came round his camera. 'I thought we were doing you first.'

'I prefer Meg to be the subject of this interview.'

'You may do, but I'll have to realign the whole shot.'

'Is that a problem?'

'No. Just give me twenty minutes.'

'Twenty minutes?'

Julian loped across to them. 'Actually, Simon, I thought the plan was to do your close-ups first and pick up any loose shots of the patients later on? After all, we've got a fair bit of footage of most of them, and time is, well, running a bit short.'

Petulance fought with vanity on Mahon's tie-dyed face. 'I thought we'd agreed I should use my intuition? That is part of my therapy. Surprise. How can I possibly obtain results if you ask me to dispense with one of my principle tools, just for the sake of . . . technicalities?' He threw a savage glance at Harry as he spoke. Julian too looked at him with something like desperation. 'What do you think, Harry? I mean if surprise is important . . .'

Harry shrugged. 'You're the boss. I should think most of the punters'll be too busy adjusting the colour to notice.'

Mahon turned on him, hands tightly clenched at his side. 'When I want the opinion of an ill-informed layman I shall ask for it.'

Harry gazed coolly down at him. 'I shouldn't leave it too long. I think you're melting.'

For a glorious moment it seemed that Mahon might take a swing at him. Even Julian looked temporarily animated, forgetting that there would be no one to film the event, but Fran, seeing her hopes of a free place on the next course endangered, came haring over to say she was calling an early break.

No one spoke much as Luce padded around with tea. Leonie sat arched against the wall, her wide claret lips pouting, eyes half-closed. Meg sat pale beside her untouched cup. Ken was searching manically for the latest instalment of his poem which turned up under Hilary's coffee, complete with round brown stain. Maureen sipped her tea, a million miles from any of them, and Isobel thought about Harry, and Leonie, and her revenge.

Julian and Simon Mahon were bickering feverishly in a corner. As a result of their colloquy Meg was put on ice. Dr

Mahon addressed the room. 'It appears,' he said in the muted snarl of a seriously angry man, 'that time is even more pressing than Julian had led me to believe. Such is the situation that we may not have time for all the one-to-ones – if we are to include this dance business,' his eyes narrowed, 'which Julian seems to feel important. We are, of course, entitled to our own opinions. After all, it is his show.'

Julian half rose and murmured peevishly into Fran's ear. Fran immediately leapt to her feet and violently refuted that it was in any way Julian's 'show' and that he merely wanted to present Dr Mahon's very fine work in a form that would be immediately accessible to the vast majority of the viewing public which, she added with sinister emphasis, was generally so unsympathetic to the plight of the mentally ill.

The group shuffled in universal rejection of the term as applied to itself.

'So,' Mahon continued with the world-weary despair of a man of principal, 'compromise must prevail. I have decided to invite Isobel to occupy my place for the next interview. We will then hold Open Forum as usual.'

There was a rustle of expectation from the others, plainly wondering if she would comply. Isobel got slowly to her feet and clumped towards the chair. Hilary looked crosser than ever, Meg relieved.

She sat down and laid her crutches neatly beside her on the floor. Mahon took his place behind Harry. Isobel noticed he was rather further away than Leonie had been.

'Isobel . . . Are you quite comfortable?'

'Yes, thank you.'

'Good. Good. Now I'd like to ask you a few questions about how you came to join our little group.' Out of the corner of her eye Isobel could see Julian Joffe leaning forward, nose pressed against his folded hands. 'What was it that brought you to St Clare's in the first place, do you remember?'

'A broken ankle.'

'And how did you come to break your ankle?'

'I fell over the cliff.'

There was a slight gasp from Meg who had never quite understood the circumstances of Isobel's fall.

'And what were you doing that allowed that to happen? Were you, for instance, walking too close to the edge, not looking where you were going – thinking of other things?'

Isobel sat silent for a moment.

'I suppose so. I can't remember.'

'Try to remember, Isobel. Try to remember what happened.'

'I tripped.'

'Or slipped?'

'Or slipped.'

'Which?'

'I can't remember.'

'Can't? Or won't?'

'Can't.'

'And that is your story?'

'If you call it that.'

'I think I do, Isobel. You see, there are others who saw you there that day. Who say you seemed perfectly well aware that you were close to the cliff's edge, that in fact you seemed to walk directly towards it, rather than along.'

'No. That's not true.'

'They say it is.'

'They're lying.'

'Are they, Isobel?' Dr Mahon half rose in his seat. 'Or is it you, Isobel, that is lying? Because you can't bear to face the truth.'

'That is the truth. It was an accident.'

'And I suggest to you that it was not.' He paused dramatically. 'That it was a deliberate effort to end your own life. Foiled only by the presence of a projectory some twelve feet below the point at which you fell.'

Isobel said nothing.

'What is your answer to that, Isobel?'

The air prickled with anticipation.

'What do you say to that?'

Isobel gazed at her leg. The once pristine plaster showed signs of fatigue. Blurred grass stains and the dull grime of street dust had taken their toll on its snowy expanse. They'd taken their toll on her too. Richard and Jenny, Harry, Mahon, now Leonie ... Where did it end? You got rid of one lot of problems and a new crop was waiting to greet you. Closing in on you – just as Mahon was closing in on her now.

She looked up straight into the camera. Straight into Harry's eyes. 'I was trying to kill myself.'

Mahon paused to let the effect of her words sink in. 'But you've always denied that was your intention. You have maintained throughout that the whole dreadful accident was just that – an accident.'

'I lied.'

'Why did you lie, Isobel?' A note of ill-concealed excitement had crept into the psychiatrist's voice.

Isobel hesitated. 'It's not something you want people to know about.'

'So why are you telling us now? Why, Isobel?'

She closed her eyes. 'Because I can't bear it on my own any longer. I can't bear living a lie.'

'And what brought you to this awful crisis in your life?'

'I don't know. Things got too much for me, I suppose.'

'Was it anything to do with . . . your age.'

Isobel stared unseeing into the camera. 'I think it may have been.'

'The fact that you were forty. Which is seen as a low point for so many people – women particularly?'

'I suppose so.'

'But how do you feel now, Isobel? You're still forty. You can't get away from the fact.'

'I know that now.'

Dr Mahon's voice sank to a purr. 'Do you feel that you would ever be tempted to do something like this again?'

'I don't think so.'

'But you can't be sure?'

'You can never be sure of anything.'

'True. Very true. But why do you feel less likely to try to take your own life now than when you first entered the hospital?'

Isobel gazed thoughtfully into the camera.

'Because it bloody well hurts too much.'

'Cut,' said Julian.

*

Harry caught hold of Isobel's arm as she was edging her way round the door. 'Don't go yet. Wait for me.'

'I think Anita's calling us a cab,' she said awkwardly, for some reason not wanting to meet his eyes. It had been all right in the hothouse artificiality of the group, but here, alone, she felt nervous – frightened, even – at the prospect of being asked to account for her outburst.

Harry finished packing away his stuff. As always his face said nothing. He should have been an actor, Isobel thought. He gives nothing away. For someone who had been the object of a declaration of passion, the subject of a major confrontation, and the recipient of a lover's suicidal confession, he looked remarkably like a man who had spent the afternoon filing envelopes.

He pulled the door open. 'I'll buy you a drink.'

'I don't want one.'

'Well, I bloody well do.'

'I'm going with Anita. I told you. In the cab.'

Harry shrugged. 'Please yourself. She'll give you a harder time than I will.'

There was truth in this.

'What about Maureen? Aren't you giving her a lift?'

'I can't take the shopping on the bike.'

'You tell Anita, then.'

Harry shook his head in disbelief. 'Stay there.'

Isobel sat down and waited for him to come back. They stopped at a pub near the village. Isobel had orange juice, then seeing Harry's double whisky, wished she'd gone for something stronger. 'Was it that bad?' she asked with false bravado.

'Pretty near.'

'I thought that was what you told me to do. "Strike a blow for the nutcases".'

'I didn't mean you to go native.'

Isobel felt slightly shocked. 'You didn't believe all that, did you?'

Harry regarded her thoughtfully. 'I believed Leonie,' he said at last, with the tiniest hint of malice.

Isobel glowered at him. 'Well, I hope you've sharpened your thumbscrews,' she said. 'You should have gone to

Tesco's with Maureen. They sell catering packs of honey.'

Harry burst out laughing. 'And for a moment I thought you were jealous,' he said.

Isobel smiled cautiously. 'Ridiculous cow. Mahon was annoyed, though, wasn't he? Do you think he thought she fancied him?'

'Mahon's the type who thinks every woman fancies him.'

'Bit like you.'

'Thanks very much.'

'Only because it's true.'

'Please God.'

Isobel reached across and put her hand on his knee. 'Well, I fancy you. Isn't that enough?'

Harry took her hand and kissed her fingers lightly. 'I suppose it'll have to be. Come on. I'd better take you home before the helicopters come looking.'

'Again.'

Harry sighed. 'Again.'

Isobel felt oddly light-headed on the way home, as though a great weight had been lifted from her. She stared at her right leg stuck out in front of her on the bike with something like contempt. All this time she had thought it was the plaster dragging her down, but it hadn't been at all. It had been the conspiracy of silence. Her own conspiracy. The hurried denial to Richard. The obstinate rebuttals to Robertson. The embarrassed joking with Eleanour's teacher . . .

Now she had done it. She had given them what they wanted, and far from it damaging her, it seemed to have given her some sort of status. Even Jock had offered her a humbug in recognition of her services to Trial by Television. Julian had been positively glowing in his congratulations. Hilary had said it had taken some fucking balls. Praise indeed.

Only Harry had remained aloof from the sensation. Watching silently through his camera. Observing, objective, detached.

And it was for him that she had done it. To prove – what?

That she was not afraid to die? Or that she was not capable of living? Pretty useless, either way.

No, it had been revenge on Leonie for daring to presume she could take her man, and on Julian Joffe for his pretentious voyeurism in the name of Art. But most of all it had been revenge on Mahon, for imagining he could poke his viscid little fingers into the recesses of her mind. Disgusting. It was worse than being raped. How wonderful it had been to play him at his own game. And win.

Did Harry understand all this? He must do. It was he who had set her to it in the first place. And if he didn't, there was no more she could do. He must live with it as best he could. Just as she had had to. Salvation comes from within.

Richard heard the roar of the Suzuki and almost ran to the window as Harry and Isobel came sweeping along the road and clattered to a halt in the driveway.

He watched silently as Harry lifted his wife off the bike and kissed her lightly on the cheek, before swinging the machine round and zooming away in the direction of Eastley.

Isobel came towards the house. Her face was glowing, not merely from the wind but with a sort of serenity. Something Richard had not seen for a long time.

Something's happened, he thought.

Chapter Twenty-six

'The man's bloody mad.' Richard, torn between righteous indignation that his wife should ride around the countryside on the back of another man's motorbike, and genuine concern for her mental and physical health, paced up and down the sitting room, slapping a rolled up newspaper against his hand for emphasis.

Isobel watched him mildly from the settee. 'Do stop stalking up and down like that. You're getting on my nerves.'

Richard stopped abruptly. 'Oh, well, I beg your pardon. I suppose it must be terribly irritating to have a husband who cares about your safety. I suppose you'd rather have one who lets you go tearing about the countryside till you end up in intensive care?'

'I thought I had,' said Isobel rather sharply.

'Oh god, Isobel. Don't start that again. Look, try to see it from my point of view. What if you'd fallen off? He wasn't doing twenty when you came up the road. Do you want to spend the rest of your life in plaster?'

Isobel shrugged. 'Well, you'd like it, wouldn't you?'

'What? Oh, that. That's a fantasy, Isobel. There's a distinction, in case you didn't know.'

'I didn't,' she retorted coldly. 'It's never been very apparent in this house.'

'Isobel,' Richard sank down on his haunches and took both of her hands in his, 'I know I'm not perfect. I know I've let you down sometimes. But can't you see, I'm worried about you? How would you feel if you thought I was off risking my life, just to impress some . . . some woman I didn't give two hoots for? I mean what would you think of me?'

Isobel looked at him. 'I'd be very surprised,' she said. 'And I wasn't risking my life. I was perfectly safe.'

'You don't know that. You've never been on one before in your life,'

'Yes, I have.'

'When?'

Isobel hesitated. 'A long time ago. Before I knew you.'

'Exactly. When you were young. You're not a teenager anymore, darling. You're forty. You've got to try and be sensible. What got into that bloke's head I'll never know. I suppose he's suffering from arrested development. Most of those media types are.'

'Don't talk about Harry like that. He's not a "media type", he's a professional cameraman. I bet he's got more to show for his life than you have for yours.' She snatched her hands away.

Richard rose slowly to his feet and gazed uneasily down at her. 'I daresay you're right. So he doesn't need your scalp as well, does he?'

Isobel picked up the *Radio Times* and scanned it earnestly. 'I don't know what you're talking about.'

Richard watched her. The church clock chimed six. 'I'd better go and fetch the children,' he said.

'Yes.'

'What will you do when this is over?'

'What?'

'The television business? Your ankle? Riding around on motorbikes?'

Isobel raised her eyes and looked at him. 'I expect I shall think of something.'

Richard nodded and sighed. 'I hope so,' he said.

Jenny was annoyed. It wasn't that she minded doing anyone a favour. Quite the reverse. She'd lost count of the number of times she'd run errands for Marjorie Bennett or Diana, in fact most of the people in the office seemed to have asked her to do something or other for them upon occasion – never with any offer of recompense – and she hadn't minded because she liked to be useful. But this was really going a bit far. Ashford was miles away. And to ask her to take the afternoon off, when she was running so short of holiday, just to chauffeur Anita and her instruments to some studio, goodness knows where – it wouldn't be near the health shop, you could be sure of that, which was really the main reason for going to Ashford as far as she was concerned – seemed to her a bit of a cheek. Particularly since it had cost her forty pounds to have the clutch put right after her friend's last expedition in the car.

Of course that was why Anita had asked her to take her this time. She was terrified of doing any more damage. And really it was rather a small car to expect her to drive. Especially since she was used to an automatic. And this was her big chance. It would be churlish of Jenny not to help out. After all, it was a one-off. If anything did come of Anita's contribution to the series then Jenny would make it quite clear that she thought a car of her own should be one of Anita's priorities. And it would be nice to think she'd helped a composer at the start of her career. Who knew? Perhaps in fifty years there would be a suite named after her.

Jenny rang the office and arranged to have the afternoon off.

Isobel picked up the phone and dialled Maureen's number. Maureen answered. 'Hullo, it's Isobel.'

'Isobel, did you want to speak to Harry?'

She was momentarily shocked by the question, then realised that it was perfectly innocent. 'No. It was you. I know it's very short notice. I just wondered if you fancied coming over for lunch today?'

There was a pause. 'Thank you. That would be very nice. What time would you like me?'

'Whatever suits. Half-past twelve? How will you get here? Can Harry give you a lift?'

'No, he was off to Ashford at first light. That Julian really gets his moneys-worth, doesn't he?'

'Seems to. Fran always looks on the point of total collapse.'
'Yes. Mind you, she strikes me as one of life's worriers.'
'Wrong kind of job for her, really.'
'She'd be just as fraught ironing handkerchieves.'
'I expect so. Do you know where we live, by the way?'
'First corner past the pier. Harry told me. Pebble Cottage.'
'Shingle. Are you going to get a cab?'
'I'll get a bus. I've got my pass.'
'It stops about two doors down. I'll look out for you.'
'Right. Bye for now.'
'Bye.'

Maureen arrived in excellent time. Isobel had made a lopsided quiche, the tilt due to her inability to hold the dish level while she put it in the oven. It was, however, the first bit of genuine cooking she had done since her accident and she was pleased with the result.

'I thought we could eat outside, unless you'd rather be in?'
'No, I love al fresco meals. Al fresco anything. I don't think I was meant to live in a house. A cave would have suited me far better. Open to the stars.'
'And the elements.'
'I suppose so. I'd still prefer it.'
'Do you want some of this wine, or would you like something else?'
'Wine would be lovely.'
They settled in the garden chairs.
'That must be coming off soon,' Maureen indicated Isobel's plaster.
'A week. I've timed it perfectly. End of filming, end of leg. Come to think of it, I don't know why Julian's so worried about a grand finale. He could have had the ceremonial removal of my plastercast.'
'Like cutting the cake?'
'Yes. Or they could have cracked a bottle of champagne against it. That might have been more significant.'
'More painful, too, I should imagine.'
'Do you think we'll have a party at the end?'

Maureen looked at her glass. 'End of what?'

'The series. The therapy sessions.'

'They won't finish just because the film crew does.' Isobel realised suddenly that this was true. 'I never thought of that. But I mean, surely you won't go on with it once this television lark is over, will you? I thought we were only sticking to it because they wanted the same people.'

'Is that why you go?'

Isobel felt slightly guilty. 'I don't know why I go,' she lied. 'I think it's all tied in with my ankle. I got roped into it by accident to start with, and then I decided I might be able to get something out of it – not from Dr Mahon's mail order psychology, you understand. It was purely a selfish motive. Most of mine are.'

'Like throwing yourself off a cliff?'

Isobel leant forward and picked up the bottle. 'You didn't believe that, did you?'

'You were very convincing.'

Isobel laughed. 'I meant to be. No, like not throwing myself off and pretending I had.'

'You certainly made Simon Mahon's day.'

'I certainly ruined Leonie's.'

Maureen smiled. 'I wondered,' she said. 'Harry's very fond of you, you know.' Isobel looked at her. It was impossible to tell what she knew or did not know. Isobel didn't want to be the one to ask.

Maureen stood up and wandered over to the lawn. 'I like this garden,' she said. 'I love gardenias. You've got masses.'

'They grow like weeds here. You must take some when you go.'

'Thank you. I will.'

Isobel struggled up. 'I'll get the lunch things.'

'I'll help you.'

'Do you think you'll keep going after Julian and his mob have gone?' Isobel asked again as they carried the food outside. For a moment Maureen said nothing and Isobel wondered if she had heard, then with a small dismissive shake of the head, Maureen said, 'I think I've got what I was looking for.'

'I shouldn't think that's very much. I can't see how anyone

gets anything from it. The man's a charlatan. And a bully. Poor old Meg'll probably end up a complete nervous wreck. I bet she's the other one.'

'Other what?'

'Suicide. Attempted. I was one, you see. Or so they liked to think. But there were two. Although I suppose dear Leonie's capable of the grand gesture.' She began to giggle. 'I bet she took a full-page advertisement in the *Mercury* before she did it.'

Maureen smiled. 'Poor Leonie. Nothing a good roll in the hay wouldn't cure, as we used to say.'

'Yes, well, she should find herself a man of her own,' said Isobel with sudden fury, adding hastily, 'I bet she's the sort who only falls for married men.'

Maureen helped herself to salad. 'A good marriage is a rare commodity,' she said thoughtfully. 'I was very lucky in mine.' Isobel was silent, thinking there was very little she could say to this.

'Harry misses his daughter,' said Maureen suddenly. 'I do know that.'

'It must be hard,' Isobel agreed, 'being separated from your children. However rotten things are.'

'I would think so. Separation is an awful thing.'

After lunch Isobel picked Maureen a huge bunch of gardenias. She had asked her to wait till Richard came home so that he could give her a lift. He was due back about four that afternoon because he had to go to a business dinner in the evening, but Maureen declined, saying she had a bit of shopping to do and wanted to be back before Harry to make sure the water was hot, as he always looked like a coalman when he'd been any distance on the bike. Isobel thought how happy Maureen looked when she spoke of Harry. She supposed she did too, and Leonie. Perhaps he had that effect on people, women anyway. She wondered how his ex-wife looked when he came to visit their daughter. They must be reasonably good friends because he seemed to go up there fairly frequently and had never hinted at any particular disruption between the pair of them. Other people's lives.

What a small patch of them was visible above the surface. Even the people you thought you knew best, you hardly knew at all. Perhaps it was better like that.

The children came home, were introduced to Maureen and allowed her to buy them large ice creams, under the pretext of escorting her to the bus stop. At the gate Maureen turned. 'I have enjoyed talking to you,' she said. 'It's helped to clear one or two things up.'

'Oh?'

'Yes. I just wasn't sure, you know, about the things you said yesterday.'

'Oh, that. Well, I hope I've set your mind at rest.'

Maureen smiled. 'Yes, you have,' she said. 'Goodbye, Isobel.'

Isobel watched her go. She looked more sprightly then she had of late as, flanked by Patrick and Eleanour, she led the way into the newsagent's to buy the ice creams.

Richard arrived home shortly afterwards. He had decided to give Jenny a miss this evening. Isobel was his chief concern at the moment. She had evidently got some sort of crush on this Harry bloke, albeit nothing could possibly come of it. No man in his right mind was going to start fooling around with a woman with one leg in plaster, particularly when he knew her husband was quite capable of breaking every bone in his body. Richard subconsciously flexed his muscles. But he did pose a slight danger, a) because Isobel should not be riding on the back of a motor bike in her condition, and b) because she was in a very vulnerable state emotionally at the moment. She obviously felt that she had to prove that she was still capable of the kind of crazy things she had done when she was young, like riding pillion on a motor bike. He couldn't for the life of him think when she might have done that. He'd known her off and on since she was eighteen so it must certainly have been before that. Also she might well be experiencing some sort of need to prove her continuing attractiveness. Women of her age often felt like that. Which might in turn lead her into making a fool of herself with this Peters bloke. No, he must devote a lot of care and attention to his wife over the coming weeks. Or at least the next ten days or so, till that blasted film crew were off the scene.

'Hullo, darling. Nice day?'
'Yes, thank you. Maureen came to lunch.'
'Maureen? From the hospital?'
'Yes.'
'You didn't say she was coming.'
'No. I just rang up and invited her. It was a spur of the moment decision.'
Richard eyed her suspiciously. 'Just her?'
'Yes.'
'Oh. Good. Did you have a nice lunch?'
'Quite. I made a flan.'
'Very nice. Has she gone?'
'Yes.'
'Pity. I could have given her a lift.'
'Yes, I said you would but she wanted to do some shopping. She's got Harry staying with her.'
'Harry who?'
'You know. Harry Peters, from the film crew. The one with the motorbike.'
'Did he come too?'
'No, of course he didn't. He's in Ashford.'
'What's he doing there?'
'How should I know? Something to do with the editing, I think. Julian's got to go to Africa so everything's a bit rushed all of a sudden.'
'Africa? Is Harry Peters going as well?'
'Not that I know of. I hadn't really thought about it. Would you like me to ask him?'
'No need for that. You're looking very pretty this afternoon. That colour really suits you. What do they call it?'
'Cream.'
'Yes, well, it suits you. You look very . . . young . . . er . . .'
'Thank you, Richard. Would you like a cup of tea?'
'Yes, please. Shall I make it?'
'If you like.'

'Look, I'm sorry about this do this evening. I don't think I can get out of it.'

Isobel looked at him in some surprise. 'Why should you want to?'

'Well, it's not very nice for you, being left on your own all day and then all evening as well.'

'I wasn't on my own. Maureen was here.'

'Oh, yes. Well, quite. It's just I don't want you to feel you have to invite people round just to fill in the time, if you see what I mean.'

'I didn't. I'm very fond of Maureen. I was jolly lucky she could come.'

'That's what I mean. You must get awfully lonely.'

'Richard, we've been over all this before. I don't get lonely. I'm not a lonely person. I like my own company, strange as it may seem. I am perfectly happy to spend the evening alone. Besides I won't be. Patrick and Elly are here and there's a play I want to watch on television. I promise not to get drunk or blow my brains out or whatever else you imagine four hours out of your company will induce me to do.'

Richard looked doubtful. 'I don't suppose you'd like Diana to pop in?'

'Frankly, no.'

'I just thought . . .'

'What is this, Richard?'

'Nothing. Just that I thought, you know, with being on your own so much, you might be missing . . . you might start thinking . . .'

'What?'

'Oh, nothing. I'd better go and get changed.'

Isobel watched him reverse the car out of the drive, the children kneeling either side of her to wave goodbye. 'Where's Daddy going?' asked Eleanour.

'To a meeting.'

'Who with?'

'Oh, some people at work.'

'Does Jenny work for Daddy, Mum? asked Patrick.

'No. He sometimes does business with the people where she works though. Why?'

'Just wondered. Whose friend is she then? Yours or his?'

Isobel hesitated. 'She's all of ours. She's what's known as a family friend.'

Patrick accepted this. Eleanour was slowly unravelling the fringe of a fraying cushion. 'Only Daddy's allowed to kiss her sometimes, isn't he?' she commented placidly.

Chapter Twenty-seven

The Nine O'Clock News had just ended when Isobel heard the screech of brakes outside. For a moment she thought it was Richard, back early, but the frenzied rapping on the door made this seem unlikely.

She pulled herself up, cursing since she would miss the beginning of the play, and went out into the hall. It was not quite dark outside and she could just make out a narrow frame against the frosted glass. She hoped to god it was not Diana, complete with happy thoughts and a sack of cast-off potato skins.

Anything but. There in the porch, face puffy and blotched with tears, stood Jenny Holt.

'Jenny! Whatever's the matter? Come in. What's happened?' She thought suddenly of Richard, and his anxiety that she should not be alone that evening. He hadn't ditched Jenny, had he, realising that she would make a beeline for Isobel? She had long distrusted Jenny's almost incestuous desire to be friends with her. Was this what it had all been leading up to? A sisterly shoulder to cry on? A shared burden of grief? Some hope, thought Isobel impassively. If anyone had walked into this it had been Jenny. It was time she grew up.

Even while she was thinking these things Isobel was leading the weeping Jenny into the sitting room, all hopes of her play now abandoned. 'Come and sit down and tell me what's the matter. Has there been an accident?' she asked with sudden sharpness, realising that Richard might at that moment be lying unconscious in some ditch.

'No, no ... That is ... it was an accident ... I didn't mean to see it. At least I did, but I didn't know. I never realised. When I said I wanted to watch, it was only curiosity. I never dreamt ... Oh, Isobel, I'm so ashamed. Can you ever, ever forgive me? I was such a fool. I wish it had been me. I do truly. Please believe me, I never meant ... it never occurred to me ... and please, please don't blame him ... Please try to understand, it didn't mean anything. It was all my fault.'

'Do you want a drink, Jenny? Would that calm you down, do you think?'

'No, no, I've taken enough from you already.'

'Well, half a glass of brandy isn't going to make much difference. Or would you like a cup of tea?'

Jenny's face registered flickering hope.

'Stay there while I go and put the kettle on. Here.' Isobel handed her a wodge of paper hankies from the box kept ready for the children. Passing the other room where her play was now in full throttle, she wondered if she had time to pop a video in and record it. She decided against this, however, on the grounds that it looked as though she were in for sufficient drama that night.

When she came back Jenny was sitting hunched on one end of the settee. She looks like a teenager caught smoking in the cloakrooms, thought Isobel, pouring herself a generous brandy. 'Are you sure you wouldn't like one of these?' Jenny looked up and shook her head violently.

'I'm afraid you'll have to fetch your own tea. I forgot I couldn't carry hot drinks.' To her dismay this brought forth fresh torrents of misery from Jenny, who looked as though she must be reaching the point of dehydration. Isobel took a large swig of brandy, then crossed to the settee and sat down beside her. She waited for a lull in the sobs and said quite firmly, 'Jenny, if you don't tell me why you're crying, I can't help. I can't even forgive you if that's what you want me to do, if I don't know what I'm forgiving you for.'

Jenny rocked from side to side. 'You never will anyway. You couldn't. No one could. I'll never forgive myself.'

This was becoming monotonous. Isobel half wished that

Richard would come home. Let him deal with it. That would serve him right. Keep him on the straight and narrow for a few weeks too, probably. Not that she cared. Or perhaps she did. She didn't know. She became aware that Jenny was trying to tell her something. It was extremely difficult to follow since Jenny stopped no more than four words into every sentence and began another one. She wondered if she should introduce her to Ken. They might be able to come to some arrangement whereby Jenny did the first part and he completed the remark. Like consequences, only not so amusing.

'You see, if Anita hadn't asked me to drive her, I'd never have gone in. But the studio's right out of town and there was absolutely nowhere for me to wait, so she asked the director if it would be all right for me to sit in the sort of waiting room while they were doing their recording, and he said he thought that would be all right.'

Isobel was tempted to ask 'In his own voice?' but thought this might confuse matters unnecessarily.

'Anyway they were gone such a long time and there was no coffee machine or anything and I'd had to work through my lunch hour so that I could have the afternoon off. I've got to go in at eight again tomorrow,' she added, momentarily distracted by this morbid thought, 'and then this man came out and asked if he could be of help, so I explained what I was doing there, and asked if he knew how much longer they were going to be, and he seemed to think it might be quite some while,' Jenny did not think Harry's 'fucking forever, love' was necessarily intrinsic to her narrative, 'and I asked if there was anywhere I could get something to drink and he showed me where there was a machine, but the thing was it was inside the studio and I had to creep in at the back, and Anita was just playing her pipes, so I couldn't use the machine till they'd finished, and so I just sat down, and while I was sitting there they put this film up on the screen and it was . . . it was . . .' Isobel felt like the victim of a shaggy dog story.

'What was it, Jenny?' she probed patiently. Then, 'Get to the point, can't you?'

The theory that a shock will cure hysterics went right out of the window as Jenny collapsed anew.

Isobel watched her for a few moments. The brandy had a very soothing effect on her. She felt detached and slightly bored. Jenny looked so very like a character from a soap opera, hands clutching and reclutching, hair tousled, face shining with glycerine tears. Except the tears were real, there was no doubt of that. Whatever could have happened to make Jenny, whose emotional depth she had always likened to a road marking, so unhappy? Perhaps she had run over a pigeon on the way to work, but that had nothing to do with Isobel. No, this was definitely connected with Ashford and the television series. She stiffened suddenly. Had Harry screwed her in the back of the studio, up against the drinks machine? If this was to be her confession she, Isobel, would personally fetch Jenny's tea from the kitchen and throw the boiling liquid in her face. If she had laid one finger on Harry . . .

She became aware that Jenny was quietening down a little. She was now at the shiver, sniff, swallow stage. This in turn would presumably lead in time to coherence. Not yet though. Watching Jenny swaying rhythmically to the sound of her own mucus Isobel began to wonder if the noise was perhaps a mantra. She rose. Jenny started violently.

'Jenny, why don't you go and get your tea, before it gets cold, then we can talk,' she said kindly.

'Whatever it is I'm sure you'll feel better when you've told someone about it.'

Jenny rose and crossed the room like a sleepwalker. Isobel took the opportunity of her absence to replenish her glass. She'd forgotten how beautiful brandy was. Beaming beatifically she settled herself on the couch and waited for Jenny.

The humble pad of moccasined feet along the hall heralded her return, black tea trembling in her hands. 'I'm sorry I was so long,' she murmured meekly. 'I was afraid of spilling it on your lovely carpet.' Her voice broke as a fresh supply of water came trickling from her eyes. Isobel sighed and reached for the box of hankies.

'Never mind my lovely carpet, Jenny. I want to know what's bothering you.' She took a breath. 'Is it about Richard?'

Jenny hiccupped violently and the tea leapt from the mug on to her lap. Isobel mopped her up, although her skirt was now so wet and the drink so cold that the operation seemed mainly superfluous. She decided that some sort of prompt would be necessary if this were not to turn into an all-night sitting.

'Jenny, I know about you and Richard.'

This time Jenny dropped the cup. Isobel closed her eyes as the younger woman went down on her hands and knees and blotted the rug with her skirt. She was half tempted to say that she would send for Mrs Beasley in the morning if Jenny were that bothered about the state of her furnishings. Perhaps she had gone about it the wrong way. Perhaps she should have let Jenny tell her in her own time. These things should not be rushed. Elementary psychology. Even Simon Mahon had subscribed to that theory. At least he had until it had threatened to interfere with his debut as Mind Show Host.

She leant forward. 'Jenny, please get up. It doesn't matter about the rug, honestly. You didn't come here to clean the floor, you came to talk to me. Richard will be back soon. Would you rather wait until he got here and we can discuss it all together?'

This had the desired effect in that Jenny shot off her knees like a bullet from a gun and, clutching feverishly at Isobel's hands – she only just managed to save her brandy – besought her not to let Richard in until Jenny had said her piece and gone. This struck Isobel as a totally admirable proposal, since the prospect of Richard prowling the streets, barred from his own house while his mistress informed on his every aberration, appealed to her greatly.

'Now,' said Isobel gently, 'you were telling me about the drinks machine in the studio.'

'No,' said Jenny desperately, 'the machine didn't work. I think they'd forgotten to refill it or something.'

'Is that what upset you?' Isobel strove to keep the edge out of her voice.

'No. It was the film. You see, I know I shouldn't have seen it – it was a total accident.'

'Yes, yes. I realise that. What exactly did you see, Jenny, that has upset you so much?'

Jenny looked at her, wide eyes round with despair and hopelessness. 'I saw you.'

Isobel gasped with relief. 'Is that all? I know I'm not the most photogenic person in the world, Jenny, but I never thought I could occasion quite such misery. What exactly did you see?' Jenny's mouth was working but no words were coming out. Isobel looked at her.

'You saw the interview, didn't you?'

Jenny nodded.

'You said ... You said ... you tried to ... Oh, Isobel, how could you? How could you let us make you that unhappy? I didn't know, you see. I'm so stupid and blind, and I *loved* him so much, you see. I couldn't see beyond that. You always seemed so ... contented and ... and peaceful. As if everything was all right. Sometimes I almost thought you knew and you didn't mind, and all the time ... Oh, Isobel. I shall never, never forgive myself. Never, never.'

Her head sank low and for a moment Isobel feared a renewal of the tears, but even Jenny's metabolism could not work in overdrive forever and she merely sat, face in hands, as in some elaborate game of hide-and-seek. Surreptitiously Isobel reached for her brandy. She took a deep gulp and wondered what to do. If she forgave Jenny openly she ran the risk of her eternal gratitude, or alternatively of her taking it carte blanche to carry on the affair with all its attendant aggravations. If, on the other hand, she played the aggrieved wife, who knew what Jenny might do in her present state? She didn't think she would go as far as trying to kill herself too, but she might well have a nervous breakdown or something and lose her job, which would be a bit unfair considering it was mainly Richard's fault – of that she felt sure. She could hardly see Jenny instigating an affair with anyone, let alone a man like Richard. She became aware that Jenny was watching her, almost eagerly. It was as though, having said her piece she was now waiting for marks out of ten.

No faults for performance, thought Isobel, you cunning little drip! But she was no slouch, either, if the effect of the film were anything to go by. Perhaps they should join forces to wreak some terrible revenge on the prodigal husband. Not worth it, she decided. She suddenly felt very tired.

'Jenny,' she said, 'I want you to make me a promise.'

'Anything. Anything.'

'I want you to promise to say nothing about this to Richard.'

'But . . .'

'Or anyone else. In fact, I want you to forget all about it. The film, tonight, everything.'

'How can I? I shall never forget it as long as I live.'

Isobel eyed her grimly. 'If you don't, I can't answer for my future actions.'

'Oh, Isobel,' Jenny seized her in genuine panic, 'don't say that. Please don't say that. I'll do anything you say. I promise. I'll never see Richard again. Anything. I'll leave the district. I'll give up my job.'

'There's no need for anything like that, Jenny. Listen to me for a moment. Let me speak to you, woman to woman.' A slight glow of hope entered Jenny's forlorn eyes. 'You've done a horrid thing, there's no doubt about that. But so have I. You wanted to take Richard away from his family . . .'

'I never wanted that. You must believe me, Isobel. I never wanted him to forsake you and the children. They're such lovely children.' A fresh batch of tears were on their way.

'Yes. Well, let's leave that, shall we? The point is, what I did was even worse. It was an act of revenge. I didn't think about the possible consequences. Of Richard having to manage on his own. Of the effect on the children growing up without a mother.'

'I would have helped him,' murmured Jenny through her tears.

Isobel resisted the desire to throttle her. 'Now, no one we know knows about that interview yet, except you and I. Richard doesn't even know. I want you to promise me to say nothing to anyone. I know they'll find out in time, when the film's transmitted, but that could be months, years even from now.'

Isobel put on her frail but courageous face. 'I've been ill. I've been hurt. Sometimes I've wondered if I'm going out of my mind. But time is a wonderful healer. I think maybe this accident may turn out to have been a blessing in disguise – perhaps for all of us. Richard has come to appreciate how important his home is to him. You have realised just how much damage an extra-marital affair can do to a family. And

I have had time to come to terms with my own weaknesses and failings. Perhaps this is Fate's way of offering us a new beginning.'

The perfect thing would have been to have taken Jenny's hands and kissed her lightly on the forehead, but Isobel was afflicted with a sudden distaste for Jenny's pastel skin. Besides, Richard had done more than enough in that direction on the Day family's behalf.

She heaved herself to her feet, determined to bring the confidences to a close. Jenny rose like someone in receipt of a vision. 'Thank you, Isobel.'

'There's nothing to thank me for.'

Jenny gave a small deprecating laugh. 'Oh, but there is,' she said. Impulsively she flung her arms round Isobel's shoulders and hugged her. An aura of peaches and salt water assailed her. 'Thank you for being you.'

Isobel staggered slightly under the onslaught, but regained her balance in time to see Jenny rushing blindly from the room. At the front door she turned and, gazing with total honesty at her erstwhile rival, said meekly, 'My greatest wish is that I shall be like you when I'm forty, Isobel.'

And mine is that you get four flat tyres on the way home, thought Isobel, watching her bumping away down the road.

'God, that was boring.' Richard, flushed with wine and a very good dinner, came lumbering into the television room. 'Good play?'

'Not very,' said Isobel. 'I turned it off.'

'Oh poor you. So you've had a boring evening all on your own.'

'I wouldn't say that,' said Isobel.

Chapter Twenty-eight

'I've got some news.' Harry stood leaning against the porch, much the way he had that first day, when there had still been time to stay friends.

'So've I,' said Isobel, hoping his was more cheerful than hers.

Despite all, she had been shaken by Jenny's confession the night before. That ridiculous charade with Simon Mahon was obviously more convincing than she had realised. Even Maureen seemed to have felt some doubts about how much of it was invention. 'What's yours?'

'Maureen's going away for the weekend. She asked me if I'd like to stay down. Have the place to myself. Keep an eye on things. It's quite a rough neighbourhood round there.'

'What are you saying?'

Harry walked past her into the hall and shut the door. 'I'm saying, can you get away? Pretend you've got a sick aunt, anything. Spend the night with me.'

Isobel stared at him. 'I can't. How can I possibly? At the weekend? In Maureen's house? You must be mad. I couldn't do that. It would be so deceitful.'

Harry shook his head. 'You don't understand. She wants you to come.'

'How can she? Harry, you haven't told her, have you? About us? Oh, how could you?'

'I haven't told her anything. She just knows, that's all.'

'How can she know unless you told her? I certainly haven't. Unless that maniac hypnotised me when I wasn't looking and dragged the whole thing out of me. Did that happen?'

'Isobel, believe me, I haven't told her anything. She didn't say in so many words. She just said "treat it as home".'

'Yes, but that doesn't mean . . .'

' ". . . and invite someone round if you want to". She's not daft, you know. She knows what's going on.'

'You can't be sure of that. Anyway, if she knows, presumably so do all the others. But we've been so careful.'

Harry smiled. 'We haven't been at all careful, actually, Isobel. But that lot are far too wrapped up in themselves to notice anything outside. Maureen's different. She's a friend.'

Isobel sighed. 'I know she is. That's why . . . Oh, this is hopeless. Anyway, I couldn't get away even if I wanted to.'

'And you don't want to?'

Isobel leaned her head against the door and closed her eyes. 'I didn't say that.' She felt Harry close to her, the rip of his leather jacket as he unzipped it, the tang of his skin, the indescribable desire that overwhelmed her in his presence. Perhaps Renate would have the children on Saturday . . .

'What was your news?' asked Harry. They were lying on the spare room bed drinking warm beer which Isobel had forgotten to put in the frig. She put her hand to her head. 'It's not really news. I had a visit from Jenny last night.'

'Who's Jenny?'

'Richard's mistress. The one I told you about.'

'How many's he got?'

'This is serious. I don't understand the ins and outs of it, but it turns out she knows Anita Craven – the music woman – and Anita must have asked her to give her a lift to the studio in Ashford, and she had to miss lunch or something – I don't think I was listening at that point. But anyway she says she asked some bloke where she could get a drink and he said there was a machine inside the actual recording area, and when she got in they were showing my bit with Mahon, and so of course she got completely the wrong end of the stick – as she always does, may I add – and assumed it was the real thing and that I'd tried to kill myself because of her and Richard. So she came round to confess and beg my forgiveness and goodness knows what else.'

'Did you give it to her?'
'What?'
'Your forgiveness.'
'I can't remember. Probably. I was getting to the point where I'd have given her the Crown Jewels just to get rid of her.'

'What about Richard? Where was he while all this was going on?'

'Out at a business do, thank god. I don't think I could have coped with the two of them repenting. Why are you looking at me like that?'

Harry continued to gaze at her. Finally he shook his head. 'Maureen was right about you.'

'Why? What did she say?'

'She said she'd never seen anyone who fought her feelings so hard.'

Isobel spluttered with laughter. 'But that's absurd. I haven't exactly concealed them from you, have I? I haven't concealed them from Dr Mahon either, if it comes to that. Why should Maureen think that? She's quite wrong.'

Harry traced her face very lightly with his finger, stopping by the tiny lines around her nose and mouth. 'I don't think so,' he said. 'This is a very stiff upper lip.' He kissed her and rolled off the bed. 'I'm off.'

'Where? Ashford?'

'Birmingham.'

'Birmingham? But I thought you were staying down.'

'Just a quick trip. I'll be back tomorrow evening. I'll give you a ring then. Try and fix it for the weekend.' He winked at her. 'I'll make it worth your while.'

Despite herself, Isobel found herself blushing. 'I can't promise,' she said uneasily. 'I may not be able to get away.'

'I know. Do you think I should put Leonie on standby?'

The pillow hit him as he was halfway down the stairs.

Isobel watched him from the bedroom window as he rode away into the sunshine. A knight in shiny leather. And she was the prisoner in the tower, chained by her leg and her upbringing and her home and her family and her complete inability to be herself, except for those few precious seconds when she had seen the world for what it was worth and made her decision accordingly. Those few precious seconds before she fell.

Richard was worried. He had absolutely no objection to the children spending the night at his mother's. Quite the opposite. They hadn't been to stay since Isobel's stop in hospital and had mentioned the fact dejectedly to him more than once. It was a good idea.

What really bothered him was Isobel's declared intention to go and visit an old school friend, Melanie Harper, whom she knew he couldn't stand. Why this weekend of all weekends? True, he had mentioned that he had bumped into Marjorie Bennett again and that she was proposing to stop by to talk to Isobel about her 'Sewing for Albania' project, but that was no reason for Isobel to leave the county for twenty-four hours. Or was it? It really had been a bit silly of him to admit that they would be around. And Isobel wasn't going for a whole day; just Saturday afternoon till Sunday morning. Come to think of it, she'd been planning to visit that dratted Harper woman before her accident. It might be just as well to get it out of the way. After all, once her ankle was better there'd be so much for them to do together. Richard would take up tennis again. He liked it better than squash, and the women were a lot prettier in general. Not that that signified because he was going to be in love with Isobel again. He rather thought he might be already.

This might also be a good opportunity to make a tentative break with Jenny. There was still one more Tuesday afternoon to go, but the arrangement so far had not proved an unmitigated success; Jenny had actually brought work home with her last time, and he seemed to be spending more time under her car bonnet than her authentic Silesian quilt these days. Yes, all in all he thought it might work out quite well.

'How will you get to Melanie's if you go?' he enquired.

'Train, I suppose. I can get a cab down to Eastley.'

'Nonsense, I'll drive you to the station. I'm just wondering if I should take you the whole way. It won't be easy for you on crutches if you've got luggage as well.'

'I won't have any luggage,' Isobel said quickly. 'It's only

for one night. Clean knickers and a toothbrush, that's all I'll need.'

'Even so.'

'Richard, think about it,' said Isobel with an air of desperation, 'if you drive me all the way there, you'll have to come in. You can't possibly travel a hundred miles and just turn round and go back. And I'll have to catch the train home on Sunday anyway, so what would be the point?'

Richard wavered. 'I still don't like to think of you . . .'

'Melanie will meet me at the station. It's arranged. I shall ring her from Eastley to tell her which train I'm catching and she'll come and fetch me at Haslemere. It couldn't be simpler.'

'Well . . .'

'And I want to finish my library book. It's due back on Monday, and you know I can't read in the car.'

'I suppose it'll be all right.'

'Of course it will. There's no real need for you to drive me to the station, either. The local chap's quite cheap.'

'No, that I will do. I want to make sure you're safely on the train.'

'Oh, Richard, what a fusspot you are.'

'Maybe so, but I'll feel safer knowing you're on your way.'

Isobel sighed. 'If it makes you happy.'

'Half an hour!' Richard, already hot and bothered from another road diversion, stared accusingly at the man in the ticket office. 'I thought they went at a quarter to.' He turned to Isobel. 'I thought you said you checked.'

'Yes, I did. I must have been looking at weekdays instead of Saturdays. Look, there's no need for you to wait. You get on back or you'll miss the Test Match.'

'I've missed most of it already,' said Richard despondently, forgetting that he was about to be parted from the woman he loved.

'Well, you go. There's bound to be a hold-up on the road by the roundabout and the longer you leave it the worse it'll get.'

'Bloody rallies,' muttered Richard. 'Why can't they save

someone else's souls? What's wrong with a few Sussex souls for a change?'

'Did you want a ticket or not, sir?' the assistant asked wearily from behind the grille.

'Yes, yes.' Richard fumbled for his wallet.

'No, hang on, darling.' Isobel dragged him aside. 'I think I'll call Melanie first. Make sure everything's all right.'

'Why shouldn't it be?'

'No reason. I'd just feel better if I did.'

'Right, I'll wait.'

'Honestly, there's no need. You get on home. I've got masses of time. I shall probably get a cup of coffee and wait in the buffet on the platform.'

'Supposing she's not there?'

'She will be. Look, if you're so worried, come across with me to the phone box.'

'Yes, all right.'

The two of them crossed to the kiosk and Isobel manoeuvred her way in. Carefully she consulted her diary and, turning her back on Richard, dialled Maureen's number. After what seemed an age she heard Harry's voice. 'Hullo, it's me,' she said in the preferred modulation of the Haywain Players.

'Are you coming?'

'Yes, Richard's just seeing me off at the station. The train's at a quarter past two so he's not going to wait,' she enunciated with the clarity of someone addressing a congregation of lip-readers.'

'You're at Eastley?'

'Yes, that's right. About a quarter past four, I should think. And I can catch a train about ten tomorrow.'

'Ten minutes. I'll be with you in ten minutes.'

'See you soon. Bye, Melanie.'

'Melanie!' They were lying on Harry's rug under the cherry tree that sheltered Maureen's garden from the prying eyes of her neighbours. 'I should have thought you could have thought of a better name than that.'

'She's the only one of my friends Richard really detests. I

don't like her much, actually, but I've known her since school and she's had a bit of a rotten time of things. Husband deserting her, had to sell her horse to pay the mortgage; her business isn't doing too well, either.'

'What's she do?'

'She sells handmade jewellery. Got quite a few out-workers – did have. She's had to lay half of them off.'

'Sounds like you were in for a jolly weekend.'

Isobel smiled. 'I feel very guilty. Lying to Richard. I keep thinking there's going to be ring at the door and there he'll be, full of wrath and righteous indignation.'

Harry looked at his watch. 'You've got two hours till the cricket finishes. We'll expect him after that. Meanwhile,' he leant over her and began to undo the elegant, 'visiting old schoolfriend's blouse.'

'Harry, not out here. I'm sure people can see.'

'No, they can't. They're all watching cricket.'

'Not everyone watches cricket. You don't.'

'I do normally. It's only because you're here I'm not.'

'What's that supposed to mean?'

'It means,' said Harry, reaching his hand up her skirt and slowly rubbing her pudenda, 'that anyone who's not watching cricket is doing this.'

At precisely ten past six there was a frantic ringing on the doorbell. Isobel was in the kitchen inspecting Harry's provisions for their dinner. She froze as Harry, who was searching Maureen's cupboards for a corkscrew, cursed and went to answer the door. 'Don't let him in,' squeaked Isobel, hiding first behind the kitchen door and then, with a stroke of desperation, inside the broom cupboard, which hardly had room for the hoover, let alone a full-grown woman with a leg in plaster.

From inside her hiding place she heard the sound of voices, one high and semi-hysterical, the other gruff.

'Come in,' she heard Harry say. 'It's in there. Do you want me to call them?'

It certainly wasn't Richard. Isobel crept furtively from the cupboard, knocking over a mop as she did so. Again she froze. Nothing happened, however, and the ping of the phone being replaced marked the end of the invasion as the couple, still talking nervously, hurried back into the street with Harry following.

Isobel peeked round the door. The front door was wide open. Yellowy-white smoke was billowing plenteously along the street. Cautiously she crossed the hall and peered out. The street was full of people standing in agitated clusters on the opposite pavement. Harry was nowhere to be seen. From the ground floor of the next-door house acrid flames were pouring, the whole of the front garden blackened by the heat. The bay of sirens heralded the arrival of the fire brigade, shortly followed by an ambulance and two police cars.

The firemen set to work. The fire was clearly less serious than had at first appeared for they managed to control it remarkably quickly. The ambulance had stopped some way along the road. It was then that Isobel saw Harry. He was standing by an elderly man who seemed to be in some distress. Harry spoke to the ambulance driver and then turned and led the way into someone's house. The driver returned and summoned his colleague, the two of them carrying a stretcher into the house and reappearing with a large red-blanketed lump which they duly placed in the vehicle. Harry came out and said something to the old man who followed the stretcher into the ambulance. The driver shut the doors and, sirens blaring, set off in the direction of St Clare's. Harry exchanged a few words with one of the firemen who were now clearing up their equipment, then hurried back towards where Isobel was now standing in full view of the neighbours in Maureen's front garden. She had realised by now that the presence of a strange woman with a strange man at number forty-two was no longer a front page item for the people of Clitheroe Gardens.

'It's the same bloody woman.' Harry emerged from the bathroom rubbing himself with a towel. 'She must be mad. Kettle without a plug. Sticks two matches in the socket and tucks the wires in. The fireman reckons she did it on purpose.'

'Perhaps she wanted the insurance.'

'A few more minutes and she wouldn't have needed it. Taken the old man with her as well. He was in the front room watching cricket.'

'Let that be a lesson to him,' said Isobel, then felt guilty at her levity. 'Was the woman all right? I saw them putting her in the ambulance.'

'Smoke inhalation. They reckoned it wasn't too serious. I tell you something, I wouldn't want to live round here with a nutter like that on the loose. You'd never know where she was going to strike next.'

'Poor Maureen,' Isobel agreed. 'It must be pretty unsettling.'

'Maureen is going to move. She told me.'

'Oh? Where to? Did she say?'

Harry shook his head. 'She was a bit vague about it. I think that's why she's gone away this weekend. To have a look around. She said something about the west country. She comes from Devon, apparently. Hadn't been back there for years, she said. Not since her husband got ill. She said they got married down there. Planning to retire there, too, till things went wrong. She could do worse.'

'I hope she doesn't find it's changed too much,' said Isobel. 'She deserves to be happy. I still don't understand why she goes to Mahon's circus. It can't be doing her any good. She's better adjusted than anyone I've ever met.'

Harry was silent for a moment. 'I don't think she had much choice,' he said. 'Doctors.'

'Bunch of bullies,' said Isobel without enthusiasm. 'I shall be so glad to be free of them all. Four more days and I shall be rid of this damn plaster. D'you know what I'll do? I shall do cartwheels all round the town. I shall be able to wear shorts again. Just imagine. Shorts. No I shan't. I'm going to have this one horrible skinny white leg. I shall never be able to wear shorts again. My life is over.' She sank dramatically on to the bed.

'I'm forty years old and I can't wear shorts. It's all too much. I shall kill myself.'

Harry who had been laughing, stopped and frowned at her. 'Don't say things like that.'

Isobel looked at him. 'It was only a joke. God, Harry, you don't think I meant to do it as well, do you? I don't think I can bear much more of this. What do I have to do to prove it was an accident? Lead a party of experts up to the cliff and show them how it's done? Drink too much, stand too near, look too close . . .' Her face suddenly crumpled at the memory of what she had seen that day.

Harry put his arm round her. 'Don't think about it anymore. It's done now. Over. As you say, you'll soon be free. Mind you, I don't know if I want to make love to a woman with two legs.'

'Pervert. I'm dreading it actually. You'll hate me. One brown leg and one white.'

'You've got that now.'

'So I have. It's not the same though. I wonder if I could get some of that leg makeup. My mother used to use it when she couldn't afford stockings. Bright orange, as I remember. She used to draw seams, too. Right up the back of her legs. They were always crooked. I could never work out what she was doing, till her sister came to lunch one Sunday, and of course she had the real thing, being married to an accountant. Mother was so jealous, bless her. I remember that. She could hardly take her eyes off them all through lunch. She kept taking surreptitious peeps at them under the table.'

'Whereas if it had been you, you'd've known how to get yourself a pair of stockings.'

'Are you casting aspersions on my chastity?'

'Yes.'

Isobel stretched. 'You're probably right. I'm starving. What are we going to have for dinner?'

'Steak. Is that all right?'

'Wonderful.' She laughed.

'What are you laughing at?'

'I was just thinking, if it hadn't been for Richard wanting steak that night we'd never have met up in the pub and all this . . . Oh god, Harry, I do feel guilty, you know. Poor Richard. All by himself at home. The cricket's over now. Whatever's he going to do with himself all evening? Would you mind very much if I gave him a ring? Just to say I've arrived safely and everything? Would that be all right?'

Harry looked decidedly annoyed. 'No, why not? Invite him over. There's enough steak. We could have a barbecue in the remains of forty-four.'

'Don't be so horrid. All right I won't. I just thought if I gave him a quick ring it would make things look more . . . real, if you see what I mean.'

Harry grinned ruefully. 'You're right. Come on, I'll give you a lift downstairs. I'm going to start cooking anyway.'

He deposited her in the sitting room by the phone. Isobel noted how neat everything was. She wondered if Maureen had been spring-cleaning. She didn't look an obsessively tidy woman. Far too sensible for that. But the whole house was immaculate, there was no denying, even with Harry in situ. Slowly she dialled her number. The phone rang for several moments before Richard answered. He sounded rather breathless. 'Hullo, Richard.'

'Isobel? Where are you? What's happened? Are you all right?' So much for reassuring him.

'Of course I am. I just phoned to say I'd arrived safely and everything's fine.'

'Did thing meet you all right?'

'Yes, she did.'

'Good. What time train are you catching tomorrow? I'll meet you at the station.'

Isobel paused. 'I'm not exactly sure. You know what Sunday trains are like. I think there's some trouble with works on the line, Melanie said. Don't worry. I'll get a cab. I'll be home by one, I promise. If not, I'll give you a call.'

'Are you sure?'

'Positive. How was the cricket?'

'The what?'

'The cricket. Did you get back in time to see some of it?'

'Oh, yes. Not bad. Not too good. Pretty bloody useless really. Look, darling, I must dash. I've got something under the grill. See you tomorrow. Have a nice night.'

Isobel swallowed. 'Yes. All right. Goodnight, Richard.'

'Goodnight, darling.' His voice dipped. 'I love you.'

'What?'

'I said, I love you . . . Isobel . . . are you still there?'

'Yes. Goodnight, Richard.' She replaced the phone. Harry

appeared at the door with a large glass of wine which he handed her. 'Everything all right?'

Isobel accepted the wine and stared at it dolefully. 'Yes,' she said. 'Everything's fine.'

Chapter Twenty-nine

'Richie . . .' Richard put down the phone and turned towards the kitchen where rather large plumes of smoke were issuing from the direction of the stove. 'I think this meat's nearly done.'

Richard leapt and tore towards the kitchen where Jenny, in scalloped apron, was prodding nervously at the charred surface of his prime porterhouses.

'Jenny, for god's sake, what did you put them under the grill for? I told you to let me cook them.' He snapped off the gas and gazed in mute fury at the crusty steak.

'I'm sorry. I was only trying to help.'

'Well, you haven't helped. You've ruined them. Look at them. They're burnt right through. Christ, woman, don't you know how to cook a steak?'

'I don't like red meat,' sniffed Jenny, the tears beginning to well in her eyes. 'It's not good for you.'

'It's better than eating coal,' said Richard crossly, then noticing her tears, put the pan aside and went to comfort her. 'Poor Jenny. Did I shout at you? I'm sorry.' For a moment he wondered if this fatherly approach were the right one. Jenny was gazing at him with such lapdog adoration that he wondered whether perhaps he should not have continued to bellow abuse at her. You never knew with Jenny. She was the kind of creature who rather thrived on being trodden on.

He wished Isobel had not phoned. She had made him feel guilty, although his motives were, for once, entirely pure. He had brought Jenny here to explain to her that now that

Isobel was nearly herself again, he had made the difficult decision that he must try to mend his marriage.

There had been faults on both sides, of that there could be no doubt, and Jenny had been to him, in this time of trial and isolation, a beacon of succour and support – she would like that – a tower of strength, even. He would always remember their time together with joy and affection, but she must understand now that he had no choice in the matter. Isobel needed him and he must stand by her. So it was he had made his painful – heartbreaking? No, not heartbreaking – he must exude staunchness and determination or she'd find a chink and be in there, forgiving him and agreeing to wait. He must make a clean break – painful decision that they must part, at least in the physical sense of the word.

What kind of a man would he be to hold on to her, when he would never be free to give her what every woman has a right to expect from her man – a home and family? He could bear it no longer. He had seen the look in her eye when she had told him about Diana's decision to have a fatherless child. That was not for her. She must not end up like that, bitter, alone, on the shelf.

'Do you forgive me, darling?' Jenny was watching the various changes in Richard's expression with some alarm as he ran through his proposed oration.

'What? Oh, yes, of course I do, Jenny dear. Now be a pet and wash that lettuce for me, will you? There's not much you can do to ruin a lettuce.'

Jenny bit her lip and crossed to the sink where she was soon rather fiercely tearing the leaves from Richard's Cos and flinging them recklessly into the salad shaker.

'That's a good girl,' murmured Richard, under the impression that he was soothing her troubled feelings.

The two of them worked in silence for some minutes. Richard had extracted an emergency steak from the freezer and was busy chopping garlic with which to douse it. Jenny finished the lettuce and began to make water lilies with the tomatoes. To the casual observer it would have been hard to credit that these two people were on the verge of a major turning point in their lives. For Jenny, too, had come with a purpose, equally pure, equally distressing. Her heart had sunk when she saw the scarlet oozing greaseproof surrounding her supper. For a moment she had been smitten with the ignoble thought that Richard had bought it intentionally, knowing how much she disapproved, but such calumny was immediately retracted as she remembered that it was she, and not he, who was about to break off their affair.

She had brought a side salad of dried bananas and watercress and a bowl of pumpkin mousse which Diana had given her last autumn and had lain in her freezer cabinet ever since. Dear Richie deserved something nice for his pudding. Isobel never seemed to have anything but ice cream or cheese, both very high in cholesterol. Isobel. She shuddered unconsciously at the memory of Wednesday's encounter, then stiffened her shoulders. This she would do for Isobel. For sisterhood. For womankind.

'Are you chilly, dar – Jenny?' asked Richard, noticing her trembling frame.

'No. That is, I might just get my shawl.'

'Shall I get it for you?'

'Oh, would you, Richie d –?'

'Of course.' Richard fetched the paisley confection and draped it carefully round Jenny's shoulders. She stood meekly still, like a child being dressed by its nanny. Richard's manner was totally in keeping. He watched with satisfaction as her small hands wriggled free of the folds and adjusted the turtle brooch at her neck.

'Ready to eat?'

'Yes, please.'

Jenny washed her hands.

'Jenny . . .'. They were sitting on the patio watching the last of the sunset. Richard was being bitten by gnats but decided not to make a fuss about it, since he had fixed this setting in his mind as the most suitable for what must inevitably be a painful interlude.

'Yes?'

'I have something to say to you.'

'I have something to say to you too, Richard.'

'Oh. Would you like to go first? That was a very nice mousse, by the way,' he added, fearful that future opportunities to praise it might not be forthcoming.

Jenny sighed. 'No. You go first.'

Richard cleared his throat. 'This is going to be very difficult.'

'Not as difficult as mine.'

'I think it will be.'

'It won't.'

This tit-for-tat trading of calamities might have continued for some time, had not Richard, irritated, resolved to grasp the nettle and prove the superiority of his claim.

'It's all over,' he said abruptly, staring directly ahead and resisting the urge to slam the midget which was gorging itself on his ankle.

There was a pause.

'What is?' asked Jenny ingenuously.

Richard frowned at her obtuseness. 'Us. You and me. I'm sorry to break it to you this way, but it can't go on. I have to think of Isobel. She's been very ill. I have to try and help her, for the sake of our marriage – the children. I know this must come as a terrible shock to you, and I want you to know that I will always cherish the memory of our time together. We can still be . . .'

'Wait a minute, Richard. Are you saying that you want to break it off with me? To end our affair?'

Richard was temporarily shocked. He had never heard Jenny speak so sharply before.

'Er . . . Yes, I'm afraid . . . You see, Isobel needs me . . . You're young, you've got all your life before you . . . I shall always remember our time together.'

'Yes, all right, Richard. So shall I. I do think you might have let me say something first.' Jenny pulled her shawl tight around her. 'I have to tell you, Richard, that you have an awful habit of overriding other people's opinions. It's not very attractive in a man.'

Richard sat back, stunned. 'I beg your pardon,' he said weakly. 'I thought it would be best to get it out in the open.' His tone softened. 'I realise this has come as a great shock to you, Jenny. And maybe I haven't been as tactful as I should. I just happen to believe that these things are best got over with, if you see what I mean. I certainly didn't mean to upset you – more than I had to, I mean. I shall always remember . . .'

'Yes. You said that. The thing is, Richard, it was all over between us anyway.'

'What?'

'Yes. That's why I came tonight, even though I knew Isobel would be away and that you could only have one possible purpose in mind. I came to tell you that I had reached a decision.'

'What sort of decision?'

'You're doing it again. I wish you'd let me finish just one sentence in my life.'

'I wish I thought you were capable of it,' said Richard, caught off-guard.

'Thank you. The decision I have come to is that I must give you up.'

'You give me up?'

'Yes. I have thought long and hard about this, Richard. I know how much pain it will cause you, believe me. But you have a wonderful wife in Isobel, and wonderful children . . .' Jenny began to sniff, caught up in the pathos of it all. Richard sat stiffly apart from her. 'And you owe it to them to try and make a go of your marriage. You don't know what a jewel you have in Isobel,' she warmed to her subject, 'and you're a fool to put her love for you at risk this way.' She paused. Richard poured himself more wine and stared grimly ahead.

'I know what I'm about to say will hurt you, Richard . . .'

'Don't count on it,' Richard muttered morosely.

'But I'm a young woman. I've got all my life before me, and you're . . . well, you're well into middle age, aren't you?'

This could not be allowed to pass. 'I most certainly am not and I resent you talking about me as though I was some clapped-out post office counter clerk! I might remind you, Jenny, that you're very nearly thirty, a spinster and likely to remain one, so let's have a bit less of the "over the hill" syndrome, please.'

Jenny pouted. 'I knew you'd be cross. Diana warned me.'

'Warned you what?'

'That you couldn't stand being reminded of your age.'

'What the fuck's it got to do with Diana?'

Jenny gave him an old-fashioned look. 'By the way,' she said sweetly, 'you needn't worry. You're not on her list.'

'Her what? What list?'

Jenny continued to look at him a trifle smugly. 'Her list of potential fathers. She's worried your sperm count might be too low.'

Richard became aware that his mouth was opening and closing like a fish. Jenny reached for her mineral water and sipped demurely. 'I'll tell you something,' said Richard when he had regained control of his lips, 'Diana doesn't need a fucking list, because the only way she'll get a man to father a child on her is to spray him with cock starch and tie him to a tree.'

Jenny sipped more vigorously. Seeing that he had offended her, Richard calmed down a little. 'Jenny,' he said softly, 'we shouldn't be quarreling like this. This should be a very precious time for us. Our last supper. Not that we can't have supper in the future, you understand, but not alone, together like this. We've made a very brave decision – both of us. We are doing the right thing. We are putting Isobel's welfare before our own happiness . . .' A sniff rent the dark air. Gently he edged a little closer and put his arm round Jenny's shoulders. The slightest tremor greeted his touch. 'These have been wonderful times. Magic. I shall never forget them as long as I live.'

'Neither shall I.' Water began to plop rhythmically on to Jenny's skirt. Richard wondered if it was raining.

'Why don't we go inside? You must be getting cold out here.'

Jenny rallied herself, wiping her eyes on the corner of her shawl. 'I must go.'

'Must you? Why not stay and have a cup of coffee with me? Just for old times' sake.'

'I can't.' Jenny was in full flood now. 'Can't you see, I have to go. I can't possibly stay now that's it's . . . over.'

Richard carried the tray into the sitting room. 'There. Have one of these.'

'Oh, Richie, After Eights. You are naughty.'

'I know, but I bought them specially for you. I'll only have one.'

'So shall I.'

*

'Car all right now?' Richard, surrounded by empty After Eight slips, helped Jenny back into her skirt. He was pleased he'd taken the opportunity to do this one small thing for her. After all, they had been lovers for quite a while now and it was always better to end these things as they had begun. It gave a sort of symmetry to things, a certain air of destiny, which helped to assuage any lingering feelings of guilt.

Poor Jenny was taking it very well. Far better than he'd dared hope in fact for, although he knew he could handle her, he had rather feared an outburst of hysterical weeping and pleading which would have been distressing for them both. Thinking back, she had behaved remarkably well. That one fruitless little effort to make him think that *she* was giving *him* up had been rather touching in its way. Yes, she was a good little creature. He would miss her. Still, he had made the right decision, of that he had no doubt.

Jenny slipped into her sandals. She would have preferred not to have succumbed to Richard's advances on this one last occasion. Once a decision had been made it was best to stick to it, she always felt. Still it had done no harm, since they both knew it was for the last time, and the poor man had looked so pathetic, sitting there eating chocolates and talking about wheels coming full circle and so forth. She wondered how Isobel would cope, having his undivided attention. She didn't envy her any more. Richard could be very selfish and babyish sometimes. Particularly in his insistence that it was he and not she who was breaking off the affair. Never mind, it was done now. She shivered with satisfaction and gathered up her shawl.

'Good night, Richard,' she said gently. 'And yes, the car's fine, thank you.'

'Good. Good.' He led her through the hall to the front door and opened it for her.

'Don't bother to come out. You'll get cold.'

'Nonsense. Of course I must see you to the car.' He padded across the gravel in his socks, cursing at the sharpness of the stones. Jenny opened the door and got in. She wound down the window and gazed up at him. 'Well, goodbye, Richard. I shall always think of you fondly. I hope everything goes well for you and Isobel.'

'Yes. Thank you. I'm sure ... that is ...' He bent awkwardly and kissed Jenny's cool forehead. 'Goodbye, Jenny. And good luck.'

'Thank you,' said Jenny, and smiling an enigmatic smile, drove out of the drive and away along the road. It was nearly midnight. She was looking forward to tomorrow. Lunch with Diana and a chance to inspect her list.

Richard watched her go, then went inside. He was tired. All this being a decent chap was pretty exhausting. He wondered how Isobel was getting on with the dreaded Melanie. She'd probably come back completely drained. Still, all in a good cause. What a charitable pair they were.

Chapter Thirty

'Isobel.' Isobel turned. She was sitting by the window of the bedroom, staring out at the moonless sky. She could smell the drizzle in the air. The night was close and sticky, disappointing after the sunshine of the day.

'Sorry. Did I wake you?'

Harry was leaning on his elbow. 'It's hard to tiptoe in full armour.'

Isobel smiled. She could hardly see him, just the vague outline of his body under the white sheet. 'What's the matter?'

She turned her head to the window again. 'Nothing. I'm a bad sleeper. I forgot to warn you.'

Harry swung his legs over the edge of the bed. 'It's so damn hot. I don't know how you bear it with that plaster.'

'Not much longer.'

'No.'

Harry reached for the glass of water on Isobel's side and, dipping his fingers into it, splashed his face. He got up and came over to the window, then sat down on the small wooden chair opposite Isobel and took her hands in his. 'Are you sad?' For a moment Isobel said nothing, then slowly she nodded. From nowhere she could feel tears pricking her eyes. She was glad he couldn't really see.

Harry pressed her thumbs. For once he seemed at a loss for words. 'Bit of a mess, isn't it?' he said at last. Again Isobel nodded. 'You did understand, didn't you? That it couldn't last?' asked Harry softly.

Isobel wiped her eyes. 'I suppose I did. I didn't think ahead. I never do.'

Harry smiled and touched her face. 'Best way to be. You'll be all right, Isobel. You've got Richard and the children, they love you. And pretty soon you'll have your leg. What more could a sensible woman ask?'

Isobel smiled in desperation. 'That was the other thing I didn't tell you,' she said.

Harry rose and, putting his arms round her, squeezed her to him. 'You wouldn't like Shepherd's Bush,' he said.

'I might.'

'Come to bed.'

'While I've got the chance, you mean?' She looked up at him and was shocked to see that he was crying, then realised that it must be the water from her glass.

They made love with the slow intensity of people on the verge of separation, struggling to record what they felt, bottling up their passion for future use – to be dispensed in measured doses, according to need.

'Why did you bring me here?' asked Isobel at last. 'I wish to god you hadn't.'

Harry didn't look at her, but stared straight at the ceiling, stiflingly close to their heads. 'So do I,' he said tonelessly. 'It was a mistake. I wanted to . . .' But he never finished the sentence and, gradually, in the darkness, they fell asleep, arms lightly touching.

Rain had set in with a vengeance when Isobel woke up the following morning. It was difficult to reconcile the soggy patches of grass backing the houses of Clitheroe Gardens with the soft green lawns of Saturday afternoon. Everything looked downtrodden.

Harry was still asleep. For the first time she noticed how long his eyelashes were. They gave him a childlike appearance, although the lines on his face seemed deeper than she remembered. She lay on her side and observed him. Somewhere a telephone was ringing. She didn't think it was Maureen's and eventually the sound of clumping feet next door confirmed this.

Either the sound or her staring had penetrated Harry's subconscious for he opened his eyes and lay looking at her for some time before he spoke.

'Well, Lady Chatterley, what would you like for breakfast?'

'I usually have toast.'

Harry rolled on his side and scooped her towards him. 'And I usually have two vestal virgins and a slice of bacon.'

Isobel laughed in spite of herself. 'I was once a Brownie sixer. Will that do?'

Harry groaned in frustration. 'I suppose it'll have to. Do you have your sex badge?'

Isobel shook her head and struggled slightly. 'I was very good at knots,' she said, 'and if you don't get off my leg I shall probably demonstrate.' Harry was undeterred by the threat.

Isobel was pleasantly surprised by the degree of ardour he managed to muster at such an early hour of the day. It was a long time since Richard and she had made love before lunch time, let alone before the first cup of tea.

'What time do you have to be back?' asked Harry carelessly as Isobel scraped the toast over the sink.

'One o'clock, I said. But I'll need to go down to the station before that. I'll have to get a cab from there, you see.' Harry nodded. He opened the frig and extracted the butter. Isobel noticed how the inside of the frig shone. 'Maureen's awfully houseproud,' she said. 'Somehow I hadn't expected everything to be so orderly. Not that I thought it would be a mess, you understand, but not this tidy either.'

Harry acknowledged this. 'She's not usually this neat. I think she must have had a clear-up specially for you. Perhaps she wanted to impress you.'

Isobel laughed. 'Hardly. Besides, she's seen my house. She knows I live in a tip.'

'It's not a tip. Anyway you've got children. You can't be tidy and have children.'

Isobel shrugged. 'Some of my friends seem to be able to.'

Harry shook his head belligerently. 'Not possible.'

'When's Maureen coming home?' asked Isobel to change the subject.

'Don't know for sure. Tomorrow some time, I think. I'm

up at Ashford all day. The sooner that twat goes to Africa, the better.'

'You're not going with him?' asked Isobel nervously. Somehow losing Harry to Shepherd's Bush seemed slightly less awful than losing him to the Third World.

'No bloody fear.'

'What are you doing after this? Have you got anything lined up?'

Harry nodded. 'I'm going to Current Affairs, BBC, for three months. After that I don't know.'

Isobel said nothing. It would be so simple for him to say that they could continue to meet, especially when her ankle was healed. She could easily arrange to go to London for the day, or he could come down to the coast. It was only a couple of hours away. Less on his bike. But Harry suggested none of these things. Obviously a job was a job. When it was over it was well and truly over.

'Do you get on with your ex-wife?' she asked suddenly. Harry looked up in surprise.

'Not very well. Why?'

'I just wondered because you obviously see a lot of your daughter, so I sort of thought you must get on with her mother, that's all.'

Harry gave a bitter laugh. 'Is that what you thought?' he said. 'No, she's remarried. To tell the truth I like her husband more than her. She's usually out when I go up. She works, you see. Shifts. I try not to bump into her too often. Better that way.' He stared moodily into his cup. Isobel didn't ask him any more.

She tidied up as best she could so that Maureen wouldn't be disappointed by the state of the place when she came home. Harry helped her, but their conversation concerning his wife seemed to have cast a shadow over his earlier good humour. Isobel wished she had never mentioned her, but it was too late now, and anyway, it was probably only indicative of the whole situation. Harry had decided to end their affair and any reminder of the ties and thralls of marriage only served to harden his resolve. He ordered a taxi and they drove to the station about twelve o'clock. The rain was now falling in torrents. As they came into the town Isobel noticed the bedraggled yellow bunting round the bandstand, along with several washed-out posters. She peered through the steamed-up windows and gurgled with laughter. Harry looked at her curiously, his face beginning to soften.

'What are you laughing at?'

'Those posters. It's that Apocalypse 2000 mob. All about Kent disappearing under water. Judging by this rain there's probably something in it. Barnbridge – twinned with Atlantis. How does that sound?'

Harry nodded. 'Pretty good.'

'Richard says they cause more pollution holding up the traffic, still they must be nearly through by now. They seem to have been here forever.'

'How long's forever?'

'Oh, five or six weeks at least.'

Harry looked at her and smiled for the first time since breakfast. 'Here's to the next forever,' he said. The cab swung into the station.

'How was it?' Richard, Patrick's raincoat over his head, came hurrying out to meet the station cab. Isobel paid the man and let Richard help her into the house. 'Fine,' she said. 'Has it been raining here all morning?'

'And half the night. What was it like with you?'

'Not too bad. It was quite dry till we got to Tunbridge.'

Richard was shaking Patrick's mac over the kitchen floor. 'Strange,' he said absent-mindedly. 'I put on the Surrey/Hants match this morning, and they said the pitch was completely water-logged.'

Isobel crossed slowly to the sink and poured herself a glass of water.

'Strange,' she said.

Chapter Thirty-one

'Mrs Day. How are you? You're looking much better, I have to say.' Mr Robertson with an expression halfway between a new prime minister and someone who has left the gas on under the soup, rose to greet Isobel. 'You've been to x-ray and I must say the results are most encouraging.' He waved a brown envelope at her as though to remove any lingering doubts. 'So now I'm going to send you along to get the plaster removed, and then we shall be able to see if you need another.'

'Another?'

Any hope that five weeks under Simon Mahon had eradicated thoughts of suicide were rapidly swept aside as Robertson saw Isobel's face change from equity to despair.

'We can't be entirely sure that the bone is strong enough to support the leg at this stage. It is sometimes necessary to replace a plaster for a week or two . . .' He noted anxiously that the reduction in time did not seem to have had the desired effect.

'I'm not having another.'

'It may not be necessary.'

'I don't care if it is. I'm not having one, and that's all there is to it.'

'Mrs Day, five weeks is not a very long period for a fracture to heal . . .'

'I don't care.'

Mr Robertson sighed. He wished he'd never mentioned it now. Mahon had specifically asked him to postpone the Day woman's appointment till after the final recording, fearing any change might give rise to unnecessary difficulties, but he had over-ridden him, partly from professional pride, and partly because the deal that had finally been struck with that pretentious heap of metaplasm, Joffe, meant that the best St Clare's could hope for was a new mobile phone for the women's wards and a possible venetian blind for the night sister's office.

'Well, perhaps the best thing would be for you to go along to Surgical and have this one removed. Tell the nurse you're to come straight in when you get back, will you? I don't want to keep you hanging about.' He smiled. Isobel threw him a lancing glare, and hobbled off without another word.

The young houseman in charge of the plastering unit attributed her out-thrust chin and furious eye to a natural nervousness. 'Don't worry,' he quipped, 'we hardly ever cut people's legs right off.'

'You might as well,' returned Isobel, by now convinced that another five weeks' incarceration lay ahead of her. Not that she would let them replaster her ankle, she would rather die, but even from this balanced viewpoint it was patently clear that problems lay ahead if that bastard, Robertson, wanted to replace the damn thing.

Presumably he had to get her consent, but maybe he already had it. That thing she had signed between the pre-med and nirvana had probably given him the right to amputate up to her cranium, should the mood so grab him. Visions of herself, held down by sweating juniors, while the bobbly consultant entombed her in a plaster chrysalis, vied with the vision of Harry, storming into the operating theatre on his Suzuki, flies undone at the ready – this was getting ridiculous. She was beginning to wish she hadn't had that vodka before she left home this morning. Still she had needed Dutch courage. Robertson was not the worst of her fears. She still had to face Harry. Harry for the last time. It sounded like a song. Perhaps she should write a poem on the subject. It could hardly be drearier than Ken's and Leonie's. She toyed with various rhymes before deciding that it was probably a great deal worse than Ken's or Leonie's and with this modest conclusion, found that she was outside the door marked 'Surgical. Strip' to which she had been directed.

She tapped on the door and was admitted by the same Australian nurse who had rescued her from Simon Mahon's first session so many lifetimes before.

'Hullo,' said the girl, plainly not recognising her. 'You for us?'

'My plaster's got to come off,' said Isobel.

'Right. With you in a tick. D'you want to sit over there?' She pointed to a row of green plastic chairs. Isobel didn't. She wanted her plaster off now. The question was plainly rhetorical, however, for the nurse had shot away to a cubicle where the unmistakable sound of a chain saw could be heard above the muted buzz of medical chat.

She picked up a magazine. 'My Life Without The Man I Love' screamed the headline. She put it down.

'Mrs Isobel Day.' She was escorted into the cubicle.

'Nice day,' said the youth to whom Isobel's entire future happiness appeared to be entrusted.

'Me or it?' asked Isobel.

The houseman frowned then grinned in comprehension. 'Oh, yep. Sorry. Bit of a daft remark.'

'Can I ask you something?'

'Of course. Go ahead.'

'How does that thing work?' She indicated what was very clearly an instrument of death in the young man's hands. He laughed. 'Not the way you think, I would guess. It doesn't cut at all. It just vibrates its way through.'

Isobel eyed it suspiciously. 'Do you sell very many?' she asked.

Isobel's ankle had mended.

She didn't know, any more than the doctor who removed the plaster knew. He was on Surgical for the week. It bored him. He wanted to be a gynaecologist. He sent her back to Mr Robertson who felt and squeezed and probed, then said the bone was mended and that Isobel did not need another plaster.

He spoke as though she had won the Best Pressed Flower Contest. He was pleased and proud. She was ecstatic.

A walking stick was furnished to relieve strain on the as yet weak and floppy muscles. Isobel was given an appointment for four weeks' time, mainly with a view to regaining the walking stick. A surprising amount of them went missing. Her crutches were reclaimed.

Isobel limped along the corridors on a cloud.

Contrary to her fears, her leg was not white with a sweater's worth of matted hair. It was pale, a trifle flakey, and decidedly thin, but it was a leg, and it was free, and so was she.

Passing the elephant-shaped bin, with 'Please Feed Me' emblazoned on its belly, she reached into her bag and, scattering the contents, extracted the tights she had packed that morning, and flung them into the ever-open mouth beneath the trunk. Then, retrieving her purse and her Polos, she continued on her triumphant way.

'This is most inconvenient.' Simon Mahon, hands entwined behind his back, paced two steps to the left and two to the right in a creditable imitation of the circle dance. 'She should have been here by now.'

Julian looked at his watch and whispered something to Fran, who immediately added a few more creases to her frown and rushed towards Luce, waving a pencil with magisterial impetus. Luce's natural pallor deepened and she hurried over to where Anita was trying, with brute force, to attach a new reed to one of her instruments.

Isobel saw her eyebrows rise in some astonishment and then alarm as she realised the import of Luce's message. They were going to have to go without one of the dancers. Time was at a premium (surely Julian's chosen epitaph), and if Maureen did not arrive within the next ten minutes they would be obliged to shoot the final reel without her.

Alternatives were canvassed. Anita wondered whether Luce or Fran might be willing . . .? In the first united decision of their professional lives, the two refused. Anita next thought she might take Maureen's position herself, then realised that she was responsible for the accompaniment. Luce was dispatched to search the hospital. Perhaps Maureen was stuck in a lavatory. She returned alone.

Isobel was curious. She wondered that Harry had not said anything. He must know where she was. Might even have brought her himself. Perhaps this was part of a plan they had hatched to stitch Mahon up at the last moment. She felt vaguely hurt that she had not been included, but the euphoria of her puny ankle was too strong to cloud her spirits for long.

Harry had not spoken to her since her arrival, but then he very rarely did during Mahon's sessions. Too much the professional, she thought indulgently, watching as he bent over the camera. Somehow the idea that this could be their last meeting had no hold over her emotions. Her leg was better, she was free. Anything was possible.

'I really think we must start without her,' said Mahon at last, angry eyes glinting behind his metal frames. 'It's not as though it was a significant part of the programme.' Isobel saw Joffe's eyebrows shoot up. He didn't like to be told. 'Just do the best you can,' Mahon continued. 'I want to get on.'

'Where is Maureen?' Isobel whispered as she lined up in front of Harry.

'Don't know. She wasn't back when I left this morning. Must have decided to stay down there.'

Isobel glanced at him, but Harry's face was impassive as always. 'I've got my foot back.'

'So I see.'

'What d'you think?' She wriggled it coquettishly.

Harry smiled very faintly. 'You're a different woman,' he said. And Isobel realised that he meant it.

The circle dance was danced. It had its own momentum, irrespective of the lack of Maureen or the presence of the five other participants. It was, as Julian had prophesied, a conclusion. A symbol, rather than an event – the message he intended his programme to deliver. He was too experienced a film-maker ever to have thought a simple recording would furnish him with the material he wanted. Even as the others blissfully watched the footage so far completed, Meg gasping anew at Isobel's revelation, he was rehearsing how to intersperse the groaning with the cry of a Caucasian wolf, the confessions with monochrome stills of Belsen. 'A Film by Julian Joffe'. Nearly in the can.

And while the actors watched, so too did Vera Beasley, newly recovered from her smoke inhalation and prowling the hospital in search of economy bars of soap, and dusters left unguarded behind radiators.

On tiptoe she watched, drawn to PSY 1 by the fitful wail of music and the flickering light of the screen. And as she watched, eyes bright as fireballs, she saw that nasty Day woman from Shingle Cottage chattering desultorily into the camera, framed by a back projection of the cliffs around St Margaret's. So that was her game. Pretend indifference and then turn up on telly and claim the credit for warning the world about the approaching cataclysm. Mrs Beasley moved away. There was no justice. She picked up a thin red notebook lying beside the swing doors, and opened it. 'My Life', she read, 'by Isobel Day'. With a smile of supreme malice she dropped it into the elephant's mouth.

The room was empty. The crew had gone off with Julian to discuss final editing and continuity. Simon Mahon was upstairs in Hugh Robertson's office, arguing over his expenses. Hilary and Leonie had gone to drink herbal tea then gin at Leonie's flat, and Ken was across the road, waiting for his bus.

Meg's husband, unusually, had left work early to pick her up, and they were now on their way to the garden centre, despite a threat from Mrs Gaskell Senior to fade away and die if no one was there to give her her pills.

Isobel sat in the little hospital garden. The sun was still high but the heat was beginning to recede. She gazed at her ankle, anxious and affectionate like a mother with a wayward toddler. She wondered where Maureen was. Probably sunning herself by the banks of some West Country river. She smiled at the thought. Poor Simon Mahon. Man is not a machine, came into her mind. Even the luckless Meg seemed to have found some kind of life without him.

She wondered where Harry was. Up there somewhere in one of the tinted glass consulting rooms, saying nothing and thinking about a cold beer. Or her. Beer, probably. She wondered if he would go back to Maureen's that night. Whether he would stay, or just pick up his things and go. Whether he would come to say goodbye.

'Isobel.'

She turned and smiled. 'Behold.' She extended her leg.

'It's beautiful. Perfect. Better than ever.' Isobel rose a little awkwardly and reached for her stick.

'Are you all right? I mean, can you manage?'

'Of course I can. I could dance a flamenco if you asked me to.'

Richard smiled. 'Perhaps tomorrow.' He led her gently back through the corridors to the car.

It was shortly after nine when the doorbell rang. Richard went to answer it. He came silently into the sitting room where Isobel was trying ineffectually to mend Patrick's trousers. 'Someone to see you.'

Isobel looked up, surprised. 'Where?'

'At the door.' She rose and went into the hall. Standing in the porch was Harry.

'Harry! What are you doing here? I mean, come in,' she tried to sound normal. 'Whatever's Richard up to, leaving you out here?'

For a moment she thought he would refuse, but wearily he stepped into the hall. She saw that his dark eyes were empty of emotion. He just looked tired, defeated ... Not like anyone she knew. My god, she thought. He does love me. He's come to have it out with Richard. They're going to make me choose. But the thought gave her no satisfaction because she knew that there was no choice. That was for books.

She became aware that Richard was watching them.

None of them spoke, then Harry, still with the same exhausted demeanour, passed his hand quickly over his forehead and said, 'I thought you would want to know, Maureen is dead.'

Even Richard, armed as he was with fears and suspicions about Harry's designs upon his wife, was ill-prepared for this. He stepped aside. 'You'd better come in,' he said, one arm instinctively around Isobel. She covered her face with her hands.

'No,' she whispered in agonised disbelief. 'Not Maureen. No. Oh, no, not her.'

Richard led her to the couch and sat her down, then crossed quickly to the drinks cabinet and poured them all a brandy.

'What happened? An accident?' He handed Harry a glass. Harry shook his head.

'I went back to pick up my stuff. I was going back to London for the night. I stayed there sometimes during the filming.'

Through her tears Isobel could see he was uncertain how much to tell Richard. 'Maureen wasn't there today,' she said quietly. 'I think she said she was going away for the weekend.'

Harry nodded. 'Devon somewhere. I expected her back yesterday. When she didn't come I just assumed she'd decided to stay a bit longer. She was thinking of moving back there, you see, since her old man died.' He paused and took a gulp of the brandy. 'Anyway, when I got back this afternoon there was a police car outside.' He was silent for a moment then took a breath and continued. 'It seems it was suicide. She left a note. She'd even told them I'd be at the house. It was all very tidy. She must have been planning it for sometime.'

Isobel couldn't really grasp what he was saying. Why, of all people, should Maureen kill herself? It must have been a mistake. But the note? 'How did she . . .?'

'Pills.'

'It must have been an accident. An accidental overdose. Maureen wasn't like that . . . I mean, she was here – only last week. We had lunch together. She was fine. She wouldn't do something like that. I know she wouldn't. She was my friend.' The two men sat in silent commiseration as Isobel curled over in despair and sobbed. 'She was my friend. Oh god, why would she do that? Why? I could have helped her. I didn't know. Why didn't I see it? Why am I so useless?'

Richard put his arm round her as she rocked helplessly to and fro. 'You're not useless. You couldn't have known. It's very sad, but it's not your fault. Or anyone's. If someone's made up their mind, there's nothing you can do.' He stopped suddenly, as though someone had hit him in the stomach.

Harry said dully, 'I think it was something she'd intended for a very long time. We talked about it once or twice, just in a roundabout way. She was very positive about everything. Try to understand – for her, it wasn't an act of despair, it was an act of. . I don't know what you'd call it . . . love, maybe? She always said that if life had nothing left to offer it was better to move on. "Try something else", she said. She couldn't make much sense of life without her husband.'

Isobel wiped her eyes. 'Yes, but that's normal with bereavement, isn't it? She would have got over it in time. If we'd helped her. If that bugger Mahon hadn't made everything seem so pointless and ridiculous. Who sent her there, anyway? No wonder she killed herself. If someone's depressed the last thing you want is to surround them with a bunch of lunatics. Ask me.'

'Don't say that.'

Isobel had never heard Richard shout like that before. She stared at him, shocked. Richard calmed himself.

'I'm sorry. We've all had a shock. I think perhaps it's a bit late to be talking about all this. We're all tired.'

Harry stood up. Richard turned to him. 'Thank you for coming to tell us,' he said awkwardly. 'Perhaps I could get in touch tomorrow . . . about the arrangements? You say you're going back to London tonight?'

Harry shook his head. 'No, I'll stay down till things are sorted out. I'll be at the Collier's Arms.' He reached out and touched Isobel's hand. She longed to grab his hand and kiss it, but she did nothing. Richard watched in silence, then escorted him to the door.

When he came back Isobel was clearing away the glasses. 'I understand now,' she said quietly.

'Understand what?'

'Why the house was so tidy.'

Richard closed his eyes for a minute. 'Come to bed,' he said.

Chapter Thirty-two

The funeral was on Friday. Richard took the morning off. They met at the crematorium. A cousin of Maureen's husband had been found in Wiltshire and had made the journey up by rail. He stood a little apart, talking to the solicitor who, as trustee, had made the arrangements. Isobel approached the cousin and told him she and Richard were friends of Maureen. He looked at her without curiosity and mentioned the weather and the difficulties in travelling cross country by train, then returned to his discussion.

Harry made no effort to address him. He had a dark jacket on and grey flannel trousers. Isobel thought she hardly recognised him as her leather-coated lover. She thought also that she would die without him, she wanted him so much.

A curate appeared and ushered them kindly into a waiting room beside the chapel. It was cream and square and contained one of those dreadful plastic flower arrangements prevalent among the deposit slips in banks. They sat round the walls. The cousin was becoming more animated as he discussed the charms of Clitheroe Gardens to first-time buyers. Isobel stared at him, unable to associate his presence with their own.

The solicitor had said no flowers, but Isobel had gone out early, before the children were awake that morning, and picked an enormous bunch of gardenias which she had handed over to an attendant when they arrived. She had no idea whether he would attach them to the right coffin. Somehow the possibility of a queue had not occurred to her, but here they were, waiting their turn, while whoever had booked the ten o'clock said their farewells and departed in the gleaming black limousines they could never have afforded to celebrate a life with.

'Are you all right?' Richard squeezed her hand.

'Yes. You'd think they could do better, wouldn't you?'

'Who?'

'I don't know. Whoever runs this place. Plastic flowers. The place must be overflowing with fresh ones. You don't suppose they cook them as well, do you?'

The solicitor looked shocked and the cousin frowned. The curate appeared again and said if they would like to follow him.

The chapel was bright and smelled of furniture polish. Richard and Isobel sat one side and Harry and the two others sat opposite. The curate said a few words about parting being a temporary thing. Isobel assumed he had presided over Jim Hart's funeral as well, for he mentioned the pair of them almost as though they were still a couple, which presumably they were now. Unbeliever though she was, this comforted her. It seemed a lot more bearable to think of Maureen reunited with the man she loved than left to grieve in silence for untold years on earth.

There was a discreet cough from the back. The coffin was in place, borne carefully by four of the undertaker's assistants. Isobel caught a quick glimpse of the cousin frowning anxiously. I hope it costs the lot, she thought savagely, but looking at the plain pine panelling, she knew that it had not. She turned away as the coffin passed. It looked so small. She wondered if Maureen had room in there. Perhaps she was curled up, the way she had seen her during Mahon's exercise sessions. She had been happy then. Isobel hoped she was happy now, then remembered she didn't believe in the After Life.

The bearers placed the coffin on the platform and for the first time Isobel noticed her gardenias, sprawling drunkenly on the top. Not at all like a florist's bouquet. She looked away. The curate murmured the blessing. From somewhere in the corner came a taped organ rendering of 'Abide With Me' as the red velour curtains hissed apart and the coffin began its slow descent into the fire. Isobel bit her tongue at the ludicrousness of it all, then bit it harder in an attempt to stop the tears.

Outside they shook hands with the curate. The cousin and solicitor nodded to them and drove away in the solicitor's smart car. Harry, Richard and Isobel stood together on the gravel driveway, looking out over the perfect green of the valley. A wind was rippling the grass like water and there was rain in the air.

Richard put an arm round Isobel. 'I think we could do with a drink,' he said.

Isobel wiped her eyes. 'Yes.' She looked at Harry. 'Will you come?'

He considered for a moment then shook his head. 'I think I'll get back,' he said. 'I'm off to Birmingham. It's not a journey to do when you've had a skinful.'

Richard nodded in some relief. 'Some other time, then,' he said to preserve the form.

Isobel threw him a scorching look. 'When? At my funeral? How many other times are there likely to be?'

Harry turned away and began to walk round the back where his motorbike was parked. Isobel half-ran, half-hopped after him.

'Isobel . . .' Richard's desperate voice was lost on the wind.

'Harry, wait for me.' She caught up with him. 'Don't just go away. I know you've got to go. I know. I understand. Just don't go and not say anything.'

Harry reached for his helmet. 'Better this way, Isobel. Try not to be sad about Maureen. It's what she wanted.'

Isobel caught hold of his arm. 'What about me? Do you ever wonder about what I want?'

Harry pulled his arm away, then relented and put his hands gently on her shoulders. 'I know what you want, Isobel. And it doesn't exist.' He gave her shoulders a light squeeze and swung himself on to the bike.

'Let me come with you.'

'Don't be daft.'

'I don't mean all the way. Just give me a ride. As far as the town, anywhere. I've never been on a bike with two whole legs. I told Richard I had but it was a lie. Please. Just so I know there's life beyond the plastercast.'

Harry looked at her for a moment, then reached behind him for the spare helmet.

Richard, standing by the car, for once completely at a loss, looked up in alarm as the motorbike ripped past him and out into the flow of oncoming traffic.

The curate, seeing the man crying, came to offer what comfort he could. Richard dried his eyes and drove away shamefaced. The curate watched him with sympathy. A man who could cry could believe. If only he had had a little more time. Odd how he had kept calling Mrs Hart 'Isobel'. He was almost certain her name had been Maureen.

At the turning for the cliffs Isobel thumped Harry's back. He slowed down and stopped just below the ridge by the war memorial. Isobel eased herself off the machine. 'This will do.'

'You're miles from anywhere. I'd better take you home.'

'No need. Richard will come and find me.'

'You can't be sure.'

Isobel laughed, quite unmaliciously. 'No, but I think he will. If not I'll get a cab.'

'You won't get one up here.'

'You're forgetting something, Harry. I can walk. Now, hadn't you better be going? I expect your daughter's waiting for you. What's her name, by the way? You never did tell me.'

'It's Isobel,' said Harry. 'I was filming some history play when she was born and that was one of the characters. Coincidence, eh?'

Isobel nodded in defeat. 'I hope she has better luck with it than I have.'

Harry shrugged. 'I doubt it.'

'Well, at least you love her. That's more than I ever managed.'

'Love isn't everything.'

'You don't think so?'

'I know so.' Harry flung one leg over the bike and revved the machine viciously. Isobel wondered if she threw herself in front of it he would stop, but with her luck he'd probably go right over her ankle again, and really it wasn't worth it.

He swept away and down the hill then turned and roared back towards her. Isobel didn't move. The machine screeched to a halt within feet of her.

'I'll tell you something, Isobel two, you talk about love. I love my daughter. I love her so much that I travel up and down the bleeding M. 1 twice a week to see her. The only problem is, I never do see her. Because if she has the slightest idea that I might be on my way, she clears out. She can't stand me. And would you like to know why? Because I buggered off and left her and her mum when she was seven, and she's never forgiven me for that, and it looks like she's never going to. So next time you plan how you're going to run away and live with me in Shepherd's Bush, just ask yourself how your little girl's going to feel when you've gone. And your son. I tell you now, it ain't worth it.'

Isobel watched him go, for hours it seemed, until he was well out of sight. The threatened rain had not materialised and the sky was beginning to clear. Slowly she turned and made her way up to the ridge, past the war memorial, past the National Trust emblem and the man falling backwards up the rock face.

The sun was warm as she sank by the edge and peered down across the bay, just as she had done on her birthday. There was no one down there now. She remembered how she had lain, with her bottle of champagne, first on her back and then on her front, and watched the stream of coloured blobs shimmying around below her, and how those two ridiculous specks rolling and pumping behind the protection of the large blue Saab had suddenly stopped being funny and become Richard and Jenny – she of the open-plan earlobes – and how she had stood up and waved to them, waved like a woman possessed until the bottle flew out of her hand and she had had to decide in a millionth of a second, whether to reach for it or not.

She looked around. It was exactly the same. The sun, the sky, the memorial. She had no champagne, but then she didn't really need any. She was high on grief, the most powerful narcotic of all. Gazing back at the ridge, she remembered the tiny dots of Mr and Mrs Jamieson as they lumbered over the hill. She wondered what would have happened if they hadn't been there that day. Perhaps she should have written to thank them? Thank them for what? Five weeks in plaster? Simon Mahon? Jenny's confession? Or Harry, and the bluebell wood, and Maureen, and Richard, contrite and loving, and beginning to show his age.

She looked around once more, but this time there was no one there.

Mrs Jamieson carried the coffee into the front room. 'Clearing now,' she said. 'We could have gone for that walk.'

Mr Jamieson, intent on the racing, nodded. 'Too late now,' he said. 'We can always go tomorrow.'

Patrick and Eleanour stood at the door of their parents' bedroom. They had never seen Daddy cry before. Gradually they edged forward till they came within his eyeline. Still they said nothing.

Suddenly Richard lunged forward and grasped them to him. They stroked at his head supportively, just as they had seen Mummy do when Daddy had had too much beer.

'We love you, Daddy,' murmured Eleanour in a passable imitation of an Australian accent. Patrick made a sick-in-his-pocket gesture to demonstrate the inefficacy of this, but Richard was glad of his daughter's protestation in whatever language she cared to give it.

Patrick jerked his head to Eleanour as their eyes fell on the open black box spilling shreds of oyster silk and dead dandelions all over the duvet. Eleanour gasped involuntarily at the sight of so much naughtiness. No wonder her father was crying. 'It wasn't me,' she swore defensively, 'Rainbow's Honour, Daddy.'

'It wasn't me, either,' added Patrick, alarmed at the implication. 'Have we had burglars, Daddy?'

Richard shook his head wretchedly.

'Aren't you very well, Daddy?' asked Eleanour, uneasy at this change in family order. 'Shall I get Mummy?'

Richard stood up and went to the window where he made a great show of removing a thumb print with his handkerchief. 'Mummy's not here,' he said croakily. 'Why don't you two go and see if there's anything on television? Then I'll get tea ready.'

Eleanour opened her mouth to ask if they could have two biscuits to keep them going, but was so severely nudged by her brother that she almost fell over the bed. The two of them went downstairs.

Richard stood for a few moments longer looking out over the garden. He could still see Isobel's uneven footprints where she had walked across his potato patch to cut the gardenias that morning. Make the most of those, he thought tormentedly, once it rains I'll have nothing left.

He returned to the bed and collected the wreckage of his birthday gift and stuffed it into the waste paper basket. Then he went into the bathroom and washed his face. God, I look old, he thought, catching sight of himself in the mirror. To think I had a go at her for being forty. And that bugger she's gone off with, he's the same age. Forty. It's nothing. They've got their whole lives before them.

It's not only bad luck to smash a mirror, it's very dangerous, as Richard realised, agonisingly picking the splinters out of his hand, and very expensive, as he found out when he came to have it replaced.

It also muffles sound, which is why, when he opened the door and saw Isobel standing there, her navy suit spattered with mud, a look of acute fatigue on her empty face, he wondered for a moment whether it was he and not she that was going mad.

'I broke the mirror,' he said at last.

Isobel nodded. 'I thought you had. Or the window.'

'It was the mirror,' Richard confirmed.

Isobel sat on the edge of the bed. 'Sorry I was so long. I walked.'

Richard stared at her. 'Walked where?'

'From the cliff.'

'Walked? But it's five miles, near enough. You've got a broken ankle.'

Isobel smiled a weary smile. 'Not any more,' she said. She

wiggled her reclaimed leg at him, wincing as she did so. 'Good as new.'

Richard stared stiffly down at her. 'What about . . . Whatsisname?'

Isobel looked away. 'Gone.'

'Where?'

'Back to London. Home.'

'I thought you were going with him.'

'No.' Still she did not look at him.

Richard gave a short laugh. 'Have you come to get your things? Is he picking you up, or do you have to make your own way? It must be hard to move house on a motorbike.'

This time Isobel did look at him. 'He's gone, Richard. It was nothing. A flirtation – holiday romance – whatever you call them. I'm sorry if you're upset, but you've hurt me, too, you know. It doesn't help to be forty and know your husband is screwing a woman half your age.'

'Jenny's not half . . .' He stopped. They looked at each other. Very slowly Isobel extended her hand to him. Richard took it. 'I love you, Isobel. I love you so much.' He sank down on the bed beside her.

Isobel put her arms round him and held him to her. 'I know you do, Richard.'

'And you love me, don't you?'

'You know I do.'

Richard buried his head in her belly and for a moment was perfectly happy. When he looked up he saw that his wife's eyes were tightly closed, as if she were trying not to cry.

You have been reading a novel published by Piatkus Books. We hope you have enjoyed it and that you would like to read more of our titles. Please ask for them in your local library or bookshop.

If you would like to be put on our mailing list to receive details of new publications, please send a large addresed envelope (UK only) to:

Piatkus Books: 5 Windmill Street
London W1P 1HF

The sign of a good book